THE KALIFEE

SUSAN CHAPPELL

CITIOFBOOKS, INC.
3736 Eubank NE Suite A1
Albuquerque, NM 87111-3579
www.citiofbooks.com
Hotline: 1 (877) 389-2759
Fax: 1 (505) 930-7244

Ordering Information:
Quantity sales. Special discounts are available on quantity purchases by corporations, associations, and others. For details, contact the publisher at the address above.

Printed in the United States of America.

ISBN-13:   Softcover   979-8-89391-778-9
                  eBook   979-8-89391-779-6

Library of Congress Control Number: 2025913304

THE KALIFEE

As it begins…

The earth in this future time had changed with all the fighting, hightech war, and general abuse and neglect of the planet. So much of the earth was inhabitable currently. There were many areas that were radioactive, and so much was lost, especially technology. But some humans, animals, and green growing things survived in small areas. Imbalance was everywhere. Now there were many more women than men. It was always thought that all the wars, skirmishes, ambushes, hostile engagements, guerilla warfare, and any other phrases of fighting was the cause of our demise. That seems logical. No one seemed to want to look at how we had all had treated the only home we have. Sometimes it is hard to tell if someone is running toward something or away from it. But no matter how far a person runs, they would still be on this planet. After all, it is round, and we carry us with us no matter where we go.

With this imbalance the women seemed to suffer the most. Many men became more irresponsible doing as they wished. As by their nature, women want a husband, a baby, and to make a home for the most part. Some men want that also. There were just not enough men to go around, and besides men seem to prefer that they were so much in demand. Women tried sharing for a while, but there was little success, and many women became more vulnerable. They were exploited, pimped, and sold right along with very young girls into slavery. They could be an indentured servant. Some women were executed for being of no service to men. It was a very sad time. Women could work as nurses, maids, medics, indentured servants or go work in the pleasure houses, but they also could be sold out right if they fell in anyway. For many women, their earnings were not their own; it would belong to the man, whether it was a husband, a father, a brother, the man who owned her, or the man who sold her. Some women ran away. Trackers were hired to find them. Roaming camps began to form by these women to have some kind of refuge for these runaways. Many had lost their way, and many more were joining the ranks of the lost. The women out numbered the men by a large margin. They were like gypsies, staying on the move. This made it harder for the bounty hunters to find them. They lack skills, like fighting knowledge, and just plain old organization. These ladies depended more and more on each other. The bonds became strong.

Education of women was not a priority and was even discouraged by most. Everyone knew women were inferior in some form or fashion. They were not considered whole people. Even women themselves had, for the most part, bought into these ideations that sounded oddly male in tone. Phrases like "you know how women are," "men are just superior," "you know women are weak and they're just not as smart as men," "women just can't have real friends," "let a woman do it and she will screw it up"—this all was the norm, common consensus no matter where one might go.

After many years of things getting worse, devolving into anarchy, turmoil, chaos, violence, and murder of any females for any reason a male saw fit, gender imbalance was at an alltime high. Rape gangs had begun to spring up. Slavers would haul in women to the selling block naked. Some women chose to fight back. The women that fought back would take some hard beatings and rape, even death. Slowly women began to organize, to come up with training. They would help each other with moving through these areas. Slowly they became good at hiding in plain sight and even taking out a rape gang or at least a few of these rogue males. The element of surprise was so good. They had developed single suits in camouflage containing over ten small concealed weapons made perfectly for a woman's hand and physique. They never trained or slept in the same place twice for a very long time. These few women lived in the bushes for the most part. The tribes were kept in small numbers, making it easier to move at a moment notice. They became excellent hunters. Hunger is a great motivator.

As time went on, the name Kalifee was used for these women. Guerilla warfare was their specialty. Kali came from the Hindu goddess. This terrifying image of a blue female that killed demons cut off their heads and wore them as a necklace. This was not exactly what they would have chosen. It was a derogatory and demeaning slang that some of the more educated males used, "That's a Kali." Later, the fee was added as a shortcut to belittle females even more—that women were "fees," not female. The ladies of these wandering tribes began to accept this name and used it themselves. At first it was just to make jokes. Then it was adopted as their name. After all women did not have a last name. They had the last name of their fathers and their husbands. So in actuality, the feminine last name was lost. Many thought that females never had a last name at all. Finally, the name Kalifee stuck. After many years, the name was made official. The image of the warrior goddess became an image that many feared and hated. This seemed to work well. Even some goddess worship sprang up. It was considered a private choice religion, and public displays were discouraged.

After many, many years, the Kalifee had evolved into a large organization of women. They were determined to have order and a permanent central headquarters, and eventually they did. It was built with escape routes that would strategically place their attackers right where they wanted them. Women in the Kalifee were educated, fed well, and trained to fight, not like men but like women. Yes, they were not as strong as men, and they handled weapons differently, but they grew into fearsome fighters with techniques developed over time that were deadly enough. They developed a breeding program. Some women became highly trained courtesans taught to control most any situation with the men through sex; some were specialized performers, exhibitionist, healers, and dancers. They continued to travel around like gypsies and to maintain the ability to move on an instant's notice. Other women and some men joined them in times of trouble. No woman was made to do anything she did not want to do, but all had to learn defense. Women have never been safe, and the Kali knew this in their hearts. No woman was forced to do anything they did not want to do. Kalifee developed highlevel specialized training. No woman, child, or man wanted anything material. It made their sisterhood strong in their values, and they were a sisterhood and growing stronger every day. This, of course, brought on jealousy, fear, and a need for some to put these women in their place, which could be the grave. Some Kalis chose to live in permanent structures. All structures were strategically planned out so it would be hard for anyone to raid them and take any of them. Field maneuvers would continue. The Kalifees would not lose what they had learned, and some still lived in small traveling tribes. Their military genius was real and so necessary for them to survive. At present they were the main force that controlled the most habitable areas left on this earth.

As this story opens, Niea, a commander with the Kalifee, was ordered to go to the Gabba region. The area was a thick forest and had small agricultural lands. Technology had been lost for the most part, but the Kalifee had developed gamma ray devices for several purposes. They also had devices that were solar power. They shared the solar power knowledge with others, but the gamma rays were theirs and theirs alone. Of course, this caused more jealousy. The fighting prowess of the Kali women was truly a deterrent against attacks. They stayed command ready. Small teams were developed to move on anyone who would attack them. Many people were afraid of them and kept a respectful distance.

Niea had boarded the liner that was to take her to the outlands of Gabba. It was a localrun liner business, and what a ragged piece of "I hope we get there in one piece" it was. It was a rough flight, and Niea got no rest, but there would be time for that later. The total mission was not revealed to her. It never was. It was a tactic of the Kalis to protect them, and for the most part it would. But circumstances don't always suit secrets, do they?

When the liner landed, Niea could not be more grateful. It was one bumpy ride. It was a small liner with little room with odors of a barn. She waited until the other passengers were off the liner, and she got her small bag and stepped to the passageway. A large very dark muscular man bumped into her. She stepped back eyeing him. She was ready for a bit of hand-to-hand combat if that was called for—that was what she could do among other things. But the dark man flashed a winning smile. "Sorry, beautiful lady, I meant no harm."

The pilot entered the cabin. "Is all okay here?"

Niea said, "Yes, all is well." She held her gaze on this large charming man. She was starting to get a feel for him.

The large dark man said with a heavy island accent, "All is well. I will accompany the lady if she wishes. You are going to the hostel?" She nodded. Then he looked at Niea, and she knew, somehow, he would never try to hurt her. She felt he could be trusted. She could trust her instincts. They had never failed her.

She turned to this dark huge man and said, "Yes, please escort me, sir."

He bowed graciously, saying, "After you, pleasing lady." She got her bag and walked off the liner. He walked up beside her and introduced himself, "My name Jamal. What is yours?"

Niea smiled at him and said, "Niea. Pleased to meet you, Jamal."

They walked in silence for a few moments then he said, "Shall we go?"

Then she said, "To the hostel it is."

Jamal said, "There is only one." He laughed that infectious laugh, and it reminded Niea of someone she knew all too well.

As they walked, Jamal said, "Shall we jog? I need the stretch. How about you?" Niea nodded and took off. Jamal was right behind her. It was about two miles, which was nothing for Niea, and Jamal stayed right with her. When they arrived at the hostile Jamal was a bit out of breath. He said, "Well, you are in shape. But a Kalifee warrior would be able to outlast most anyone."

Niea stopped dead in her tracks, "How do you know that?" She was not wearing her single suit. She had no Kalifee markings of any kind on her.

Jamal laughed again, that incredible warm hardy way of his, then said, "It is all over you, dear lady, but don't worry. I'll keep your secret."

She said, "Let's go inside."

Jamal said, "After you, my lady," and opened the door for her. He called out, "Miguel, you here?"

Miguel answered back, "Jamal, that you?" Jamal yelled, "'Shoo is!"

Miguel came out of the back. He had been working on a drain and was quite dirty. He came out wiping his hands, saying, "I'm dirty." He stuck out his hand for a good shake with his friend. Jamal grabbed him and hugged him. "Man, it is so good to see you." He added, "Want ya to meet a friend of mine."

Miguel turned and froze. "Hello." It almost sounded like a question. He was taken back by this beautiful woman. Jamal gave a sly smile. He could see that Miguel was overwhelmed by this magnificent woman. Jamal said, "You got a real drink around here, my friend?"

Miguel turned and reached into a cabinet just behind him and pulled out a bottle of homemade wine. "Are you two together?"

Jamal answered with his big grin, "No, I just met her at the station." Jamal had a way with women and people. Miguel wondered if maybe they were here for a bed together. Miguel handed Jamal the bottle and three glasses and said, "Serve it up, my man."

Niea said, "I will be outside for most of the night setting my chargers. Got to get them loaded."

Jamal said, "Okay," and served up the homemade wine. Miguel dipped up a stew he had made. Miguel almost stumbled, but he caught himself and said, "Well, don't you need to eat something?"

Jamal was excited. "Your cooking is the best. If you were a woman, I would take you as my cook."

Miguel said, "Let me get cleaned up." Jamal poured up three glasses and handed Niea one and set down one for Miguel. Then he went to get them all a bowl of stew, came back, and handed each one a bowl. They all ate and drank their wine in silence. It was clear that the food and wine were just too good.

Jamal said, "This is crackin', Miguel."

Niea said, "Did you make the wine too?"

Miguel nodded. When they were all finished, Miguel gathered the bowls and spoons, retuning them to the kitchen area; washed up ever thing; and cleaned himself up some more at the sink. Jamal laughed, then he pulled out his harmonica and said, "Great! Me and Niea will go sing some songs."

Niea shook her head no. "I don't sing well." She drank some wine. And then she drank some more. It was excellent. Jamal started playing his harmonica, a slow-moving piece of blues. Niea started a low hum. Jamal thought this lady can sing the blues. She hummed along perfectly and sipped on this fabulous wine. Niea saw that they were listening to her, and she stopped.

Jamal said, "Don't stop, dear lady!" Niea stood up and began to tone, and Jamal joined her. This went on for a few. Niea continued to sip on her glass. Then she started to giggle like a kid until she sat down in a plop in a luckily nearby chair. "I am tipsy?"

Jamal whispered in a grin, "Yes, you are. I think that is enough for you." There was more silence. Miguel's eyes were scanning Niea on and off. Niea leaned forward with her elbows on her knees.

Jamal asked, "So, Niea, you got a man, dear lady?" Niea started to laugh. "No."

Jamal said, "Why not?"

She said, "No time."

Jamal said, "So, you have a man in your past?"

Niea sat up and mumbled, "No." She placed her empty glass on the floor and sank deeper into the soft chair. Jamal looked at Miguel, giving him a sly grin, and pursed his lips toward Niea. Miguel rolled his eyes in embarrassment.

Jamal said, "What are you waiting for?"

Niea said, "The right man? I gotta wee."

Jamal said, "Maybe he is near?" Then he winked at Miguel. Niea stood up a bit wobbly. She stumbled, and Miguel caught her. She fell into him again, and he helped her steady herself. She wallwalked toward the bathroom, which Miguel had pointed toward. He waited and helped her back to his bed, where she passed out.

There was a loud knock at the door. Jamal knew he felt someone, but there was no malice. He got up and opened the door, and Miguel stood looking at Niea lying on his bed. She just might be the best woman he had ever seen, and Miguel had seen and had many women. But there was no one that compared to her. Jamal opened the door and said, "Well, hello, ladies. Please come in." In walked Cal, Zek, and Tulie fresh from maneuvers in full Kalifee warrior gear.

Cal said, "Where's the commander?"

Miguel asked, "Commander?"

Cal said, "Yes, Commander Niea."

Jamal answered with a gesture toward the back room.

Cal pushed by and went to Niea, "Commander, Commander." She shook Niea softly.

Niea rolled over, opening one eye, saying, "Ah, Cal."

Cal said, "What's wrong?" Cal was angry. Tulie and Zek were at the door in a flash.

Jamal said, "She drank a little too much wine." Cal was upset. "She doesn't drink."

From the other room, Niea called out, "I drank too much wine." Then she rolled over and went back to sleep, if one could call it that. Jamal walked up behind Cal, saying, "It's pretty good wine."

Cal came around on him, got in his face, and stared in his eyes. They were the same height. Jamal was a thick, muscular, and powerful. He did not break his gaze, then he smiled that infectious smile, and it caught Cal off guard.

Cal thought, I can take him.

Jamal said, "Oh, did not mean to upset you, pretty lady, but if you want to fight me, so be it."

Then Cal said, "Where's the wine? I would like some." The other two ladies relaxed and went to see their commander. Jamal poured Cal a drink. She sipped it at first then turned around and asked, "Who are you?"

"My name is Jamal." He graciously bowed his head.

Cal could only think that this was a real specimen of a man, a very dark man. There was something about him that rang true.

"Would you ladies like a drink of some mighty fine wine?" Both came out into the sitting area, and Miguel poured them a glass of wine.

Cal asked, "Where do we sleep and have a bath?" Miguel pointed, and Cal and Tulie followed him. Cal downed her wine then headed off behind him to the bunk room. He showed her the bunk room for the ladies and where she could clean up. Then he returned to his guest.

Jamal said, "The commander wanted to set some charges in the earlier morn."

Zek said that she would do it. Jamal offered to help. She nodded, saying, "Let me get the packs."

While he and Miguel were waiting, Jamal said, "Fine group of ladies, eh?" Miguel nodded. He was debating heavily in his mind to sleep in his own bed. There was this beautiful young woman in his bed, passed out. He decided to sleep on the floor next to the bed.

Jamal waited as Zek gathered the things she needed, and both left. She asked where a high area would be that would be good for solar loading. Jamal led the way. They walked in silence for quite a while. Jamal pointed to an area he thought would do. Zek scanned the area and nodded. This would do just fine. She said, "You know the area?" Jamal nodded and flashed his winning grin. Zek couldn't help but to be taken by him. She guessed everyone did. He was a confident, charming large dark man. In fact, he could hardly be seen at all at night. Zek found several areas that would do just fine. She would set the chargers just before sunrise. It was obvious to both that being quiet was very important, especially in a new area. Jamal had sat down on a rock, then he placed his jacket over an area near him and gestured for Zek to sit. He was a true gentleman. They sat in silence for some time.

Finally, Jamal spoke, "How about you, beautiful lady? What's your story?" There was a very long silence. Jamal thought maybe he should start first. He did wish to know these people, these fascinating women. "How about I tell you about me." Zek looked at him and smiled. She was an average-sized woman with a muscular body, thick and powerful. Jamal could see she could give him a good fight. Her eyes were almond shaped, her hair jet black, and there was a sadness that Jamal could feel. She was reluctant. After all he was a stranger.

Jamal began, "I was born on an island with a mama and a dada. It was a very good life, simple. We had enough to eat. My mama was a wonderful woman with a splendid heart. Dada was a hard man but fair. Then one day the Gogatt showed up. Why I didn't know. Turned out they were slavers looking for fresh meat to sell. They killed my parents, took me. I was nine. I was a small child for my age, so they put me in a bag and hauled me off. For the first year with them, they made me live on my own around one of their camps. I had to fend for myself. If any of them saw me, I got a real beating. I was made to go barefoot. Now I have very tough feet. Very few children lived very long with the Gogatt, but I did. So, they thought maybe I could be of some use. For the next year I was a slave boy. Then one day, one of them tried to rape me in my butt, and I killed him. I started to run and did not stop until I ran into an old woman, who was dark like me. I told her the whole story, and she hid me well. Once they gave up on me, she allowed me to work around her home for her for room and board. She taught me many things— hunting, cooking, sewing, and so on. She was good to me. She even taught me love. I thank the Spirit every day for her. Finally, one day, the Gogatt returned, and they killed her. So, I killed them all. I buried her, said a prayer over her, and left. With what she taught me, I was able to fend for myself well and have been doing well enough since." Again, there was a long silence. He could feel that she wanted to tell her story, so he sat and waited.

Finally, with a deep inhale and exhale, she started, "I was born way north of here, a colder climate. My father died when I was very young. My mother moved into a Kalifee camp, and they helped us. So, I always thought well of the Kalifee. They were good to me, my mother, and my two sisters. We worked hard. We had food and clothing. The camp move as ordered. It was a way of warding off attacks. Then one day these horrible men came and started killing Kalis. They were slavers. Right behind them was a wave of Kali warriors, and the fighting was bloody. A Gogatt grabbed me by the arm and started to try to rape me. Then this tall blond Kali jumped on his back and rammed a blade into his neck. She picked me up and took me to a tree and whispered, 'Climb,' and I did as she said." Up in the tree, I could see this mighty female warrior running toward these horrid men. I tried to keep quiet. Then I saw my mother and two sisters being dragged away by these horrible men. "I started screaming, and one of them came back for me. A smaller one climbed the tree with ease and kicked me to the ground. Several of these awful men dragged all four of us to a thicket, and the rape started, first my sisters then my mother. They did gruesome things. Things I would never know people would do to each other. They held their legs open and rammed things into them. I was fighting the small one, then the tall blond Kali came back. She took all of them out no problem. Then she told me to come with her, and I did. I've done as she says ever since. After it was all over, this incredible woman took me back to bury my family." Then, she started to cry.

Jamal put his large powerful arm around her and said, "It is okay to cry, to let it out. Let the spirit hear your pain so the healing can begin." Zek wept, and Jamal rocked her gently until she fell asleep. Just before dawn, he woke Zek. "The sun is coming, sweet lady." Zek had slept well. Jamal dozed a bit. She cleared her eyes and gave him one big grin and went to work. He assisted her as needed, and soon they headed back to hostel.

When Jamal and Zek arrived, Miguel had some hot cereal on the stove, and they ate it up. Niea was sitting on Miguel's bed with her head in her hands. Miguel walked into the room and asked if she wanted something to eat. She shook her head no and lay back on the bed. Cal came into the room with a loud voice, saying, "Commander, are you getting up?"

Niea said, "Yes, Cal." She stood up and almost fell back. Miguel caught her and helped her stand up.

Cal said, "Want something to eat, Niea?"

She gave a long exhale. "I need to eat." Cal stood quietly, having never seen Niea hung over. It was Cal who was usually hung over. Niea turned around and held onto Miguel. It made him nervous, but he enjoyed holding her for a few seconds, then he led her to the eating area and served her. Cal ate a bowl of this hot tasty cereal. She thanked Miguel and turned to Niea. "How you are feeling, Commander?"

Niea groaned, "I'm okay. No more wine for me."

Cal gave a soft laugh. "I'm not used to this. We've swapped places. What's on the agenda today?"

Niea took a few seconds to gather her thoughts and said, "Of course we have to wait for the chargers to load. Oh! I didn't place them!"

Jamal and Zek walked through the door. Jamal said, "Don't worry, Zek did it."

Niea sat looking at Zek, saying, "Something in you has shifted." Zek felt good, whole. She knew that somehow Jamal had something to do with it. She looked at him and smiled. He winked at her. Then she excused herself and asked where the bathroom was. Miguel showed her where she could bathe and sleep. Zek did all those things and went to lie down. She slept like a baby. When everyone had eaten, Miguel cleaned up the kitchen. Niea inquired about the maneuvers. Cal said they were boring. Tulie sat in silence as usual, but she never really said much. Niea had tried to get her to open up, but it wasn't happening. Tulie was their best assassin, and she was very good at it. Her lack of emotional involvement in people was very useful for such a task. Her small frame and uncanny ability to slip in and out of places was formidable.

Niea asked, "Where are we on our projects?"

Cal whipped out the collapsible sword. "Works real good, Commander! I didn't show it to anyone, okay?"

Cal had bragged on Niea in the past, so she had learned to keep their projects under wraps. Niea asked, "Think we could work on getting materials for making some more?"

Cal responded saying she and Tulie could see what was available locally. There would be no training for a few days. The maneuvers had just ended, and Niea knew without a doubt they had been grueling. Besides there were plenty of other things they need to do. Niea knew they all needed a break. Miguel had been listening and said that there was a market near where many things were sold and swapped. He also told them of waste dumps that could be helpful. Then Niea looked at Cal. "Want to go have a look? But if you need to rest, please do so." Cal and Tulie seemed excited to go. Miguel had provided for them some local clothes. Cal's long-legged self looked funny in the ladies pants he had given her. No one laughed. Cal would have torn them off. They asked Miguel where the marketplace was, and Cal was sure they could find it with no problem, so they left. They would visit the dumps later. Niea thanked Miguel for all he had done. He reminded her that this was his job, and besides the Kalifee provided all of this for this purpose. Niea said to him, "No one cooks like you. I must be grateful and appreciative for that. Would you have time to show me the place?" He nodded, and he gestured the way to the door. This beautiful dark-haired violet-eyed woman did make him nervous. He was not used to a woman making him feel this way. He had always been good with the ladies. He was gorgeous and humble. Niea found him so interesting.

They walk for a while in silence. First, he showed her the beehives he kept. She was particularly impressed with his use of organic material, especially the recycling. There was a small pasture he kept. He had said he wanted some animals someday. It was just too nice here. She could tell he was very proud of the work he had done here, but he continued to be so humble. He also had a small garden, and there was a local fellow that would help him from time to time and a couple ladies that would help him clean. Other than that, this place was all him. Niea totally enjoyed him showing her his wonderful place, saying, "I love it out here. This is the life I would have."

Miguel said, "I would like to have some dairy cows, maybe a horse, a mule—I don't know, a full working farm. It would be nice. A lot of work though." He wanted to kiss her. He had been with many women, but this one was different, special; he couldn't put his finger on it. They continued to walk in silence.

Niea said, "My team and I can help here for a while. Well, at least until the Kalifee decide what they want us to do here." They continued to walk around. He could see she truly loved this place, and that warmed his heart.

Jamal said as he walked up on them. "So, Niea, what's on the agenda for today?"

Niea whirled around. "Good morning, Jamal. Well, we can't do much. It is so overcast the chargers are going to be slow. No training.

I want the ladies to have a break. They have been on maneuvers, and a few days off would be in order. So I guess it's free time, in a way."

Jamal looked at Miguel. "You know we gonna need some meat for you to cook." He slapped Miguel on the back and laughed that glorious laugh of his.

Miguel stumbled and felt ridiculous. "Yes, we need to do just that. I have a longbow and a crossbow. Take your pick." With that they headed to the shed where the weapons were. Niea thought she might go with them, but her head was throbbing. So, this is what Cal feels.

Niea stood for a long time and watched these two fine men walk off to the woods. As they disappeared, she turned and walked for a long time around this wonderful place. She would love to live here. She knew that she could if she chose. But she had her team, and there was much work to do. There were threats on the horizon. She knew this was why they were here. When she returned to the hostel, Zek was up and eating some fruit she had found on the table. "How are you feeling, Commander?"

Niea laughed. "No more wine for me." Zek asked where everyone was, and Niea explained. Niea said, "You were different when you came back with Jamal—shifted. What happened?" Niea's observations were excellent but annoying.

"He told me his story, then I told him some of my story," Zek said.

Niea sat and looked at Zek. "What else?"

Zek said, "I cried. He held me, then I fell asleep, and when I woke, I just felt better. He is a wonder of a man, don't you think?"

Niea said, "That's so good." Her smile deepened, for she loved her ladies with all her heart. Everything she did was for their good health and that they could do their job and continue to thrive.

Zek said, "Well, Commander, I think I'm going to work out some. There are some moves I need to practice." Niea smiled at her, and she left. Niea went into the hostel and began to clean up.

When the two men returned, it was close to dark. They had a large deer. Niea met them, amazed at how fast they had brought down such an incredible animal. This always made her sad. But she knew that her people had to eat, and the best way to get protein was animal flesh. They strung the deer up and began to butcher it. Niea stood close and prayed. She had to thank the animal for giving its life for them. Jamal noticed her praying and joined her. He also felt this was the thing to do. When she opened her eyes, she saw Jamal with his head bowed. She touched his arm, and he looked at her. He was sad too!

Miguel yelled out, "Are you going to help me?" Jamal moved up on the deer, took the guts, and put them in a bucket of water. Every part of the deer would be used, no waste here. He began cleaning the innards. Miguel had started a fire with a large caldron suspended over it. After Jamal had finished bleeding the deer, skinning it, and cleaning the abdominal cavity, Miguel was ready to cut it up and put most of it in his smokehouse. He closed the door and returned with a large piece for their supper. He said to Niea, "How would you like it cooked for supper, Lady Niea?"

"What's easiest?" she said.

"Don't want to bore you with stew, but that would be the best.

I have some fresh herbs that should be good," he said. "Sounds so good, Miguel."

Miguel headed off to the kitchen to start supper. She called after him, "Want some help?" He nodded, and she followed him. He showed her where everything was and asked if she could start the water. Jamal had drawn some, and it was in the corner beside the door. He wanted to clean up before he started the stew. So Niea got the water, started the fire, and waited. He soon returned and began chopping up the fresh herbs he had gotten from the garden. Niea loved this—cooking in a kitchen, being in the country and with a beautiful quiet man. He showed her where the potatoes and carrots were. Then he asked her if she could handle a knife. She gave him a look and said, "You think?"

He laughed. Of course she could handle a knife; what was he thinking? Soon the stew was simmering, and it smelled so good. "Miguel, where did you learn to cook like this?"

He said, "My mother, sisters, and by just doing it." She said, "You have sisters?"

He said, "You might know them. They are Kalifee from the breeding program."

She was taken back. "Your mother and sisters are Kalifee?"

He said, "Yes. My mother was a high-level breeder. After she gave birth to two daughters, she fell in love with another brownskinned man and married him. They had one child, me. I don't see them much. They come here rarely. They are busy with their own lives." There was a sadness there. Niea didn't pry. He would tell his story when he was ready. He said, "It's almost ready." At that moment Cal and Tulie came through the door.

Cal said, "That smells good."

Niea said, "Get washed up, and we will eat, compliments to Miguel." She called to Zek and Jamal. Soon they were enjoying Miguel's fine stew. Once they were full, Niea got up to clean up. Miguel tried to stop her because that was his job. But Niea insisted.

Cal said, "Let her do it, or she will drive you crazy."

So finally, they all gathered in the sitting area, and Jamal pulled out his harmonica, saying, "Miguel, get your guitar." Miguel shook his head. Jamal said, "Come on, man, play us a tune. At least one." Miguel gave a shy smile and went to get his guitar. When he returned, Jamal was playing softly on his mouth harp. It was an old tune that Cal recognized. She started to sway her body. Niea knew that they were going to have a show. Cal could straight up dance and would put on a show that was something to see. Miguel came in, sat down, and started to play along. Cal wanted a drink and gestured to Zek to pour her some of Miguel's fine wine. Niea seemed relaxed and asked Zek to pour her some too, just a little. Soon the tempo turned up, and Cal drank down the wine and danced Zek a thank-you. Then she held out her glass to get some more. Jamal had not taken his eyes off her. He was more intrigued every time he was around her. Look at this tall blond woman. She could kick your ass in the morning and dance your cares away at night. What a woman, and the music was doing everyone good. Miguel was watching Niea watch Cal. She took so much joy in what she called her ladies. The heart of Niea was so warm and inviting. He couldn't, wouldn't, let her catch him looking at her the way he did. What in the grand scheme of heaven and earth was he doing? He was so drawn to her, and he wanted to run at the same time. But he stayed near where she was. Everything about her had a hold on him and the way she looked at him. Her smile, her violet eyes flashing—he needed to get a grip.

Miguel had had many women, too many to count. The ladies loved Miguel, and he loved the ladies. He often visited the traveling brothels of the Kalifee, and there was a special one, Varah. She saw very few men in her quarters. Once she had done her dance— and oh, what a dance it was—she might have a session with maybe one. Very expensive, and what she did or didn't do was totally up to her. Varah and Miguel had met at Central Headquarters years ago. Miguel thought she was from the Kalifee breeding program. Varah had always wanted Miguel ever since they were children. She would make sure that her traveling band of entertainers came to the area where he was. She did love him completely—his attentive nature, his one-of-a-kind lovemaking, and of course, the way he looked. He was stunning with his caramel skin and golden-brown eyes. There was no one other than Miguel. He was just the best and would do whatever she wanted. But she could never seem to capture his heart. He did care about her, but it just wasn't love, and that was what she wanted. Vahar wanted devotion. It is was what most women want. She could only hope to see him again soon.

Meanwhile the music and dancing had turned all the way up. Cal was moving and grooving; Jamal joined her and followed her every move. Cal couldn't help herself; she like that he could move. She loved that actually. Soon Miguel started up a slow love song and began to sing it. Cal and Jamal went for the slow dance. He was even better at this than Cal could have ever imagined. He took her in his arms, pulled her close, and began to rock her slowly. She could feel him getting very hard. She looked at him with that look. He said, "He likes you a lot." Cal laughed so hard she stopped dancing. Then Jamal grabbed her and whirled her around and around. She was starting to like this huge man. Then she thought maybe she couldn't take him. He was massive, muscular, and the best-looking dark man she had ever seen, and that wicked and indelible laugh of his! He pulled her close to him and said, "If he goes off, it's a compliment." She laughed again. She had had a few men in her life, most in a drunken haze with a couple of women thrown in, but it had been a while. Cal fanned, fatigued, and gestured she needed a drink. Jamal bowed graciously and grabbed Zek's hand and whirled her out on the dance floor. He did not pull her up on him; he thought of her more like a sister, even a daughter. So, they danced for a while, and he did delight. To watch such a large man dance was just too good.

Finally, Miguel finished up his last tune and excused himself so he could finish up cleaning up the kitchen. Niea followed to help. She was so quiet he did not hear her. He turned and there she was. He said, "Woo, I didn't hear you. Sneak up on someone, can't you?" Niea said, "Only if I have to." She went to the sink and got the water to wash up. He started to stop her, then he looked at her and bowed. She laughed. She had had only one glass of wine. Liquid courage, Cal had called it. She was feeling courageous. She stepped up on him and looked in his golden-brown eyes. He was nervous and excited. Her eyes were violet and intriguing. Is that even humanly possible? She thought about kissing him. She felt a bit inadequate. She had never done this before. She had never kissed a man, never been with a man or a woman. He was the first man she had been this brazen with, or any man.

He wanted this so bad, but he was waiting on her. She leaned back and took a deep breath. Neither one knew how to be the aggressor. Niea instinctually knew it would have to be her. He would never make a move. Niea was angry with herself, so she turned and started washing dishes. Miguel stepped up on her. Her head was right up under his nose, and he took a deep breath. It was a smell he would never forget. He almost fell into her. She knew exactly what was going on. Somebody make a move. Here we are a virgin and a lady's man. What the hell is going on? He stood there for a minute or two taking in all her smell. Then he touched her neck with his hand. This was all Niea could take. She turned and kissed him with the passion of fully trained Kalifee queen. It was more than he could handle. How could he be the first? He had to admit it was so special. He had always been with a professional. It was all he had known. His timid nature had required he wait for the lady. They loved it. It worked for him so well. But this was unexplored new territory, and he was scared. There they stood frozen in that moment that they both wanted. But neither knew how to proceed. Well, they did know, but neither let go. They stood there looking at each other. Then he kissed her and pulled her up on him. He was ready for this, and she knew it.

Then he let go, and she said, "No! Hold me at least." He held her as long as he could, then Jamal came into the room not saying a thing. This picture was just too good. It felt right in this violent world they lived. Niea looked at Jamal and winked, then she excused herself and went off to the bunk room. Jamal stood there with that wry grin.

Jamal said with a grin on his face, "How's was that? Looked really good, ay!" Miguel had a grin on his face that lit up the room. He turned and finished up the kitchen area with joy and longing.

Jamal thought, Well, this was an acceptable night. He got to dance and hold Cal, and Miguel got to first base. They had been friends for such a long time. Jamal would love for Miguel to find a good woman. He had met Miguel in the woods while hunting. They brought down a deer together. Miguel had made them some backstrap stew in the woods with some wild herbs. Of course, it was delicious. Miguel had mastered cooking in the field and at home.

In the morning, Zek got the chargers and headed back to the hostel. There she got the ladies to ready; a message had come through from Central. They were to head out to the designated area. Miguel provided a map and pointed to where they needed to go. The ladies gathered what they needed. Miguel was not keen on them going there. It was dangerous, poisonous; he really knew this could not be good. He took Niea by the hand and kissed it, asking them to please be careful. She said they would and kissed him a lovely goodbye. Jamal hurried out of the hostel, saying he would tag along, and off they went.

When they arrived, Tulie was not comfortable here. The smell of the place had triggered some old memories. Plus, their equipment was not working well. The radiation in the area was interfering. Niea could feel Tulie's deep discomfort. She tried to comfort her, but Tulie was needing to leave. But Niea knew she had to do something. So she started to gather samples. There was this strange hole, so Niea got down on her stomach and lowered herself as far down the hole as she could. Then suddenly, a puff of odd white smoke came out of the hole, and Niea breathed it in before she could move away. She began to cough repeatedly. Her complexion became pale. She did not look well. Jamal picked her up and headed back to the hostel. He ran the whole way. Niea was not heavy. He ran hard and fast. He got her to the bed in Miguel's room and laid her down. She was barely breathing. Miguel was trying to hold in his panic. What could he do? What to do? Jamal started to try to breathe for her. Cal and the others came rushing to Niea.

Miguel looked at Cal. "Who's the medic here?" Cal came forward to assess Niea. After a few moments, her breathing got a bit better. So Jamal dropped down on one knee and started to pray. He was afraid for her. He had prayed over many a dying person and animal. Miguel was in the corner freaking out. Tulie stepped up to him and took his hand. He knew she was trying to help him, steady him. It was helping a bit. He was so scared for her. He knew he should have demanded she not go. He did not want any of them sick, but why Niea? He dropped to one knee and started to cry then pray. His heart was breaking. Tulie sat down beside him, holding tightly on to his hand. Cal finished her assessment.

Cal looked at Zek. "Could you get my pack for me?" Zek returned and handed Cal a small pack. She pricked Niea's finger and traced a small amount of blood onto a very small reader she had. She waited a few moments, and a read came up. Niea's blood was toxic— way too much acid for her to survive. "We have to neutralize her blood. She's acidotic." Cal looked at Miguel. "You have any lime?" Miguel was glad to have something to do. He went out back to the garden and found some lime and returned. He handed it to Cal. "I need water. As fresh as you can get." Miguel returned with some fresh drawn water and handed to Cal. She mixed the two together. She stripped off Niea's garment and began to rub the mixture all over her. "We have to allow this to dry then wait." Miguel did not know if he could wait. His nerves had gotten the best of him. Waiting was so tortuous. He thought he was going to lose his mind. Cal covered Niea with a light sheet and stepped back. She put her hand onto his shoulder. "I know this will be hard." Miguel began to cry; she simply could not die.

Niea had a restless night. Between sweating and coughing, it was hard for her to rest. Cal stayed with her, attending to her every need. In the morning, Miguel came in to see how she was doing. Cal looked up and shrugged. Niea was still alive, and that was a start. She did not smell good. There was some bad crap coming out of her. What the hell did she get into? Miguel sat down by Cal and started to cry. Cal thought this man loved the commander. Niea came to and called out first Cal then Miguel. He rushed to her side. She took his hand. "Don't cry, my love. Cal will save me. I can feel it." Then she drifted back out of awareness. He looked at Cal with huge tears coming out of his eyes. "I know you can do this." It would take time, but Cal was encouraged. How could the commander die with so many pulling for her?

It was early dawn when Cal found Miguel in the kitchen. This poor man was so sad. She said, "Could you stay with Niea today?" He nodded. "Try to feed her. I know you can do it." Cal got Zek, and they got some masks and a couple of readers. They would return to the hole in the ground to gather some more samples. She did not ask Tulie to go; she knew Tulie had been disturbed by the area, and no Kali was asked to do anything she did not want to do. Besides, she could assist Miguel with the care of the commander. Miguel never left Niea's side except to prepare something for her to consume. She ate and drank with Miguel helping her. As always, she was amazed by what Miguel could make. It was always a delight. After she ate, she was very tried. She slept, and Miguel tore himself away to do anything for her. He gave her a bath and cleaned up the mess she made in the bed when her bowels had let go. He had combed her hair, which had started to fall out. She still had a very bad odor, but he did not care. When she got cold, he would crawl in the bed and curl himself around her to keep her warm. He cried and prayed, rocking her gently. He hummed softly some tunes he thought she might like. Finally, when Cal and Zek returned, they found him holding her ever so gently. This man was Niea's without reserve, and he was a very reserved person. Niea meant the world to him. He would do everything he could do to make sure that she did not die.

Several days went by, and Niea slowly recovered. Cal knew without a doubt that Miguel's care and the vegetables/herbs and root concoctions had helped save Niea's life. But now she was bald. All her beautiful black hair was gone, but she got stronger every day. As they waited for a message from Central, the ladies, Jamal, and Miguel got to work on the place. The first night that Niea was obviously well, she and Miguel slipped off to his room, and oh, what a night! Every thought or idea Niea had, Miguel provided a true reading of her every wish. They even got into some wild sex in the coming days. Niea began to read Miguel's every desire and that she knew what he wanted, where to touch him, and how. It was just the best. Niea never knew it could be like this. The intimacy and sincerity were mind-blowing, for there was no better way to describe what was happening between them. They would get rough. Both would show up at supper with bruises on them. If someone mentioned any of these questionable marks, they would kiss the areas in question and giggle. It was so cute and was sickening. But everyone here enjoyed the play between the two. Good medicine, as the elders would say.

They all worked at the hostel. Waiting for anything could be aggravating. "Keep busy," Cal would bark mostly to herself. Jamal kept his distance. He would occasionally wink at Cal, and she would ignore him. She saw everything he did, and if he didn't flirt with her, she would make sure she did some girl posing to get his attention, then he would look at her, and she would ignore him. Jamal saw everything she did. He would laugh to himself. He was enjoying it for the most part. He loved the way Cal looked. Her long lanky body, the way she would curl herself into a chair or on her bed. She fascinated him even into his dreams.

One day there was a bit of loud talking out front. Niea went out front, and she found herself behind what looked like lady boys, two of them, fighters, assassins, bodyguards, but whose? As Niea approached the commotion she saw the one and only Vahar. Cal called her a stunt queen. She was dressed to the nines and smelled so good. If Niea asked Vahar what that was scent she was wearing, Vahar would say it was just her. No, it wasn't, and why was she here with this entourage? She was way out of protocol. Why would anyone need such a group? Yes, they were lady boys, but they were also hightech assassins. Niea would say nothing, but Cal would probably have a throw-down fit and alerted Central. Niea stepped into the middle of the argument as she always did. She had little fear especially when she could see all around her. "What's up here?"

Zek stepped forward. "Commander, her bodyguards have weapons, and they must surrender them." The lady boys twisted their bodies like Vahar. Niea could tell they had been hanging out with her. They were also dedicated to her. They would die for her.

Vahar said, "Of course, Commander, that's not a problem." She placed her eyes—enormous brown eyes—at her two companions. One of them had six weapons on him, the other had eight. There were at least three poisons found on both. *Well, you came to play, ah? Not today,*

Satan! "So Vahar, no one expects you of any of this except all of us." Niea looked at this beauty with her head turned sideways.

Vahar did one of her coy sly moves and smiled. "I meant no harm."

Niea laughed, "Of course not." Miguel came up behind Niea. He saw who it was, and he was pleasantly surprised and somewhat delighted. Niea saw all of this. Vahar told Miguel that they surrendered all their weapons and that she never meant any harm.

Niea rolled her eyes and stepped aside. "Where are my manners? Please, you and your entourage, come on in and have a drink." Everyone followed the uninvited guests into the hostel. Niea wasn't sure, but she thought she just might have an idea why this woman was here. Would it have anything to do with the beautiful brownskinned man that ran this place? She could tell by the way Vahar looked at him. If it was not love, it was lust in its highest form. She was crazy for Miguel. Niea knew how gifted Miguel was at lovemaking. For a moment she was so thankful she had chosen the man she did. But in that moment, as she saw this most gifted queen, one from the highest order, come here for Miguel, Niea knew it would not be long before he would go to see her. Not forever, hopefully, but it would not be just one hot night with a stranger. No, this well ran very deep between Miguel and Vahar. Niea had no question that he would have to see her again. Her heart was a different story. No, the two of them made no promises, declared no exclusivity to each other. It all had been so easy. The sexual compatibility was too perfect. It scared Miguel, and it left Niea astounded. Niea had excused herself to go get some glasses and some of Miguel's wine. When she returned, Miguel was talking to Vahar. She was priming herself for Miguel and enjoying his intense stares. Niea felt things she had never felt before seeing Miguel with this woman. They obviously knew each other well. Miguel had sat down next to Vahar, put his hands on her shoulders, and lightly kissed her cheek. The whole time this was taking place, Vahar was staring at Niea with that "got you" look on her face. Niea turned as Vahar was asking Miguel something, whispering in his ear. He laughed a knowing laugh of familiarity and intimacy. This was starting to gnaw at Niea's insides. She did not like feeling this out of control. She did not know whether to cry like a baby or go running screaming into the night. They chatted for a bit, then she got her entourage and left. Thank God. Niea did not know if she could handle this anymore. Niea had cleaned up the kitchen. She turned off the flame of stew simmering on the stove and excused herself for the night. There was a full moon, and she went outside to observe. As Niea looked at the stars, Miguel stood in the shadows and watched. He wanted to talk to her, tell her that he just had to go and see. God, that sounded horrible. What could he say? He did not want to hurt this woman. He wanted to spend the rest of his life with her. Vahar had slipped him some sexual enhancing and stimulating drugs. He took them no problem. He pretty much had used something every time he was with Vahar. She expected more ever time. So far, he had not disappointed. But he did not know how much longer he could keep this up. At this point, Vahar did not seem to know that this was draining for him. His time with Niea was not like that at all. They took their time rocking each other to the ultimate experience. Niea would let her mind slip to pictures of Miguel with Vahar doing the things they did. She had to stop this. It was going to drive her crazy. Early the next morning Miguel returned from being with Vahar.

He was noticeable hung over. He did not look well. He knocked on the door where Niea was sleeping. It was just before daybreak Niea had not slept well at all. She could feel him. He was still somewhat intoxicated. She said for him to come on in, and he did. He did not know where to start. All he knew was he had to talk to her. He did not want that other woman. He wanted her. He knew that they did not make any promises to each other. But he wanted to make all the promises. This was the woman he wanted to spend the rest of his life.

Miguel said, "May I sit down?" Niea stared at him for some time then patted the bed, and he plopped down next to her. He smelled bad, from booze to whatever chemical he was trying to sweat out of his system. He also smelled of sex. He hung his head looking down at the floor. "I am so sorry."

Niea was her compassionate, composed self. She sat up beside Miguel and put her arm around him. "I love you, Miguel. I don't think anything can change that. But it seems to me you have some figuring out you need to do." Then she kissed him even as bad as he smelled. She did not know when she would get to kiss this beautiful sad creature again. She knew he had some more darkness he had to walk through. He looked at her so deeply and longingly it tore at Niea's heart. "We did not make any promises. We did not talk about the future or plans for family. We should have. It got serious between us, fast. I guess we were having so much fun we forgot to pay attention. I know I did." Niea looked at Miguel; he looked like a tortured soul. She knew he really did love her, but there was that small factor—Vahar. Niea said, "Why did you go to her?" Miguel dropped his head and said nothing. Niea took his hand, picked his head up with her other hand, and looked him in the eyes, saying, "Whatever you did was because you needed to. You were comparing me to Vahar. I know you were."

Miguel started crying softly. "I came back to you, Niea."

She looked at him, saying, "You want more from her?"

He did not answer right away. Then he said, "I don't think so." Niea knew that he was not done with Vahar. He just took too long to answer. Then Miguel reached up, grabbed Niea, and pulled her close to him. Now the crying was a heavy sighing.

Niea stayed there in his arm until she finally said, "You smell like booze and day-old fish. I hope it was worth it." He crumbled to the floor. What in the world was he thinking? He guessed that was the point; he was not thinking. He was running on pure sensation and drug-fueled debauchery. Niea said, "We will need to finish this conversation later. I have to go to Central. I am not quite well." Miguel was crying soft tears now. He wanted to kiss her so bad. What had he done? He looked at Niea and melted her heart. He was her heart. He was and will forever be her only man. "You are my only man, and I do promise to love you forever. Take a shower. You need it." Niea gave him a long-lasting kiss and left the room.

For the next few weeks Miguel just wasn't himself. He had receded to somewhere deep within himself. His heart was broken. He knew beyond a shadow of a doubt that she was his one true love. But for now, he would work on this place and stay out of the queen's shadow. He had always been fascinated with Vahar, and he knew that he might have to go see her again. But he could feel that no one could take Niea's place. Niea packed her things. She and Cal headed off to Central. They were excited. Their new ideas were about to make a debut. Once the ground car was loaded up, they took off. Cal drove. Niea didn't like Cal's wild driving. But she knew they would be there in record time. They sang songs most of the way there. Then Cal asked Niea about what was going on with Miguel. Niea said, "I have to slow down with him. He has much to work out."

Cal mumbled a question that Niea did not understand. She said, "What?"

Cal said, "What are you two going to do?"

Niea shrugged. "I can't keep having sex with him until he is done with Vahar."

Cal said, "I will keep an eye on him."

Niea said, "No, please don't do that. He needs to decide for himself and make his choice."

Cal said, "He will surely choose you."

Niea said, "I haven't made any decision, but this may be the end of it all." Cal understood perfectly. She was hopeful that it would work out. But all that remains to be seen. Now the focus was on their task. They were excited. So excited. Cal drove off in a burst of speed. Cal was a wild child, especially in her heart. Niea said, "I figured out some more of the particulars of the shadow suit. As one wears it, the better it adapts to your body. It also has a high resistance to hits and stabs." Cal had on the prototype. Minus a few alcohol stains, the suit looked good. One of the new features was that the suite could hide its wearer in the shadows. The undetectable opening at the pubic area also worked very well, and every suit was to be fitted to each woman/man. It was also much better at dealing with preparation. (But I have sports socks and clothing that wick away the preparation. It is advised that way.) It was so special to have these projects to look forward to. Then she thought of Miguel, and the sadness was too much. She was moving forward and needed to do so. She just couldn't truly let go. Such was love.

The presentation went well. They especially liked the sword. It would collapse into a small flat handle. That thing was a marvel. Niea was jumping with joy. She couldn't wait to see these incredible things that her team had come up with. She never took total credit for the things her team made. But in actuality, she was the sole mastermind of all this. Cal couldn't be prouder to be a part of this crew. They shined like a diamond, all because of Niea's brilliance and her incredible heart. Everything Niea did was for her ladies. Cal liked that she would do anything that would help her ladies to do their job and come home with her. Niea always put herself out in front in the action always. She was one of the most selfless people Cal had ever known. If this Miguel hurts Niea, he would have to answer to her, and she knew she could take him. Cal said a silent prayer for Niea to find her happiness in love. Cal knew Niea was happiest when she was with her ladies and they were safe. Such was her heart. A path of the heart she walked without hesitation.

All had gone well at Central. Their products would take Central some time to put into action. Central always took their time to get it right. The particulars would be worked out with Niea. No, she did not write anything down. She had prefect recall. All the information in her brain could be accessed with little prompting. As she and the Kalis worked out what they needed for these projects, Cal drove back to the hostile. She sang most of the way home. When she arrived, Miguel was serving a bit of deer chili. She gave him one hell of a look. She was not going to make it easy for him.

The days came and went. Miguel got up early and stayed busy all day. There was a lot to do. Jamal had gone hunting and had not returned in many days. Miguel hoped he had not met with an accident. They all walked the woods looking for him. Finally, he tried to put that out of his mind, so he worked. Two weeks had gone by slowly. The ladies helped Miguel do whatever had to be done. Cal would help some time. There was no wine, and Cal was down, but she was good help. She was strong as any man and clever. She was like Niea. They both liked things to work right. They were going to need some parts. Well, at this time, that meant they would have to scavenge the many waste pits that seem to be a click or two in any direction. Cal began to write down what she thought they needed. Pretty much anything metal. She and Zek decided they would go. Miguel made them a map of the surrounding dumps. Zek thanked him. Cal gave him the stank face.

One night, when all was quiet, Vahar showed up at his back door. He was obviously nervous. He knew Niea would not be back for a while, but he was not going to get involved with her anymore. She had what he liked. He resisted. She stepped up to him and asked in her provocative way, "Are you sure?" His breathing quickened, along with his pulse. He looked down at her. Her body, breasts—so curvy, so womanly—the way she smelled, and her sexual prowess sent him wheeling.

Miguel said, "I can't do this."

Vahar grinned that sly smile. "Oh, she won't let you play?"

Miguel stepped away from her. "It's not that. I love her."

Vahar rolled her eyes. "Oh! So it's love, is it? You know, Miguel, I love you. What about that?" He shook his head and stepped farther away. He was having a hard time not taking her right here. She stepped up to him and put her hands on his ass, gently rubbing his buttocks. She knew this was a weak point for him. If only she could get to that prostate, she could get to him. She knew exactly what she was doing. She wrapped her fingers onto his buttock, slowly massaging the opening to his rectum.

Miguel jerked away from her. "Please, Niea—Vahar," he said, quickly correcting himself.

She was angry. "Okay, I get it, I'm not Niea." She was hurt, furious, and determined to get even in some way or form. She would make it happen, no matter the cost. As she left, she brushed by Miguel. She dropped a couple of pills in his pocket. She thought to herself that this would make him come to her. Once she could get Niea hurt and hurt good, she would take her prize. She got back into the ground car where her two lady boys waited. "How did it go?" one of them questioned.

Vahar nodded with satisfaction. She knew she would win even if Niea had to die. In that moment she didn't even care if Miguel never spoke to her again; she was going to win.

A little later that evening, Miguel sat out on the edge of the small lake out back. He heard some moaning. He searched it out. There was a large man lying on a thicket. Miguel went to him. It was Jamal. *Oh my god!* He rolled him over. Jamal had several serious wounds. He had to get him back to the hostel. He saw Tulie, Zek, and Cal coming across a small field. He waved furiously. Zek and Tulie came running, Cal not so much. When they got to Miguel, Zek screamed. Cal quickened her pace and was there in no time. She was horrified. This looked like a Gogatt's nasty work. Miguel and Cal picked him up and carried him to the kitchen area. Tulie quickly wiped down the kitchen table with cleaning solution. They put him on the table with great care. Tulie and Zek cut his clothes off. They were ruined anyway. Then they all started cleaning him up so Cal could start with her assessment of his condition. She looked at Miguel. He had already brought dressings, a gentle cleaning liquid, and some ointment. The two of them went to work on saving Jamal. He was going to need internal and external stiches. Miguel went to the kitchen area, gathered some deer sinew, and sterilized it the best he could. He found several sewing needles and dropped them in some hot water. He turned up the fire and brought the water to a boil. As he got everything ready, they found eight wounds on him that needed closing. He was in and out of consciousness.

Miguel was concerned with Jamal's pain. He turned to Cal. "If we are going to go deep on the stitching, he's going to need something for the pain. I have a bottle of whiskey. Maybe we can get that down him." Cal nodded and wondered if he had been holding out on her, but in this moment, she was glad they had something for Jamal. Even though she was mean to Jamal, she really liked this beautiful big dark soul. Cal and Miguel worked for hours sewing up Jamal. They were able to get him inebriated enough to interrupt the pain. It was early in the morning when Jamal regained consciousness.

Jamal saw Miguel through one eye. "Ah, it's good to see you." Then he gave that million-dollar smile and asked for Cal. Why he asked for Cal, Miguel didn't have to wonder, even though Cal was so hateful to him, doing those provocative girl poses, teasing him relentlessly. She came to the door. "Jamal! You're awake!" She seemed genuinely happy to see him better. That was infantile to Miguel, if someone cared. Why would a grown woman act like hormonal raging teenager? Cal smiled a thin smile, walked up to the bed, and took Jamal's hand. "I am so glad you are still with us!" Miguel was glad and disgusted at the same time. Cal needed to grow up. Jamal patted the side of the bed for her to sit. She did and hung her head. She was ashamed of how she had been acting. Her emotions have been on a roller-coaster ride through hell. She was desperately trying not to drink. It was stinking hard. He asked her how she had been and what she was going to do today. Miguel thought she wouldn't be a raging bitch today. All Miguel wanted was for Niea to return. He asked Jamal if he needed anything. Then he got him something to eat. Jamal had a hard time feeding himself, so Cal fed him. *Now isn't that sweet,* Miguel thought. *Tomorrow she might poison him.*

All of them knew this kind of attack could only come from the Gogatt. They were a particular nasty piece of work. Torture was their specialty, and it was some of the worst seen. They were a very large group of men, if that was what one could actually call them that. They produced nothing. They plundered, raided, raped, tortured, and maimed. They were very nasty, especially with women of any age. Jamal told Cal he had killed eight of them to get away. He was sure that other groups of them might be headed this way. Cal's brilliant strategical mind kicked in; she needed to do some surveillance. She was not sure when Niea would come back. She talked with Zek and Tulie about making a trip. Tulie offered to go. Cal liked this idea. She and the master assassin could slip in, do some surveillance, slits some throats, and get out. This was what Cal needed, and she was glad for it. She and Tulie gathered ever thing they needed. They would travel light and run most of the way. No ground car could get through that terrain. She was excited. She was in her element. Jamal asked her to come to him before she left. He asked her for a goodbye kiss, and she gave him one. It made his day. They took off.

When Niea arrived at the hostel, she was aghast. She was glad Cal and Tulie had headed out to do surveillance. Tulie and Cal would dispatch as many as they could, get the intel they needed, and get out. The Gogatt had done horrific things to almost everyone she knew. They were the Kalifee's and ever one else's biggest problem/ nightmare. Miguel was overjoyed to see Niea. He wanted to kiss her, but he waited for permission. She really looked beautiful with her short-cropped hair. It had fallen out when she had gotten so sick. She looked into his warm golden-brown eyes, and she knew he had really missed her and wanted to talk. That would be done later. Now she had to check in on Jamal. Jamal was feeling a bit better and sat up in bed. He told her about the incident, and she questioned him just as Cal had done, gathering as much information that she could. She asked him if she could do anything for him. He said to bring Cal back soon. She chided him. Cal was mean to him. She suggested he ignore her. It would be for the best. Jamal said in a voice filled with pain, "I'll try."

A bit later, when Jamal had been all attended to, and everyone settled into their late evening places; Niea was sitting in the front room working on a new project. Miguel knocked at the door. She invited him in cordially. He pulled a chair up as close as he could to her. "Niea, hear me out."

She nodded.

"I don't know how to unhurt you, but I want to try. You are the most precious thing I have ever known, and I will do whatever it takes to have you as mine. I love you, and I have never felt like this about anyone ever."

She looked at him for a very long time. So long he almost got up and left the room.

Finally, Niea said, "You know I love you too. It was almost in an instant for me. Love at first sight. Who knew?" She sat there for another long period. She was gathering every feeling, every thought so that she would say it right. If she was to get back into bed with him, the air must be clear between them.

Miguel jumped in, "I will not get in bed with Vahar again ever!"

Niea thought for a moment. "That would be necessary. But I don't think that is the heart of the matter." Miguel looked at her with a question in his face. Niea continued, "I wanted you. I had never had any sexual experience. You seem so perfect. You are one of the most beautiful men I have ever seen. You have a beautiful heart. You are humble, giving, and kind—everything I ever wanted in a man. But you haven't totally owned who you are. Let me explain." Miguel's heart was soaring, but what exactly did she mean? She moved in very close to him and kissed him lightly on the lips. Then she took a deep breath and took in all of him. "I am not here to put conditions, standards of living on you. I see before me a man that might have an addiction. I think I know that you have had many trips to this woman and women like her, using whatever is available to numb the unsettling emotions that rides through a person of your character. You have to numb yourself to perform, and I get a feeling of what you have been doing most of your life." His head dropped. Niea looked at him, took her hand, and brought his chin up. "Hold your head up. That's what needs to be done. You must be proud of who you are and what you are. That lifestyle doesn't serve you at all. I

think you have become addicted to it."

Miguel tried not to drop his head again, but he did. "Niea, I am not smart like you. My mother left me at fourteen here to do what I could do on my own. I'm just this guy that no one really knows and can fix a few things. That's all."

Niea couldn't help it. She stood up and put her arms around him. He started to cry. She held him for quite some time. Finally, he sat up and looked at her. Niea said, "You don't think you are good enough. There are not enough substances in this world to give a person self-worth. In truth, if you don't love yourself, it will be hard to love someone else. A person who lacks self-caring will inevitable sabotage themselves, doing things to mess up their life to drive good things away. I have a great example—Cal." He knew that she was right and very insightful. She looked deep into his beautiful face. "There's more. You think you are not smart. You belittle what you do. Humility and self-depravation are very different. I have never seen someone who could fix anything like you can. Do you have a how-to book on any of these things you fixed or someone who taught you how to fix things?" He shook his head no. Niea continued, "Hum! Imagine that. You are brilliant. Oh! I also most forgot, you made concoctions out of roots and herbs that helped restore my health." She sat with him, letting him take this all in. She didn't want to preach. She remembered, "Cal told of how you stitched up Jamal. She said you were better than her. She's trained. Are you?" He wanted to drop his head, but he didn't. This is what she means about owning. She had done this so many times with Cal, and it would work for a while. She did not know about Miguel. He didn't seem to have that nasty side that Cal had these days, but there was something else with Cal. Maybe she was feeling threatened. This strong, capable warrior had an unloved child inside. Once again, if you don't love yourself, how the hell can you love some else?

They sat for a while. Miguel sat holding Niea's hand, running over everything she had said, and yes, he could remember a lot of what people say for verbatim. He did learn fast and could do things other people couldn't. He pulled her close to him and laid his head onto her neck. Niea said, "Balancing the dark with the light—that's what it all about."

Miguel said, "But you don't have any dark."

Niea sat straight up, put her hands on his shoulders, and said, "Oh, yes I do. You seem to know me quite well, but you have not seen the rage and the depression." His face showed a question of needing details. She said, "You have not seen me fight. I call her the Kali killer. I have learned to channel this rage into a fearsome fighter, and she is a beast. The rage helps me ward off the depression." He was sitting up straight looking intensely at her. He understood. He kind of felt he had turned his anger at his mother into self-hate.

Miguel said, "I know Vahar is not good for me. She's a master manipulator. I believe she loves me, but her love must control people. She will come for you. She will be back."

Niea thought before she said, "Let her come, but be prepared." He saw what she was talking about deep in her eyes. This commander was no ordinary commander. He stood up and held out his hand, and she took it. She was excited the minute he pulled her up on him. She was wet. This was her man. He picked her up and took her to an area in the back away from everyone. He had prepared a mat that both could sleep on if that was what they would do. He could still hear Jamal if he needed anything.

The lovemaking was epic. He was with his woman, and she was the light of his life and could love him like no one else. They would sleep for a few hours then either she would crawl up on top of him or any other configuration they would find themselves. This was heaven on earth. Miguel felt himself tingling all over all night, whether they were asleep or in the throes of passion. They did get some sleep. She woke before dawn and went to check on Jamal. He was snoring softly. She and Miguel ate breakfast.

It took several days for Tulie and Cal to find the Gogatt camp. As they walked and talked about Jamal, they realized it was hard for either of them to believe that Jamal had come so far as seriously wounded as he was. He had serious inner strength. It was daytime when they arrived, so Tulie and Cal found some very heavy bush area. Before they took a nap, Tulie would use the advantage of her small shadow self and get a count of how many men, tents, weapons, and what else they might have with them. Cal kept a lookout. They went in on their bellies. To communicate, they had small voice router the team had developed a while back. It was very quiet and could only be used at close range. Once Tulie was satisfied she had what she needed, she returned to their rabbit hole. They planned their attack and then took a nap. They woke just before sunset. They checked all the weapons in their suits. Cal had on her shadow suit, which meant she could work with Tulie getting into the campsite unseen. Tulie was a natural shadow warrior. One day Cal knew that Niea would unlock the mystery of Tulie. What marvelous things their commander had created. Cal had been thinking long about her behavior. She wanted to hang her head and cry. She remembered what the commander said to her so many times, "Hold your head up, remember who you are, own every part of yourself, balancing the dark night of the soul with the glorious being of light you are." Cal admitted to herself she truly liked Jamal. Why she could not or would not let him in, she did not know, or maybe she did not want to know.

It was finally dark, so the ladies crawled out of their hiding place and headed to the Gogatt camp. They barely made a sound. They went to a crouched posture for a bit. When they got close enough, they went back on their bellies and crawled close enough to stay hidden. Cal would follow Tulie. She was the master of shadow fighting. This would be the first time the shadow suit would face a real battle. When all the Gogatt had gone to sleep except the guards, the two ladies crawled into the camp and took out the two guards in silence. Then one went right and the other left. Slowly they entered each tent and began the slaughter of these foul beasts. At one point Cal was struck from behind inside one of the tents. The light from the low fire had caught Cal's suit just right, and she got struck. Tulie knew something happened to Cal and made her way to assist her. Tulie got under a flap at the edge of the tent. She rolled in right under the Gogatt as he was rolling Cal over. In the next instant, Tulie thrust her thin blade right into his genitals with a twist and a jerk. He fell onto the knocked-out Cal. Tulie stepped forward into the light to see about Cal. The last standing Gogatt saw Tulie and came screaming into the tent with sword flashing. He swung his sword at her. She disappeared into the shadows. He turned to find Tulie's blade going up into his throat. Now they were all dead. Tulie held still and listened just to make sure the silence was real. When she was absolutely sure, she went to Cal and tried to get the Gogatt off her. He was way too big for her to move. Suddenly Cal came to, yelling a warrior's yell, and heaved the nasty vermin off her. He flopped over dead. Tulie wiped her knife off on him; he was the one who got shit and blood on her knife. The other one lay there with a hole punctured in his throat. They were all dead. The two ladies gathered all maps and any other thing they thought helpful and took off. They ran for several clicks until they felt safe and stopped for the night. Tulie found a small stream that seemed fairly clean, and they washed up. Cal was amazed the blood from that fool on top of her washed away as if it was nothing. And the suit seemed to dry within seconds. Not until all was settled when they were ready for sleep, and eventually they did sleep. But first they took turns reliving their victory. Tulie was always so animated when telling her stories, and they were always good. They woke before dawn, ate the wraps Miguel had made, and took off. It would be another day before reaching home base. Cal was still thinking about her behavior. She sure some of them had referred to her as the bitch from hell. Cal hated bad language, but at this point she knew the phrase flying bitch suited her just fine. She could not do as Niea suggested. Niea had asked her many times to come and talk to her before she drank. Saying Cal was stubborn was an understatement. Cal knew all this, everything Niea had ever said to her. The truth was that Cal would rather drink alcohol than anything else. She understood what Niea had said to her many times, "Dis-ease in the spirit becomes disease in the body." Cal could feel the alcohol was taking a lot of her strength and focus. When Niea and she would practice, Niea went all in. It had made them all much better fighters facing Niea. But Cal could feel that she would not do well up against Niea these days. It was hard enough to face Niea when she was on top of her game. Cal knew it was time to face her demons.

Cal and Tulie arrived the next afternoon, exhausted but elated. They had some real interesting intel to show Niea and Zek. They both got a shower. Miguel had rigged up one inside the bunk house where they stayed. It had hot and cold running water with a finespray shower head he had found in a dump and gotten to work. They loved it. Everyone ate a fine meal Miguel and Niea prepared. As they all sat and ate, Niea could tell something was different in Cal. She was so pleasant with everyone. Niea guessed she needed the action to hone her focus, and that would help her remember who she was and the fine job she was capable of doing and doing well. But it was more than that. She had been so excited to see Jamal up and about. He was moving a bit slow. But he had survived one hell of a journey. Cal couldn't help but marvel how far he came with no help, as wounded as he was. Everyone was impressed with that. Stories like that were what Kalifee legends were made of. When supper was over, Jamal was feeling tired, so Cal helped him to bed. She sat with him; he played his harmonica. Cal didn't get up and dance. She didn't need to be the center of attention for a change. He asked her to tell him some war stories, and she did. He fell asleep. She covered him then kissed him on the forehead and went off to bed.

In the morning Niea wanted to hear all they had. Tulie and Cal told of how they had accomplished their mission. They showed Niea the maps. It seems they were a small band of marauders sent to check out the area. It appeared they were planning to move into this area at some point. When they planned to move here was not clear. But they were coming. Central would have to know as soon as possible. When they would get here, no one knew. But everyone knew exactly what they were going to do when they got here. The commander was concerned. They would have to start planning and be prepared. Niea went to send a message and hoped it would work. She sent the message and was waiting for Grandmama to respond. The atmosphere had an effect on how fast the communicator would work. The mood at the hostel was tense and somber. Niea felt that they had a little time; after all, Tulie and Cal had killed them all. It would depend when they were found or missed. Gogatts were infamous for going off on raids on their own. Niea thought they needed to spread out and scout for other Gogatts. They needed to be ready. Hell was coming. She sat everyone down and discussed her idea. Cal thought maybe they needed some reinforcements. Now they had to wait for orders. Niea still wanted to do some scouting of the area. Miguel thought that they could go in different directions paired off in twos. Maybe that was too risky? Decisions, decisions, what would they do? Maybe they should at least give Central time to respond. They all stood quiet, unsure. They really might need backup. Then Miguel spoke up, "I know this area well. I will go northeast. That is where others have come from in the past."

Niea did not like this but he was probably right. "I will go with him," she said. The others did not answer. All stood in quiet pondering this situation. She suggested that two of them go to Gabba and see what they could find out there.

Cal spoke up, "I will go to Gabba. The others can stay here. Someone has to see to Jamal."

Tulie spoke up, "I will stay with Jamal. He can move around on his own now. I will see to his other needs."

Miguel said that he had started a hidden area he needed to show them. Niea wanted to see this hidden room. Miguel led the way. When they were all in his room, he asked everyone to look for this area. They all looked around moving things, inspecting the floor, walls, ceiling, and furniture. Miguel had very little furniture. After everyone had looked, taped, knocked on, and even hit, no one found anything. Then Miguel had them follow him out to the odd area off the main hallway. He took his foot and put it under the floorboard. They heard something open in his room. They all went back into the room. Still, no one saw any opening. Everyone looked puzzled. He moved to the side of a closest, tapped on the wall, and slid through an opening. Once inside, it closed. He opened it up and came out. They all went in. It turned out to be more than a room. It was a tunnel that led to a shed he had out back about a hundred feet from the hostel. It was an escape route. It was not complete. Niea wanted to see the shed. The shed would hide any movement away from the hostel, and a thick wooded area lay just behind it. Niea finally said, "Looks like this could work." So, everyone agreed. They all readied up. Miguel and Niea went northeast. Cal and Zek put on local clothes, got in the ground car, and headed off to Gabba. Tulie saw them off. Jamal was in a deep sleep.

Miguel and Niea ran for a good ten miles then stopped by a stream to get some rest. After a good rest, Niea climbed a tall tree to get better look. She had a small strong spy monocle. Taking her time, she did a full 360 and saw something. It looked like an old campsite. She scanned the area again looking for signs of traffic. She shimmied down the tree, and Miguel was there; he had something for her to eat. He had a small fire with water to make a stimulating tea so they could move at an optimum pace. Niea always marveled at him. He was so good at everything. He anticipated what people needed, and he would have it there for them. Niea still had trouble realizing this man was hers and she was his. He had been used so sorely by the queen Vahar. She had been one of the Kalifee's finest. Niea didn't know the whole story. She hadn't asked. It made her too angry. Nothing good was going to come of this. Niea knew this wasn't going to end well. She also knew her job was to keep her people alive and healthy. Vahar was coming. Be prepared; one of their own was on the hunt. Someone would have to die. It would not be her or her precious Miguel. If she lost him, the rage would be too much. She drank her tea and ate the protein wrap he gave her. She kissed him passionately, but lovemaking would have to wait. They headed out to the old campsite. It might be a Gogatt camp, but maybe not. They would be able to determine that when they got there and did an investigation. They waited a few for the tea and protein wrap to kick in, and they took off.

Cal parked the ground car outside of Gabba, and they walked. It was a pleasant enough place. Cal, like Niea, preferred the outlands, open country. They walked at a fast pace, deciding not to run and be a little obviously all sweaty and out of breath. The strolled easily like locals. The people looked relaxed. There was no reason to excited and scare anyone by asking questions, especially about seeing any Gogatt. So they kept their eyes open and blended in with the locals. They decide to do a bit of shopping and keep their ears tuned into any interesting conversations. Zek was so much better at this than the impulsive Cal. But Cal had been trying lately. She knew she had been somewhat out of control. She also knew if she didn't calm down, Central would call her in for an assessment. Their psychological evaluations were grueling. She wanted none of that. So she followed Zek's lead and chilled. They walked about the settlement looking for signs. But there was really nothing at this point to indicate any Gogatt had been anywhere near here. If the Gogatt had been anywhere near here, this place would be torn apart with bodies everywhere. So they listened, watched, and waited. Zek heard some whispers about Gogatt being seen further north of here but nothing else. So at dusk, they headed back to the hostel.

Jamal had slept late. He did not like that. But he knew he had to be patient. He would not be alive if it weren't for Cal, Miguel, Zek, and Tulie. Tulie brought Jamal some of Miguel's chili. It got better with each day. Only Miguel could make anything so delicious. Jamal couldn't be happier. He had known at the very start there was something there with Niea and Miguel. That first look between them was just too good. Niea was glowing when she looked at Miguel. After all the women Miguel had known, he found the perfect lady. Jamal could feel something bad was coming. He hoped he would be on his feet when it did.

Tulie was such a quiet creature. Most of the time you would not know she was there. Jamal would love to get her to open up. He called to her. She was sitting in the room with him. No one would have known. She was the master of shadows. Tulie said, "You don't have to yell."

Jamal laughed. "Little lady, you startled me. I'm gonna get up and walk to the kitchen." She handed him a cane she had found. He went slowly, making sure he did not injury himself anymore.

Tulie stayed close, saying, "If you fall, don't fall on me." There was hot water, and Jamal tried to make himself tea. Tulie pointed for him to sit down, and she got him some tea. They sat together in silence for a good while. Then Tulie spoke, "Do you think I'm weird?"

Jamal was taken back a bit. He said, "Aren't we all a bit strange?"

Tulie said, "You know what I mean."

Jamal looked at her, "You are very unique, and I like you."

She smiled but had so much more to say. "I am not sure how to say this, but I am a misfit."

Jamal's forehead crinkled. "What?"

She started, "When Cal found me, I was in a dungeon. These people had put me there and couldn't find me. My shadow beings protected me and continue to do so. Cal sat and waited for me to show myself. No, these people didn't really want to harm me. They wanted me sleep with men while pretending to be a child. I couldn't do it. If I am to have a lover, it would have to be of my choosing. Cal sat quietly.

Niea joined her. Finally, I came out and sat down between them. I could tell they didn't want anything from me. They wanted to help me. So I just sat there and cried. Niea and Cal were there to help me. When I couldn't cry anymore, they asked me to go with them. I did. For some strange reason, I trusted them. Niea kept trying to get me to tell her about my past, but that is as far back as I can remember. You are a fine man, Jamal. One of the finest I've ever seen. If I was interested in a man, it would have to be a man like you." Jamal's heart felt the love that Tulie had for him. He didn't feel he should say anything. He waited for Tulie to continue. Finally, she said, "Cal, Zek, and Niea started to train me. They had to get me strong, feeding me proper food and giving me proper care. They are wonderful ladies. I would probably be dead if it wasn't for them. There is a terrible past before the dungeon. I don't remember it. Although when Niea got sick from the smoke, the smell triggered memories. It came in flashes. Horrible images, but nothing concrete. So, I don't know what to say about all that." She started to cry, and Jamal held her small elfin self. It was hard to imagine this person was a master assassin. Tulie asked as she turned her elven face to look into his kind face, "Do you think I'm a horrible person?"

Jamal looked at her and shook his head. "You are a special person, Tulie, and the team is lucky to have you."

She was shaking her head no. "I am a murderer!"

Jamal held her tight. "You are a protector of what is good. Have you ever killed someone who did not truly deserve it?" He gave her a look. She knew he was right. Jamal said, "It will take time, but I just know you will find your peace and your love for yourself." Jamal began to hum. Then he sang, "Amen, amen, let your light shine. Amen." He continued, and he felt the present of the Spirit and a start for the wonderful Tulie. All this was because of the incredible Commander Niea. Was there a better woman on earth? Jamal could only hope he would find a woman like her someday. Miguel was a lucky man.

Memories started to flood Jamal. He remembered going to the brothels with Miguel and how popular he had been in that setting.

Jamal had taken favor with some of the working ladies there, but it wasn't what he wanted. He wanted one special woman. Besides, there was that awful woman, Vahar. Jamal couldn't tolerate her and bowed out of Miguel's excursions to see her. Jamal knew she was using and abusing Miguel. She would pass him around among the ladies, pumping him full of drugs, sexual stimulants, and happy drugs, making him delusional to what was going on. She had prided herself on how much she controlled him and he did not disappoint. He would have several of them in a night, and Vahar would have him last after a thorough cleaning of all of him. She was his pimp. Jamal knew he saw this but chose not to see the deeper implications of his actions. Jamal knew this made Miguel feel like a man. Nothing could be further from the truth.

Once Jamal was feeling better, Tulie convinced him to have a stroll with her out back. They had a nice walk through Miguel's beautiful place, waiting for the others to report back their findings. Cal and Zek returned later that afternoon to some of Miguel's wonderful chili. They had been eating it for days, but it just kept getting better. Cal was needing a drink, and Jamal could tell. She didn't take one. She was holding on for dear life at times. Tulie made her some valerian tea, which did help. Cal was grateful. Jamal wanted to help her so bad, but he felt she really did not like him and left her alone. Actually, the opposite was true. Like Niea had said to her; "You are afraid of intimacy." Cal knew she was right. She wanted to be close to Jamal. How in this world does she do this? Niea had said just follow Jamal's lead. His heart was big enough for all of us! Her heart softened, and she asked if she could help him to this bed. He agreed. He was a bit scared. Would she trip him or help him? It all remained to be seen. She helped him to his bed, and he lay down. She asked if she could check his dressing and the wounds. There were many of them. A lesser man would not have survived such an ordeal. He was a specimen of a man. She really liked him. What in the world was wrong with her? She knew the booze had taken a lot from her, and as Niea had said so many times, "You drink to mask the pain." There was a lot of pain for Cal to work through. One reason she liked to fight was she felt whole when she was swinging a sword or her fist.

They had arrived at his bed. Tulie had made up his bed, so it was fresh and inviting. Jamal use to make silly jokes for Cal to join him but not now. Once he was settled and comfortable, she asked if they could talk. He agreed. She didn't really look at him but apologized deeply for her behavior and that she was embarrassed, and could he forgive her? He said he could, and he apologized for coming on so strong. Cal gave a thin smile; here she was the ass of the whole picture, and he apologized to her. She sat and stared at him. He asked, "What's wrong?"

Cal just shook her head. "I am the butt here, not you. You have been nothing but a gentleman." He smiled that infectious smile of his and took her hand and held it. He wanted to kiss her, but he dared not. He did not want to mess up what was happening here. He knew she could shut down on him at any time. She held his hand and felt the genuine good heart that beat under his chest. She wanted to kiss him too, but her guilt held on to her tight. So for some time, they sat holding hands. She asked if she could get in bed with him. He was shocked but nodded.

Cal laid beside him. "I am so sorry for how I treated you." Jamal was guarded; he knew Cal could be volatile at any time. He did not want to start something he could not finish, especially a fight. She lay down and began to cry softly. He was unsure how to handle this. This was new territory, unexplored in the caverns of Cal's. She was so vulnerable right now, and he knew she could explode at any time. He had to be careful; he was making head way with her and did not want to blow this. Besides, she could really hurt him. She was a master fighter, and he would not be able to defend himself if she became aggressive. He also found this exciting. This woman was dangerous. But her mood could change in a heartbeat, and she could do some real damage. But instead, she cried, and he held her. Then they both fell asleep. She was curled up in his arm. It was some of the best sleep she had had in a long time, and she didn't want to drink.

After Niea and Miguel was tired out from their run, they stopped and took a few moments to recover. They both heard voices and quickly hid in a thicket they saw. Unsure who it was, Niea shimmied up a nearby tree as quietly as she could. Making sure no one saw her, she pulled out her spyglass and had a look. They did not look like Gogatt, but the feel was that they were up to no good. She did finish up her surveillance and shimmied back down to Miguel. He had hidden himself well in some of the thicket. Niea joined him, making as little noise as possible. She used the silent battle language of the Kalifee that Miguel had picked up without being taught. She had never seen anyone pick up things as fast as Miguel, and he still clung to the idea he wasn't that smart. She couldn't help but marvel at how people do not see themselves. It was that we provide mirrors for each other so we can see ourselves clearly. They stayed quiet until the camp was asleep. Neither one of them got a good feel for these men, but they were rogue. Killing them would not be the answer at this point. They needed more information, so they waited. When they were all asleep, Miguel and Niea moved far from the camp but were close enough to keep an eye on it. Then Niea decided to crawl closer to the camp to get a better look. She counted five of them, young and more than likely could be taken or killed easily. Niea thought that maybe they would kill all but one and question him. She did not like this idea totally but wasn't sure what to do. Indecision could be deadly, so she conversed with Miguel to get his take on it. He thought that rogue males were always a bad sign. He was right. So they came up with a plan. Niea would slip into the encampment and start the killing; he would follow with the cleanup. He did not like her being put in harm's way, but she was the commander and totally capable of any job at hand. She also was the light of his world, and he would do anything to protect her. Once she had gotten account of how many rogues there were and who was their target for capture, she crawled out of the camp like a snake in the night. She found her way back to Miguel. He was relieved. She was dirty and ready for the mission at hand. They took them all down without a hitch. Niea was so impressed with Miguel's fighting style—so different from the Kali style. He had a way of slowing down at near the last moment of the strike. She would certainly have to see this later. The young pup was no more than a boy. Niea felt sorry for him getting himself involved with such horrible kind of people. But he was not saying much, and maybe he didn't know much. But he certainly knew something. Niea hoped the interrogation would not take a turn toward Cal working on him. He would not survive Cal. Niea preferred the psychological. Cal was much more hands-on.

When Niea and Miguel arrived back at the hostel, the crew were all just getting up. Niea found Cal inside lying in bed with Jamal. When she got up, Jamal seemed relieved. Niea understood. Cal was unpredictable, and she remained on the edge of violence. What in the world was going to happen with one of their best fighters? But now she was becoming a liability. She would have to go to Central for evaluation and treatment. She got out of going so many times. Niea was at her wits' end. She loved Cal. They had been friends since they were children. Niea remembered the first time she saw Cal. She was dirty and raggedy. She was found in the woods near the settlement she had lived. The Gogatt had burned it down and killed everyone. Cal was the only one alive. How? Cal had always been a survivor. She knew how to fight from the very start. When they met, Niea had put Cal on the ground. Niea had a stick she had made. She had put an electrical charge in it somehow. She shocked the crap out of Cal. Niea was one of the hardest fighters to best. She always had something extra for her opponent, some weapon or unexpected move she had that was unique and effective. Niea had helped Cal up and then flipped her. They had been friends ever since.

Miguel and Niea were exhausted. They had to pull their captive along. He wasn't capable of running like them. The discipline was not there for this young pup and probably for none of these rogue males. They chained him up in a shed in the back. Niea brought him some stew, and he ate it down. They were all hungry. Once all had eaten and cleaned up a bit, Niea and Miguel went to bed and slept deep. The interrogation would start later. Niea would try her method first. Cal would have to be last, because he might not survive if she didn't get the answers she sought.

Later that evening, Cal sat with Jamal out back watching the sunset. There was no alcohol. Cal would have to go to town to drink. Her mood was somber and quiet. Jamal was playing his harmonica softly.

She sat and drank some tea Zek had made them. She had nothing to say. Finally, Jamal stop playing and asked Cal how she was doing. She shook her head no. He could feel she was miserable. She did not have her drink of courage. She didn't even want to dance. Jamal had no idea how to help her. He knew it was an inside job, and she simply wasn't ready. She got up and offered to help him inside. He agreed, and off they went, him leaning on the capable Cal. She probably could carry him but was glad she didn't have to do so. They walked in silence, and soon he was very tried. She helped him into bed, covered him up, and kissed his forehead good night. She saw a vest on a chair and picked it up. Two pills fell out onto the floor. She picked them up and looked at them. Jamal saw her but pretended to be asleep. She threw them in her month and down her throat. Jamal said nothing. He knew it would make her mad. She was on her own. He had felt this way when he would see Miguel take the drugs that Vahar had given him. He wanted nothing to do with drugs. A little alcohol was all he could handle of anything that altered him in any way. He lay awake for a while, listening for Cal. He heard nothing from her and finally fell asleep. The pills started to kick in, and it brought the craving on—bad. Cal was going to get something to drink. She got in the ground car and took off. She arrived at the only tavern in Gabba. It was a quiet night, and there weren't many patrons. So Cal got a liter of ale and sat in the corner. She was dressed in local garb, but she stood out. She was, after all, a stunning-looking woman—tall, long-legged, blonde, and in shape. As she was finishing up her ale, a young local male offered to buy her a drink. She agreed, and he got her another liter. He was polite enough, so Cal tolerated him. She would rather have been alone, but her coin was low, and she need more to drink. He asked all the usual questions. Cal answered in the vaguest manner possible. No need to say anything real in a bar. Then he tried to kiss her, and she put him on the floor. If he hadn't been so impressed with her skill, there would have a problem, but he was amazed. "Wow, you got skills." She nodded and drank down her ale. He offered her another one. She took it of course. He wanted her to show what she did. Then she said she would rather dance. He asked the barkeep to put on some music. It was a hip-hop number from long time ago, and Cal loved it. She got up and started her show. Everyone was watching her dance. She had rhythm, style, was very acrobatic, and was a marvel to watch. They all were clapping, cheering, and buying her all the drinks she could handle. The pills were peeking, and Cal knew she was starting to lose control. She dropped down into a chair, and from that point on she remembered nothing. The blackout was coming way too soon.

She came to in the local jail. She had bruises all over her. What the hell? She had no memory of what happened once the peeking had started. It had been too much. What the hell had she taken? An officer came back to her cell. He stood back from the bars as if he was scared of her. Oh god, she knew she had beaten up someone or several someones. Niea was going to have her head. She sat up on the hard bunk and held her head in her hands. Maybe she could slip out of this and get back to the hostel before anyone would know. Then the officer spoke, "Your ride will be here be soon, if you want to ready yourself?" Ride? They got the ground car. No, they had notified Central, and they were here to get her. No one dealt with Kalis but Central. What the ef was she thinking? They chained her into a walking four-point restraint and put her in the ground car from Central and off they went.

Miguel and Niea slept for more than ten hours. They got up and washed up. Zek had some fresh meat and eggs prepared for them to eat. They needed protein. Jamal joined them, and all ate well in silence. Niea wanted to know where Cal was. No one had seen her. Then Jamal remembered, and he told the pill story. Miguel thought to himself how those pills got into his vest pocket. Then he remembered and said out loud, "Vahar!"

Niea said, "What?"

Miguel said, "She came by one evening and tried to get me to go with her, and I wouldn't. She must have slipped them into my vest pocket." Niea got up and went to the communicator. There was a message from Central. They had Cal. She was to be evaluated and treated. She had three substances in her blood. The local law had picked her up in a bar. She had beaten up four men and passed out. Miguel tried to apologize, but Niea stopped him. Cal was a grownass woman and knew better that to put anything she found in her mouth. Niea was so disappointed. She knew it was just a matter of time before Cal got herself in some real trouble. After all, she was a loose cannon and dangerous. Niea had let her get away with way too much for way too long. Niea was sad but relieved. Cal had become a liability, endangering the team's safety. Hopefully she would come back to them soon. Central might have another idea. Niea said a prayer for her long-time friend. She would miss her terribly. At least there was the incredible Miguel that could do anything and do it well. It seemed so unfair that their problems had to be his. She knew Miguel would have it no other way. For whatever Niea's troubles were, they were Miguel's too. Truth be told, Niea had been covering up for Cal way to long. She knew that one day Cal would have to face her demons head on alone.

After all of them had eaten, cleaned up, and were ready for their day, they brought the captive in for the interrogation to start. He was lucky Cal would not be a part of this. Although Tulie might decide he had to die. She would be quicker than Cal. Tulie really didn't like to see others suffer. The prisoner was brought in and given something to eat and drink. He could bathe later. He did stink. Niea started. First, name and rank. He didn't have a rank. His name was Keddie, and he had been with these males for a year. They were Gogatt, but they were an offshoot from the mainstream Gogatt. They pretty much operated on their own. Once they had proven themselves worthy, they could join the others in raiding, killing, and raping men, women, and children. The boy didn't seem to have guts for all this. He seemed so weak and still had some human emotion in him that Niea felt like saving. They did not have a particular direction to head in. They were wanderers. They would not be missed. Niea was sure that the ones Tulie and Cal killed would be missed soon enough. The Gogatt were coming this way. How long before they arrived was still unclear. The Kalifees would be ready.

Cal had arrived at Central four hours later. She was dirty, still hungover, and remorseful as the day was long. She knew she had screwed the pooch on this one. But she knew she would have to face her crap sooner or later. She was no fool. She just acted like one too much of the time. She was questioned by a team of women that were, for the most part, psychologists—addiction experts, they say. Addiction was a problem everywhere. The Kalifee had its problems too. Cal knew she had to take her medicine like a champ. She answered all their questions as best she could. Then they let her bathe, eat, and get some rest. Tomorrow would bring the beginning of a long period of treatment.

The young pup was kept chained for several days until Niea was sure he was not going anywhere. He had not eaten this well in a long time. He was horribly thin, malnourished, and needed some human kindness. Niea had him sit down and tell her his story. These marauders had killed his ma and pa. They chained him up and dragged him along. He was given little food and nothing else. He cried like a small child. He took to Niea. He had never seen a woman so beautiful, smart, and caring as Niea. He asked her a hundred questions and listened to anything she had to say. He thought Miguel was the luckiest man on earth to have such a woman. He had never seen a Kali woman, before much less a commander.

Niea missed Cal, but life goes on, and one does what one can to keep going. Miguel comforted her as much as he could. He knew this was hard for Niea. They were sitting out back when Keddie approached. He waited a proper distance until he was told he could approach. He had remembered something he heard long time ago. The Gogatt were planning to take over this area, enslave all farmworkers, and kill all the rest except for some of the women. They would be used as breeders/ slaves. They want children. This was very different for them. All women would be their whores to do with as they please no matter how many children they had for the Gogatt. He hated the idea that they would make Niea their whore. She smiled at him, telling him he had nothing to worry. She could take them all out. He believed her. He had seen her take out the ones at his camp. He felt like he loved the commander. Niea had always had this effect on men, especially young impressionable ones. Some days he would follow her around like a puppy.

The team started working on the hostel. They needed to finish the hidden room and the escape route. Miguel had the idea of booby-trapping the escape route in three different places. Niea was always enthralled with Miguel's ideas. He was a natural. But living here alone as long as he did, he had to have some talents, or he would not be here. They finished the traps and the secret room. They reinforced the wall on the outside and in. They installed weapons that could be fired remotely. Jamal was much better now, and he was a master at construction. He was so strong. He missed Cal but was glad she was gone. She would surely have messed things up the way she was going. The kid Keddie helped a lot. He was proving to be an asset. He took instruction well and never gave any lip. He hardly left Niea's side. He was devoted. Miguel took him under his wing. No need to fight over how he felt about Niea. Instead, he made him his ally. Smart. He taught him how to cook, hunt, and use a longbow. The boy was hungry for any attention and information. Keddie had gained weight and looked more like he should have looked. He wasn't a bad soul at all. Niea had known this about him from the start. His only drawback was the way he looked at her. But Miguel knew that Niea would never allow anything from this child but respect, or he would surely be dead. Miguel would make sure of it.

Months went by, and still no Cal. Niea didn't know if she was coming back or not. They all missed her. Nobody missed the drama. But Niea would do everything in her power to have Cal returned to her. She missed her terribly. The place was ready. Now training of the pup needed to start. All of them needed to have their skills honed to perfection. Jamal needed more rehab. So Niea, Zek, and Tulie set up a larger training area out back. They started with the basics of just getting in shape, stretching Jamal, weight training, then sword skills, hand-to-hand combat, knife defense, and running. Keddie was a good runner. It would take a lot more training for him to be a good fighter. He preferred Niea to teach him. She was so patient and kind to him. Miguel and Jamal were rough, but he understood. He needed to be ready; the battle of his life was coming. He would be happy to die for Niea. Miguel was well aware of how the boy felt for Niea but was not threatened by it. Niea was his woman, and he could not love her more. He hoped one day they could start a family. That was what they both wanted. Late at night, when they were in bed, Niea often cried about the world they lived in. If it wasn't for all these people close to her, she would be so resentful, angry, and depressed. But she had her crew, and she loved them with all her heart. They kept her going. She prayed for the day Cal would come back to her whole.

Early one morning, Miguel had Niea down on the bed preforming some of his oral magic on her. Keddie came rushing through the door. He froze. He had never seen such a beautiful nude woman splayed out before him. Niea quickly grabbed the cover and pulled it to cover her. He could still see her exquisite form and continued to stare. Miguel got up and slapped him on the back. He came out of it and said there was a blond lady with short hair and a large butt outside with two men dressed like women. Niea wanted to throw up. It was Vahar. She wasn't going to give up. She got up and put on the lovely dress Miguel given her and readied herself for what was coming. Miguel whispered in her ear, "Later, my love. It's my favorite." She adored him doing it to her. He was accomplished. All three of them went outside. There she stood with her lady boys. Niea said, "You are right, Keddie, she does have a large butt."

Vahar's lips tightened. It made her look angry and old. "Well, I see you have my dress on."

Niea said with a sly grin on her face, "No, Miguel gave this to me. You didn't want it, remember?"

Vahar circled Niea. All went on point to assure no violence occurred. Vahar said, "Well, if you like looking like a bumpkin, I guess it suits you."

Niea laughed. "Well, bumpkin it is. What do you want, Vahar?"

Vahar smirked. "I came for what is mine, and if I don't get it, who knows what I will do."

Niea started to answer. Miguel stopped her. "I got this."

Vahar said, "So, when did we become a man?"

Miguel stepped right up on her and looked down on her. "You smell like an old pair of shoes." He looked at Niea and winked then smiled a kind of evil smile. He was going to rip Vahar a new one. This whore needed to be brought down a notch or two. He started, "You know I have not smelled bad since I stopped screwing around with you."

"So you think you are a man, don't you.?" She snarled at both of them.

Miguel smiled that evil smile again, saying, "It took a real woman to make me into a man, not a disgusting piece of whorehouse pimp like you."

Vahar was livid. "How dare you! I sold you to anyone who wanted you, and you never disappointed. You were a good little whore giving up that ass like you were told. You love it." In that moment Niea realized she needed him for coin. Vahar was going broke without him. Nothing good ever comes out of using all those drugs. Surely Vahar had to know this on some level.

Niea chimed in, "Well, well, well, the pimpet is sliding down the hill. You do smell like something old and worn out. Maybe a good douche, Vahar, and you could make some coin off your huge vagina." The lady boys were confused. Vahar had told them something so different, that Miguel would come along without any problems. Vahar looked at the lady boys, seeing their disbelief. She felt foolish. How dare any of them make her feel this way. She slapped both of her escorts in the face. Both were shaking. They had never seen this side of Vahar. But then again, they had never seen anyone put her in her place so well. And Miguel had changed. He held himself so different, like a warrior prepared for anything. He looked a person dead in the eyes. He used to drop his head. He hardly talked to anyone. He had indeed become a man, and Vahar couldn't handle him like she did in the past. He was a man now, and Niea had helped him move into who he really was.

Vahar recovered some of her sass and said, "So did you enjoy the pills I left you?"

Miguel was contrite. "No, someone else found them, so your little plan to get me back on the crap failed."

Vahar hissed, "You little punk, I'll have your ass in a sling at the whore house and my customers will be wearing you out. But before that, I will have your Niea killed right in front of you." When Keddie heard she would kill Niea, he jumped and grabbed her around the throat. Miguel pulled him off. He looked at Keddie and nodded, that it was all okay.

Miguel said, "It's time for you to go. There will be no reason for you to return."

Vahar started to leave then turned and said, "I'll be back, and Niea will die in front of you."

Niea laughed at her, "I don't think so, musty woman. You don't have the skills."

Vahar hissed again at Niea, "I will watch you die with Miguel under my wing. I don't dirty my hands with such trash."

Keddie jumped again. Miguel stopped him. He did appreciate the pup's devotion to Niea. She was special to all of them. But Vahar was sneaky and devious. She could have a blade in his gut before anyone even knew what happened.

Miguel had a full picture of the beast she had become. He said, "Well, it's time for you to go. Don't come back at any time, and if you do come back, bring some humble fish pie with you. We will share it with the fish at the bottom of the pond." Vahar turned to leave. She looked back for her assassins to follow. They were frozen still in shock. Who was this horrid woman? Both of them wanted to stay.

Vahar screamed at them, "Come along now!" She had lost her composure and wanted to kill them too. *Later*, she thought. *I need them right now.*

Meanwhile at Central, Cal had been through intake. She had to be medicated due to the bootleg substances they found in her blood, and she was going through some kind of hellish withdrawal. She had told them she had not been drinking as much as she usually did. Nonetheless, her blood had high amounts of alcohol, ecstasy, and a sexual stimulant.

She was toxic. The combination was dangerous. If they had not picked her up when they did, she would be in real bad shape. She was kept in the infirmary for almost a week until she was stable. Then they moved her to a single room where she could be observed. She felt horrible. She was weak and kind of disoriented. Within another week she was clear enough to get around on her own. Her movements were limited by the Kalis. She could go to the library and read as long as her brain would let her. She found some real interesting information there on the computers. She knew of the laptop Miguel got to work. It had speakers and something called a video cam recorder. Cal was fascinated. Could she get this computer to video to the one at the hostel? She would have to ask permission.

She wanted to see Grandmama. Would that be allowed? She asked, and it was granted.

Theodosia, one of the advisors to the Califia had grown quite jealous of the leader of the Kalifee. She didn't like her popularity and her casual manner. Theodosia wanted Cal to be isolated. She didn't want her to contaminate anyone else. Grandmama would decide what she could do and where she could go. Finally, she got an audience with Grandmama. When she saw the grand lady, she ran to the leader of the Kalifee, picked her up, and whirled her around. Theodosia followed Cal into the office of Grandmama. When Grandmama saw her, she informed her that this was a private meeting with her granddaughter.

Theodosia said sternly, "That's not your granddaughter." Grandmama reminded the old bat that she had adopted Cal years ago, and she stomped out.

Cal rolled her eyes. "Some things never change."

Cal put her grandmama down after she kissed her many times. Grandma said, "It is so good to see, you my beautiful granddaughter. Sorry it has taken me so long to grant you an audience, but I have been too busy. Isn't that sad? Too busy to see my own granddaughter."

Cal said, yawning, "I probably was not in good enough shape for a visit from Grandmama."

Grandma said, "You look good now."

Cal said, "I feel much better." Permission was given for Cal to take one of the laptops she had found and work with it all she wanted. Finally, she believed she could get a message through to Niea. After several days of struggling, she got through. A young man answered and went to get Niea. Niea ran to the laptop; she was so excited. She screamed so loud when she heard Cal's voice. Miguel came running. He thought something was wrong. No, it was his lady hearing her friend's voice.

Niea voice was so high-pitched. "How are you?" Cal told her of her ordeal and that she was improving every day. She did not know when she could return. She was still in treatment. She told Niea about her adventures in the library and wanted the code off the laptop they had. She believed with Miguel's help, she could get the video cam going. Miguel was able to find what Cal asked for, and soon they all could see Cal and she could see them. Niea was ecstatic. This was sweet.

Miguel worked on the laptop using the code Cal had provided. Finally, success. He called everyone to join around the screen. Cal could only see Miguel and Niea. She told them they look good. Keddie was introduced, and he told Cal he couldn't wait to meet her in person and she could train him to use a sword like her. Zek jumped in, throwing Cal a big kiss, and Tulie squealed with joy. Niea stuck her face back in front of the screen. Cal seemed down. Where was Jamal? She wanted to see him, talk to him. Cal had tears in her eyes. Then Jamal jumped in. Cal screamed, "Oh my god!" She was overjoyed to see his beautiful dark face. She wanted to know if he was mad at her for all her shenanigans. She knew he would forgive her, but she wanted to hear him say it. She told him how much she cared about him and bad she missed him. Everyone left them alone so they could have some privacy. Cal could not quit crying. She wanted to hold Jamal so bad. He got really close to the screen and told her he loved her and had loved her from the start. She cried some more. The connection was lost, but all of them were overjoyed. Cal would be returning to them. Cal was so sad and overjoyed all at the same time. She wanted a drink. She thought, no, she knew she had to talk to someone. She ran to Grandmama's office like a wounded child. At first, the receptionist made her wait. Cal couldn't stand it; she needed her Grandmama. She had learned that when she had the urge to drink, she needed to talk to someone she trusted. That would be family, and there was no one more family here than Grandmama. She burst through the door crying. Grandmama had not seen her cry since she was a small child. She sent everyone else from the room. Theodosia was very annoyed and stomped out in her usual way. She held Cal for a long time. Cal cried until she could not cry anymore. After some time, she said, "I got in touch with the team, my team. I saw them all. I miss them, Grandmama." She told her that she had seen Jamal, the beautiful dark man she had been so hateful to. He forgave her and told her he had loved her from the start. Niea was right; Cal feared intimacy. There it was clear as a bell ringing in a tower.

They talked for quite some time, then Grandmama said, "I think you are ready to face the music, my love." Cal stayed for three more weeks just to be sure. Grandmama would have let her go then. It was a breakthrough for Cal. She had come upon this realization on her own. The day she left, she held her Grandmama for a long time crying again. The love she felt was so healing. Cal got into the ground car, not in chains this time, and headed home with laptop in hand.

When Cal arrived, she kissed Jamal like he was the last man on earth. Miguel and Niea had made a meal fit for the great warrior she is. Everyone ate. No one drank any alcoholic beverages, but they had a grand ole time. All of them cleaned up the after their feast. Cal took Jamal to the mat where Miquel and Niea used to sleep and make love. All of them had made it look like a honeymoon suite, and Cal was thrilled. The night went so well for the new lovers. They lay and kissed for a long time. Jamal was in no hurry, just to have Cal near him was just too special. One day they would marry and have some beautiful brown babies.

In the morning all hit the training area after they had eaten a proper breakfast. They trained most of the day. Niea showed Cal the improvements to the place to see what she thought. Cal had a few more ideas, but she was impressed to say the least. The intense training went on for weeks. Niea hounded them. They had to be ready. The Gogatt were fearsome, evil fighters. Niea would not accept any death from her crew. Wherever there was a weakness, she drove in hard. She checked with Cal to make sure she wasn't driving her or the others too hard. Cal told her no and pushed even harder. The nighttime was making for love, and the daytime was made for training. After several weeks of training, they started the grueling task of running several miles a day. Cal found that Keddie could outrun her so, she took him on. He always beat her no matter the distance. The kid was a gifted runner. Keddie had taken a shine to Tulie and asked Niea if he could start seeing her. It was just too precious, him asking for permission. Niea said he needed to ask Tulie. Tulie had said she thought she like women. He said he could be a girl if Tulie wanted, and all Niea could do was laugh. Soon they were seen holding hands and kissing. Keddie did not go any further. He waited for Tulie to tell him when she was ready. He had turned out to be a delightful person with a beautiful heart, and Niea adored him like a son. The hostel had to be reinforced. Niea and Miguel started a plan on doing just that. Miguel had an idea to make two jug-handle tunnels wrapping back onto the main tunnel to lead the enemy back into the hostel, and if they came through the other end of the tunnel, it would lead them back to where they had come into the tunnel. Cal didn't totally understand how this would work, but she believed in Miguel. He and Jamal started to dig. Miguel figured out a way to reinforce the tunnels to make them difficult to collapse. He also designed a way to blow them if they had to. All of them helped digging some fake tunnels to confuse their attackers, and those tunnels would be blown easily if needed. It was a tremendous amount of work, but that stopped no one. They seemed to have plenty of time. The Kalifees had put out scouts to watch for signs of the Gogatt.

They were needing some meat, so Jamal, Cal, and Zek volunteered to do some hunting. Niea's orders were that no one hunted alone. She was comfortable with the threesome. So, the three of them packed up and headed for the deep woods. Jamal decided they would head south. Meanwhile Tulie and Keddie went out to pick some wildflowers. Tulie loved flowers, and Keddie would do anything she wanted. He loved her quiet ways. He was falling in love with her, but he didn't yet know how she felt about him, and he had not told her how he felt. They walked for several miles. Tulie loved to walk in the great outdoors. Keddie followed her like a puppy dog.

Niea and Miguel were in their room making love. Then Vahar's lady boys entered the room and blew darts into both of them. They were paralyzed but could hear everything that was being said to them. Vahar entered the room, laughing like a maniac. "Well, well, well, look at the lovers now!" She paced up and down looking at them. "Isn't this sweet."

The lady boys were nervous and wanted to run like rabbits. Babe the tall one said, "Can we get this over with, please?"

Vahar hissed, "We are over when I say we are over."

Babe said, "So get him and let's go before someone comes."

Vahar snapped, "We are finished here when I say we are! I will tell you when we are done." She leaned down over Niea and in a hissing evil voice said, "You are going to die. Miguel gets to watch and then go with me." She looked at Miguel, whose eyes looked horrified. "Your ass is headed back to the swing and all the drugs you can handle, my love." Her lip curled in a twisted smile, but there was no joy in her. She was full of rage and revenge, and her revenge was close at hand. Babe and Mauk were clearly unsettled.

Mauk said, "We can't kill her. She's a Kalifee and a commander!"

Vahar turned on him, "You do as I say, you piece of—" She decided to hold her insults until later. If they didn't follow her orders, she would kill both of them.

For some reason, the drug they had shot into Niea was wearing off fast. Miguel was having a hard time focusing. He was drifting in and out of clarity. Niea was now her sharp self. She thought she heard a noise in the back. She remained still, making sure not to give up her secret. The cords they had tied them with seemed to get tighter with movement. Niea remained still, not wanting to give away her state of awareness. There was another noise. Babe and Mauk were anxious, nervous. They both wanted to run. Vahar locked her eyes on both of them. They were going to do what she wanted them to do. The lady boys now knew she wanted to kill a Kalifee commander. They would get in deep trouble, maybe even executed for such an act. They both froze. There was someone here. Vahar had her eyes on them, daring them to move.

All of a sudden, Tulie was on Vahar with her long thin blade on her back. "Please move, I wish to kill you." Vahar froze. Tulie had figured out they had used some kind of dart. She stayed behind Vahar. She didn't like the smell of this woman. She just wanted to kill her and be done with it. She waited, then she whispered, "Please move." Vahar held still, waiting, but the boys didn't move. Niea had broken away from her restraints and tackled Vahar. Vahar got a small cut across her back as she hit the floor. Niea had one of her arms behind her back.

Niea said in a hoarse voice, "What the hell do you think you are doing?" Vahar laughed an evil laugh that was disturbing. Niea knew she was mentally ill. She needed to take her to Central. She should have reported Vahar a long time ago. That was one of Niea's weaknesses. She let people get away with way too much, but not this time. Vahar had to be stopped before she killed one of her team members. Keddie burst into the room. He wanted to make sure Niea was okay. He knocked the boys to the ground with a flying tackle, jumped up, and snapped the sword on them. Cal had loaned it to him to practice with. He loved this sword. It was pure genius, and it worked so well. No one had seen such a weapon.

Keddie said, "Shall I kill them, Commander?"

Niea shock her head no. She said, "Tie all three of them, and if she tries anything, kill her." Keddie gave a snap of his head, indicating he knew what to do.

Niea communicated with Central. They wanted them there as soon as possible. All three were bound tight and put into the ground car. Miguel was still out. Tulie tended to him. He was really groggy. Miguel had worked on the ground car, and it would go really fast. Keddie and Tulie helped Niea secure them for safe travel. Niea was going alone. They loaded them up, and she took off.

Tulie and Keddie slept together. But there was no sex. Tulie still wasn't ready for relations. Keddie was willing to wait. He loved the little woman. She was special. Tulie heard Miguel moaning, and she went to see what he needed. He was sitting up holding his head.

Miguel mumbled, "Where is Niea?"

Tulie said, "She took those three killers to Central."

Miguel mumbled again, "My head is killing me." He fell back into bed and slept all night.

In the morning, the hunting party returned to find out what had happened. Cal was thoroughly peeved. How dare that B try to hurt any of their team. Vahar, the stunt queen, needed to be tried and executed. She had no opinion about the lady boys. They were pawns. Vahar would have killed them anyway. How dare that B! She was going to kill Niea. She was a stupid woman. Why would she? She was crazy. She needed to die.

Jamal, Cal, and Zek butchered the deer and put the meat in the smokehouse. Miguel was still hung over from the dart. He was no good today. Maybe he would be better tomorrow, he hoped. He missed Niea. He couldn't help it; she was just everything to him. Tulie bought him breakfast in bed. He ate as much as he could and laid back down. Cal came to his bed side and questioned him about what had happened. He wasn't sure once the dart got into him. Cal was angry not at him but at that brazen B. What in the hell was she thinking? Cal was so glad Niea had acted fast. Niea just gave too many breaks to people. She checked the communicator. No message yet. Cal needed to get busy. She found Jamal, and they went to work on the tunnel Miguel had designed.

Once at Central, the prisoners were secured in the cells provided for people, criminals like them. Niea filled out the report and did not leave out anything. She even reported the threats. She knew that should have been done earlier. If no one liked that she had waited, she would deal with that later. It was nice at Central, all the creature comforts one could want. It was not like the hostel. But Niea always loved the country life, the outlands. She liked roughing it. She liked/ loved being with her team, although she had been groomed to work for Central. No one could deny her skills as a Kali commander. She got a massage and took a tub bath. In the morning she felt nauseated, and her lower abdomen hurt. Later she started bleeding. It was not time for her period. She went to the medical center. They checked her, and she was having a miscarriage. She cried the rest of the day. They believed it was the dart. Other than losing the baby, she was in great shape. She contacted Cal later that day. She informed her of what had happened and would be staying a few days to recuperate. Miguel was asleep when she called on the laptop. She wanted him to get some rest; the drug had been much harder on him.

Niea returned to the hostel. Miguel saw she was down. She didn't want to tell him. But that night, while in bed, he had started to kiss his beautiful woman, then she stopped him and told him what had happened and why. He swore he would kill Vahar with his bare hands. He slept close to his Niea, holding her like there was no tomorrow. In the morning, he was still off. Cal did her quick check of his blood. He needed something to help clear out the rest of the dart sedative out of his system. He had an idea of some herbs and roots that would do the job. Tulie and Keddie went out and got what he needed from where they had found all the wildflowers. He made himself a large drink of beets, ginger, and turmeric. He drank it down. After a few days of his concoction, he felt so much better. All he could think of was choking Vahar to death. He was obsessed with the idea. She had killed their child, that stupid woman.

The tunnel and side tunnels were coming along well. Tullie and Keddie had found some crude oil bubbling out of the ground a few clicks from the hostel. Miguel knew where some phosphorus could be found. He would make some fuses and rig a bomb to blow the tunnel if the time came. Niea loved the idea.

The meat in the smokehouse was getting low, and some of the team decided to go hunting. So Cal, Jamal, and Miguel set out to hunt deer where tracks had been seen. Keddie and Tulie decided to go deeper in the woods and look for roots and herbs. Niea and Zek set into making some explosives out of the crude oil and phosphorus they had. They used small amounts and tested it out back. They were finally satisfied at the results and decided to take a mud bath. It was one of Niea's favorite.

A message came in from Central. Some Gogatts had been seen north of their position. The Kalifees had taken on several of these bands of Gogatts much farther north and needed Niea and her team to check out this band south of the main fighting. Central believed they were up to something that needed immediate attention.

In the morning, Niea and Zek packed up, left a note, and headed north. They stayed close to the forest and thicket so as not to be seen. Within two days, they found a large encampment of Gogatts. It was not clear what they were up to. Intel reported they didn't have any female slaves, and they were traveling with more equipment and supplies that had been seen in the past. Niea was instructed to get as close as possible but to use extreme caution. There was quite bit more of them in one unit than had been seen in the past. They usually moved in small bands of ten or so and usually had slaves.

The Gogatt treated their slaves much worse than they treated animals. They fed and kept their animal; slaves were allowed to starve for the most part and were beaten for pleasure. These rogue males were less than human. They were by far the worst thing that had survived in this so-called modern age.

On the second day of their travel north, they found this large camp of Gogatts. Zek and Niea watched for hours from a thicket just south of the camp. As reported, there were no slaves. This was indeed unusual. The Gogatts were famous for doing as little work as possible. They produced nothing. They raided, plundered, burned, raped, destroyed, demolished, and made a stinking mess of anything they touched. And there was no stench. This camp was different. It was clean, orderly, and there was no foul smell. Niea was intrigued. They watched for the rest of the day. The Gogatts were doing their own work. The camp was neat. The men looked washed. What had happened? Niea had to go in. She couldn't decide to tell Zek. Maybe it would be best not to say a word. She advised Zek to head back to the hostel, and she would remain here and just observe. There wasn't much they could do here but watch.

Zek was not keen on the idea, but Niea was the commander. At dawn, Zek headed back to the hostel. Once she was gone, Niea devised a plan and fell asleep on a tree limb. Later that day, she fell as the limb broke, screaming all the way down. Two Gogatts came running and found her scratched up as hell and dragged her back to the camp into their leader's tent. There she lay until their leader returned, and they threw a bucket of water on her. She wondered why it wasn't piss. She sat up and slowly looked around. They all stood back. She wondered if they were going to start the rape, but they all just stood there looking at her. Even with all the dirt, leaves, and general grit she had on her, she was beautiful. Most of them had never seen such a woman. She kept her head down, waiting for a sign of some kind. They had not even searched her. She had over ten weapons and several poisons on her. She couldn't help but wonder if these were even Gogatts. Then a tall man stepped up close to her and put out a hand. Things had gotten strange. What in the Spirit's name was going on? She slowly looked up. He was holding an outstretched hand to help her up. She looked down waiting for some kind of joke. All she could think of was to get ready—this could be the battle of her life. He spoke, "May I help you up, dear lady?" She crinkled her forehead and looked at him, then she handed him her hand. He gently helped her up. She was stunned. She had no idea what was coming. She remained ready for a killing spree. He smiled a warm, inviting smile and asked if she would like a bath. She nodded, and he instructed some of the men to set up a warm bath for her and to leave them. All was done as he had ordered, and he turned around and told her to take her time and enjoy the warm fragrant water. It smelled like jasmine. She undressed and stepped in the tub. It was wonderful. He never turned around. She soaked until she started to wrinkle. Finally, she stepped out and dried off with a soft clean towel. She found a dress he had left for her. Was she dreaming? What was all this? A set up for a ritualistic killing? Who knew? She dressed and kept her suit close to her. If she was going to have to get out of here, she would need it.

Niea sat down and said, "Sir, you can turn around if you want."

He did and smiled, saying, "You are one exquisite-looking woman. Who are you?"

She said, "I'm Niea. What is your name?"

He smiled again. "Leit. Glad to meet such an extraordinary woman." He graciously bowed his head. She was actually flattered. He was a gentleman.

Niea had to ask, "Are you Gogatt?"

He said, "Yes and no. Yes, these are Gogatt men, but I am of a different breeding. I am their new leader. I wish to change the face of the Gogatt."

That word *breeding*—why did he use that word? Niea said, "You have certainly done something. I was sure I would be raped repeatedly and killed. I really don't know what to say."

Leit said, "No one is going to hurt you. You are Kalifee. What is your rank, and why did you allow yourself to be captured?"

This was no dummy. She smiled and said, "Commander, and I just had to see what the hell was going on in this camp."

"Commander, how old are you?" He was dazzled by her smile, smitten.

Should she lie? No. "I am twenty."

"What kind of commander are you?" He was amazed at her. She must be a low-ranking commander to be out here on reconnaissance on her own.

Niea laughed just a little. "I lead an away team. We explore, invent, and move in if we have to."

He understood. This woman had a high position in the Kalifee, the freedom to make her own decisions. Still, what was she doing alone? He wondered. "Where is your team?"

She said, "Quite a few clicks from here."

Then he asked if she was hungry. He decided not to question her any further, and he would just have a wonderful evening with a beautiful woman. It had been a long time since he had enjoyed the company of such a woman. Maybe never.

They shared a meal. It was fair, but she had been spoiled by Miguel's cooking. She wished she had not thought of him. It made her ache deep in her heart. She didn't like being away from him. He felt the same way. They were bonded.

Finally, Niea said it was late and she was tired. Leit showed her a mat he had the men prepare for her in a private area of this tent, and she slept but lightly. She was not sure when all this would change. She felt that Leit was sincere in what he said. There was a sense of authenticity, sincerity, but there was also something hidden. There was something more he wanted from her than just companionship or to share an evening meal. She needed more time, and at this point she was sure she could get it. Caution at every turn—that was the ticket.

When Zek arrived at the hostel, the hunters had not returned. She bathed and went to sleep in the bunkhouse. She was awakened in the early morning. They had returned and were butchering the deer. She got up and made her way to the kitchen. There was Miguel, looking for Niea, hoping she was behind her. When Niea did not show up, he quickly went to his bed. It was still made. He went to the bunk room. No Niea. He came into the kitchen.

He said with a bit of alarm in his voice, "Where is Niea?"

Zek turned around and shrugged.

"What? You don't know." He was too upset to say it lightly.

Zek said, "She sent me back here. That's all I know."

Miguel's worry went into panic. "What the hell! You left her there by herself!"

Zek said, "I did what my commander told me to do."

"Were there Gogatts?" His voice was shrill.

Zek nodded her head in big yes. "A lot of them."

He was almost yelling, "What do you mean a lot?"

Zek said in a matter-of-fact way, "It was a very large camp. It was clean and orderly. I guess she went in."

"What! And you left her there?" He went to jump on her. She sidestepped his advance, pushing him to the floor with a thud.

She yelled, "Someone, get in here now!"

In ran Cal and Jamal. They secured Miguel on the floor. Cal said to him in a commanding voice, "You are not to attack your own kind!" Then she turned him over and socked him in the jaw, and he went out. He lay there for several minutes. They stood over him waiting for him to come to. Finally, he sat up rubbing his jaw.

Miguel looked at Cal and said, "Sorry."

She was angry. "Sorry, you tried to attack one of your own kind, a Kalifee warrior. That is not allowed. You should spend thirty-plus days in the brig for an attack like that." He dropped his head and started to cry. Cal just shook her head and backed up.

Miguel said, "Aren't any of you worried?"

Jamal said, "We have to trust the commander. She is a very capable soldier. You must have faith, my man!"

Cal said, "He's a wussy." She walked away and went back the chore of the deer.

Jamal said as he put a hand out to help him up, "Come, man, get up and pull yourself together." Miguel wiped his face with a cloth he had in his back pocket and grabbed Jamal's hand. As he got up, he started to cry again. Jamal said, "You gotta get it together, man. Do you think Niea would like to see you like this?" Miguel went to his room, lay down, and cried. Cal could hear him and shook her head. What the heck was wrong with him?

Later that evening, Cal was in the small office area that Niea used. She communicated to Central that Niea was in the large camp with the Gogatts, she believed. Then she learned that Niea had been instructed to observe all if she could, safely. Cal did not like this at all, but orders where orders. They were soldiers first always, and if Miguel couldn't get his head around that and act like a soldier, she didn't know what would happen to him. If he was at Central, they would have thrown him in the brig, and when that was done, he would have been sent to boot camp for at least six months. Cal knew what she had to do. Maybe Niea had been too easy with him. He had never known love in his whole life, and this was throwing him for a loop.

A bit later that evening, Miguel knocked at the door where Cal sat going over some plans Niea had. She did not look up and said, "What is it, Miguel?"

He apologized for his behavior and said he was going to look for her. Cal cautioned him, but he was determined to find her. She wished him good luck, and as he turned to leave, she said, "For what it's worth, I feel the same, but a soldier has to remain strong for the sake of all of us. I love Niea just like you do. I never knew of love until her." Miguel knew this was true.

Miguel said, "I have to get out of here for a while."

Cal said, "If you go looking for Niea and you find her, please don't jeopardize her in any way." She looked him dead in his eyes saying, "Please, Miguel." He nodded and left.

He wandered for hours. He was headed north. Cal's words echoed in his head, and he knew she was right. He had to trust her, her training and her brilliance. She would come back to him. But for now, he just could not go back to the hostel.

In the morning, Niea woke up. She had slept a soldier's sleep of one ear and one eye on the surroundings. But nothing happened. She would need some real sleep soon. She waited until she heard noise outside the tent and got up and put on her single suit. Then Leit tapped on a tent pole, and she said for him to come in.

Leit said, "You are up early. I have some breakfast for you. You have to be hungry." She was and took the food graciously. She wanted to know this hidden agenda he had. She felt it even stronger this morning. She sat to eat, and he asked if he could join her. Of course. He sat, and they ate in quiet. When all was finished, he called for the plates to be cleared, and they came right in looking at Niea with wide eyes. He smiled. All his men could see she had a prize of a woman. Niea felt this. She was some kind of accomplishment. That was fine. She felt this had something to do with that word he had used—breeding. The rest of the day was spent him showing what all he had done and how well all this had been going. He was aware of the fighting in the north. He wanted to avoid fighting. He wanted to negotiate. He wanted his men to produce, to have a society, a settlement, children, and some kind of future that had purpose. There were no women with these Gogatt. Niea was prepared to offer something, but she needed to communicate with her team and with Central.

All was quiet at the hostel. They continued to prepare for attacks. The word from Central was the fighting had concluded for now. The Gogatt had pulled back for some reason. No, there had been no word from Niea for Cal or Central. Cal was able to talk to Grandmama with the two hooked-up laptops. In private, they both expressed their concern about their Niea. But both knew Niea was capable of doing well no matter the situation. They prayed together and gave their love to each other.

Miguel wandered for days. He found himself at a bordello. His heart felt like it had broken in a thousand pieces. He needed to be numb. He went where he could do what he knew best, drugs and sex. His old stomping grounds of self-deprecation and here he was. He felt sick in his heart. He would have to fuel up before he could get into any kind of sexual debauchery, depravity. There was one woman there that knew him and Vahar. She asked Miguel about Vahar. He spat on the floor. All he could think of was choking that filthy woman to death. He still had not spoken a word. He had no words to speak. The ladies were having a slow night, so all attention was focused on this beautiful brown man. He was very sad. He was given his usual cocktail of the best booze, a sexual stimulant, and ecstasy. He had some coin, but as usual, the ladies were taken with his beauty. The one that knew was quick to tell of his sexual prowess.

He spent the night pleasing these women, and they all loved him. But it didn't feel like love. Toward the end of his stay—which could have been days, he did not know—he asked for a woman that would do to him what that filthy woman used to do to him. He found a practitioner of the Greek art of anal, and she was good. It took a lot for him to find an orgasm. She went as far as needed, and he had his moment. Then he was spent and passed out. He woke in the a.m. She tried to care for him, but all he wanted was for her to penetrate him again and again.

She was worried about his rectum. He took the wand she was using and tore into himself. Then all at once he was a mess back there. She would go no further.

He begged her to kill him through his rectum. She started to cry. He had gone too far. She left him to find a medic. When she returned, he was gone. Again, he wandered. Somehow, he found himself near the hostel, but he was afraid to return. But what was he supposed to do? He passed out. He was bleeding from the rectum. He had wanted to die. He felt like a piece of worthless manure.

Later that same day, Keddie and Tulie went for one of their walks. Keddie was still waiting for Tulie. He was close to giving up. He thought she was ready for some kind of love. He cared too much for her to give her an ultimatum. They walked around in silence, then he said, "You ready to go back?" She shook her head no and kept walking. She wanted to say how she felt. The horrors of her past were stalking her. All that stuff that happened before they had found her in the dungeon were lurking. Keddie couldn't take this anymore. He needed to know. He took her by the hand and said, "I love you." She wanted to tell him, but she couldn't. Then they heard some buzzard cawing and arguing. They both turned and saw buzzards picking at Miguel's backside. Tulie screamed, and Keddie gasped. He chased the buzzards away and yelled for help. Jamal came running. He froze in his tracks. He was horrified. The buzzards had been picking at Miguel's rectum. Oh my god was all he could think. It was more than anyone could handle. Cal heard the commotion and came running. Even she froze. Once they all found their composure, Miguel was taken back to the hostel and placed on a table. Cal knew they were going to have to do something. He would certainly die. He had to be infected and had internal bleeding. Who knows until she took a good look? They cleaned him up and placed him on his left side. Cal and Jamal worked for hours to see what they could do for this poor wretch. Keddie, Zek, and Tulie assisted as needed. When it was all done, all they knew to do was pray for the Spirit to help this lost man.

Jamal volunteered to stay with Miguel. He didn't leave him or sleep. All he wanted was for Miguel to live and try to learn something.

Wasn't that what trouble was, a lesson for learning where your light was? As Jamal had heard, the dark defines the light; without the dark, one could not define their light. Jamal prayed and sung for Miguel to heal, to find his light, to find the love of self, to be whole. As he had heard Niea say, one must be balanced and focused for the job ahead.

Within a few days, Cal was running out of anti-infectives to give Miguel, and he was going to need at least a few more weeks to help him get better. She went to Miguel and questioned him about what they could find around these parts that could be used. He thought for a while and came up with a formula—aloe vera, slipper elm bark, and sulfa. Tulie knew where to get aloe vera, and Jamal had seen some slipper elms when he was hunting. He also knew where to get some sulfa. It could be heated down until digestible. It was gathered by the crew and made up each day for Miguel. He drank it down and slowly healed.

When Cal knew he was better, she came to him to talk. He seemed ready to hear what she had to say. Cal started off with wanting to know if he wanted to be part of this team. If he didn't, she said they could pull out tomorrow. He said he did. This was the first family he had ever known. She looked hard at him. She wasn't sure he knew what being a soldier in an away team for the Kalifee meant. She asked, "Do you know what I am asking of you?"

Miguel took a while to answer. "I think so."

Cal kept looking at him hard. "I want you to know what you are getting yourself into. It's a lot of hard work."

Miguel looked at her with deep regret at what he had done, and he was so appreciative that they had saved him. "I need to be toughened up. I know that. All of you have done so much for me, and if I don't get my act together, I could get us all killed."

Cal was glad to hear he saw he was an integral part to this team. "We need you whole, focused, and strong. You are our think tank even if you don't see it or won't see it. You have seen how we prepare this hostel, and you have guided us the whole way. Miguel, I can't have you falling apart on us right when we need you the most."

He knew she was right. "Cal, I want to change if I am ever going to be a good husband to Niea and a father to our children. That won't happen, not the way I am now. I have to put all this crap behind me. How could I turn away from the truest thing I have ever known?"

Cal started, "When you are well, fit, we will start. I am not sending you to Central for boot camp. We are going to boot camp you right here. You agree?"

He nodded. "Just don't hit me so hard again."

She laughed. "Get ready, man. I am gonna hit you with everything I have."

Niea spent a day taking looks and whispered insults from Leit's men. She pretended that she didn't hear them, but she didn't miss a thing. She remembered every word. Finally, when she could not take another slur, she went back to the tent. She was carefully considering what to do next. As she sat with her eyes closed running all the events over in her mind, Leit walked in. "How are you, dear lady?" She nodded. Then Leit asked her to have some lunch with him. They ate in silence. She wanted to ask about the word he had used, breeding, but thought better of it. She was trying to hide a lot here too, especially her readings of him. She continued to hide her apprehension. She needed to appear to take him as he presented himself to her. He was not a bad-looking man. There was something kind of soft about him, and he certainly knew how to treat a woman. Not like his men at all, who obviously did not like or respect women. Then she decided to ask for a tour of the camp, and he said he would accompany her. She really wanted to observe without chatter from him. But she decided that she did need a guide. She kept her eyes wide open and mouth closed. He could do all the talking and did just that. Niea listened with full attention. She would remember every word he said. She would be reporting to Central all she had seen and heard here. She felt that it was all very important.

They shared another average meal. Niea tried not to think about Miguel's wonderful food. It would make her miss him too much. Later that evening, she watched the sun set in the west. Her thoughts wandered to when she had met Miguel and how fast they had fallen in love. Once again who knew that such a thing could happen? It had been so wonderful, so complete. She still wondered at how it had all happened. There were certain things here she really liked—the warm scented baths and some of the clothes Leit gave her to wear. She knew he was developing a thing for her. It would go nowhere, but she couldn't let him know there was no hope. She and Miguel were for life. She would never love another. She knew that for sure.

In the morning, she felt sick, her stomach hurt, she was itching, and she was sweating profusely. What in the world had she gotten into? She ran everything through her head using that analytical mind of hers. The only thing she could come up with was that one of them had slipped her something in the food. Was it Leit? She truly didn't know, but she had her suspicions. She needed to go to Central and have them check her out. She certainly couldn't fight in this condition. She had to remove herself as a target. When Leit came into her tent, he seemed truly shocked she was so sick. He offered to take her anywhere she needed to go. No, that would not be necessary. She would leave in the morning if she was well enough. She finally got a message to Central. They would send a liner to pick her up in the morning. No need to tell him how she would be traveling. She didn't need anyone following her!

Miguel had improved and was ready to start training with Cal. First, she had him run with Keddie. Slow at first. Day by day, they ran. They stretched. Then the rigorous training would begin. Cal would work on his upper body strength. He found some old weights at one of the nearby dumps, and they pumped iron daily. From morning to night, they worked. He improved wonderfully. He never complained. He gave his all, and Cal became very proud of him. She withheld compliments and continued to train with him along with Zek, Tulie, Keddie, and Jamal. So far no one could outrun Keddie. He still wasn't much of a sword wielder or fighter for that matter. He was very thin. Miguel came up with some protein wraps for the team and had made some deer jerky. Keddie slowly started gaining weight. Miguel referred to Cal as Commander. She was in charge until Niea returned, she reminded him. Cal had gotten a message from Niea. She didn't tell the others. Niea was ill with what had been slipped to her. No need to share this. She needed Miguel to stay focused. It did seem a bit mean to keep him in the dark, but she had him focused. He needed to stay that way. He was good at everything, and that could make him lazy. It could make anyone lazy. She was harder on him than anyone. He knew he needed it. At night, in his room, he would cry for Niea, but in the day, he kept it to himself. He was making something special for his beloved lady. The days were made for grit and the nights for longing. He kept his tears inside. No one saw his pain. No need, he was becoming what he had always wanted to be—a warrior!

When Niea arrived at Central, she was not well, but she walked straight to the infirmary and lay down on the exam table. She told the medic her symptoms and everything else that had happened. When her blood came back, they found some real suspicious substances. One of them for sure was a fertility drug; the other was something that was trying to change her DNA. The medic was very worried about this. This description was something that the medic was sure only the Kalifees' highest scientist knew about. The how and why of the description of DNA would be gibberish to a regular person. She went to her communicator and got Grandmama down here. They talked to themselves so Niea couldn't hear them. She told Grandmama that Niea was lucky her metabolism worked so fast, or she would be dead or deeply changed—serious stuff. They kept Niea for four weeks until all were satisfied that she could return to the field. That was where her heart was, with her team and Miguel.

Grandmama and Theodosia were going over all the reports. Grandmama held no emotions back even in front of Theodosia. The woman was a hard-hearted, flawed, and extremely small-minded.

But deal with her, she must. The head of the right factions of the Kalifee would be dealt with much more in due time.

But first, Niea needed to be commended for her uncharted bravery. Theodosia hated that any of Grandmama's crew would be commended for any achievements. Her hatred for Grandmama and her so-called daughters made her a furious, twisted woman and even more shortsighted than ever. Why Theodosia held such resentments and animosity was a mystery even to Theodosia. And how in the world did such a woman get such a strong hold on this organization? It seemed to Grandmama that Theodosia hated strong, independent women. She seemed like a misogynist. This made no sense to Grandmama. What the hell was wrong with this disgusting woman? How could one hate their own sex, and how did such a woman get to such a powerful position? Grandmama was quite old, but she would be damned before she allowed this half a human to take over her beloved Kalifee. Niea would be at the ship helm of the incredible Kalifee command, and if Grandmama had to kill Theodosia, so be it. The consequences were high for killing any Kalifee, no matter the rank or status.

Training kept escalating. Cal put more and more on Miguel. He was getting stronger and quicker. Cal had noticed he had a very different kind of fighting style. He had only been using what Cal and the others taught him. Now Cal wanted to see if he could show this other style. Had he developed it, or was he taught it? Miguel was unsure how to show his slowed-down movement. He thought he had learned it from his stepfather. Cal stepped back and watched as Miguel tried to remember how they had started the training. Cal asked many questions about the stepfather. Where had he learned this style? What area was this man from? The questions never seemed to end. Finally, Miguel said that he would just show her some of the beginning moves, so onto the fight area they went. There he went slow at first, then Cal started to push for more aggressiveness. Miguel had learned not to let her get under his skin and remain patient, moving slowly around Cal with his sword drawn. He knew this would make her jump at him first. She struck hard and fast. He countered, and she stumbled from the blow she tried to deliver. Again and again she tried to hit him with all she had. Her patience was wearing thin. He counted on this. He kept his composure and his stance with his eyes locked on her. Unknown to him, Cal had instructed Zek and Jamal to jump out at him full force. He parried both. Jamal's weight worked against him, and both of them hit the ground with a thud. Cal shook her head. She was going to put this brown man on the ground if it was the last thing she ever did. Her gaze was intimidating to say the least. She had bloodlust in her eyes. Miguel held firm in his intent, gaze, and movement. Cal looked away and sighed in frustration. He let up on his stance, and she went for him full force. Miguel barely got out of her way. She turned so fast it was hard for him to see which way she was coming next. She was almost on him when he dodged, turning his sword so that the flat side came across the back of her head, and she went down with a thud. He waited for her to get up. He said her name several times. Nothing. Jamal went to Cal and took her in his arms. She was breathing but was out cold. He carried her into the kitchen and put her on the table and tried to wake her. She was out. He looked at Miguel and Zek. Miguel had a deep look of regret as he stared at Cal. He didn't realize he had hit her so hard. Jamal tried and tried to wake her. He looked at Miguel. His eyes had big tears in them. He was so worried for Cal. Jamal had always known to let Cal be the warrior that she was. Miguel had not been able to do this so well. But now he needed Miguel to see to Cal. Miguel understood. He started to undress her, and Jamal assisted. He checked the response of her pupils, and he checked for doll's eyes. He ran the handle end of a knife on the bottom of her feet. He was looking for any neurological response that would indicate brain injury. So far, she was just unconscious. But that was not a good sign in itself. They helped her to his bed, and Jamal sat with her. Miguel knew he had to be like Jamal, standing back and letting Cal do her job. This was how he needed to be with Niea. They were warriors first and foremost. Miguel looked at Jamal. He had no blame for Miguel. There was much here for Miguel to learn.

In the morning, she woke up. Her head was killing her. Woo, he had hit her hard. Miguel thought she was going to be mad at him. But instead she grabbed and hugged him. She was impressed.

No one other than Niea had ever knocked her out cold. Jamal had not left her all night. He was tired but overjoyed. Cal did have the hardest head he had ever seen. There was a large lump on the back of the head. Cal just had to show it to everyone. It was a trophy she was so proud of. Miguel was relieved, but maybe she needed to go to Central for a more complete checkup. She assured him that if her symptoms get worse, she would go, but for now did he have a potion for her throbbing head? He quickly got some herbs together and made her a delicious drink. He made her one three times a day until she was feeling much better. She was so proud of him. He still couldn't believe she was so elated.

When they went back to the practice floor, Miguel was tentative with his fighting. This upset Cal. She got in his face and yelled it out of him. She kept yelling, "Fight, soldier!" Finally, he did just that. They fought for an extended period until neither one could go any more, and Cal gave a truce and slapped Miguel on the back. She was beaming. For now, his style would remain his style. Her head still hurt. Miguel could see this and made her another potion. It did work well. He convinced her to rest, and she did. Jamal checked her neck and gave it an easy realignment and that helped tremendously.

One evening, Cal got a call from Niea. She would be returning in the morning. Cal decided not to tell anyone, especially Miguel. Only thing was, Miguel had been standing near the door and heard the whole conversation. He kept it to himself. He was getting a bit wiser. All he cared was she was well and returning to him and the team.

In the morning when she arrived, he kept his distance until she had greeted her ladies, Jamal, and Keddie. She knew Cal had trained him well. He presented himself to her like a proper soldier, then he gave her a wink, and she smiled a thin smile. Tonight would be a different story.

Miguel had prepared a feast with the help of the crew. Niea always marveled at the way he made everything so good. Then she started her story about Leit and the difference in the Gogatt hoard he had with him. She told of the substances that had been found in her blood. Leit had seemed sincere in the act of not putting anything in her food. But how did these Gogatt come across such a thing? Surely, they knew nothing of DNA, much less descripting, but Leit did this, Niea was sure.

Miguel made little eye contact with Niea. He was concealing his worry for her. He knew he had to do as Jamal did, let his lady be who she is and do the job she was trained and lived to do. She told them of all the differences and that she had been stunned that she had not had to fight at all, although she had fought for her life after ingesting what was in her food. She had an idea. She wanted all of them to go meet Leit and his men. Maybe they could strike some kind of agreement. Miguel was not keen on it, but he kept it to himself. At least he would be there to help protect her if needed.

Cal sat and listened but was unsure about this deal or agreement. Why not just kill them all? That would be best. Niea asked, "We could put on some kind of show, feed them, get them drunk, then explore the camp." She was delighted. Yes! "We will dress in our war garb. Jamal will braid all of our hair, and Miguel will make his fine food. We'll get them drunk on Miguel's fine wine. Then we will entertain them like a proper traveling Kalifee band of gypsies." Niea was excited. Cal not so much. Zek and Tulie seemed up for the challenge. Jamal just shrugged, and Miguel just raised his eyebrows. But it was on. Niea was the commander, and all began to prepare. Niea sent a message to Central. It was on.

That night Miguel spoke low and slowly in bed. He wanted to be careful not to show anything but agreement to do as his commander ordered. But as her man, he was filled with apprehension. Who was this Leit, and had he made sexual advances toward Niea? She assured him Leit had been a complete gentleman. He just had something that Niea needed, and the Kalifees needed to know. This describing of DNA was something only a few science types would know anything about. Miguel thought maybe this Leit was somehow connected to the Kalifee. Who else would have such a thing, and what was the purpose of it? Too many questions—dangerous.

It was exciting to get all this together. Jamal had all their hair looking sharp. The ladies had on their single suits. Jamal and Miguel dressed like soldiers on parade. They all looked so good. They loaded up the ground car. It was full. Jamal had his harmonica, Miguel had his guitar, Cal had the laptop with some of her favorite music, Zek had a small drum, and Tulie had some finger cymbals. Keddie would assist as needed. Niea was so proud. They loaded the meat and herbs and wine, and off they went. Cal drove. They headed northeast as Niea directed. They arrived midmorning just outside the camp and took a break to stretch and get some water from a stream. Niea directed the way. She wanted to go into the camp alone, but the others did not like this idea. So after they had rested, drank some water, and made sure they all looked good, they walked into the Gogatt camp like the fine Kalifee performers they were. All Kalifeeians loved live shows.

The Gogatt men pulled their weapons. But Niea walked right on in looking at each one. They remembered, and one of them had spiked her food. They had to be careful not to eat or drink anything from them. One has to be very careful of the dance and its steps if you're going to dance with the devil. She strolled in as if she owned the place. They kept their weapons ready. Leit had heard the commotion and exited from his tent. He was delighted to see Niea. He took her hand and kissed it. Miguel remained neutral. Jamal was watching him out of the corner of his eye. He thought Miguel was getting the hang of it. He was cool as they come. He knew Miguel wanted to break Leit into pieces and probably would.

Niea and Leit disappeared into Leit's tent, where she told him what she had in store for him and his men. Leit was delighted. She needed a place to set up, and he showed them the prefect place. There were no tents in the area. The terrain was even and actually had a good 360-degree view around where they would set up the tent. She was pleased. She returned to her people, and they went to work. The Gogatt men wanted to watch, but Leit sent them to finish their work. There would be plenty of time this evening to see everything. Leit was sure these men had never seen a Kalifee show. They were all in for a real treat.

Niea and the ladies decided the order of the show. They all helped set a designated performing area. Miguel and Keddie began the preparation for the feast. The wine was stored in a cool area.

Miguel had brought some sedating herbs that would be added to the wine the Gogatt would drink. He was careful to cleverly mark these bottles. They would start the show with Niea welcoming everyone and having them eat and drink. She was very good at getting people to relax.

She was the perfect choice for this job. Cal would have told them to eat, drink, and don't be bunch of jerks.

When the food was ready, the ladies gathered the bowls that Leit had the men provide and began to serve. They had their own cups for drinking. Cal grabbed the special bottles of wine and started to serve. Niea didn't think this was wise. But Cal made that tongueout eek face at her, and she stepped back. Jamal started the music for her, and she began to dance for this very unlikely crowd. All eyes were on Cal. Her long legs and unpredictable movements were amazing. She filled the cups in perfect rhythm, making eye contact with every one of them. They were mesmerized by this tall blond exotic creature with prefect rhythm and moves they had never seen. Once the wine was poured, Cal placed the proper bottles on the tables with these men and went to the back. Now it was Jamal and Miguel's turn to play some music. The Gogatts seem more comfortable with men preforming for them. They just weren't used to women being anything but dirt under their feet. They clapped and sang along with these two. It went well. Then Niea, Zek, and Tulie came out. As Zek drummed, Tulie played her finger cymbals, and Niea danced. Miguel had never seen her do this. He was enthralled, wow! He didn't even watch the Gogatts and Leit. He couldn't take his eye off her. She began a shimmy with some popping and locking. Where did she learn such a thing, and why hadn't she shown him her dancing? The men went wild. They had never seen such a woman and such a dance as this. It was the finality. They ended with Cal joining in, and all four women shimmied down and bowed deeply. The men got to their feet, and the place was turned all the way up. Jamal put on some R and B he had found on the laptop, and Cal began to serve wine, giving a new provocative pose with every pour. Niea joined Leit, and he hugged her and was overjoyed at the show they had put on. The men were drinking and enjoying the shenanigans of Cal. It wasn't long before Leit's men were getting way drunk. Niea noticed Leit was not drinking. She asked if he wanted some wine. She had a glass in her hand she had been sipping from. He did take it and a sip. He gestured for her to join him in his tent. She picked up a bottle. It didn't have the mark, but she believed it would do, and she joined him in his tent. Miguel held his angst close inside. He didn't want to mess this up, but he didn't like that ass anywhere near his Niea. He had to trust her.

In the tent, Leit did drink. He really liked the wine. Niea was careful to act like she was drinking. She was able to pour out some of the wine when he wasn't looking. Leit went on and on about their show. "Wow! So this is your away team." He was very interested. He wanted to know all. Meanwhile the others began to clean up and pack up. They left the wine and food for them. Most of the men were sleeping it off somewhere. Some were still trying to drink. Soon they were all about out. Cal and Jamal started to dance slowly. He loved to hold his woman close to him. Her wild self had charmed the crap out of these beasts. He was so proud of her. He could only hope Miguel was proud of Niea and not worried. Hide that jealousy. No need for those emotions; they only bled off energy and hindered love. But Miguel was keeping his possessiveness to himself. He was growing up. Jamal had to admit that he wouldn't like Cal going into that tent with that man. She would probably kill him anyway.

Soon Leit was a bit high and tired. He lay down and patted the mat for Niea to lay with him. She sat and watched until he was passed out. Then she joined the others, and they started their search of the camp. There was a small wooden box Niea retrieved from Leit's things she thought that might be helpful. She and the rest of her crew were quiet and careful to replace anything that they disturbed. Niea found some chemical formulas that where intriguing. She memorized them they could be reported to Central as soon as possible. Cal found some pills and pill-making supplies. Cal took small separated samples of everything she found. Once they had exhausted their search, everyone found a place to sleep. Niea found Miguel and kissed him. She had missed him as bad as he had missed her. She was so proud of him. She told him she was sorry he had gone through that. He shook his head, telling her she should be ashamed of him and his behavior. He had jeopardized everything. How could he be a good father, husband, if he gave in to such alarming actions. He had to change, and he had.

Niea lay with her head in the crook of his arm, then she rolled over and mounted him. He slowly rocked her on top of him, exciting her so. Then he slowly penetrated his beautiful woman. He was in his element and was exhilarated that his talents were for Niea and hers alone.

In the morning they were up long before the Gogatts. Niea went to Leit's tent and lay down on his mat as if she had been there all night. He woke, apologetic for falling asleep on her. She was secretly glad she didn't have to deal with any of his advances. She smiled warmly at him and offered him breakfast. She didn't have enough for all his men. He wasn't expecting such a meal, much less breakfast. He followed her to their camp and enjoyed the most delicious breakfast he had ever had. He wanted to meet each one of her team. He was intrigued. She began with Cal, fighter extraordinaire and exciting dancer. Then Miguel, who introduced himself as the cook. Niea laughed. Then Jamal chimed up as the hairdresser. Leit was intrigued with Tulie as the assassin. Zek was introduced as the woman who could make anything and as a fighter of great talent. Keddie was off in the woods gathering some herbs he had seen. Niea was glad. There might be some of the men who remembered him. She was sure he had done that on purpose.

Leit asked Niea to walk with him one more time before they left. They walked, and he asked her when she would be returning. She wasn't sure. He said they would be moving farther northwest soon, and he really wanted to see her, spend time with her. Niea knew he really liked her, but he wanted things she knew she would never give him. But she would see him again. She assured him of that. She returned to her crew. They were packed and ready to go. Niea made sure Leit knew they had left the food and wine for him and his men. He was genuinely grateful. Niea noticed how he was looking at Miguel with no shirt on and a small loin cloth flapping in the breeze. No one could blame him; Miguel was stunning. Even heterosexual men noticed Miguel. Niea wondered at his attention, although it was obvious, and Miguel gave him a show without giving away he knew what he was doing. Again, with Cal driving, they made it back to the hostel in record time. In silence they unpacked the ground car and made their way to take a nap. None of them had slept much. Niea contacted Central and informed them of what they had found. They wanted her to report to Central in person, and they had her inventions ready for them to put through a trial period. She was excited. She and Miguel would take off in the morning. That evening, when all was quiet, she and Miguel were lying on their bed. She asked about him putting on a show for Leit. Miguel just shrugged. Niea admitted she was always excited about Miguel's sexual past and marvelous abilities. She loved he had been with so many women and knew what to do for each of them. He smiled. And what was he doing to Leit? He grinned even wider. She slapped him in his chest with the back of her hand. He laughed hard and teased her with some of the "unintentional" poses he had done for Leit. She loved looking at him. "Tell me, what were you doing?"

He laughed. "You don't know."

Niea pushed him. "Miguel! You were trying to entice him."

Miguel was having too much fun. "I didn't have to entice him! He was already there. Might be able to use it later. So, you like that I have had a lot of women?" He attempted to do a shimmy while laughing.

She was getting agitated. "Yes, I find it exciting that you have these abilities. You know how to please a woman. What about a man?"

He kept smiling. "I don't really know. Too messed up, too many evenings. Tell me about your excitement."

She was a bit embarrassed. He loved the flush of her cheeks. "Your virginity is showing." She hit him hard this time. He grabbed her and threw her on the bed and went down on top of her. He whispered in a husky voice, "So what excites you the most?"

She squirmed under him and giggled like a schoolgirl. "I love that you can rock any woman to completion. It's hot."

He flipped her over and began to take her clothes off, sliding his hands slowly over her every part of her body. Once she was completely nude, he asked, "What else, my love?" He already knew. He pulled her onto his face and slowly explored ever part of her. She screamed with delight. Then he would enter her then remove himself and lick her there. Again and again until Niea thought she would lose her mind. She came over and over again.

She was almost out of breath, saying, "What about you?"

He smiled and pulled her down onto him slowly. "When do you want me to? It's all for you, my beauty." At that moment, both of them went into completion. It was not just sex. It was the completion of their very souls, forever united in the grace of what a woman is to a man and what a man is to a woman—the essences of the Great Spirit within all beings.

In the morning, Miguel and Niea headed to Central with the samples. Niea's perfect recall and the excitement of the sling sword and the shadow suit would be there. They were both excited. Miguel drove. They stayed in silence for the most part. Niea was running everything through her head to make sure she had it in order. The drugs/powder samples that Cal had found were packed to retain their integrity. They would go straight to the lab. Niea would recall to Grandmama everything she had scanned with her perfect recall memory. She was so grateful for this gift, and it was a gift. She had done nothing to create it or train for it. It was just there with her focusing on the task. Miguel knew what she was doing and did not interrupt. How could a man headed nowhere end up with this woman, these dedicated people? He was by far the luckiest man on earth. He had found true love, he had found his warrior, he had found his purpose. *Thank you, Great Spirit.*

When they arrived, Niea would talk with Grandmama alone. The lab was on the samples. Grandmama and Niea made a chart of all Niea had remembered. It was definitely a way to rescript DNA. This Leit was definitely a geneticist or a chemist, or he was working with one. He must be watched. Niea told Grandmama where they were headed. He had to have something to do with these substances Niea had gotten into in the outlands of Gabba. The word breeding may indicate he was from the breeding program of the Kalifee or he himself was engineered. No matter where he came from, he was now on the Kalifees' most dangerous list. He was obviously developing some kind of genetic weapon. Grandmama shuddered at the thought.

The lab had reported that one of the white powers was an improvement on the rescripting substances found in Niea's blood. This rescripting was definitely targeted toward women, the feminine basis of life. Whoa! So some evil genius planned to change women at their core. Certainly, the why of it was clear—control. So many men had controlled women or tried to control women throughout history. The fear of women was ever prevalent in so many men. This confused Niea. How could this be beneficial to anyone, especially men themselves? The only way to enter the earth was through the female. Don't men and women balance each other in a dance of life?

Niea needed a distraction from all this. She wanted Grandmama to meet her magnificent Miguel. Yes, they would all have supper together. Right now, she and Miguel would go out into Central and take in the sights. She found her love down in the grand atrium and kissed him, whispering, "I love you." He grabbed her and whirled her around. He had gotten so strong.

They walked the promenade. It was beautiful. On a corner stone he noticed her name. She tried to pooh-pooh it, but he insisted. She had designed this plaza, the buildings, the escape routes. A few years ago, it had all been destroyed, and many Kali men, women, and children had died. Now it had many escape routes, and when the enemy got in, they would be trapped. It was all Niea's design. She was just too modest. He chided her that she needed to own her truth. She laughed. It was the same words she had said to him.

They found a small tavern and got something to eat and drank some really nice Kali wine. Niea told Miguel his was a bit better. He could be a legend here with his cooking talents was what Niea told him, but he had better stay out of the brothels. He laughed. Then Niea thought he was probably already a legend in the Kalifee brothels. They both had a buzz, and Niea wanted to show him the gardens. He already knew she had designed them. They strolled slowly, taking in all its beauty. Then Niea gasped. Miguel said in question, "What's wrong, love?" Niea pointed a low held-out finger. Miguel slowly turned his head. Oh my god! It was Vahar sitting on a bench.

She was dressed in a worker's outwear, but she wasn't working. She did not see them. Niea and Miguel turned and quickly walked the other way. What in the world was this murdering whore doing here? She was supposed to be executed. She had tried to kill a Kalifee commander. Kalifee had a strict rule: no Kalifee was to injure another Kalifee. In fact, none of them was to kill or injure anyone that was not a threat to life and limb. Niea had assumed she had been executed and had not inquired about her outcome. Niea didn't know what to feel. Miguel was fuming. He wanted to choke this slime of a woman for way too long. Niea had told him that she was sure Vahar had been put to death. Niea's mind was blown. She would have to wait to ask Grandmama what the hell was going on.

They showed up at Grandmama in some outfits they had bought in the square. Miguel had picked out her dress, and it looked wonderful on her. She had dressed Miguel. She thought he would look good in anything. Not on her, she had slender build, and some things just didn't look right on her. As a young girl she always thought she was built like a boy. Miguel assured her that no keister he had ever seen was the curvy voluptuous stellar piece of perfection like her derriere. Grandmama invited them both into her quarters. She marveled at how wonderful they both looked. Niea could tell she was taken with Miguel's looks. She wanted to know all about Miguel. He told her everything except his brothel experience. She might already know. She knew his mother. They ate the meal and drank the wine; both were really good. Niea just had to chime in about the superior culinary delights of Miguel. She offered that they cook for her tomorrow. Once the food was gone, they all sat quietly sipping on the lovely wine. Niea said, "I saw Vahar in the garden." Grandmama could tell Niea was angry. She definitely had a reason to be majorly peeved.

"Seems like Vahar has some very influential people or person in a high position." Grandmama was having a hard time looking at Niea. She felt horrible that that woman was still living after trying to kill her granddaughter.

Niea huffed, "Theodosia!"

Grandmama was disgusted. "Yes. They put Vahar to work, but Vahar doesn't do physical labor. She only knows sex and using men sorely. So, she sits in the garden all day. No one has anything to do with her. She looks like hell. She doesn't exercise and contributes nothing. It is a tragedy. I have never liked that woman, but she made the Kalifee a lot of coin. She had begun to slip with her contributions, and I believe she is quite mad, crazy." Niea questioned Grandmama about the circumstances around Vahar. Turned out Grandmama knew everything. She knew of Vahar's manipulation of Miguel for her coin. She assured Miguel she had no problem with his past. She had a past of her own. She considered him a victim. She knew how his mother had abandoned him. It had been Grandmama that arranged for Miguel to have the hostel. She had been aware of his talents for some time. She was so pleased with him being with her granddaughter. Niea sat there in wonder. Grandmama had her finger on the pulse of them all. She was truly a phenomenal woman who had enough love for them all. Niea couldn't be prouder. Miguel just sat there speechless, flabbergasted. This woman was a true leader, the caretaker of the Kalifee people.

Miguel had one question: "Did you arrange for me and Niea to meet?" She just shook her head no. He didn't believe her. He was staring at her. She winked at him. He and Niea kissed and hugged this tremendous woman. They thanked her and reminded her that they would be cooking for her tomorrow night. As they left, neither of them said a word.

When they returned to the beautiful room that Grandmama had arranged for them, they stood out on the balcony looking at the lake below. Neither knew what to say. Miguel felt that Grandmama had been his guardian angel, and he loved her so. She was a spectacular woman.

They got ready for bed. Both were quite stunned. Niea lay on the bed and looked at Miguel. She had never done to him the wondrous thing he did for her. It was her time. She pushed him down onto the bed. She looked into his golden-brown eyes. "It's my turn. You must teach me, oh erotic master."

He smiled, saying, "First, I must know. Does Grandmama know everything?"

Niea was as baffled as he was. "I guess so."

He looked at Niea. "So she knows I'm going to teach her granddaughter fellatio?"

Niea started to laugh. "Yes, and it better be good. Grandmama expects the best from her grandson!" He smiled and felt so warm in his heart. He was a part of this incredible family and had been for some time now.

He showed her a few things, and Niea took to it. She loved it. It was a joy to please her man the way he pleased her. He kept stopping her. He was so excited. He wanted it to last somewhat longer than a few minutes. She slowed down and tenderly licked the end of him, the side of him, all of him. She was so good at this; his mind was blown.

When it was all done and he was spent, he lay there stroking the hair on her vulva and tenderly kissing her neck and shoulder. He had never known happiness and acceptance, but here he was. He was so excited for every day that awaited him. Had Grandmama sent her to him? He would believe so no matter what. Both of them fell into a deep sleep.

Just before dawn, Miguel sat upright in bed. He had a vivid dream about killing Vahar. It was real. He could smell her. He could feel her venomous touch. He could hear her shrill voice. He jumped up obviously disturbed. Had he actually done it? No, it couldn't be. He had been here all night. Niea woke, wondering what was wrong. He told her of his dream. He felt he had been awake, present in his dream. He had all the sensation of being there in the moment. He had felt Vahar dying as he choked her. They would see Grandmama later, and he would tell her of his most disturbing dream. But for now, they would have a breakfast and avoid the garden. They spent their day by the lake and then in the library. They both loved to read. Niea found some very technical info on DNA and rescripting of DNA, but not much more.

They returned to their room and found new clothes that Grandmama had delivered. It was an exquisite gown and leather pants and a silk shirt for Miguel. They fit perfectly. of course they did. They bathed and dressed. Miguel braided Niea's hair, and she braided his. They stood in front of the mirror and marveled at how they looked. Grandmama had some scented oils for both of them. There were Niea's favorite wildflowers in a wonderful country bouquet, just her style. Miguel had a rosemary boutonniere, which he loved. They both knew they were getting married. There was a knock at their door. Their carriage was there being pulled by a Friesian horse—Niea's favorite. They were taken to the open-ended chapel. Grandmama met them there and took both of them by the arm. She whispered, "I can't wait for you two. You would probably have had children and would never have gotten married." The music started. It was an old piece from many hundred years ago about love making us true. It was perfect. She walked them down the aisle, kissed both of them on the mouth, and stepped in front of them. She gave the most wonderful sermon on love, devotion, and sex. She then pronounced them married. They kissed, and the party started. There were many Kalifee there in their finest. The bride was separated from the groom. Grandmama took Miguel by the arm and guided him to a private room and sat him down. Niea was taken to the main ball room, where she was to receive wedding gifts from all the Kalifees there. Grandmama had this planned, leaving nothing out.

Grandmama just looked at him for a very long time. He just sat there and looked at her. She had something to say. "I will not keep you from your wedding night, but I am sure you and Niea started that many nights ago." He looked at her with a sly smile. She knew. "I have much to tell you, my son. You had been alone for some time, and that part of your life is done. You are very important to me as well as Niea. Yes, you are to protect her and help keep her alive, but at no time are you to endanger yourself to the point of death. Niea and I need you alive. Do you understand?" He nodded. "You are to travel with her whenever you can, especially if Cal isn't there. We have some important things that are coming to light. You and Niea, I believe, have captured the interest of this Leit. We need to know him as well as we can. I don't ask either of you to do anything you cannot see yourself doing, but please entice him. He may or may not be the constructor of this very dangerous DNA rescripting. I need to know where he is getting this information. A battle is coming. We have all our fighters in full readiness. You are ready for this, I know." Miguel nodded. "You are my pivot. We will communicate outside the knowledge of others. Can you do this?" She looked hard at him. He nodded again. "Good, let's join your exceptional bride and this fabulous party!"

Miguel realized in that moment that he was now and would forever be a major player in keeping the Kalifee and its values alive. He knew his purpose, and Grandmama was there to guide and assist him.

It was the most wondrous party seen here in a very long time. They all drank, sang, and danced. It was late in the night when all was done. In the morning, Niea and Miguel gathered their things and headed to say goodbye to Grandmama. She was in a conference but came out and kissed both of them. She told them to take care of each other and that their pictures would be there before they were. They took off singing and chatting the whole way. They were so happy. Niea hoped that her people would not be mad at not being at their wedding.

It was glorious. Everyone was so happy they had gotten married. All knew they would have never really done it on their own. They had a great party that night. No alcohol was present. The food was leftovers from Miguel's fine cookery, and it tasted better than ever. They all sang, danced, and looked at pictures of their fine wedding that Grandmama had sprung on them. It all was so prefect. Miguel and Niea looked so happy.

Several days went by, and they all seemed satisfied with the hostel. The work was done. They all could relax for a bit. Training would start again in a few days. A message came through for Miguel from Central. Niea was amazed. Who was messaging him from Central? It turned out to be Grandmama. He spoke to her over the laptop, and she wanted him there as soon as possible as long as all was well at the hostel. She also wanted him to bring Jamal.

What? Jamal was taken back. What would such a powerful woman, the leader of the Kalifee, possibly want with him? He was reluctant.

Miguel reminded him she was the high command, and were they not her soldiers too? Of course she was. Jamal felt unsure, but how could he refuse?

Grandmama had said tomorrow was just fine with her. So the two of them got in the ground car and took off. Jamal was visibly nervous. Miguel tried to reassure him, but he had never met, much less requested an audience with, such a high-level woman. Miguel had never seen Jamal like this. They drove in silence most of the way.

Miguel went straight away inside and was escorted to the office of Grandmama. That was what everyone called her. Jamal stood back. Grandmama walked up to him and looked him dead in his eyes and said, "I don't bite, and I rather enjoy large handsome men. Please have a seat. Can I get you some refreshments? I have some very good wine." Miguel asked for the wine. He did like her wine. Jamal sat and said nothing.

Miguel said, "Please, my friend Jamal needs some wine." She left and returned with two full glasses and gestured for them to drink up. They both drank hardily. Miguel said, "How have you been, Grandmama?"

She smiled so warm and friendly at Miguel. "Just fine, my son." She looked at Jamal and said, "This is informal. Please sit back and relax." Jamal did as he was told and smiled that infectious smile of his. She had taken to him. "I have asked you here because my granddaughters speak so highly of you. Cal is in love with you, and I want to love you too, so let me."

With that, Jamal put his hand out and said, "You honor me, sweet lady." She took his hand, and he kissed hers.

She looked at Miguel and said, "You were right, he is a fine man." She could read people, Jamal saw that. He looked into her heart and was warmed immediately. This was no ordinary woman, nor was she an ordinary leader.

The talk was easy for a bit, and then Grandmama moved into both of them and said, "The brothels can be fun, but they are a hard lesson at times." Miguel tightened. She said, "Relax, Miguel, I am talking about me. That is where I started. I was a brothel worker. I was good at it. I liked it. I do love being with men—one at a time of course. I worked my way up to exalted queen, choosing my clientele for my own pleasure. I have always loved love no matter how it came." They were on the edge of their seats. "I made the Kalifee many, many coins. They asked me to run the brothel. I was good at that too, running the show, talking to people. I moved up. I chose a man to be my one and only, and we had Niea's mother. He was killed as Niea's mother was killed by the Gogatt. This did something to me, made me focus on how to stop these vermin. I now had purpose. I needed that. When my daughter and husband were taken from me, I went into a very dark place. A lost and angry heart needs a purpose, or it will destroy itself. For a long time, I allowed myself to live in the pain. Love and pleasure are important, but one must look to the well-being of all living things that are left on this planet. You two gentlemen love my girls, and they have a very important job, a mission. With your love and devotion to these women, you are now on that mission too. Is this good for you? Is this what you want for your path, your journey?"

Miguel and Jamal sat in silence, then they looked at each other. Love had brought them to this moment, this declaration. Miguel said, "There is really no life for me but dedication to my Niea and to this life of purpose."

Jamal thought for a while, then he said, "There is no life without the woman that has chosen me."

Grandmama was not sure of his statement. She looked at him with a wrinkled brow. "I am not sure of what you have said."

Jamal looked at her. "I have prayed my whole life to have the woman that God chose for me. Maybe that's just a simpleton way of looking at things. But I know beyond a shadow of a doubt it is Cal. It is not because she is wild and formidable, although those things excite me beyond comment. She is the finest woman I have ever seen. She has the wildest biggest heart I ever felt. Beyond a shadow of a doubt I felt it, true love, and it was complete. When I stand before God, I can say I have known love."

Grandmama sat looking at Jamal with awe. He had described love as it should be. A single tear rolled down her cheek. She sat up and said, "You are my son, and one day you will wed Cal. I need the same statement from you that you will stay alive above all else." She looked Jamal hard in the eyes. "I need you to protect Cal, but never are you to die. I need you alive. We need you alive. You will never sacrifice your life. You are to find a way to always stay alive. Do you understand?" Jamal nodded. "Now, gentlemen, I have much work to do. Will you come by tonight and dine with me?" They both agreed. She kissed them both and excused herself.

Jamal and Miguel spent the rest of the day taking in the sights and looking in the shops. Miguel bragged about his bride designing this place and showed Jamal the corner stone. Jamal had never been to Central and was looking at everything, taking it in like a small child at the fair for the first time. Miguel had lived here until he and his mother moved into the hostel. His mother lived here now. Jamal suggested they go and see her. Miguel just shook his head no. He knew that would not be such a good idea. Miguel was wondering if Grandmama had some more to say to them. They would find out tonight. Jamal bought some beads for his hair braiding along with bands for the same purpose. Before they went to Grandmama's, he braided and beaded up both their hair. He always marveled at the shape of Miguel's head. His head had many a bump and knot on it from too many hits mostly from the Gogatts. He always said he had a hard head, and he thanked the Spirit for it.

That evening they dined with Grandmama. She was the most gracious hostess. They ate and talked of Kalifee legends. Miguel told the story of Jamal returning to the hostel with such horrific injuries. Grandmama had to see the scars. She was truly amazed at the inner strength this man had. As she touched his scars, she said, "You know, my son, you will need all that strength to deal with my granddaughter." He knew she was right. Cal could be difficult to say the least. She had a horrid time talking about her feelings. Grandmama took a long breath in and out then started, "Maybe I know too much, but you are going to need each other more than ever. I'm sure I could have said all this on the video you have at your place, but I need you here to know you hear me clearly." She thought for a long time, looking back and forth at these men. "You have to promise me, Miguel, that if either of you gets lost in your own darkness, you'll come for each other." She was looking directly at Jamal. Jamal wondered what she knew. She was certainly an energy reader, and he could see she was very concerned for him. "I am going to need both of you to report to me, especially if one of you is lost." They both nodded.

Jamal said, "What do you know, Madame?"

She said she didn't see details. She just knew the personal darkness was coming especially for Jamal. She wanted them both to always know of the other's needs. They agreed, and Jamal remained quiet. He was trying to get a feel of what she was seeing, feeling, and needed so to tell them. He did see some of it, but he knew that he and Miguel could get through anything.

Grandmama showed them her private art collection. It was very old, the most spectacular thing that either one of them had seen. A *Black Madonna* was at the center. Grandmama noticed that Jamal was fixated on this image. He was close to tears looking at the Madonna holding her white child. Grandmama said, "You like the Madonna!" Jamal nodded. He couldn't take his eyes off her. His heart was captured.

Jamal said, "Tell me about this, please."

Grandmama was so pleased he had taken to the Madonna. It was her favorite. It was an ancient glorification of the divine female. She wasn't sure where to start. "It is the holy mother and the Christ child. Very precious to me." She was so glad to talk about the divine female. For her it was the heart of the Kalifee. "There are many stories of how she became to be black. Black like you, dear man." He smiled and continued to take in all the Madonna.

Miguel had continued to walk slowly, looking at all the priceless images that Grandmama had collected. The wonder had brought both of them to silence. Then he stopped in front of a bird that looked as if it was on fire. The stitching was spectacular, with red and gold flames. Tears were coming out of its eyes.

She was looking at Miguel staring at the bird. "It is called the phoenix. Legends of this magnificent bird can be found in the ancient countries of Egyptian, Greek, Persian, Greco Roman and Jewish fables and literature. Its tears are shed to heal the mind, body, and or spirit."

Miguel wanted to know if he could use this image. Then he asked, "Where did you get all this?"

She said, "You can use any image you find. I found the Madonna in a vault. I opened it, and she was there!" She saw the pure admiration in their faces. "I have also been to many dumps. Dug for hours, completely enthralled and energized. It is sad to me that these treasures have lost their meaning to society. I wish to restore them to their former glory. So much was lost at the hand of the two-legged creatures that almost destroyed this beautiful home of ours. I will never believe they knew what they were doing, killing their home and ours. It would be hard to fathom that people can be so shortsighted!" They all stopped in front of an image of a blue female warrior wearing a necklace made of severed heads of demons. Grandmama smiled. "Kali, the Hindu goddess, a fierce feminine power, both destruction and creation, death and rebirth. A force of nature. She also is the embodiment of sexuality and violence and considered a strong mother figure. She is feminine energy, creativity, and fertility. The wife of the great Hindu god Shiva. I would love to have the image of her stepping on him." Miguel examined it thoroughly. He wanted to remember everything about her.

When the evening was over, she hugged and kissed them and told them to contact her if they needed anything or just needed to talk. They agreed and went to get some sleep.

In the morning, they drove back in silence. Jamal was feeling some foreboding, but it wasn't in his nature to hover in bad or negative feelings. Miguel knew his spirits would lift and patted his leg, giving him the look of reassurance. Jamal closed his eyes, and the rocking motion of the car lulled him to sleep. Miguel drove on toward their home.

Once back at the hostel, Niea and Cal wanted to know everything. Miguel told them that Grandmama wanted to meet Cal's man, her soon-to-be son-in-law. Cal knew Grandmama liked him. Who didn't? Jamal had a magical heart. Neither of them said anything about her warning. It would throw Cal for a loop. Miguel wouldn't tell Niea either. She would worry way too much. He and Grandmama had spoken about Niea's weakness—one being Cal. She didn't report so much of Cal's behavior. She always tried to fix things herself. Niea had let Miguel off the hook with the whole Vahar situation. If Cal hadn't been able to step in and train Miguel, he more than likely would have ended really losing his self in drugs and brothels, even some sorry death. Every time he felt overwhelmed, his weakness would have gotten the better of him. Miquel and Cal's emotional instability are not Niea's responsibility, but she did enable the ones she loved the most. Cal could put being a warrior first, and that what was needed the most especially at this time.

Later that night while Miguel was holding his bride in the dark, he did whisper to her that Grandmama was concerned they all stay close, especially emotionally, and support each other. Niea agreed. She knew she needed to be stronger emotionally, especially with Cal. Tough love was not easy for her. Miguel felt so solid inside himself these days. She knew that all of them could depend on him. He also told her that the two of them were going to try to get close to Leit. Intel on him was needed. He was dangerous. His pursuits must be known and stopped.

Niea pondered the Leit situation for several days. Miguel would come to get her to come to bed, if not to sleep, so they could have some love. She always loved how he approached her. She could imagine him with one of the courtesans. They would melt just like she would. He was so hard to resist with his gentle ever-present style. He gave all of himself. How could any woman resist that? Impossible. She remembered having to make the first move. He was just too respectful and very shy. She had known he was a ladies' man. She told him that all of her stumbling was to get him to hold her, kiss her, and show her the ways of love. He admitted he was so nervous when he met her. He had never been nervous with any woman. He had felt so foolish.

How would they proceed? Word came back from Central that a large band of Gogatts had been spotted northeast of Gabba. Could that be Leit and his crew? Niea and Cal went out to have a look. They drove and drove, scouting for any signs of them. If they had been anywhere around here, there should be something, anything! If they were covering their tracks, they were doing it well. The ground car needed charging. They would have to stay the night and part of the next day. Niea sent a message to the hostel. Miguel would worry himself stupid if she didn't. Cal didn't think she should have to check in with him so much, but she understood. Such is love. Especially for a man so taken with a woman as Miguel was. Cal could only hope she could be so devoted to Jamal like Miguel was to Niea. Certainly, she wanted too, but she did love fighting more than anything. She needed the focus.

Once the car was ready to go, Cal saw some covering that didn't look right. With further investigation, she knew which way they went, due north. They decided to follow. Niea got a message from Grandmama; they had a lead on Leit. He was with a very large band of Gogatts. They were heading due north, and she wanted them to follow but not engage. Some Kalifees were headed that way also. Cal wanted a big piece of Leit. She would have to share with Miguel.

Meanwhile Grandmama had her hands full with Theodosia. Seems she was moving in hard on some changes she was trying to introduce. She wanted the away team to return to Central. She saw no need since the enemy was headed north and that hostel was in the south. That team needed to go. Her motivation was from a place of resentment. She hated anything that made them look right or good or even necessary. She had been successful in stopping the making of the shadow suit and sling sword, claiming they were just too expensive. Grandmama, in secret, had several made. And even if the worrisome Theodosia found out, it would be too late. She sent a message to the hostel that they could come and pick them up. Zek said she would go. She took the local liner and walked into Central. She thought that would be wise. She wanted to make sure Theodosia and her group of tight asses knew nothing.

Zek arrived early the next morning and asked to see Grandmama. The grand lady was so glad to see her. She motioned from her balcony for Zek to come up right away. She knew that Theodosia would be here soon to say something. How did she get any work done spying on Grandmama? Grandmama grabbed Zek and hugged her. "You look marvelous and more beautiful every time I see you." Zek blushed and kissed her on her cheek. "Let us hurry. We will be having unwanted company soon."

They stood looking at the suits and swords. Grandmama was thrilled. Zek reminded her that it was all Niea's design. Grandmama smiled. "But you and your team made them first." Grandmama knew that Zek was a master at construction. She reminded Zek that her skills had done much of the sewing. Zek nodded. But it was their team that worked as a unit on all their projects. Grandmama shared with her that Theodosia wanted to dismantle their team. Zek seemed worried. Grandmama assured her that it would not happen anytime soon, but it was a strong possibility once this Gogatt Leit situation was put down, and it would be put down.

Grandmama pulled out a comfortable chair and motioned for Zek to do the same. She asked her about her love life. Again, Zek blushed. Grandmama knew Zek's choice would be a woman. She assured Zek that she had known all along. Niea was right; there was very little Grandmama didn't know.

Grandmama packed the suits and swords in a trunk quickly. Zek assisted. Grandmama called for assistance to carry it. Zek knew she could carry the trunk, but she could feel Grandmama wanted her to get out before that god-awful woman came busting in sticking her crooked nose where it did not belong.

Zek arrived at the hostel carrying the trunk. She could hardly contain her excitement. They were going to have fun trying the suits on and getting accustomed to the sling swords. She was disappointed when she found out Niea and Cal were not here. She would love to see Niea's extraordinary silhouette in any single suit. She would also like to see Miguel's face when he saw Niea in her suit. Her body was perfect.

Tulie, Jamal, Keddie, and Miguel were so surprised when they found a sword and a shadow suit in the trunk for all of them. It was like birthday presents around the house. Jamal had a bit of a fitting problem, but Zek was able to get him adjusted, and he did look marvelous in it.

Miguel jumped around like he had never gotten any kind of present. He didn't share that he had never had any presents given to him, not even from his mother. The swords took a bit of work for each of them to work correctly. The sword would adjust itself to each of them as they practice with them. The sword could be adjusted with practice and actual fighting. They could use each other's swords, but their own would work best for them, and someone who had never used one of these swords would have a hard time getting it work at all. Tulie found the note Grandmama had left. It reminded all of them that they were to stay alive, and these marvelous creations would certainly aid in doing just that. They all spent the rest of the day practicing using their swords and stepping in and out of shadows. Zek yelled out, "Good job, Niea, wish you were here."

Miguel waited patiently on the outside for a word from Niea, but on the inside he missed her so bad. He lay in his bed that night and recalled every moment they had had sex. How in the hell did he ever do what he used to do in all those brothels? He felt ashamed, but on the other hand, his girl liked his past with all those women. Then he remembered they were married. He got even more excited thinking about his exquisite wife. He like the ring of it. He never thought in a million years he would be married, much less to a woman like Niea. His entire being warmed to a strong tingle. No one could have told him that he would be with the love of his life. He had never felt love for any woman. He closed his eyes and saw her violet eyes smiling back at him.

Niea and Cal spent the day tracking the covered tracks of the band of Gogatts traveling north. They had left the ground car due to the terrain being too thick for the car to get anywhere. The car could charge up and would be ready when they return. They spent an hour or so covering it from detection. The roof had to be left open to gather sunlight. They would have to travel on foot until they got close enough to use Niea's spyglass. Miguel had found some lens in a dump he had been exploring. He had made the glass capable of switching lens so she could change her viewing distance. As always, she was thrilled at what he had done. His mother was never impressed with any of his accomplishments.

The absolute opposite was true with Niea. She marveled at everything he did. She said one time that his mother must be so proud. He said nothing, just shook his head in a quiet no.

The two ladies walked for miles in the thicket, making sure they made as little noise as possible. They must remain hidden. Finally, they found a gang of Gogatts. It was not a large group. The foul beasts had some female captives. These poor creatures were in horrible shape. Dirty and unfed, of course. Niea and Cal knew they had to rescue them. Central was about thirty clicks east of them and would be contacted as soon as the job was done. She was appalled at how these filthy men treated these women. They were even horrible to each other. She watched everything they did. Tonight, she signed to Cal. Cal was ready to foil these bastards. How dare they treat any woman this way? How could anyone be so lacking in the heart department?

Niea watched as they brutalized a woman, kicking her repeatedly until she passed out. She was bloodied from head to toe. They took turns raping this woman, and then they peed on her, laughing. Niea didn't want to watch, but she wanted to gather as much info as she could. As soon as these brutes ate and were getting sleepy, Cal and Niea made their way into the camp on their bellies. They went so slow so they wouldn't make a sound. They finally made it to the women and woke them one by one, making the sign for them to stay quiet. Each woman was freed and told in a hushed voice to make their way out of the camp and wait for them. One woman stayed with them holding her fist up, ready for a fight. They understood. Cal motioned for her to follow them. An extra set of fists would certainly be helpful.

They entered the tent in Kali stealth. They were all sleeping, and there was no guard. Cal put her foot on the throat of one of them and pushed hard on his larynx. He grabbed at her foot, and she stomped him in the face, crushing his nose. He was choking on his own blood. Cal stuck out her tongue, wobbling her head back and forth, and gave a silent, absurd laugh. One of them was sleeping on a chair. Niea garroted him from behind. He hit the ground with a thud. This woke another one, and the woman with the fist punched him hard in the breastbone.

It made a loud cracking sound. Then Cal drove her sword into his chest. Another one jumped Niea from behind and took her to the ground. As he landed on top of her, she had turned a long knife so it would pierce his abdomen. Cal pulled him off her and struck him again just to make sure. The last one swung at Cal. She sidestepped, punching him in his ear. Blood gushed out. As he fell forward, she kicked him in the balls then stabbed him in the kidney area. Now that they were all dead, the three of them took off to where the others waited. All four of them needed medical attention. Cal checked each of them and did what she could. She didn't have her med pack. Cal would wait here with them, sharing her deer jerky and water with them. She was sure they had not been fed anything. Niea took off to get the ground car. Cal motioned for them to sleep. They all waited in a partial sleep.

Just before dawn, Niea returned with the car and took these wounded women to Central. Once there, she and Cal took them to the infirmary. The woman's hand was broken. She asked if she could go with Cal and Niea. They agreed to wait for the medic to set her hand. This would be a great time to go see Grandmama. They cut through the garden and saw Vahar sitting there. Cal walked up to her and punched her in the face, saying, "Get a job, you worthless whore!" Vahar started screaming. Cal was laughing long and hard. Niea tried to hold back a laugh but couldn't.

Vahar was holding her nose, yelling at Cal, "You broke my nose, you fucking brute!"

Cal couldn't stand to hear foul language, especially from a woman. "You foul mouthpiece of garbage. How dare you talk that way? You are the worst excuse for a woman and a whore I have ever seen." Now Cal was right up on her, ready to beat the living hell out of her. Theodosia came running up on them, threating to have Cal arrested. Cal turned on Theodosia with a snarl, "This piece of human excrement should be dead, executed for trying to kill a Kalifee, and a commander at that!"

Theodosia stepped in between them, saying, "It was never proven her intent was murder."

Cal turned on Vahar again and spit on her. "I'm not done with you. You better stay alert because I will be waiting, watching, and ready to pounce." Cal could see she was horrified, so she laughed, sticking out her tongue at Vahar like a court jester. Niea was tickled as she and Cal walked off. They made jokes and laughed all the way to Grandmama's.

When they got to her quarters, they were still amusing each other about Vahar's expression. Grandmama had watched the whole thing and was proud of Cal for not killing her on the spot. If she had, Theodosia would have jumped at the chance to have Cal arrested.

They told Grandmama what they had found at the Gogatt camp and what they did. No, they hadn't seen any sign of Leit and his crew. They had covered their tracks well.

They had a nice visit with Grandmama. They told her about the woman that helped them take down the Gogatts. Both ladies had a bath, and Grandmama had some clean clothes brought to them. She knew their sizes well and what they like to wear when they were not in their fighting grab.

They returned to the infirmary. The lady had two bones set in her hand. Other than a few bruises, she was good to go, and she was ready to go with Cal and Niea. One of the women was in surgery, the one that had been so brutally kicked and beaten. The other two had several broken bones, and one had a serious concussion. She could have suffered some irreparable brain damage. Cal and Niea would check on them later. There was always room for anyone treated so horribly and needing help with the Kalifee people.

The lady was given antibiotics and instructions on caring and rehabilitating her hand. She was in pain but was excited that these two fearsome fighters were waiting on her. She kissed the two ladies waiting for treatment and wished them well. She didn't even know their names. The gratitude she felt was making her cry.

Niea was so sad seeing these women, any woman that had been brutalized for just being a woman. It was what drove her to be the best fighter and to be surrounded by the best. Her ladies were some of the most fearsome fighters in the Kalifee today.

The three ladies walked in silence to the ground car. Niea held all her questions until they were on their way. Once in the car, Niea was wondering if Cal's driving would be a bit too scary. But she took it easy on their new lady. No need to let anyone see all of Cal's wild ways at once, if that was even possible. Her mind wandered its way to Miguel and that he was now her husband. He was so beautiful and kind. He was a marvel of a man.

Niea went first. "What is your name, dear lady?"

She answered, "Marguerite, but I am called Margo."

Niea smiled. "I'm Niea, and this in Cal." Cal flashed her devilmay-care grin and kept driving.

Margo said, "So you are Calandra?"

Cal said, "Just call me Cal."

Niea was curious. "Calandra? What does it mean?"

Cal said, "It means my name is Cal!"

Margo chimed in, "I believe it means wildflower. Marguerite is the name of some flower. Can't remember what kind."

Niea seemed pleased. "I like that." Cal gave one of her many clownish faces and of course stuck out her tongue.

Margo wasn't finished, "You know that there are several ancient images of Kali the Hindu goddess sticking her tongue out. I believe it is after she kills demons. The one I remember best is where she has several severed heads strung onto a necklace wearing it around her neck."

Niea was intrigued. "I've seen that. My Grandmama has one of those images in her collection."

Margo said, "I would love to see that!"

Niea grinned. "That can be arranged, but first, you must heal that hand. Then we have to start your training. You, dear lady, are going to be one heck of a fighter. You already know how to throw a solid punch."

Margo was pleased. She couldn't be happier. She was with some of the most fearsome fighters she had ever seen. They were fair and lead from a place of heart.

Niea said, "So where is your family? You have any kids? Is there a husband?" Niea hoped she wasn't asking too many questions.

Margo looked out the window and started to shed huge tears. She said in low tone, "They are all dead."

Niea caring heart reached out. "Do you want to talk about them?" Margo nodded. Niea waited until Margo was ready to tell her Gogatt tale of misery.

Margo wiped away her tears. "I was married to a man that was a good man. It was an arranged marriage. I didn't love him, but I respected him, and he loved me. I hid my real self away. I was in love with a woman, a healer, an artist. It was forbidden by my people to have same-sex love. The Gogatt showed up and killed them all. I fought them, so they kept me for their further entertainment. When you two ladies came to our rescue, they had already started on one of the women. I didn't know any of them, but I had been praying that someone, anyone, would come to our aid. Then there you came ready to take these subhumans out. I am indebted to you until my last day."

Niea was crying. The story was always the same, full of horror and totally unnecessary violence. This was what drove the Kalifee and created trained killers like herself and Cal. These rogue males must be very afraid of women on a level that was incomprehensible to Niea. Where did all this fear and hatred come from? Niea reached out and held Margo's hand. Margo gave her a smile full of joy and pain. The pain of complete loss. The joy of being found and finding real friends.

They rode in silence for the rest of the trip. Niea continued to check on Margo. Her instincts told her that Margo was a very strong, intelligent, and capable woman. Why would anyone want to hurt her or any of them? At that moment, she felt a little guilty for having such a wonderful, loving man as Miguel. She decided to have gratitude for him, not guilt. That was just too wrong.

When they arrived, she ran to Miguel and kissed him with all her passion, respect, and desire. He was a bit taken back. She missed him just like he missed her. "Hello, wife." He pulled her close to him and buried his head into her neck. He had always loved the way she smelled.

Introductions were made. The team welcomed her, and she could fight once her hand was ready. Margo was so happy to be with these people and for the training they were going to give her. She said a deep prayer that the Spirit would make her worthy.

They ate some of Miguel's deer chili and complimented him on his skill. He apologized for the leftovers, but it did taste better after it had sat for a few days. His refrigeration was working, and he was glad.

That evening they played music, danced, and sang, but no alcohol was served. Cal was wanting a drink or two, but she knew that was not a road she wanted to go down. When did she ever stop at two or three? There was no stopping until she was out. She could only hope and pray that she was done with booze. She had to be honest—drinking and fighting were her first loves. Jamal deserved better than what she had inside of her. Knowing him like she did, he probably already knew. He was deeply empathic just like Niea. They both seem to know what she was feeling long before she did. What in the world had she done to deserve such devoted people in her life? Tonight, she danced, entertaining everyone. But deep inside she wanted to be drinking more than anything. Everyone who had tried to help her wanted her to talk about her feelings, to talk about her past. Either she couldn't remember or wouldn't remember, but she had never told anyone how she stayed alive when everyone in her village was slaughtered. She carried her survivor's guilt deep in her tender heart. Yes, she had tender heart and hid it well in all her clowning. She could pull up the memory of her past, but she would definitely need some serious alcohol consumption to deal with the pain.

After Cal had danced and delighted everyone, she sat alone, quiet and reserved. That was very un-Cal like. Niea didn't like seeing her number one so withdrawn, but all she could do for Cal was to love her and pray for her. She was trying her best to stay sober. How sober was she? Maybe dry was a better way to put it. Niea also noticed Jamal watching Cal's every move. He did love her, but he had been pulling away, staying busy. He just didn't want to hurt Cal. He knew she had been through a lot. He always put the needs of others before his own. He seemed to be waiting on Cal to disappear one evening and head to the local pub. He knew that alcohol would always be lurking and available. Cal had to fight her demons head-on one day, and it wasn't going to be pretty.

As the days passed, Margo's hand was coming along nicely. Miguel had made some herbal remedies that helped with the pain and with inflammation. Niea could not believe that a man with such talent had had such a poor image of himself. Surely his mother had much to do with that. Anyone with the looks that he had would have been cocky. But not Miguel. He was so humble and helping. He kept his eye on everyone and attended their needs as they presented themselves. He was so quiet and unassuming. How had Niea been so lucky? He had taught her so much in the bedroom that she could be an exalted queen with what she knew of love, all because of him. The way he touched and held her was more than she ever expected. When she would feel down or out of sorts, she would think of him and would instantly feel better.

Keddie had backed off from perusing Tulie. He felt that she didn't want much to do with him. After all, she was a high-ranking Kalifee fighter and assassin, and he knew he couldn't fight so well. He knew he was not up to her status. He stayed busy helping whoever needed help. He was hoping maybe he could help with something he was good at, like running. It came naturally to him. He wasn't sure how to help anyone with running. Niea was always there for him to talk with about what he was feeling. He adored Niea. What a kindhearted woman, and she could fight. Better than Cal. He had heard the stories of their fights. Niea would not argue with Cal. She would just say, "All right, Cal, let's take it to the mat." He couldn't wait to see that—two strong, highly trained warrior women going at it!

All the team members had taken to Margo. Jamal was wanting to hear her story, but he would wait until she was ready to open up. She and Miguel used a language that only Niea seemed to know some of. It sounded like English, but there were other components, like Spanish, Italian, Spanglish, or something else. Niea payed attention and was intrigued. They were talking about some woman, but that was all she could get out of it at this time. When she asked Miguel what they were saying, he said that Margo would need to talk about what she wanted to say. It wasn't right for him to repeat anything anyone told him if it was told in confidence. Niea respected that, and she did feel a bit left out. She had the strong tendency to stay up with all her people and their needs—something she had definitely inherited from Grandmama.

One evening Margo and Miguel were sitting talking in this language, and Niea got a bit put off. Miguel could read his lady better than anyone. He looked at her and said, "You want to join us? We'll speak regular English." Niea moved in close and said, "Please continue, and it doesn't have to be English." She was starting to get the gist of their conversations. Margo continued to tell her story in this mixed-breed language. Niea understood she was talking about love and was much more comfortable in not using English. The word *love* had so much meaning when used in the language of her youth. Niea said in a teasing way that she was after her man. Margo smiled at her and said in her language that she was in love with a woman, and the head of their tribe had not taken to this and sold her. The Gogatt had bought her, and her life had turned to a living hell. They had returned and killed her husband and two children, bringing their heads to her as a souvenir. She had shown them no emotion, and they left her alone for a while. She was sure they were going to keep her as a slave. She had hoped they would give her a good fight and she could die killing at least some of them. Being a slave is worse than death.

Niea, using her language, asked if she needed to return to her village. Margo shook her head no. She was pretty sure they had all been killed. She had overheard some of the Gogatts talking about going back to get her girlfriend. She continued saying she prayed that Schade had gotten away, especially with her talents. Niea was intrigued. She absolutely loved getting to really know her people.

Margo went on to say that she was sure Schade had gotten away, especially with her abilities. Niea had to know what abilities. Margo told her of her sorcerer's training, that she had been raised by shamans and trained in the ancient ways. Margo told of how Schade foretold of the Gogatts coming. She had warned the people, but no one would listen or heed her words. "She wanted me to leave to take my children and go. It all happened so fast. The Gogatt were on us." Niea wanted to know if Margo wanted to look for Schade. Margo was certain she would find her.

That night around the dinner table, the laptop went off. There was a message, video style, from Grandmama. There had been attacks north of Central, and they believed the Gogatt and some other fighting force were headed where they were. She asked them to keep the laptop up and running so she could talk to them at a moment's notice. She asked them to stay put and if they thought they needed to leave to message her immediately. This put all of them on point. Everyone readied their suits and prepared their weapons. Cal tended to sharping everyone's sword. She showed Margo how to operate the new swords with a flip of the wrist to open it. It would take some time to get it just right. They all decided to sleep in their shadow suits. Tulie had a shadow suit and tried to offer it to Margo, but the size was all wrong. No one slept well that night. Niea stayed by the laptop. She wished it was more mobile, but it had to remain near the receptor Miguel had rigged up. Miguel had been trying to figure a way to do just that. Miguel wanted to sleep near Niea. She was so restless, and she didn't want to disturb him. Someone needed to get some sleep. She waited all night to hear from Grandmama. At dawn, a message come through that Central had been breached, but the invaders had been caught and were being interrogated. Niea felt a bit better. Her plan had worked, and all were safe for now. The design of Central had served its purpose. She finally went to sleep across Miguel's lap, and he carried her to bed.

All the people at Central were very unsettled but was glad that the security system that Grandmama's Niea had designed was working so well. Theodosia and her faction were very quiet. She was not used to real action and decision. This was not good for her. She looked weak. Her narcissist self couldn't handle being looked down on, and she disappeared. Grandmama didn't seem to notice that she was not there to be a real pain in the backside.

Grandmama checked in with her girls several times a day until some order could be restored. She was glad that they were not here.

She needed them right where they were. She felt the Gogatt and these other fighters would be returning to the south of Gabba, especially to the place where Niea had gotten poisoned. The substances found in Niea's blood had surely something to do with the manufacturing of the descriptor.

Niea slept for a few hours and got up, groggy and unsure of this waiting. They were action people—soldiers, a response team. She hated waiting around, but this was part of it. She had to be patient. After all, she was the leader, the commander, and had to set an example for the others. They all hated waiting. They all would rather have a tough battle than sit and wait.

Cal continued to sharpen swords. The sling swords needed little adjustment. So she got out the older swords and worked on them. This always helped her to stay calm and focused. She and Margo got one of Miguel's longbows and some arrows, went out back, and practiced for hours. Even Cal's arms got sore, and she could switch from left to right with no problem.

Miguel made up some packs for field eating. They could be cooked or eaten straight away. He had some deer jerky packed up nice and tight. He had to keep himself busy like everyone else, anything to keep the nerves in check.

It was days before they got a message from Central. The news was not good. Many Kalifee field solders had been killed. Ceremony to honor the dead would have to wait. The bodies were coming in body bags on liners from the north.

At night, they waited by the laptop for any message, but it seemed like the Gogatt and their newly joined crew had been pushed back for now. It would probably be awhile before they could regroup and head south again. They did not have a central headquarters. Scouts were put on patrol to keep an eye on them and their movements. At present, repairs were being done on Central, although the damage was minimal.

Cal decide to up the training. They did their usual strength, stretching, and cardio training. Cal was particularly interested on some new guerrilla techniques that were more suited for the shadow suits—

anything to help her smaller crew have the edge. So each day was at least six hours of rigorous training. They all did well, and Cal was proud of her folks.

The waiting was starting to get to all of them, but Grandmama's orders were clear—stay put. Niea was having a particular problem with waiting. She started having dreams, nightmares even. She wanted to go to Central for the ceremony to honor their dead, but she heard Grandmama loud and clear. Sleep was getting fitful and she could only do an hour or so and she would be up pacing the floor, sitting, crying, not knowing what to do. Miguel wanted her to take something to help, but she refused. When she closed her eyes, she would see mutilated children, pregnant women with their breasts cut off, and their unborn babies cut from their abdomens. She would wake crying, even screaming.

Early one evening, Miguel came to her. He was very concerned for her health. She was starting to look haggard, and the crew was getting edgy. Something had to be done. He had made a concoction of valerian root and chamomile. He drew a bath with lavender in it. Now the trick was to get her to relent. She could be very stubborn at times. He found her out back in a small shed sitting all by herself, despondent. He stood there for a while looking at her. Finally, Niea looked up and said, "What is it, my love?"

He held his hand out for her to take, and she did. "I have a bath for you. You haven't had one in a few!"

She gave him a thin smile and said, "I know." He wasn't going to take no for an answer.

She put her hand in his, and he led her to the tub he had prepared. It was just right. He had the laptop set up with some soothing music. The lavender was wonderful to smell. She knew she had been failing as their commander, and this thought made things even worse.

He handed her the drink, and it was good. She sipped it slowly and tried to relax. Miguel said, "Stop beating yourself up. You are only human after all." He was right. She had always been an emotional creature, but this was just too much. She hoped her crew could forgive her. Of course they could. They all loved her so much.

Miguel started to wash her hair slowly, rinsed it, dried it, and wrapped her head in a towel. Then he began massaging her feet, and that felt so good. The tension was more than she had realized. He moved all the joints in a gentle range of motion. She slid down into the water, and he began to wash her body. It was getting him excited. She did have a magnificent body. She had always said she had a boy's figure. Miguel assured her that there was no boy who had the buttocks that she did. This always made her smile. He rubbed her shoulder and found knotted muscles that he gently worked out into relaxation. He was so turned on, and she knew it. But she was getting sleepy, so she slowly stood up. He wrapped another towel around her body, and he helped her out of the tub. He dried her off and escorted her to bed. Once he was sure she was asleep, he returned to clean the tub. Now he was off to the kitchen to prepare some food for tomorrow.

He was in the kitchen when Cal showed up. She was wondering if he could make her one of those concoctions for sleep. He prepared it, and she drank some. She lifted her cup and said, "May the sun shine on your butt in the shade." He gave her a curious look.

She said, "Don't ask me. I didn't make this crap up." She drank it down then kissed Miguel on the cheek and went to bed. Miguel was thinking that was so un-Cal like, but he liked it. After all, she was his sister-in-law.

Early in the morning, Niea rolled over and found Miguel sleeping on the floor. She knew it was so she could sleep. She stroked his back, and he rolled over. She giggled. "I see someone's ready for action." His smile was so warm and inviting. He crawled into bed with her and held her for a long time. He was so glad to see his lady looking and feeling so much better. He started kissing her on her neck, which he knew she couldn't resist. Soon she was on top of him, and all he could do was think of something else. It had been a long time, and he missed making love to her. It had been hard for him to recognize the worrisome creature she had become.

The next day it was raining, so training would have to be done indoors. Niea got up, went to the laptop, and found a video message from Grandmama. The fighting had started up again. So far, the Gogatt were getting pushed back. But she was sure they would be headed their way soon.

Niea and her crew checked everything. Weapons, placements of explosives, the tunnel, food stores, the tower—all was checked and rechecked. Niea felt confident that all was ready. Now for the waiting, and as it turned out, it wasn't long.

Early one morning Keddie was out for a long-distance run and took an arrow to the shoulder, but he was in peak condition and ran for five clicks with an arrow in his person. Cal got the arrow out. The boy was tough. He hadn't taken anything for pain. Once all was done that could be done for him, Niea ordered him to stay in the hidden room with the laptop and wait for reports. He wanted to go with them, but he wasn't much of a fighter with two good arms. So, he did as he was ordered. Shadow suits were adorned. Margo fit fairly in Keddie's suit. They all gathered for a Kalifee prayer, holding on to each other, and as Niea always said, "You all will follow me home. That's an order." They bowed their heads and held on to each other for a moment of silence then gave the Kalifee battle cry and headed in the direction Keddie had come from.

They arrived at a Gogatt camp in no time. All got down on their bellies and slowly crawled to the camp, staying absolutely quiet, knowing that their success and well-being depended on it. Niea went up a tall tree that had good cover and pulled out her spyglass. Yes, oh yes, it was pure Gogatt. She didn't see any women, but they were either killed on the spot or they had them chained up in some other tent. They would need to get a closer look. Orders were understood. Kill all the Gogatt you can and stay alive. Central had all the prisoners they could handle.

Niea and the others decided to wait until night to attack. That would be their best advantage. It hadn't failed them yet. Tulie volunteered to go in first and do some surveillance on the setup of the camp. She was, after all, a shadow warrior, assassin supreme.

Tulie got in and out without a hitch. She counted maybe fifteen or twenty, and there were children in one tent chained to a log. That was unusual, very out of character of these monsters. But deal with it they would. If it was safe, they would take the children to Central. But first, the Gogatt must be killed.

They decided to take the larger tent first. Tulie would shadow her way in and start her work with her needlelike blade. She would take them out one by one, and the shadow beings would escort them to their hell. After all, they made their own hell as we all do. We make our own reality, day by day and minute by minute with each thought and action.

Tulie had complete trust in her shadow beings. They had been with her since the beginning. The only being she trusted as much was Niea, her commander, a pure beam of light and love in a very dark world.

Tulie would slow her breathing and her heart rate before she entered their tent to do her sacred duty. After all the killing had a sacred purpose—not only to avenge all those so maliciously tortured and brutally killed long before their time but to assure these monster would rape, maim, or kill no one else. She knew this long before she took the consecrated oath of the Kalifee.

Once Tulie had slowed her heart rate and breathing down, she stepped inside the tent with stealth magic. She was amazing. Niea would stand in quiet reverence, feeling the slow heartbeat of her amazing friend. So brave.

Once they heard the groans and moans of death, the rest of them entered the tent. Jamal went for the biggest one, hurling him to the ground and cutting his throat clean and smooth. Although these vermin did not deserve such a clean and painless death, Jamal was not one for torture. His heart was just too kind to desire such a dark pleasure.

Margo, on the other hand, might have enjoyed torturing them, but that was not their mission. But if interrogation was performed, she would definitely want to be in on that. She had one of the older swords and was wielding it with expertise. She brought down two with no problem. Turned out there were twenty-three of these stinky males to dispatch. It was all over within a very short time. Niea and Miguel brought down one of the smaller tents down on them and killed them as the tent trapped them on the ground. And where was Cal?

When all was quiet, a small sobbing cry was heard in the tent where the children were. They all took off to see what was going on there. Cal was found with three children in her arms. Two were dead. Niea sat down by her and put her arm around her tall, lanky number one. Cal loved children as much as she loved fighting. Niea rocked Cal as she sobbed. She got Cal to let the children go. Jamal and Miguel took the two dead children out to bury them, and Niea began to examine this very small underfed child. She was in poor health and was comatose emotionally. It never ceased to bewilder Niea how cruel these so-called men were. Niea shook out a ragged blanket she found on the ground to wrap the child up in papoose fashion. She cuddled her to the chest so she could hear the drumming of her heartbeat. After all, the heartbeat was the first musical instrument ever heard by anyone from deep inside their mother's womb. Once they were ready to transport this sad little creature to Central, she messaged Grandmama to see if it was safe to come to Central. Niea wanted to know how long it would take to get a liner here to pick this poor creature up and try to save her life as well as her spirit. Niea sat on a small rock singing a soft gentle lullaby and crying, trying not to disturb this lost and abused baby child. She hoped to be able to ask the Great Spirit someday why children had to suffer so. It befuddled her to hear the locals talk of God's love. This didn't feel like love.

Once the two dead children were buried and prayed over, they all cleaned up in a small stream near the camp. Niea washed the child's tiny face and kissed her and in her heart wished her all the best that life had to offer.

They all waited in silence for a message from Grandmama. Soon as they got the go-ahead, there was another message right behind it pinpointing the location of another Gogatt camp. This one was even bigger. Niea thought it was best to wait for backup, and it was an order from Central. Cal wanted to go ahead. Niea gave her a look that said no, and Cal complied. But she was impatient and was pacing hard. Niea patted the rock next to her. Cal sat down, not taking her eyes off this little waif. Niea gave the tiny creature to Cal. She knew this would help

Cal calm down and wait. Cal will make a fabulous mom someday. Niea knew this beyond a shadow of a doubt. But would Cal ever settle down enough? That would remain to be seen. It was a hope she held for Cal. She knew Cal would raise fine Kalifee children, especially if Jamal was there to guide her and love her.

Another order came from Central. They were to go back to the hostel and wait. The liner would be there soon to pick up the tiny patient. Cal wanted to go with the child, but she knew she was needed for fighting, and that was what she would do. Her heart would be with this little lost soul. Cal wanted to take her home with her. She could definitely skip fighting to care for this lovely baby.

The liner sat down in a clear field, and two medics came out and took the child. Niea and Cal kissed her goodbye. The orders remained the same. They were to go back to the hostel and wait. They walked in silence. Niea could hear Cal's heart breaking. She sobbed the whole way back and went right to bed when they arrived. In the morning, Cal sat at breakfast and ate very little. The waiting was going to be agonizing. Niea went to the laptop, sent a video message to Grandmama, and gave all the details of the raid on the Gogatt camp. She also told that Cal had not drank in a long time and believed she would be all right if she could get back out there and fight. It was the only thing that would keep her grounded. Grandmama reminded her that they were to stay put until further orders. Niea gave a resigned sigh, nodding. She told the others, and everyone seemed to feel the same—disappointment. It would be like getting ready to run and being told to sit down.

Later that day, Cal became restless and began her pacing. She was biting her nails and spitting out the pieces. She couldn't stand it anymore and went to get ready to leave. Niea followed her into the bunk room. "What are you doing?"

Cal grunted, "Can't wait, gotta go."

"You can't do that! You would be disobeying a direct order! You know that horrible woman will jump at the chance to have you locked up!" Niea gave her a hard stare.

"I'm going, no matter the consequences. Crap on the consequences!" She was visibly on edge.

"Cal, you could be court-martialed for such an act!" Niea knew she was serious.

"So? You have held information from Central before. Do it again!" Cal was surly, and she knew she was insubordinate. She didn't give a crap, and she had grown used to Niea covering for her.

"Cal, don't think for one minute I won't report this action." Niea was beginning to lose her patience. "I am begging you, don't do this." Niea couldn't let her get away with this.

Her surliness was becoming straight up insulting. She continued to pack her bag. She went by Niea, hitting her with her shoulder hard and curling her lip at her. Niea followed her to the kitchen, continuing to remind Cal of the act she was insisting on doing.

Cal whirled around on her in attack mode. "I gotta go. I can't just sit around and wait while innocent women and children are starved, raped, and murdered. Now the rest of you can sit on your duffs and wait for the high and mighty Kalifee to tell you what to do and when to do it. Not me."

Niea stood right in front of her. "I won't let you. I can't let you." Niea had taken all she could take from Cal. This was the last straw. Too many times Niea had left out Cal's behavior and insulants. In this moment, it was just too much.

Cal turned on her, ready to hit her. "You can't stop me."

Niea stood and stared at Cal hard.

"What, you're going to stop me? You and the rest of these do-nothings you call a team!"

Niea was beyond angry. She stepped up on Cal and said nothing. Cal yelled, "So, you gonna stop me!" Niea remained still, holding a predator gaze at Cal. "What?" Cal yelled and jumped at Niea. She sidestepped, and Cal fell hard on the floor. Niea stood over her still staring. It was a bit scary to see the commander like this. Niea didn't flinch. It looked as if she hadn't blinked. Cal got up right in Niea's face. "So what are you gonna do!" Still, Niea said nothing, staring at this woman that outweighed her, was taller than her, and was one the most fearsome fighters the Kalifee had ever seen. She pointed to the practice mat. Cal was still very surly. "I'm not doing that." Niea stood with her chest out, staring and pointing. Cal whirled toward the practice area. "All right, if that is what you want." Cal knew this was going to be a beast of a fight. She did not want to do it.

The crew was outside sitting at the picnic table. Zek looked up. "Oh my god, it is on." She jumped up on the table and flew to the other side as fast as she could. Tulie was right behind her. The rest of them looked at each other and followed the action. Niea was standing still, fierce, savage, wild, and ready to attack. Cal didn't want this. Truth be told, she had never beaten Niea, especially when she was like this. Niea had morphed into an aggressive killer, a wild animal hungry for blood. Her eyes were locked on Cal.

Cal stood ready, but actually she wanted to run as fast as she could. Why didn't she just sneak out when no one was looking, like in the dark of the night? Niea was so still that no one knew if she was even breathing, nor had she seemed to blink. The crew froze when they saw her. Each one of them sat slowly as not to break her stare on her prey. Cal looked away, and Niea socked her in her jaw. They all heard a crack. Was it her jaw or a tooth or two? Audible gasping was heard from the crew. Cal spat blood out and removed a tooth and threw it. She knew she should never take her eyes off Niea. She was in full killer mode and very dangerous. Cal began to circle Niea, summing up the situation, but she knew she was in for a real butt whooping. Niea followed Cal's every move, never flinching, staring with a low growl coming from deep inside her. Her violent eyes had turned black, and the skin under her eyes was red. Miguel was frozen, staring at Niea. Many moons ago she had told him about her beast. My god, she was more than a beast. She was a she wolf from hell, ready to kill anyone threatening her pack. Cal was rubbing her jaw, and Niea delivered a full kick to her stomach. Cal went down. Niea was on top of her delivering blows to her face and chest. Cal was able to push her off her. Niea landed on her back, flipped herself to her feet, and pulled a knife. From where no one knew. She was ready to kill Cal.

Margo whispered to Zek, "Has it ever gone this far before?" Zek's eyes were locked on the two fighters. She shook her head no. Margo was afraid that Cal was going to die today. Miguel had the same fear.

Cal began taunting Niea, talking smack, trying to get Niea to lose concentration. Niea was locked in on Cal, waiting for the next millisecond when Cal would lose focus. Cal continued to taunt, throwing insults, trying to get Niea to crack. Cal was pulling up anything she could think of to throw Niea off. As Cal chattered away,

Niea cut her across her left arm. Cal fell back, looking at her arm. Niea lunged again and cut her thigh. Cal was visibly shaken. She realized that Niea was going to kill her. Her eyes went wide, and she rushed toward Niea. Again, Niea stepped aside, and Cal stumbled even harder than before, but she recovered well this time and kicked Niea hard in the stomach. Niea gave out a small groan, got to her feet, and drove the knife into Cal's shoulder. She was down. Jamal dove in to grab Niea from her next strike. Niea whirled around on him and delivered a solid kick to his groin. Jamal hit the ground with a thud. This was all Miguel and Margo could stand. They both dove at Niea, and she rolled on the floor, taking Margo to the floor, and ended up behind Miguel and delivered hard sidekick to his kidneys. Cal had pulled the knife out of her shoulder and went for Niea's throat. Zek and Keddie got Niea by both arms, stopping Niea as she lunged, moving her out of the way of Cal's attack. When she saw the bloody knife Cal had in her hand, she stopped moving. Tulie was there with her blade on Niea's throat. "I don't want to kill you, Commander, but I will." In that moment Niea froze. She looked around at all of them, turned slowly, and then left the area.

Jamal had recovered and was standing. He was still in pain but was functioning fairly well. Miguel and Margo got to their feet. Miguel went to Cal. He motioned for Jamal to help him get Cal to the kitchen table. He had stitch kits prepared. He would need some hot water, and Jamal got that ready. Zek, Tulie, and Margo began to assist him. Margo didn't have much of any medic training, but the other two ladies knew exactly what to do. Miguel sent Margo to get some valerian root to give to Cal. She wouldn't let them cut her shadow suit, so Tulie and Zek managed to get it off her in one piece. They cleaned her up. Miguel gave her a quick assessment. He was glad to see there were no ligaments or tendons completely severed. Miguel went to work on Cal. Repair would take a few hours. But Miguel felt the outcome would be fairly good.

Once Cal was all tended to, Miguel gave her another dose of valerian root with lavender and chamomile. He gave her a good dose of sulfa for the infection that could set in. When she was finally resting well, all of them joined up at the picnic table. No one spoke for some time. Finally Margo asked, "What was that?" No one answered right away. She asked again, "Are their fights usually this bad?" Of course, Miguel, Keddie, and Jamal didn't know; none of them had ever seen them fight.

Tulie said, "No. This was really bad. I have never seen Niea so feral. So vicious. She was going to kill Cal. Cal finally pushed her too far." They were all clearly shaken.

Miguel and Zek cleaned up the area. Miguel found Cal's tooth and decided to preserve it. Maybe it could be put back into Cal's mouth. He had seen that done before. Then he decided to see if he could check on Niea. He found her on the other side of the small pond out back. She was sitting very still. He approached her slowly. She could feel him and turned to find him looking very uneasy, as if he was afraid to disturb her. She turned back around and said, "What is it, Miguel?"

He said, "I just wanted to make sure you were okay."

She said, "I'm fine."

He said, "Can I get you anything? Do you have any wounds?"

She said, "I'm fine. You can come closer. I am not going to attack you."

He stepped a bit closer, but he stayed at least an arm's length away. She looked at him. "I'm not going to hurt you."

He said softly, "That was some kick you gave me."

She looked at him. She had tears in her eyes. "How's Cal?"

He said, "She should be okay. Nothing major was injured. She will be out of commission for a while."

She patted the ground next to her, and he sat. He was unsure what to say. He just looked at her. She put her head on his shoulder and continued to weep. "I am so sorry this had to happen this way. I let myself get pushed too far, and all my anger toward Cal came out in one ugly lump. That is all my fault. I was in the wrong. I let her get away way too much. Then I exploded."

Miguel held her as she cried, then he said, "Yes, maybe you shouldn't have let her get away with such bad behavior, but as you said to me one time, she's a grown-ass woman."

In the morning, Niea went to Cal. She was sleeping in the bunk room. No one knew how long she and Jamal had stopped sleeping in the same quarters. Cal rolled over and saw Niea. Niea stood and waited for Cal to invite her in. "Come on in, Commander." Niea stepped into the bunk room. She felt awful and was totally unsure what to say. She just knew she had to say something, anything. If nothing else, she had to say how sorry she was for being so vicious. If she had killed Cal, she would have never forgiven herself.

Cal said, "Are you going to say something? You know I deserve a real good chewing out."

Niea looked at the dressings on Cal and shuddered. "I am sorry, Cal. I let my anger and resentment get the best of me."

Cal sat up and held her hand open to Niea. "I deserved it. I know I have been a major behind on the planet, and you put up with my crap for way too long. I should have been in the brig so many times, and you protected me. As you have said, so many times you enabled me. I need to go to Central and declare all my actions and insurrection, at least to Grandmama."

Niea shook her head, putting her hand in Cal's hand. "I don't want you to go, but I don't know how to proceed."

Cal pulled on Niea's hand so that she would sit down beside her. She took a few moments to collect her thoughts, then she said, "I should have been dead many times over. I am reckless, self-willed, and straight up arrogant. You are probably the only reason I am still alive or not locked up." She thought for a while. Putting her arm around Niea, she started to cry. She let her head fall onto Niea's head, and they sat together for quite some time. "It's best I leave. Maybe they can help me at Central. I am not good to anyone here. What I want to do is drink and drink a lot."

Niea pulled back a little so she could see her sister and said, "Is that why you are going?"

Cal hung her head not wanting to admit it, but she would rather be away from the team for a while. "I need to be away. I am an emotional wreck almost all the time, and I don't let anyone know. I know I could be helpful with the fighting, but for everything else, I am not so confident. I can't do anything that would benefit anyone, much less myself."

Niea stood up. "When are you planning to leave?"

Cal laid down. She was tired. "As soon as I am well enough. Would you have Miguel bring something for sleep? Hopefully that will help me with my alcohol cravings."

Niea said, "'I will bring you something." She returned and handed Cal a drink of valerian root and lavender. Cal drank it down. She smiled, curled up in her bed, and soon fell into a very deep sleep. Niea stood there looking at Cal, wondering what would become of her sister, best friend, and her number one.

There had been no fighting reported from Central for several weeks. Cal was feeling better, and she was ready to travel. Niea offered to drive her to Central, but Cal said she would take the liner. It was an awful ride, but it was much faster than the ground car. In the morning, Cal packed her things and headed out. Niea wanted to drive her to the liner, but Cal said she needed to start her journey alone. They all said goodbye, and Cal left.

Four days had gone by, and everything was quiet. Then early one morning, just before dawn, Niea sat straight up in their bed. Miguel was startled. "What is it?" Niea made the sign for silence. She had felt something, heard something. She put on her shadow suit straight away. She signed to Miguel that there were three, maybe more men just a few decameters from the hostel. They were up to no good. She told Miguel to get the others up quietly, and she was going to investigate. She was gone before he could say any more. If he had ever doubted her abilities, he didn't now. He knew she could kill them all. Plus, she knew they were coming before they got here. It had to be something more than empathic ability. He would definitely question her about it later. He went to the bunk rooms and woke each one up, quietly gesturing for them to be quiet and be ready. Trouble was here.

Zek and Margo went out on the perimeter. One went left, and the other flanked off right. Tulie did her shadow movements through the hostel. Keddie went up in the tower where one of the charges was set, along with the projectiles, and waited for the signal. Miguel and Jamal set out on either side of the edge of the hostel. They both knew Niea was probably right in behind the intruders. After all, she was the best at sneaking up on people.

One of the intruders came in through the back door. It probably never occurred to him that it was left unlocked for a reason. Cal always said that men like the Gogatt were really stupid. And this one gave himself away by his smell. He tipped in the back, stepping right into a trap named Tulie. As he stepped over what he thought was a piece of furniture, a small blade went up into his groin. This was Tulie's favorite place to take out vermin. He fell forward, hitting the floor hard. Tulie put the blade into the femoral artery, piercing several nerves. If he didn't die immediately, he would be soon enough. She stood up, wiped her blade off on him, and stepped back into the shadows and waited.

Another intruder came in through the front door. He was a bit more cautious. He had a small light that he shined about the room. He thought he saw someone but decided it must be a rat or something. It was gone before he could be sure. Then he was met with Tulie's blade to his throat. She had been standing on the edge of a small chest. He saw her and was shocked. How in the hell did this child get the drop on him? That was his last thought. He lay on the floor gasping for air. She struck him one more time in the diaphragm, slicing horizontally. He would not breathe another foul breath. The stench from these morose creatures was starting to get to Tulie. She found all the shadows she needed into the kitchen and got some lavender. She tied it under her chin and preceded on into the shadows of the hostel.

Miguel ran into one of them trying to set a charge to the side of one of the buildings, and he sliced his throat. He dragged him out of sight, which was no easy feat. The filthy man outweighed him by at least fifty kilos. Jamal saw this and gave him a thumb's-up. It was no easy feat.

Niea was out on the road. She was just behind six of them. A large dog had joined her. She always had a way with animals. This wooly creature was there to assist her. One of the Gogatt came out of nowhere, and the dog attacked him almost in silence. It was like he knew they needed to stay quiet. Another smelly man dropped back beside them, and Niea turned and shoved a blade into his spleen. Two more came at them, and the dog took one by the throat. Niea pulled a Tulie and sliced his femoral artery along with his testicles and penis.

There were several more that were standing just under where Keddie was positioned, and he dropped several large stones on them. Both were knocked unconscious. He didn't know if they were dead. He and Tulie had put those stones there when they started building the tower. One of them was still alive. Miguel spotted him and drove a flip sword into his gut. He followed Tulie's lead and wiped his sword off on the dead Gogatt. Soon all were dead that needed to be dead, and the crew met at the predetermined area. Margo and Zek had killed two of them, one each. They were all a bloody mess. But there was no casualties and no serious wounds. It was a good night.

Niea ordered them all to get cleaned up and get some sleep. They would do some reconnaissance of the area in the a.m., which was only a few hours away. Everyone got cleaned up, but no one could sleep. Miguel made a small fire that was quite hidden. They sat drinking wine for the first time in a long time, each telling the story of what had happened. They would do a body count in the morning, then Niea would give a full report to Central.

Some of them did nap by the fire. Niea woke those folks up. The body count was eighteen. They confiscated their weapons and anything of value. All that would be taken to Central later when all their work was done. After the bodies were piled up, they would be burned after the sun came up. They all went to bed except Niea. She went to the laptop and gave a full detailed report. The big wooly dog was right there at her side. She had fed him. He would get a bath later. She looked at him with so much love. He had helped her so much. They now belonged to each other.

Once all reporting was done, she and Grandmama had some private time on the laptop. She asked how Cal was doing. Cal was not there and hadn't been there. Now it was time for her to tell Grandmama what had happened between them. She apologized for not reporting on Cal all this time. Grandmama understood. She loved her girls so much. It made Grandmama sad to hear this story. But she knew Cal was not done with her darkness. They both had a moment of silence for their beloved Cal. Grandmama would put out feelers for where Cal might be, and they would bring her home. Grandmama knew she had to be careful. Theodosia was always looking for any rhyme or reason to get all of them or any one of them if she could. Grandmama was humored at the thought that Theodosia kept her sharp.

Cal wandered for days staying in thickest hard-to-see areas. No need to alert any unwanted attention. God, she needed a drink or ten. She knew she had missed the liner and had not even made it to Gabba. She wandered west for a while, did a bit of small game hunting, made a small fire, and cooked up some squirrel. Nothing would ever be as good as Miguel's cooking. But she ate it; she was hungry. Then she slept for many hours in a wonderful shaded thicket. She was sure no one could see her in here. When she woke, it was late afternoon, and she heard something coming down the road. She climbed a tall tree that had some cover to get a better view. It was a traveling Kalifee band of performers, entertainers, and a brothel. She decided this would be a good place for her to get a drink, and maybe if she was lucky, she can find a fight or two. She knew very well that she needed to find the fight first. Once she had a drink, she would be drunk soon, and fighting would be out of the question.

She watched the people with the caravan for a while to get comfortable with what was in this large group. Cal knew how to be charming when she needed to. But this was a very large caravan, and there were many Kalifee soldiers with them for protection. There had to be some fights for coin, and goodness knows Cal was in need of some coin. The last thing she wanted to do was drink off the kindness of horny men. She stayed in her perch waiting for some time. She didn't recognize anyone yet. Hopefully not—she wished to remain incognito until she had a good feel for this mishmash of Kalis. She would wait until she felt the time was right.

Just as the large tent went up, Cal decided to have a look around. She walked slowly in the crowd of people. There were mostly women, dancers, jugglers, magicians, workers, and of course the queens.

There was one woman that looked a little like Niea. Cal thought she might be from the breeding program, maybe even kin to Niea. She loved the excitement of putting up the show and then the show itself. She had a few coins, so she got herself something to eat. Drink would have to wait. She wanted to fight and make some real coin if she was going to drink the way she wanted to drink. She had herself some tea and a sandwich. It was pretty good, but again nothing like Miguel's fine food. Niea had really caught herself one hell of a man. He was so dedicated to Niea right from the start.

The woman that looked like Niea was standing near the front of the large tent. Of course, there were other tents going up, but this was the main event. Cal approached her and asked about other events that would be taking place here. At first, she said nothing about fighting. Then she asked if there would be any fighting. The woman shook her head no and walked into the tent. Cal looked around for anyone else that might know about fights and how they were conducted. She saw a little hunchback man out by one of the tents that were serving up food. They were cooking deer over a spit. It did smell good, but Cal would try that delicacy later. She asked the man several questions, avoiding asking about fighting matches. Then she saw a man that really looked the part of fight arranger. She approached him and asked about what it would take to get into one of his fights. At first, he wouldn't even talk to her. Then a man with him stepped up on Cal, and she headbutted him, knocking him unconscious. He hit the ground with a thud. She looked at the man in charge with a big grin on her face. He looked at her and motioned for her follow him. She looked down at the man on the ground. He was coming to. She offered her hand to help him up. He got up on his own but avoided close contact with her. The man in charge motioned for her to follow him. She dropped in behind him and trailed both of them to a wooded area away from the others, isolated. She liked this area. It looked right. He motioned for her to enter the tent. She let the two of them go in front of her. She was not going to let them ambush her, even though she could get away no problem. In that moment she realized that all her training gave her so much freedom to do what she wanted when she wanted.

Once in the tent, he motioned for her to sit. She preferred to stand, just in case. He spoke, "You can have a seat. We are not going to hurt you." No, no one was would hurt Cal, just not plausible. She could kill them both in seconds. She took a strategic seat. She would do one of three things—kill them both, get the hell out, or arrange a fight or two, maybe more.

The man in charge offered Cal something to drink. It was homemade whiskey. She shook her head no. "Maybe later. I need to make some coin." He understood.

He said, "What kind of fighting are you interested in?"

Cal said, "What you got?"

He said, "Bare knuckles, weapon of choice, sword, knife, or just free style and going at it. What would you prefer?"

Cal said, "Anything, anywhere, and with anyone preferably men."

He looked at her as if she were exaggerating. "So, you can handle any fighter, any situation, and any weapon?" Cal nodded and grinned her devil-may-care grin. He liked this woman. She was fearless. Now they would see if she could deliver. "All right, tonight I have several fights, if you can do more than one fight a night."

Cal was glad. She grabbed his hand and shook it. "How much if I win all fights you promote for me?"

Cal shook her head no. "I will need more than that."
He said, "The betting will bring a lot more than I can give you."
Cal looked at him. "You bet on these fights?"
He said, "Sometimes."
Cal leaned in with a grin. "You bet on me and we will split half the winnings."
He was curious. "You are very sure of yourself."
She stood up. "If you had fought as much as I have, you would know what I can do." She stuck out her hand, and he shook it. The deal was made. "How's just after dark?" He agreed and she left.

Cal would need some more protein intake, so she made her way to the food tent. The deer on the spit was ready, and she was going to get her some. She didn't have any more coin, so she told the hunchback man that she would be fighting later, and he could make some coin on her if he was a betting man. He looked at her and was intrigued. He gave her a shank, and she ate it all. Then she went to find a place to lay down and rest. She woke just before sunset. She always seemed to know when to wake up. She found a small stream and washed up. She decided not to wear her shadow suit. She kept on her plain single suit. She didn't look like a Kalifee warrior much. She looked like a tall lanky woman that was about to get her backside beat. She showed up at the man's tent. This time she asked him his name. He apologized for not introducing himself earlier. It was okay with Cal; she hadn't given him her name either. She said her name, and they shook hands. He said that his name was Jedidiah. He wanted to know if she needed anything. She did say she would like to wrap her knuckles. He got her stretchy tape and offered to do it for her, and she said no, she would rather do it herself.

Her first fight was called, and she was ready, excited. She warmed up, and this caught the attention of the audience. She thought Jedidiah would start her with a more inexperienced fighter and then go up from there. The betting was already against her. She was not worried at all. Fighting would prove her to be the champion he needed. He, on the other hand, was nervous. He had bet a lot on her. Why? He had a hunch, and after all these years of fighters, she was different. Oh, he had had female fighters before, but no one like her. She was a highly trained fighter—her stance, her swag, and that undeniable confidence was seen by anyone that looked her way. His only question was, What in the hell was she doing here? There was something more.

Cal continued to warm up, stretching and running in place.

Jedidiah came to her. "You ready, Lady Cal?"

"Just Cal will be fine, and yes. Do you want me to lose the first fight?"

He said, "No, but take it slow. Give the folks a bit of a show."

Cal grinned. "You got music?"

"Sure. Something fast with grit?" he said.

Cal stood up and stretched back. "That will do!"

He had quite a bit of music. He liked all kinds, but he knew exactly what to put on.

The first fight was without weapons. When Cal came out, the cheers were mild, and there were boos. She kind of like that. She loved proving someone, anyone, wrong. This was the perfect place to do just that. Jedidiah announced the fighters, and the gong went off. Cal pretended to be wary, moving around as if she was unsure of herself, which was a lie, but it was show time. Then the music started. It was that old hip-hop at its heart. It took her over, and she started to do some dance moves, provocative. She dropped down in front of this young chicken fighter, starting to move her hips. She looked back at him as if this was going to be somewhat sexual. His mouth was open. Cal turned and put her foot up under his chin and closed his mouth. The crowd laughed wildly. Now she was right in front of him in a wide stance, knees bent, thrusting her hips. He swung at her, and she twirled around and pushed him with her foot. He stumbled onto all fours, and she jumped over him, landing on one foot and then sitting on his back. She looked at Jedidiah. He motioned for her to do her opponent in by making a chop motion at his neck. So, she jumped up in the air, turning like a ballet dancer and delivered an aerial kick to his chest. He hit the ground with a thud. The crowd went wild. He did not get up right away, and she was declared the winner. She walked the perimeter of the fighting area holding up two fingers. Then Jedidiah sent out the next fighter. He was a bit older and hardened, not like the young pup she just fought—if you could call that a fight. This man was serious and had that predatory stare. It reminded Cal of how Niea looked at her when they had last fought. He also had a sword. She looked at Jedidiah. He held out a sword, but she shook her head no. Cal thought, I got this! Jedidiah hoped she wasn't being foolish. He swung his sword in a figure eight pattern and circled Cal. She kept her eyes on him. She thought he might try to kill her. He can try. At that moment, he lunged at her and cut her arm. It was just a scratch. Cal was glad she had someone to fight that was out for blood. She lowered her head then ducked down and twirled around, coming forward, knocking him off his feet. He stumbled, dropping his sword. When he looked up, Cal was standing on it. She kicked it back to him. The crowd gasped. He bent down, slowly never taking his eyes off Cal, and picked up his sword. He lunged at her again. She whirled around and kicked him on his back side. He stumbled forward, not dropping his sword this time. He swung his sword hard and low. Cal jumped over it. The crowd was thrilled, applauding. He wanted to put an end to this showboat woman. He swung again and again. Cal allowed him to chase her around the fighting area with moves and maneuvers that were amazing and very entertaining. He was obviously angry. Cal thought, *That will do you in, dude.* No one could channel anger like Niea. The Kalifee were trained not to use anger. It could really get in your way. He swung at her neck. She ducked and punched him square in the nose. The crowd heard the crack, and he was bleeding from his busted nose. He tried to stab the sword into her stomach. She sidestepped him, and roundhouse kicked him in his face. He was done for. He fell and was not moving. The crowd were craning their necks to see the dead man. Cal pushed him with her foot. He moaned.

Jedidiah called for a short break. The crowd was chatty as they left the tent. The excitement was just too good. Several of them went to get friends to come and watch this woman fight, dance, and entertain.

The man needed a medic. Cal offered her services. She and Jedidiah took him to the back. He had a stronger light there. She got her pack and checked his blood pressure, pulse, and respiration. He was starting to have a problem breathing. The bridge of his nose was busted up, and his jaw needed realigning. Subluxations were not in Cal's training. But Jamal had shown her some moves to put the body back on track. She had Jedidiah control the bleeding of his nose, and she palpated his jaw and shifted it without warning. She believed he had a hairline fracture there. She would have to set his nose if he was going to breathe through it again. She looked at Jedidiah and asked for some whiskey. She told him it was for the patient, not her. He brought out some whiskey. Cal was bent over the man, making sure he agreed with her setting his nose. He nodded. Jedidiah handed her another cloth. She wet it with a bucket of water that was placed for the fighters. She cleaned off his nose and dried it. Blood is so slippery. She cleaned her hands and dried them well. She slowly palpated the pieces of bone in his nose. Then with all the accuracy she could deliver in this setting, she pressed with her nimble fingers, going in different directions, and his nose was set. She packed both nasal openings with clean dry cloth. She asked Jedidiah for some tape, and she taped it in place. She instructed him to go to an infirmary and get some antibiotics. He said he had no coin. Cal looked at Jedidiah, and he reached into his pocket and pulled out twenty or thirty coins. The man thanked him. Cal told him that if he needed any more coin to come to her.

The rest of the night went great. Jedidiah could not have been more pleased. He and Cal split the take, and it was two hundred coins each. Cal got her coin and her things and was leaving when Jedidiah stopped her. "Where are you going?" Cal gestured out. He said, "No, you must stay here. I have a hot tub and some nice bedding. Please let me care for such a great fighter, a great lady." Cal smiled a warm, inviting smile and nodded. She could use a hot tub. Even Miguel didn't have one of those. Now she would have a jar of that shine, if Jedidiah didn't mind. It turned out to be stronger than Cal was to. She slept well that night.

There had been no word from Central. The fighting had stopped, and there had been no reports of any of them being seen. Grandmama thought that they had gone underground. Of course, Theodosia thought that was foolish. They were still out there. Grandmama tried to explain that she thought they were in actual caves. Why was Theodosia so disagreeable with everyone and everything?

Back at the hostel things were quiet too. No one had heard from Cal. Even Grandmama hadn't heard a word, and she had eyes and ears everywhere. The place had not been wrecked by the attackers. But Niea wanted more training, more work on the place, and ideas. Miguel was fascinated by one of the paintings of the Goddess Kali where she was wearing several bracelets on each arm. He asked Niea if those could be weapons. She thought the idea was good. She knew he could make them. So, together they set into a project of making jewelry that could be used against their enemies. They visited several dumps looking for anything that could be made into these bracelets. Miguel had figured a way to put charges in them. He thought they would be ignited by throwing and exploded on contact. Then he had the idea of a left-arm explosive and right-arm smoke screen. Niea was delighted. It always made him happy to please her. Where in hell would he be if not for her?

Jamal wanted to go look for Cal, but Niea didn't think that was such a good idea. She said, "I need all of you here. What if we get attacked again?" He knew she was right. There could be twice as many men to come here next time. He missed Cal. He loved her like Miguel loves Niea, and he could only hope she would come back to him someday. But she had to find her own way. Jamal seem to have a broken heart more with Cal than he had love from her. He prayed for her many times a day. He often cried himself to sleep at night.

Keddie had stopped trying to get Tulie's affection, but he was cordial with her. His feelings were fading as much as they could when you see the person every day. He would leave, but he was dedicated to Niea, and he still had much to learn. Niea was convinced he could learn to fight well. She just needed to find a style that was suited to him. She gave him an assignment for combing through the laptop looking at any and all styles of fighting until he found one he was drawn to.

Cal had some ideas she presented to Jedidiah. She told of her shadow suit and that she could put on a demonstration of moving in and out of shadows through the audience, pulling weapons on them and showing moves to make in defense. She also wanted to do some promotional things. Jedidiah wondered what exactly what was she talking about. She wanted different kind of fights. She could be in the nude. They could fight to the death. He shook his head no. Then she had an idea about a skimpy suit she could wear and work up a routine where she would dance, picking out an opponent from the audience. He reminded her of needing them to sign an informed consent. No, he would need time to think about her ideas and see what he could do to get these ideas moving. She was excited, and so was Jedidiah. They were going to make some serious coin.

Cal had made a friend in the main tent, a queen. Together they made a strapped suit out of stretchy material the queen had. It didn't take much material. When it was done, Cal put it on. Layla screamed. Cal wanted to know if she did that with her clients. She said no, that would depend on how much they paid her. They both had a good laugh.

Cal's performance was so good in the skimpy suit that she was asked to move it to the main tent. She and Jedidiah made a deal with the head of the show there, and Cal took the show by storm. She had an idea to make a trapeze and fly out over the crowd. Jedidiah found a fellow who could make the trapeze as Cal had designed it, and it went over with the crowds. But Cal's main focus was the fighting. She had the ability to do anything physical, but fighting would always be her main event.

Cal was fine if she was fighting or performing and focused, but time off was the worst. Jedidiah gave her a week off, and she ended up in a ditch with a broken leg and a torn rotator cuff. A young orphaned boy found her. He recognized her from sneaking in to watch the fights. He had been watching her when she left for a week. He followed her every move. Jedidiah had always let him watch the fights whenever he wanted, and he would feed the almost feral boy.

The boy gave Cal some water and ran off. She fell back down into the ditch, still sleeping it off. The boy told Jedidiah, and he got a man to help. He had a stretcher he used for the wounded. They got Cal back to his tent. He got a medic to see her. The medic was a performer with the traveling Kalifees. She had seen Cal perform. She set her leg as best as she could and put her arm in an improvised shoulder harness. No, Jedidiah would not be giving her any alcohol for pain. The medic sold him an anti-inflammatory ointment of turmeric, curcumin, and lidocaine. He gladly paid her well and went to tend to Cal. She was his champion, his star. His business would suffer without her, but he had made so much coin, he could coast for a quite a while.

The boy would come by every day to see Cal. Jedidiah could see she really liked children. One day she asked Jedidiah if the boy could stay here with her. Jedidiah told Cal how he had tried to get the child to stay with him and that he would give the boy a job. Cal believed she could convince him to stay, and she did. The boy obviously worshipped her and would do anything she asked. He called her Ma-Cal. As she convalesced, she helped the boy learn to read better and taught him math. They would sit together every evening and work on anything he would ask about. He was curious about everything. He was a hard worker. He couldn't remember his name, so Cal asked if she could call him Jay. He liked that name. So Jay it was. The name reminded her of the name Jamal. She missed him, but she felt she had saved him from so much more turmoil and heartbreak by leaving. Once Cal was up on her feet, she taught the boy self-defense. He obviously knew how to stay alive. He thought he might be ten or eleven. He lost his dad to some kind of fever. His mother had died when he was a baby. His father said she died of a broken heart. He never asked what that meant.

A few weeks later, Cal wanted to fight. Jedidiah was not sure she was up to it. She admitted that it was either fighting or drinking. That seemed to be her only choices. Jedidiah didn't think that to be true, not with a woman as excellent as Cal. She had so much more in her than those two things. He told her he couldn't stop her from fighting or drinking, but he reminded her she had done without both for almost three moons. She gave this some thought. She had been focused on Jay and healing. She had not thought of a drink in all that time. She might give up booze, but she never would she give up fighting.

A loud explosion woke Grandmama up early one morning just before daybreak. The Gogatts were here. They had projectiles and obviously explosives. Her quarters shut down. The entire building was designed to shut down in sections. There was enough food and supplies to last a year stored in each living quarter. Communication was limited, but Grandmama had made sure she could talk to Niea and Miguel. She sent them a message that they had been attacked but all was okay. The building was doing its job. She was insistent they were to stay put and not come this way. She would message them as any new developments came up. It was the old adage that no news was good news. She would expect to hear from them if needed. Still no word on Cal.

Niea would get everyone to prepare to leave in a moment's notice, but for now they were back to waiting. One day a quick message came from Grandmama. She needed them to go to the hole in the ground where Niea had encountered the smoke that made her sick. They were not to engage the enemy, just observe and report. Miguel and Keddie were out after some meat. He had plenty of deer jerky prepared and ready to go, but fresh meat was needed. So Niea gave orders that Jamal and Margo would go there and do some reconnaissance, and the other two would hold down the fort. The three of them packed up what they needed and headed out.

News reached the traveling folks about the attack on Central. Cal was disturbed. She would have to go. She went to Jedidiah and told him what was going on. She apologized deeply. He understood. He thanked her for making his business a true success. They both had plenty of coin. Cal knew she shouldn't go to Central. It would be shut down. She would go back to her team. That would be the right thing to do. She packed her belongings and headed out. Jay was right behind her. She stopped. She looked at him with such love. "You can't go. It could get bad, and you could get hurt, even killed."

Jay insisted. He would follow her to the ends of the earth. She was his Ma-Cal. After much debate, Cal gave in. He promised her he knew how to stay alive. He had been doing it most of his life. So she and Jay headed out for the hostel. It was several days' walk from here, and they would stay in the thicket. No need to call attention to a woman and a boy. He already knew how to use the thicket and stay hidden. She was impressed with his abilities. He was also good at stealing. Cal would discourage that in the future, but for now, he must show her his every trick. She had to know where his training should start. This was now her boy, and she was responsible for him.

It took them many days and nights to reach the hostel. Cal was anxious to hear from Central. The traveling Kalifee were a bit isolated. They would stay on the move until they got word where the enemy were concentrated. That was at the center of basic life skills for the Kalifee—keep moving.

When Niea, Margo, and Jamal reached the area, Niea climbed a tree with good cover and was aghast. There were hundreds of Gogatts and other kind of soldiers too. She had never seen such a gathering of their enemy. They would stay a while and try to get a better look at their setup and a count of how many men they had. She came down the tree as quietly as she went up. When she told the others, they were as shocked as she was. What in earth was going on?

Niea found another good vantage point to watch with her adjustable spyglass. So far, she had counted over six hundred soldiers. There was some kind of plexiglass covering the hole where she had gotten sick. What were they doing? What were they cooking up down there? Nuclear weapons hadn't been used on the earth in over a thousand years. She would love to get a better look, but it was just too risky. They could overrun the three of them in no time at all. They had to stay incognito. She was wondering why none of the Gogatt had returned to the hostel. Retaliation was important to them. But those particular marauders may have acted on their own, and no one knew where they were. It sure seemed that way. There hadn't been another attack. They would return to home base, and she would report all her findings to Central.

As Cal and Jay got close enough to the hostel, Jay became a bit nervous. What if these people didn't like him? Would he have to leave? Would Ma-Cal go with him? Cal did her best to reassure this sweet scrap of a child that she would always be here for him. He grabbed her hand and held on tight. This was going to be very new experience for him.

Keddie was out for a run when he spotted Cal. At first, he didn't see the little waif she had with her. The boy thought Keddie was going to attack Cal. He circled around got a large stick and started to hit Keddie. Cal grabbed the boy and held him back. "This is one of the crew, Jay."

Jay dropped the stick, looked up at Keddie, and said in a low tone, "Sorry, sir." Then he hung his head in shame.

Cal picked him up and kissed him. "You were protecting me!" Jay said, "I thought you were mad at me." Then he turned to

Keddie. "Can you forgive me?"

Keddie smiled and stuck out his hand. "Put it there, tough guy." Jay shook his hand and grinned.

Keddie said, "Let's go. Miguel has something special cooking." Cal couldn't wait to eat some of Miguel's food; it was just the best.

When the three of them got to the hostel, Niea came running toward Cal. She was overjoyed to see her. She threw her arms around Cal and cried. As the tears streamed down her face, she called out to everyone, "Cal's home!" She held Cal's face in her hands. "You okay?" Cal nodded. Niea had not seen the small boy. All she could see right now was her Cal, her lifelong friend. She wrapped her arms around Cal again and cried. Finally, Cal got her hands and held them, kissing her sweet sister all over her face. Niea looked at her beautiful number one and said, "I am so sorry for what I did. I have dreamed of you every night. Why didn't you get a message to me?"

Cal knew she should have contacted her, but she had been with traveling Kalifees, and messaging was very slow to nonexistent with the traveling. Besides, she would have come right back here if she and Niea had communicated. She had heard of the attack on Central. Niea let her know that Grandmama and the others were good. The building was holding. Grandmama's messaging was limited. She wanted to make sure there were no interceptions. There had been no intel on the Gogatt's ability to intervene or intercept any messages. So, short and sweet was the answer.

Cal smiled her hearty smile and said, "I have someone I want you to meet." Jay was behind her. She reached around and pulled him out so Niea could see him. He stuck his hand out. Niea took it, and he shook her hand hard.

"My name is Jay, and I am glad to meet you. Ma-Cal has told me so much about you." Then he stepped back behind Cal. Cal pulled him in front of her again. She wanted everyone to see her precious little fellow.

Niea got down on one knee and took his hand. "It is so good to meet you, Jay."

Jay looked up at Cal and said, "Wow, she's pretty! Not as pretty as you, Ma-Cal."

Cal picked him up, kissed him, and said, "Let's go eat. You are going to have some of the best food you've ever eaten."

Keddie led the way, and the four of them entered the hostel. Miguel was finishing with several dishes he had prepared. He did love to feed people especially his people. They always raved about his food, and they were his family. Something he had never known.

Cal wanted to ask where Jamal was. Instead she looked around for any sign of him. Niea noticed and called out for him. Jamal came through the back door and was stunned at the sight of Cal. He just stood in the doorway staring at her. Then she said, "It's me. You aren't seeing things." He simply did not know what to say. They had been on the outs for such a long time, and he never knew why. Grandmama had told him that she was a difficult person to love. She also said that she believed Cal would come around someday. He could only hope. There was no one else he wanted or needed than Cal.

Cal introduced Jay to everyone. He was really taken with Jamal. He said he had never seen such a man, so dark and big. Jamal laughed and shook Jay's hand. Miguel found a bucket, turned it upside down, put a pillow on it, and gestured for Jay to sit. He pulled up between Cal and Jamal. Miguel served the food. It was jasmine rice with curried deer meet and fresh vegetables from the garden Niea and he had grown. He also served some wild greens he had cooked to perfection. Everyone ate and as always raved about his culinary delights. Jay's face told the whole story. The boy had never eaten anything like this.

When it was all over, Jay wanted to help Miguel and Niea clean up. He informed them that he earned his keep and he would never steal from them. Everyone laughed. Jay informed them that he was serious.

Later that evening, the music came on. Miguel didn't bring out the wine. Cal asked him to please serve everyone some wine but herself and Jay. He was a little hesitant but did as she asked. He brought her and Jay a glass of root beer he made. He assured her it had no alcohol in it, just a lot of sugar. She and Jay enjoyed it very much. Jay went over and shook Miguel's hand. "You a mighty fine cook, sir! And you are quiet."

Miguel smiled. Yes, he was quieter in a crowd of people. Even though he knew these people very well, he always felt more at ease alone. Niea was a different story. He was playful and chatty with her love and support. She was so encouraging and responded so positively to every idea he had. Maybe just the kindest, gentlest badass bitch in all the Kalifees. He would never say that out loud, but she was a fearsome fighter, and he loved that. He would not want to face her, and he would pity the man that did.

In the early evening, they all joined in the back. Jamal had his harmonica, Miguel brought out his guitar, and they started in on some swing-style music. They had put out some tiki torches, which gave off wonderful flickering light. Everyone was clapping and having a wonderful time. Cal got up to dance, and Jay joined her. Niea, Zek, and Margo were girl dancing, and it was a sight. Finally, Cal's leg was bothering her, and she sat down. Maybe later she would get Miguel to look at it and see what he thought. He was a good healer, and no, she did not think of him as a medic. Medics were trained like her. He was a natural.

Jay was sitting next to Cal and whispered in her ear for her to go talk to Jamal. She shook her head no. He elbowed her in the ribs. "Why not?" he whispered. She motioned for him to come with her and walk by the pond, and he did. They walked for a bit, where Cal was sure they were out of earshot. He said, "So, why wouldn't you talk to him?"

Cal thought for a while and said, "I need to leave him alone. I have given that poor man too much grief as it is."

Jay said as he squinted his eyes at her, "You are hurting him by not talking to him."

Cal looked at this boy. "You can see that?"

Jay pressed his lips together. "Anyone can see that."

Cal questioned him further, "How do you know that?"

Jay said, "The way he looks at you!"

Cal said, "How is that? The way he looks at me?"

Jay let out a frustrated breath. "Like the way Sir Miguel looks at Lady Niea! For crying out loud, woman, you can't see that?"

She looked long and hard at the boy. She thought he was right, but she had no idea what to say to this man. They had had some incredible times together, and she did miss him. It was just that she felt that all she would do was hurt him again. Cal said, "What do I say?"

Jay round his eyes. "Tell the man you miss him. Hold his hand. How about kissing him?"

She felt so inadequate. Jay had not seen that in her ever. He had a feeling she was always confident.

He said, "Sir Jedidiah said you have swag, and a woman with swag would go in there, dance with that man, and tell him just how you feel. Now let's go. If you're gonna be my ma, I want Sir Jamal to be the pa." He stood up, grabbed her hand, and pulled her up, saying, "All right, Lady Swag, let's go." This little pistol of boy had told her what she needed to do, and she thought, *Why not? Out of the mouths of babes.*

When they rejoined the group, someone had put on some oldtime rock and roll. Jamal was dancing with Tulie, then he pulled Margo up for a few steps, then Zek, and he went round and round. Niea and

Miguel were slow dancing in the corner like teenage lovers who slipped away for the night.

Cal waited; she was standing by the rose bushes that Miguel had planted. Finally, the music went into a ballad of love. Niea and Miguel continued to slow dance, holding on to each other like they would never see each other again. Jamal was filling his glass with wine at the picnic table when Jay came up to him and pointed at Cal. "That lady has something to say to you." He took Jamal by the hand and pulled him toward Cal. Once they were face-to-face, neither spoke. They just looked at each other. Jay had had enough of this. "Just kiss her, man. What's wrong with you two?" Everyone heard this and was staring. The question on their faces was the same. Is he gonna do it? Is she gonna do it?

Finally, Cal spoke, "I'm sorry, Jamal. I never meant to hurt you. You know I love you, and I always will." With that, Jamal wrapped his arms around Cal, bent her backward, and kissed her like only the lonely knew how to kiss! They were cheered on by present company,

like they had just seen the ending to the prefect love story. It might not be perfect, but they have hope.

Jamal picked Cal up into his arms, and she snuggled her face into his neck. He carried her into their old sleeping area. He placed her carefully onto his once lonely bed. He was so happy he felt like he was going to burst. He started singing and dancing to a song from his once-upon-a-time home. Cal sat up smiling. She just couldn't believe this was happening. The rascal Jay was responsible for this. Clever boy. Cal said a silent prayer that she would never hurt this beautiful soul again. It would be horrible on so many levels. He danced over to her, stripping his clothes slowly and flashing that phenomenal smile of his. She stood up and joined him. He wrapped his arms around her waist and held her from behind. She could tell he was ready for love. But he would take his time. He wanted to rock her all the way down. He wanted to hear her scream.

Late that night, when all were asleep, the laptop went off. It was a call from Grandmama. Niea woke up and went to see what was going on. Grandmama told them that things were much better at Central. She apologized for calling so late, but she had been wanting to see them. Niea reassured that anytime she called would be fine with them, and she did speak for them all. Niea told her about what they had seen at the large hole. There were approximately six hundred soldiers, and some of them did not look like Gogatt. She had sent some samples and wasn't sure she had gotten them yet. The liner could be so slow. The samples were in the lab. It didn't look good. Could be some kind of biowarfare. The place looked like they might have large manufacturing going on in that hole. It also had some kind of clear plastic covering over the hole. Miguel stumbled in, wiping sleep from his eyes, and greeted Grandmama with a kiss. He asks if he could butt in. Of course, no son of hers needed to ask for an audience with her. He loved that she called him son. He had not ever been called that.

Niea got up and let him sit his sleepy self in front of the screen so he could see Grandmama. He had an idea. What if they blow that hole? It would have to be a large explosion. She wondered how they were going to pull that off. Didn't the explosion have to be contained?

Wouldn't want to blow any more crap into the atmosphere than what their ancestors had done. Miguel believed so, but he would have to get a closer look. It could be difficult, but he believed they could pull it off. Grandmama was worried for their safety. He promised to be very careful. She knew he could be extra careful, especially with Niea. He said that he could contact her as soon as he could work out the details. They all said their goodbyes, and the call ended. They both made their way back to their bed. He lay down and pulled Niea on top of him. He rocked her onto his considerable self. He did not enter her. He loved to watch her as she got excited. Then slowly he would rock her onto him then off. She was almost ready to go, and he couldn't take it anymore. She screamed, and both of them reached their crescendo. It always amazed him how prefect lovemaking was with his beautiful woman. The only way life could get any better was to rise every morning to see his lovely bride—naked.

In the morning, Niea gathered the team, and they had breakfast. Jay ate like there was just no tomorrow. He hugged Miguel for his wonderful breakfast. The boy had a good heart. Miguel gave him a handshake. Jay decided to go outside and do some exploring. The rest of the team helped clean up, and all sat and waited for Niea to start. She told them of the hole and that they were going to blow it as soon as possible. She wanted the team to come up with any ideas they thought would work. The covering would have to be moved to introduce the explosive, then the cover needed to be replaced or contained. Then they needed to get the Hades out of there. Niea said, "It's going to take all of us, and this will be dangerous. As you know, no one goes unless they want to, okay? But I need all of you to present your ideas, no matter how wild or dumb you might think your idea is. Okay?" They all wanted to go, but someone would have to stay here. But all of that would be decided later. Right now, they broke up into groups and bounced their ideas off each other. Miguel wanted to return to the hole and have another look. He and Niea decided to go in the morning.

Cal had the idea of her going in dancing and cutting the fool and drop the bomb down the hole. She was sure they could rig a timer, and she would get the heck out of there before the thing went off. Sounded too dangerous to Niea. She knew Cal like the dangerous way. Tulie said she could shadow her way in and shadow her way out. Leaving might be the problem. Niea was afraid that she couldn't get out in time even with a timer. Zek had a workable idea. What if they created a diversion, something that would get the Gogatt's attention away from the hole, and crawl into the camp and place the device there? It would have to have a timer on it. Niea asked what kind of diversion she was thinking about. Zek said that they could blow another bomb away from the hole. Niea liked this idea, but it would need more. It was the exit she was worried about. No one needed to get hurt or, worse, killed. Jay chimed in that he could get in without being seen, or he could fly in on a kite and drop the bomb. Niea asked him about the cover. He said oh and sat down. Margo said that they could create the diversion just before dawn, then another one in the opposite direction while the Gogatt were busy with those. They could get in, set the charge, replace the cover, and get out. Niea loved the diversion idea. Sneaky was always a favorite method of hers; it also would keep the team safer.

In the morning Niea and Miguel returned to the hole to have another look. Then Miguel had an idea. There was some kind of cave around. He believed it could be accessed into the hole allowing them to get in and get out safely. So they went to Gabba. It was closer than going back to the hostel, getting the ground car, and then driving to Gabba. So they took off running. Besides, the ground car was being charged. With all their training, they ran at an amazing pace. It wasn't long before they reached Gabba. Miguel led the way to the city archives, where all the maps of the area were kept. They looked for hours, then Miguel found an old dusty map which he believed was the cave he was talking about. The proprietor of the place wanted more coin than they had. Miguel offered a barter of deer hides, cook a meal, or anything the man thought he might could accept. He said he was sorry, but it wasn't his decision. So, they returned to the hostel, running the entire way. Niea was going to contact Grandmama and get her to send them some coin. Miguel ask her to wait. He wanted to try to get it here at the hostel if he could. Niea knew he wanted to be completely self-sufficient, and she understood that.

Cal and Jay had warmed up some deer curry and wild green. Everyone sat down to eat. Jay wanted to know why Miguel's food tasted better the more it sat. Niea told them what they had found out and that they needed coin to get this old dusty map. Cal got up and went to her things and came back with a hand full of coin. She asked how much they needed. Niea gave her a curious look. Where did she get all that coin? She even had more! She would be questioning Cal later. Anyway, Cal had not said where she had been and what she had been up to.

Later that evening she knocked on Jamal and Cal's door. "Come in, Niea." Cal knew exactly who it was and what she wanted. She also knew she was going to get third degree from Commander Niea. She and Jamal were in bed, and Niea gestured if she could sit down. Cal moved over to give her room. *Here it comes.*

Niea took a few moments, looking intently at Cal. "Where did you get all that coin? How much do you have? What have you been doing? Where were you?"

Cal put her hands up. "Hold on. I'll tell you."

Niea didn't wait. "Where have you been? And did you get hurt? I see you limping."

Cal didn't want to tell her anything. She still felt a bit ashamed of how she had left, the fight they had, and her getting so drunk she ended up in a ditch with a broken leg and a torn shoulder.

Jamal excused himself and went to the kitchen for a drink. He did not want to hear Cal's story. He knew Niea would be able to get it all out of her. And besides, he didn't want to hear if she had slept with any men. That was something he thought better left unsaid. It would be just too painful for him to hear.

Niea was waiting to hear it all. She knew she would have to pick it out of her, and she wouldn't leave until she had all the tea. So Cal needed to start pouring it out. Niea sat there and stared at Cal. Cal started shaking her head. She didn't want to fight Niea, the daughter of Satan.

Finally, Cal knew she was cornered. It was time to spill it, and she knew it. She told how she had walked for hours once she knew she had missed the liner. She had wandered for days and found a large group of Kalifee performers. There were many tents. She tried to bore Niea with too many details. She could tell Niea would wait all night for her story. Finally, she told her everything. Niea just sat there and shook her head. Then she said, "You have one large pair of balls on you, Cal!"

That was true, but Cal had always flown by the seat of her pants. Her devil-may-care, scared-of-nothing attitude led her to some dangerous places and situations. Maybe that was because of her feral past. Staying alive no matter how bad the odds were.

In the morning, Miguel went to Gabba and bought the map. While he was there, he stopped by the market to pick up some supplies. They had some real nice fresh vegetables and some spices he wanted to try. He had enough coin left to buy his bride a gift. It was a necklace with an unusual stone in it. He thought Niea would really like it.

In the morning, Miguel went over the map. It was not clear exactly where the cave led, but it was close enough to where they needed to go. They would have to explore the cave first. Miguel could only hope it would not take too much time. He had another problem. Whatever was down in that hole needed to stay in that hole. They would need to have an implosion, and it needed to go straight down. He and Niea discussed how they were going to do this. They had everyone to gather out back to discuss how they were going to do this. In the morning, they would gather supplies.

Zek and Margo headed to Gabba to buy rope, climbing hooks, and some kind of headlamps. Jamal and Keddie went to get phosphorus. Jamal would make sure it was a yellowish solid because it could ignite spontaneously. They also would need some crude oil. Miguel packed up enough deer jerky and canteens of fresh water that would last them for four to five days. He was still unclear how to get it to implode. It has to blow down. Charges would have to be set low into the hole. They would need some kind of breathing devices. There was no telling what was down there.

Niea decided that only two of them would go into the cave. Hopefully they would be in and out in two days. Miguel would run a line from where they entered the cave to where they ended up. No one needed to get lost.

Eventually they found the area. It was full of soldiers, Gogatt, and these other fellows. Niea got a really different feel off these men. They felt human, caring. It just didn't add up. She would get to the bottom of this; she simply just had to know. Miguel and she signed that they would have to go back. It took half the time to return to the entrance. They returned to the designated meeting place. They weren't going to have to find another way into the hole to place the charge. They would have to try a diversion. Two more charges would be set away from the primary target. They left for the hostel.

Early in the morning, before sunrise, they left for the hole. Jay had to go so all of them packed up the needed supplies and headed for the kaboom area, as Jay called it. Margo found a good place to set the first charge. Zek went several clicks south to set the second charge. They set the second charge to go off a few minutes after the first. They waited. One went off, then the other. It looked to Niea that the enemy had all gone to investigate. She took off with the charge. The cover was gone, so she went running by the hole and threw it overhanded into the designated area. She kept running as far and hard as she could. She ran right into some Gogatts and their companions. She sped up, and they took off after her, but no one could catch her. She ran south for many clicks and was exhausted. When she stopped, she drew her sling sword and readied herself for battle, and sure enough there were four Gogatts. She went into a killer stance, keeping her eye on the prey. She was a bit out of breath, but she knew how to slow her heart rate and her need for oxygen. They circled her, and she dispatched them one, two, three. Number four took off running. She looked around to get her bearing. She was not sure where she was. Then she saw and heard a Gogatt coming for her full force. She took off, collapsing her sling sword so it was just a handle. But this time they had a heavy net and threw it over her. She was caught. Then they knocked her unconscious. She woke up in a large cave with Gogatt and these different fellows around her. The Gogatt were mad and wanted to kill her right way. She stood and got the net off her, popped out her sword, and started attacking. Some of them, especially the non-Gogatt, just watched. They had never seen a woman fight, much less one that was so wild and capable of killing them all. Niea took one more blow to the head, and she was out. When she woke, there were nineteen dead Gogatts and a few of the other fellows. She was tied down, and the rape was about to start. It was their ritual to rape a woman until her soul was gone. They were dropping their pants and pulling out their penises. There were gonna be a lot. As the first one mounted her, she cut him with a razor blade she had in her mouth. So, the next one avoided her mouth. She got her leg loose and kicked him in his balls, and he was out of commission. As they tried to tie down her leg, she got her arm out of her restraints and cut two of them in their face. None of them wanted to go up on her. She was now completely freed from all restraints. She killed too many to count. They got her again. This time they drugged her. They really liked their victims conscious so they could enjoy their terror. But with this one, it wasn't going to happen. They would have to ritualistically rape her without their full enjoyment. Many of them would not be able to keep an erection. Too bad.

The crew sat at the designated area; the only member that was not there was Niea. Cal was hot, but she calmed herself down and asked who would follow her. She was going in to get Niea. Miguel stepped up, and rest of them followed. She asked Jay to wait at a distance, and he agreed.

When they got to the cave, they entered the cave slowly using their lamps. This had to be where their main camp was. They all started looking around. There was food cooking over a fire. Cal felt they would be back soon. So she asked everyone to find a hiding place and follow her lead. She got herself a bowl, dipped up some of this gross-looking food, and took a seat. She put her long legs up on the table and waited. She started singing and tapping out a tune. Soon some of the herd that was going to rape Niea showed up. One of them yelled at Cal, "What are you doing?"

Cal looked up, puckered out her lips, and poured the bowl of food onto the floor. "What is this crap? Smells like scat!"

One of them yelled for her to get her boots off the table. She looked at him and started to laugh. Then she jumped up on the table. Miguel took this as a cue. He came out acting like he just had to clean the crap up off the floor. Cal started to tap-dance on the tabletop. Jamal started a drumming beat with a barrel he found. Zek and Margo started sing in the cave, and it sounded like angels from heaven. Tulie shadowed her way through the men, and the carnage started. As they started to drop dead one by one from her needle knife, fear grabbed them. One yelled, "Killer ghost! Run!" They looked like rats abandoning a drowning ship.

Some of them ran to where Niea was being raped. The team followed at breakneck speed. When they all saw Niea being raped, each one of them got out a sling sword, and the blood began to flow. Miguel was particularly wild. He had to get to Niea. There was one beast still on top of her. He kicked the living hell out of him. He was dead when he hit the ground. Later Cal would remark that was the first time she saw anyone kill a demon back to hell in one kick.

When it was all done, there had been several of these other men that had helped them kill the Gogatt. Cal wanted to talk to these men and ask them what in the hell was going on with them turning on the Gogatt. She wasn't sure if she liked that or not. Of course, it was nice that they helped them, but were they the kind of soldiers that turned on those that had employed them?

Their leader stepped out. He had manners. First, he apologized for their mistake in following these horrible men. They didn't know enough about them. They had no idea that they treated women this way. Their women were at home with their families. Cal thanked them for their help, but their commander needed care, and that was what they needed to do now. Miguel picked up Niea and started to carry her back to the hostel. The leader said they had a ground car and could get her back sooner. Miguel was wary, but he did want to get Niea back as soon as possible. Cal spoke up; she and Miguel would ride with the leader, and she asked what his name was. He apologized. He said he was Malik and he would be happy to take all three of them where they needed to go. The rest of them would follow on foot.

Niea was still out cold. She had a head wound. Miguel started a neurological exam on her. Her pupils were round and reactive. No doll's eyes. She was negative with the Babinski test on the bottom of her feet. Her breathing was slow and heavy. Her heart rate was regular.

When they got back to the hostel, Miguel gave Niea a bath, soaking her in warm soothing water with lavender. His beautiful wife had been through a horrific ordeal, and he was so sad in his heart, but he was here for her. She drifted in and out of awareness and finally went into a deep sleep. He covered her with a light sheet, kissed her on her forehead, and prayed to the Spirit for his woman.

Cal had to ask Malik about him and his men turning on the Gogatt. She was appreciative they had helped, but what was that? He told her that he and his men knew nothing of their hatred and was appalled at what they had done to Cal's commander. He also told Cal how Niea had fought, and he had never seen a woman fight like that. He was impressed. Cal accepted this but felt she would have to be wary of these men.

All the team members had returned. This was what Niea always said was a successful mission. Her team came home with her.

Miguel was in the kitchen warming up some deer chili. There was enough for all of them to eat well, and as always, the food was just so good. They all ate in silence. No war stories, they were all so sad, worried, and very pensive. What would someone say anyway in a situation like that. Each team member thanked Malik and his men for their help.

In the morning, Miguel woke up and found Niea sitting in front of the laptop staring. He asked what she was doing. She wanted to talk to Grandmama but just did not know what to say. She sat there staring at the black screen with slow, quiet tears rolling down her face. She looked at Miguel and said nothing.

Then Niea said, "I don't know what to do. I am not sure what happened."

Miguel said, "You were attacked and raped."

Niea looked at him. "Can you forgive me?"

Miguel was astounded. "Forgive you? For what?"

She lowered her head and said, "For being unclean, raped, defiled."

Miguel wrapped his arms around her and said, "None of this is or was you fault."

She pushed away from him asking him not to touch her. This hurt him to the marrow. All he wanted was to hold her and reassure her. But he turned, asking if she needed anything. She shook her head no. She felt so different. She felt weak and dirty and definitely not worthy. She didn't feel like she could be her team's commander. She just knew she had let everyone down, and now she just wanted to sit and hopefully disappear.

Niea spent the rest of the day sitting staring out the window. It was raining hard. She watched the sheets of water running down the windows and listened to the rain hitting the tin roof. She did love the rain. It did make her feel better. She cracked the window so she could feel the cool breeze and the spray of water on her face. She spoke to no one for the rest of the day. She sat in her silence like a shadow of a human.

Each team member came by to see how she was doing. She had little if anything at all to say. The mood was somber, and Niea knew they should be, could be celebrating if it wasn't for her. What could she say to any of them, especially her kind, gorgeous husband? She sat until her legs started to swell. She started walking as if she didn't care about anything. She found herself in the woods and became disoriented. That was when the hallucinations started. She thought she was back in the cave fighting the Gogatts. They grabbed her, threw her down. She kicked and screamed. She remembered it all, and it was reality for her. She got really scared and started to run. She ran until she was exhausted.

Back at the hostel, no one could find her. Miguel and Cal got some lights and went to look for her. They both knew her favorite place and ran there as fast as they could. Cal saw her crumbled on the ground, dirty and talking incoherently. She was still in the cave in her mind. They both tried to pick her up, and she went wild, kicking, screaming, and hitting. Thank the Spirit she had no weapon. Getting her back to the hostel was no easy feat. She would try to attack first Miguel then Cal. They would restrain her and try to talk her down. She would apologize then drift out of consciousness.

Cal and Miguel got her inside, and she finally accepted a drink Miguel had made for her. It would help her sleep. She was shaking and needed to settle down. Her mind was driving her crazy. When she did get to sleep, it was fitful. Miguel slept on the floor next to the bed. During the night Niea woke, she thought she was in the cave and being attacked. She jumped onto Miguel and stabbed him high on the chest.

He yelled for help as he tried to hold off her attack. "It's me, Niea, Miguel!" It was as if she was looking right though him, staring and screaming. Soon, the whole team was awake. Cal was the first one to come help Miguel. He was bleeding profusely. It looked like she had nicked an artery in his shoulder. Cal threw a cloth at him and told him to hold pressure. He wasn't looking good. Cal needed to tend to him, but it was taking all she had to hold Niea. She was a woman possessed. Jamal flew into the room, slipped in Miguel's blood, and fell.

Cal yelled, "Someone hold her! I have to see to Miguel. He could bleed to death in a matter of minutes." Jamal got a large blanket and wrapped it around Niea to contain her. He had blood all over him, but he held onto her with all his might. Damn if she was going to kill anyone here if he could help it. She was one strong woman. It took all he had, and he was very strong. Once she was a bit calmer, Tulie got her to drink the valerian root. She wanted to see Miguel. What had she done? She started sobbing.

Cal was able to tack the artery, but Miguel was going to need a little thing called surgery. Niea would need to go to Central too. Cal was very uncertain how long the stitching would hold. She secured a wrap around his arm and across his chest. Miguel didn't want to go to Central. Cal leaned down, getting as close as she could, and gave him that look that said "you're going." He nodded.

Cal decide to take both of them to Central. Niea was dangerous and needed help as much as Miguel. Miguel didn't want to take Niea. What would they do to her? How do they treat soldiers whose minds are so warped? What kind of drugs would they give her? How would they deal with her when she became violent? Cal gave him that look that he knew so well, and he knew Niea needed help. What if she kills him or one of their team? It would mess her up forever.

Cal went to get their ground car, and Malik said they could take his car. It was faster. He had souped it up. Cal had Niea in walking restraints. Miguel didn't like seeing his lovely bride chained up, but he knew it was for the best. If Niea did kill one of them, she could be commented and declared unfit.

They loaded up into Malik's car, with Niea and Miguel in the back. Cal sat up front with Malik. She asked him questions about what he had done to this car. It was fast, and the stirring looked like it was way improved. She asked if she could drive it. Sure, on the way back.

They arrived at Central early in the morning. They went straight away to the infirmary. Miguel was assessed and taken to surgery stat. Niea sat in a viewing room to be watched. She was starting to amp up. Her restraints had been removed, and she was pacing hard. Her pupils were looking dilated and black. The predatory gaze was turned on anything that moved. Her observer was a young male intern. He was getting concerned about her. He called for help. Niea was hitting the observation window hard. It looked as if it would break. Cal and Malik were in the waiting room and heard all the commotion. Cal knew Niea was either going to injury or kill somebody or somebodies, maybe even get hurt bad herself. She tried to go into the observation area but was denied. She begged them to let her back. Finally, there was so much commotion that Cal was able to get back there. Niea had knocked out two techs and was attacking a third. Cal came up behind her and was able to put her in a one-person hold. They would have to get her a shot soon. Cal would not be able to hold her for long. With Niea's fighting abilities and the superhuman strength that came from adrenaline and psychosis, Niea could not be dealt with easily.

Finally, the tech came with the shot. Niea was kicking, screaming, and twisting about. The needle wasn't landmarked well, but the tech was able to plunge all the medicine into Niea. Cal still had her in the hold, and the tech motioned for her to follow. They put Niea in a more secure room with double plexiglass for observation. A mattress on the floor was all that was there. This room was for people with homicidal ideations, and Niea certainly met criteria.

Once Niea was out, Cal left. She had to talk to Grandmama right away. She asked Malik if he wanted to come. He nodded and followed Cal. He marveled at the place as they hurried to Grandmama's quarters. He asked Cal who was this Grandmama. Cal said she was the leader of the Kalifee, and she was her adopted mother and Niea's grandmother. He had heard of this woman. He was pleased and nervous to meet her.

When they got there, Grandmama was having breakfast and offered them something. Neither of them felt hungry, but Grandmama insisted, so they sat down with her and ate. Cal proceeded with their story. When she came to the part about what happened to Niea and what Niea did, Grandmama was stunned. She didn't know what to say. She wanted to see her granddaughter right away. She called down to the infirmary. Niea was sedated right now, but they would certainly call her as soon as they had anything to tell her.

The infirmary called. Miguel was going to need a blood transfusion. They needed a consent form signed. All three of them left right away for the infirmary. Grandmama signed the form. She was his mother-in-law, and that would do. She wanted to see him, but he was still in surgery, unconscious. She asked them to call her as soon as they could.

Cal and Grandmama went back to her quarters. Malik was waiting in the reception area. When he saw them, he stood and lowered his head. Cal stepped up to him and said that Grandmama would like to formally meet him. She thanked him for helping her daughters and their team. He expressed that he owed them a debt. He explained how they how joined the Gogatt and how that had been a true mistake. Grandmama invited him to finish a meal with her and Cal, and he graciously accepted.

Late that evening, one of the surgical team called. Miguel was out of surgery and recovered enough. He would love to see her and Cal. Malik excused himself to go find a place to sleep, and Grandmama said no way. He could use one of her guest rooms. He thanked her and went off to bed. None of them had slept much since they recued Niea from the Gogatt.

Miguel was weak but elated to see both of them. Grandmama and Cal gave him a kiss on the cheek. He wanted to know about Niea. Grandmama informed she was resting. They had to sedate her again. The sadness in his eyes told the whole story. They sat and talked about all that happened. Grandmama was so proud of the team. They had blown the hole where the Gogatt had been cooking up the substances to bring down the Kalifee and killed so many of these monsters. It was getting late, and Miguel needed to sleep. They kissed him good night. The tech came and administered him a sedative so he would rest all night. The surgeon came out to speak to Grandmama. He was fairly certain he could be discharged in a few days, but he would have to take it easy. His subclavian artery had been nicked pretty good. Whoever tacked it did a fine job. Grandmama smiled and looked at Cal. Cal gave a thin smile.

The surgeon turned toward Cal. "You did one hell of a job, soldier. You can scrub with my surgical team anytime, and I mean that!" It was always disconcerting to see Cal become humble. She never did like compliments. She did what she did as she was trained to do. The surgeon stuck out his hand, taking Cal's hand in his, and shook it. He smiled a broad smile, nodding with admiration. "I am always impressed with great emergency skill, especially in the field where you have to operate on a wing and a prayer." He bid them good night, and they left for Grandmama's in silence. As they walked through the door, Theodosia came in behind them.

Grandmama was not in the mood for this trying woman. "What in hell's name are you doing here?"

Theodosia curled her lip in a cold hiss. "Well, aren't we in a good mood."

Grandmama looked her in the eyes, and Theodosia darted her gaze. Truth be known Theodosia found Grandmama very intimidating. "So, I hear your granddaughter and son-in-law are in the infirmary wounded from their little trials of war."

Grandmama said, "Look, we are all tried. What do you want?"

Theodosia knew this could wait, but she was hoping to get a dig in on the grand lady. "Are you going to be present at the council meeting in the morning?"

"Yes, Theodosia, I will be there." She went to her front door and opened it for Theodosia to leave. At that moment, Malik came through the door looking for a restroom.

"Oh, excuse me. Just looking for a place to have a wee." Malik didn't want to interrupt, but he had to go.

Grandmama pointed to the hallway. "Second door on the left, my good man."

Theodosia rolled her eyes. "Keeping company are we!" Grandmama hated the way she used the all-encompassing we. There was no we to it. Theodosia was a lone pimple on the butt of the Kalifee. Grandmama was sure that one day she would pop it.

"My dear Theodosia, he is here with the away team. You can leave now!" Grandmama was dead serious. If this woman wouldn't leave, she would have Cal remove her, and Cal would love that.

Grandmama went to a cabinet and pulled out a bottle of wine. Then she looked at Cal. Cal smiled and said, "Please have yourself a glass of wine."

Grandmama was truly contrite. "I am so sorry, Cal." Cal laughed, went to the bar, and poured two glassed of wine. Grandmama's eyes got big.

In that moment, Malik came through the door. Cal turned and asked, "Would you like a glass of wine?" He nodded, and Cal handed him and Grandmama each a glass. She looked at Grandmama, smiled, and got herself a glass of hibiscus tea she found in the ice box. Then she motioned for all of them to take a seat, and they did.

"Excuse me, ladies, but who was that woman?" He had a perplexed look on his face.

Cal giggled and said, "She is the thorn in my Grandmama's butt."

Malik said, "I know her. I have seen her before."

Cal said, "It wasn't at one of the traveling brothels. I'm sure no one would want that pinched-face gargoyle." She and Grandmama laughed.

"No, it was at one of the camps." He was nodding to himself. He was sure it was her.

Grandmama leaned forward. "You saw that woman at a Gogatt camp?"

"Oh, yes, several times." He was still nodding as he ran through his memories.

"And you're sure it was her?" Grandmama was locked in on what he had just said.

"She would come there and talk with that man. The one that is very different from the Gogatt. She would bring a satchel with papers and some kind of substances. He would give her coin. I had to take the coin bag to her ground car a couple of times." He was still nodding.

Grandmama was still trying to wrap her mind around this. Cal sat there with her mouth open in shock. Neither said a word for several minutes.

Finally, Grandmama, looking at Cal, said, "Who do you think this non-Gogatt man is?"

Cal asked, "Was his name Leit?"

Malik thought for a while and said, "Yes."

Cal stood up and looked at Grandmama. "Shall I go get her?"

Grandmama said, "No. And believe me, Cal, I want a big chunk of her butt too. And we will share that, but we are going to need more evidence." Cal knew she was right, but she wanted to smash her head right up her own buttock.

Later that day, Miguel wanted to see Niea. One of the techs helped him into a wheelchair and took him to the psych ward. Niea had been so nervous, pacing the floor, unable to sit down and relax. She was on one-one level of observation. Her tech was a sturdy young man that was assigned to watching her. She had been downgraded from a two-one. Niea and adrenaline were hard to handle. But she had been doing quite well. She did appear to be amping up. Then she saw Miguel in the wheelchair and started to cry. She got still and focused. Her dear sweet Miguel was here. The tech was relieved. He didn't want to have to manhandle this capable woman. Besides, she was too beautiful to hurt in any of these holds taught by management. Safety care? What a joke.

She stood quietly looking at Miguel with huge tears in her eyes. She had almost killed her only love. She would have gone really crazy if that had happened. She waited patiently, and the door opened. She waited for a staff member to instruct her. The tech led her to the visiting area and motioned for her to sit. Miguel's tech brought him in and warned about his wound, to be careful. Niea nodded. She looked at her tech about, pulling up a chair. He nodded, and she pulled her chair up slowly. She never took her eyes off Miguel. Her heart was soaring, pounding. She sat slowly and reached for his hand. Her tech was going to remind her of the no-touch policy, but she was being so respectful he just couldn't do it. It was so sweet to see two people this much in love. They reached for each other's hand and intertwined their fingers. Both sat there just looking at the other. Niea didn't know what to say. She whispered, "I love you." Miguel smiled and whispered it back to her. The tech had never seen such a visit with any of the patients he had been assigned to—so sweet, gentle, kind, and quiet.

It wasn't long, and Miguel got tried. Niea looked at her tech and asked, "May I kiss my husband goodbye?" He nodded with a warm smile on his face. She pulled her chair up real close to Miguel and placed her lips on his, and huge tears came again. They both breathed each other in and whispered words of true love for each other. The rest of the day Niea was in a great place. Miguel was the magic that she needed.

Both of them were healing well. Miguel was to be discharged in a few days. With Niea, it wasn't clear when she could be released. Her days were good. She had been sitting with other patients, listening and helping. She was no stranger to looking deep into others and pulling out want they needed to hear about themselves and what they were ready to hear. But the nights were a different story. She would awake and think she was back in the cave being raped repeatedly. There was this one tech that had a rapport with Niea. Most of the techs were afraid of Niea by reputation and from seeing her in action. She had put four techs out on medical leave. She would have never hurt any of them in her right mind.

Niea was out in the courtyard lying on the grass staring at the sky. The manager of the unit wanted Niea off the ground. No one wanted to deal with her. The man that was assigned to Niea wanted to change assignments with anyone who would take her. So, this stocky young man stepped up. He said he had a rapport with her, but he had to be allowed to deal with her the way he knew would work. The manager said that he didn't mind, but he needed to keep her calm and cooperative. He reminded everyone that this woman was a commander of the highest degree, her Grandmama was the leader of the Kalifee, and she was a fearsome warrior. She also hallucinated repeated trauma and had gone through horrific things that were hard for any of them to imagine.

Miguel came to see Niea. He was walking perfectly and looked so good. He had prepared some food for everyone. The manager called to ask if he could do this, and they agreed. He was allowed to set up in the break room. He had made a roasted turkey with all the trimmings. He had made some ginger beer with no alcohol in it. They allowed him to eat with Niea at a corner table. The staff took turns coming in to eat, and there were many repeat trips. When all were full, Miguel made up several go home-plates for the staff. They all got together and thanked him for such a meal. They had never eaten this well. He finished cleaning up. They allowed Niea to help him. She whispered to him it wasn't home, but this was what she loved to do with him. He grinned and said he hoped he would like to do other things with her. This seemed to bring her down. So he quickly added when she was ready and not a moment sooner. She smiled slightly. The tech allowed her to give him a real goodbye kiss, watching out for any tattletales.

Miguel returned to Grandmama's. She had turned her kitchen over to him. He cooked for her daily, and she was thrilled. She also insisted he stay at her quarters. It was a fine place, many rooms with much privacy. Miguel had a large room with a private bath. That he wasn't used to. At the hostel, there was a one large bath area. He had rigged some showers, and there was hot running water with two toilets. He hoped one day he would build a home for him and Niea separated from the hostel.

Later that day, he went for a walk in one of the many gardens at Central. It was beautiful here. His favorites one were the ones his wife had designed. It was almost as beautiful as her. He would come here daily, sit, and mediate. Niea had taught him how important it was to do just that. He made a ritual of it. It did make a big difference in his mood, and he felt aligned after he had done it. On this day he was sitting in his favorite area with eyes closed. Then he heard a familiar voice. He turned and was speechless. It was Vahar coming his way. What the hell? He felt so good, and now her. He remembered what Niea said to him many times, "Don't let anyone steal your joy. No one can really touch your soul unless you let them."

Miguel acted like he didn't see her, like she didn't exist. She stood in front of him for several minutes, and without looking at her he said, "What is it, Vahar?"

She wasn't sure what to say so she said, "Hi." He just looked at her and said nothing. She sighed and said, "Of course you are still mad at me, and I don't blame you. I didn't want to kill either of you. I love you, Miguel. I always have." He continued to look at her. He remembered what Niea had said many times to give others their say, listen well, and then tell them what you need to say. His expression said go on. He leaned back and laced his fingers together behind his head. She sat down beside him, dropped her head, and said, "You know I would do anything for you. We grew up knowing each other. I thought we would be married someday. I hear you and Niea are married." He just looked at her. He couldn't imagine any kind of marriage to her. What would have he been? Not much. All she ever seem to want was him to be performing for coins.

His silence made Vahar nervous. "Say something, please." He thought of his beauty Niea and smiled. Vahar was uncomfortable. "Say something!" He laughed a little. He had a diamond in his mind, and it wasn't Vahar.

Finally, he said, "You love me?"

She moved a bit closer to him, knowing this always had an effect on him, but not now. Why? "What are you thinking?"

He kept smiling and said, "What would that have been like, I wonder."

She said with a tear in her eye, "I do love you, Miguel. I have loved you since we were children."

He nodded slowly. "So, you call all that happened between us love. Interesting. That is not what I would call it," he said.

"What do you call it?" she said so sincerely. Miguel knew she was a very good actress. She convinced every man she had that she loved them.

He stretched his back, saying, "This is a fine day, isn't it?"

She was perturbed. "Answer me, please. What did we have?"

Miguel couldn't quit smiling. "You were a damn fine pimp." With that statement, he laughed just too much. She wanted to slap him. She resisted.

"You know, Miguel, I gave you so many opportunities. You could have all the women you wanted. You got all the sex and drugs you wanted, and it cost you nothing." She was hurt now. "How could you be so cavalier after all I had been through for you?"

Miguel's amusement had turned to curiosity. "What do you mean what you have been through?" He should have known she could only see herself and her needs. Her narcissistic tendencies were definitely showing. "So, what indiscretion have I shown you?" He was sincere. Vahar found his manner compelling.

She took a deep breath, giving her breasts an extra thrust. This always made Miguel look at her body, which she knew drove him crazy. He did seem to notice her attempts to get him interested in having sex with her. She took another deep breath, this time in frustration. "I just thought we would get married and have a family someday."

Miguel resisted the urge to laugh, but he wanted to. "Vahar, you always said you never wanted children. It would ruin your figure. You never talked about a future for you and me. You don't even know me that well. There was never enough time. You were too busy selling my ass to the highest bidder, collecting coin for the right to view my sexual prowess or doing you at the beginning and the end of every night. I had to take sexual stimulants to keep performing on the level you expected. If all this had continued, I would have been dead before I was thirty years old."

She sighed again. "Why didn't you tell me?"

He laughed. "I did, and you chose not to hear me. Vahar, you paid little attention to me. My needs were never met when I was with you. I preformed, and you got paid. That's all it was. You never figured out or asked why I came around less and less. It was all killing me on so many levels."

Vahar said, "I can make it up to you. Whatever you want, I'll do it. You are the only man I have ever loved."

Miguel looked her dead in the eye. She was used to him not making eye contact with anyone. "Vahar, I am happily married to Niea. She knows me, and her love is healing and complete."

She was upset. "You're married?" He nodded, with a warm glow she had never seen. "You are so different."

"Yes, I am, and the Spirit has given me another chance at being a complete loving husband and man. She is the best woman I have ever known." He smiled.

Vahar sneered, "She doesn't know about your past with me. About all the debauchery you have involved yourself in and how wonderfully you took it up your rectum over and over again."

He just looked at her and shook his head. "She knows everything. She knew me without me telling her anything. She knew I was a lady's man. She looked into my soul and found love. I didn't have love for myself. She showed me how. She accepted me totally."

Vahar looked sick and said, "She almost killed you. Is that love?"

Miguel shook his head slowly and said, "She has been through a horrific experience with the Gogatt. Beaten and raped repeatedly."

Vahar said, "She's dangerous. I hear she has hurt several workers in the unit where she is being held. What if she injures you again, messes you up so bad you can't work or even live?"

Miguel was growing weary of talking to this woman. Whatever he saw in her was so gone that he couldn't even remember what it was. It was sex, but he couldn't see that now. There was nothing more between them. "Vahar, you don't know anything about me."

Vahar believed she could make her point, but honesty prevailing, she couldn't think of anything she really knew about him. She said, "Like what?"

He smiled again. "Did you know I am great cook? I can fix anything or build anything. I belong to the finest away team of the Kalifee. I am a warrior, a medic, and a man. I am not a sex toy or a servant. I don't do anything I don't want to. With you and the drugs you provided, I went down many roads I would never have ventured on in my life."

She had never known him to brag or talk about himself. "Who told you all this?"

He continued to smile. "No one. I actually figured it out with the help of Niea."

She was taken back. She said, "You are so different. You hardly even talked to me. Your silent sexiness drove me wild. I thought you didn't want to talk. I though you just wanted unusual experiences."

He had started to remember all the wasted nights in her care, if one could call it that. "You never asked me what I wanted. We never talked about sex, love, marriage, children, or a home. You were slowly killing me. So, if Niea does kills me, it will be a much finer death than dying in one of your brothels with someone's fist up my ass."

She had never heard him be so frank, so straightforward. He wasn't the same man that had submitted to her every whim. She had to admit to herself he was a fine man and not just the way he looked. Niea was one lucky woman.

She stood up and said, "All I know what to say, Miguel, is that I am sorry. I am a very self-absorbed person. But please remember that I do love you and always will. I am glad you and Niea found each other." As she walked away, she realized in that moment that she had grown and was actually appreciative to learn about him. She knew beyond a shadow of a doubt she had truly done Miguel wrong. He didn't watch her walk away. He closed his eyes, and all he could see was Niea's beautiful, loving face. He thanked the Spirit for sending him what he needed to be whole. He also prayed for Niea, and he said a prayer for Vahar. May she find her happiness.

Niea had a real bad night. She was hallucinating and lashing out. She had taken down one tech that had to go to the emergency department. The night manager of the unit called in the tech that had a way with her. Yes, he would come in no problem. Thank God. When he arrived, she was screaming Miguel's name. They had her in the seclusion room. No restraints. She was not hurting herself, and no one wanted to go in there and try to hold her.

The stocky man got a report from the manager and went to the plexiglass window and waited until she saw him. She was elated to see him. She wanted to see Miguel. He reminded her that it was night, and everyone was sleeping. She accepted this. Could he please take her outside, and could they look at the stars? He asked the manager. They agreed but asked him to keep her as calm as he could. He opened the door, held out his elbow for her to take, and escorted her to the courtyard. She was so sorry. She didn't know his name. He introduced himself with a formality that she liked. "My name is Serge. So nice to meet you, beautiful lady." He bowed, and Niea giggled. They walked to the courtyard, and Niea ran to the grassy area and lay down. Serge reminded her that they didn't want her to lay on grass. She begged. He said, "I can get a blanket for you to sit on." Niea wanted to feel the grass. He gave in. He delighted in her love of nature and people. He could tell she loved him as well. What a pure spirit, and she had been through such an awful ordeal. He was working a lot of overtime, but he never seemed to mind coming in for just her. They had spent a lot of nights together. Sitting quietly, mostly. Tonight, they talked all night. Neither seemed tried nor bored with each other. She was concerned with him not getting any rest. He assured her there was nothing he would rather be doing than being here with her, and there was overtime pay!

One evening, Serge would be coming in later. He had called the unit to let them know. It was after supper, and Niea was feeling afraid. She was having flashbacks. The faces of her attackers kept flashing in her face. The tech assigned to her was a fairly young girl, and she was obviously leery of Niea. She asked Niea if she needed something for her nerves. Niea never answered; she was seeing the horrors over and over in her mind. She started pacing, barking out orders, screaming, then she collapsed. The young tech was unsure what to do. The lead came and helped get Niea to bed. They put her in soft restraints, and an injection was given. She would sleep through the night. Serge was called and asked if he could not come tonight but come in the a.m. He said he would.

Later in the night, Niea had woke up in a cold sweat. Somehow, she got out of the restraints and was running around the unit screaming and fighting someone that no one could see. The team was able to restrain Niea and get an injection in her. It helped maybe a little. She was still obviously hallucinating, trying to fight off her attackers. The manager came out to see her and let the techs know that Lady Niea was going to surgery. An order had come through for her to have a frontal lobotomy. The manager was concerned. Yes, the order was signed by Grandmama. He called her quarters, but there was no signal. He tried to get a message through to her. He was stalling. This was not right. He wanted to talk to Grandmama to confirm this order. It would make Lady Niea into a vegetable.

Finally, the medication started to work, and Niea settled down some. She was still talking to someone that wasn't there. She was begging for them to stop and let her go. She wanted to see her husband and her team.

The manager had stalled for over an hour, but he couldn't get in touch with Grandmama. He saw Serge coming in. He quickly filled him in on what was going on. Then he had him go to Grandmama's quarters, find her, and bring her here, stat. Serge took off. He knew he could find her.

The manager was getting nervous. Then he saw that awful woman Theodosia coming down the hall. What in Hades does she want? Theodosia approached the counter and wanted to know who was in charge here. He stepped up and got ready for an ass chewing.

Serge found Grandmama in her quarters. Something was wrong with her communicator. He informed her they needed to hurry and why. She put on her running shoes and took off. Serge stayed right with her. The grand old lady could run. When they got there, the team was strapping Niea to a gurney. She was sedated but still somewhat conscious. Her body had always metabolized substances faster than most. She saw Grandmama and Serge push the swinging doors open in gangster style. Grandmama had her eyes locked on Niea. "Where in the hell do you think you're going with my granddaughter?" Then she looked at every person in the area. She was angry. Everyone froze and stepped back. And there she was, the cold sore at the center of this attack on her Niea, Theodosia. Grandmama instructed the team to untie her granddaughter. Then she turned her full attention to Theodosia. "This is your doing!" Theodosia just stood there with her pursed mouth and self-righteous sneer. "What do you have to say for yourself?"

Theodosia said, "We can't have this woman up here attacking staff. Do have any idea how much we are spending on compensating our injured staff? She is dangerous and needs help. Obviously, you aren't going to do the right thing."

Grandmama was livid, but she held it well. "First, there is no we. You have nothing to do with this infirmary. If the coin is what bothers you, I have plenty and will be glad to donate. But that's not it, no! Do you even know what a lobotomy will do to a person's brain? No, you don't. You hate me and my little family and will do anything to hurt us." With that, Grandmama stepped up to Theodosia, got in her face, and whispered, "You're done for."

Grandmama turned toward Niea, who was sitting up on the gurney still a bit groggy. Serge was holding Niea's hand. She wanted to stand up. They both assisted her to her feet. She was wobbly but doing okay with their assistance. The three of them went outside to the courtyard. Grandmama wanted to take Niea to her quarters. Niea thought that she would be safe here, especially after that shit show. She informed Grandmama that she was still getting triggered and hallucinating, especially at night. They all sat and talked until Niea felt she could stand. Grandmama thought it was a good idea if the lovely Serge took Niea for a walk in one of the small gardens. Niea liked that idea. Serge helped Niea to the lavatory so she could get cleaned up and put on a dress. They left the unit arm in arm.

Grandmama was talking to the manager, thanking him for getting in touch with her. Theodosia heard him call her Grandmama. She stood there looking at Grandmama.

"What is it, Theodosia?"

Theodosia pursed her self-righteous lips even more. "That is not your title. The proper name is Califia. It means queen. These people are not your relatives."

Grandmama had had enough. She remember that she needed to get copy of the order for the lobotomy. She knew Theodosia did it. Grandmama turned toward the pursed-lipped bag of wind. "The Kalifee is my family, you halfwit." Theodosia said nothing, turned, and walked away. Another missed opportunity. One day she would rid herself of the Califia and these showboat women. Grandmama— who ever heard of using such a name, like she was the mother of them all? It made Theodosia sick to her stomach. Her granddaughters were good at everything they do. This made her sick too. She wanted to see them all destroyed, even if that was the last thing she would ever do. No, she did not want them dead. How could they suffer when they are dead?

Miguel entered Grandmama's quarters. She told him what Theodosia had tried to do. He was seeing red. How could someone be so cruel? That operation would have destroyed Niea's brain. If she had done that, he knew he would have to kill that hateful woman.

Niea had a wonderful afternoon with Serge. They walked around the gardens and visited a small artisan shop. Then she wanted to see Miguel, so they went back the infirmary. Miguel was waiting for her with some supper he had cooked. She ate it and was delighted as usual. He was still angry at what had almost happened, but he kept his fury to himself. The manager approached Miguel and Niea, saying he was sorry. Miguel thanked him for calling Grandmama. He had saved his Niea.

Niea had been doing well. The nightmares had settled down for now. Miguel thought Niea would be safer at the hostel. Grandmama agreed. She knew Miguel would take care of his beautiful wife no matter what. He had little to no ego. Everything he did was for others.

Grandmama couldn't be more pleased that he was her Niea's husband. Grandmama had known she would find a man perfect for her.

In the morning, Miguel and Grandmama went to get Niea. She was excited and scared. She didn't want any more tragedies. She said goodbye to the staff. Grandmama had an envelope for each of the techs that had cared for Niea. It was a healthy dose of coin. They would be pleased.

Just before they left, there was a knock at the door. It was Malik. He had seen Theodosia again at the edge of Central talking to a man he believed was in the Gogatt. The man had been seen with Leit. He had a different look than a usual Gogatt. They were exchanging papers for coin. Grandmama really wanted to know what the old bat was up to. She always hated to see Niea go, but she would be safer away from where Theodosia had any influence.

They took their time driving back to the hostel. It seemed like a long time ago when they had driven here. Cal had returned to the hostel to her Jamal and Jay. Miguel thought they were doing so much better since Cal had her a son and had not had a drink. His sweet Niea slept most of the way. He pulled over by a small pond and spread out a picnic he had prepared for the trip. Once everything was set up for his bride, he woke Niea with a kiss. At first, she seemed scared, then she saw it was Miguel. They ate and kissed. Niea said she was not ready for lovemaking. She asked Miguel if he minded. He smiled and said that he would wait forever for her. Hopefully it would not be that long. But that didn't matter; his Niea was alive and well.

Cal saw them getting out of the car and came running. She grabbed Niea and whirled her around. Then she held her close. Her baby girl was back. She picked Niea up and held her in her arms. She placed her on the ground and lay down beside her. Cal whispered in her ear, "You're my baby girl." Niea looked at Cal and grinned. She nodded and kissed Cal on the mouth. Miguel was watching all this. It was kind of a turn-on.

The rest of the crew were so glad to see her. Niea did looked thin, but she looked healthy and happy to be with her crew. They ate, sang, danced, and had wonderful time. Jay had a bunch of wildflowers for Niea. He hugged her and told her she was the bravest person he had ever seen. She felt that she used to be a brave person. But possibly her fighting days were over. Only time would tell, and the Spirit would guide her where she needed to go.

Niea woke in the middle of the night screaming and holding a knife on Miguel. He was lying on the floor. He was out cold. Cal had come through the door ready for a battle with Niea. She had no weapon. She was not going to go that far, she hoped. Jamal was right behind her. Cal said, "What's going on, baby sis?"

Niea turned and saw Cal. "I don't know?" She looked down at the knife in her hand and dropped it. Then she saw Miguel sprawled out on the floor facedown. "What have I done?" Cal stepped in close and opened her arms to Niea. She jumped into her Cal's arms and held on for dear life. Cal motioned for Jamal to see about Miguel. Jamal picked up Miguel and took him his bed. Cal looked him over and found no wound. Niea had knocked him out cold. There was a bump on the back of his head. Jamal iced it and sat watching him as he held the ice on Miguel's head. Jamal had Miguel on his side in case he was to vomit. He was starting to come around. His head was throbbing, and he could hardly turn his head. Jamal asked Miguel if he could manipulate his neck. He agreed and had him to lay on the bed, and he palpated his neck. He found some sublocation along the cervical spine. With several adept moves, he realigned Miguel's neck. The relief showed on Miguel's face. Maybe Niea had come home to soon. He hated that idea. At least she didn't stab him. That was an improvement. He would take that any day over not having her here with him.

They could hear Cal in with Niea. She was rocking her and singing lightly. Niea wanted to see Miguel. Had she wounded him again? Cal called out, and Miguel answered. He said he was fine. Niea's body had gotten tight again. Cal held on to her as she tried to get away. "Aren't you, my baby girl?" Niea started crying and buried her head into Cal's neck. Cal continued to rock her baby sis. Then she kissed Cal on the lips. *Yes, I am your baby girl,* she thought. Niea started wiggling in Cal's lap.

Cal asked, "What is it, baby sis?"

Niea said, "You remember baby girl, don't you?" Cal grinned from ear to ear. Yes, she remembered. One of the games they used to play a lot. Niea jumped up. She had to see Miguel. "Catch me if you can." She took off and flew into where he was lying. "You okay?"

He just looked at her and nodded. Niea looked over her shoulder. "I gotta run. She's after me." She took off. Cal came bounding down the hall and saw Niea. The chase was on. Cal doubled back and hid in a closet. She jumped out and caught Niea by the waist, whirling her around and held her close to her. Then she kissed Niea lightly on the neck. Niea giggled and pretended to try to get away. She put arms around Niea and brushed her lips slowly on Niea's neck. She swooned and began to arch her back in pleasure.

"Why run, baby girl? You know you can't help yourself." Niea wiggled free, laughing like a child having too much fun. She tried to run again. Cal caught her by the arm and whirled her around. Niea jumped up, wrapping her legs and arms around Cal, slowly rolling her hips. Cal said in a low, husky voice, "You know you love it, baby girl." Niea yelled out in ecstasy. "Look at you, baby girl. You hot little mink." Cal held on to Niea, rocking her ever so slowly. Niea looked to be in pure ecstasy. Finally, Niea relaxed in Cal's arms. Cal continued to nuzzle Niea's neck and carried her to Miguel and her bed. She asked Niea if she could give her to her husband. Niea nodded.

Cal said to Miguel, "You want to hold our baby girl?" Miguel had a funny look on his face, but there was a big fat yes in his eyes. Cal sat Niea down on the bed, kneeled, and pressed herself between Niea's legs. Niea scooted herself up on Cal and again wrapped herself around her. She was breathing heavily with what sounded like passion. She was moving herself on Cal, shifting her hips ever so slowly. Cal stood up with Niea's legs wrapped around her. She blew on Niea's neck, and again she cried out in rapture. Miguel couldn't quite believe what he was watching. Cal looked at Miguel. "Hold our baby girl. You have to be sweet to her. She's as hot as a blade over a fire." Niea had nestled her face into Cal's neck. Cal looked at Miguel. He was spellbound by what he was watching. Where they intimate? No. It did seem like some kind of sex therapy. Cal was not participating in the ecstasy, but Niea was. This was their baby girl play. Niea was still holding on to Cal and breathing heavily. Cal stood up holding Niea. Her pelvis was pushed up against Cal, and she was moaning. Her legs were shaking, and she cried out. Cal motioned for Miguel to stand up and take Niea. He took her. She was hot and purring. He kissed her neck, and she cried out again. She was soaking wet between her legs. He looked at Cal. Cal nodded encouragingly. "You know what to do. Just do it at her pace. Don't let her run away. Baby girl needs this."

Miguel laid Niea down on the bed and said, "How's my baby girl?" She giggled. She looked up at him with those large deep violet eyes. Cal watched for a few more moments and went off to be with her man. After all that, she was going to need some of Jamal's largerthan-life love. He was a powerful big man, and she wanted him bad right now.

Orgasm had eluded Cal most of her sexual life. Jamal had given himself wholeheartedly to her, and she had found with that and their love, she could have an orgasm. She could have another one. He knew just how to love her. Thinking about him was just the best. But she would rather have the real thing in its totality. Cal had all but given up on sex and true love. She also had believed that orgasm was brought on by the use of sexually stimulating drugs. She did not like the aftereffect of those drugs; alcohol was her romance. Alcohol blotted out her emotions. Funny she didn't want to drink and hadn't for a very long time. She was thankful and gave the Spirit all the glory.

Miguel lay in bed holding his girl. She had been very still. He kissed her on her neck. She moaned then touched herself, smelling her fingers. He looked at her with a crooked smile. He took her fingers and smelled them. He went deep into her smell. She was delicious. He asked a silent request to touch her with his fingers. She smiled and took his hand and placed it on her mount of Venus. She was so wet. He touched her tenderly. She opened her legs and thrusted her hips.

She pushed onto his fingers. He let her guide his hand into her warm, wet heaven. Miguel knew how to sustain an orgasm, but this was just too sexy. He had had many women and knew instinctively what each of these women wanted, needed, and how to get them there. But Niea was so different. Everything they did felt like the first time. And this was blowing his mind. Niea kept his hand on her as she rolled over on her back. He put his fingers in his mouth. The taste was just as good as the smell. He got between her legs. She scooted her way down to his penis and testes. She rubbed her breasts all over them. Then she licked and suckled every inch of him. She made her way back to his mouth and sucked on his tongue. Her legs were splayed open, and he buried his head in her warm wetness. Niea was in ecstasy. He has the most talented tongue ever. She couldn't help but have powerful orgasms. With all that, he sat up and smiled so tenderly at her. He lay down on his back. She straddled him and slowly lowered herself onto his generous penis. She rocked him ever so slowly and another one. He finally couldn't take it anymore. He came so hard it almost rendered him unconscious. Niea was worried for a moment she had hurt him. He opened his eyes and smiled. "Life begins in Niea!" She laughed. She thanked the Spirit she had not killed him. She couldn't wait to meet their babies. She hoped to have many, and with this activity there was no doubt they would be able to have lots!

Jamal and Cal were lying in bed. He was kissing her neck. Then he lay back, pulling his Cal close to him. As always, loving Cal gave him all he needed in this world. He had to ask what she and Niea were doing earlier. Cal snickered, wondering if she should tell him her sorted escapades of her teenage years. Why not? This man seemed to be able to take anything from her and continue to love her. She explained that she had become sexually active at sixteen, promiscuous. She would come home from being with a boy, and Niea could smell it on her. Niea had always been the nosiest little thing. Cal explained what she had done, and Niea was curious. She wanted Cal to show her what the boy had done to her. Cal said no, reminding Niea that she wanted to wait to meet her husband and then have sex. Niea begged, saying just the kissing and stuff. Niea said she needed to practice. Cal said no and went to take a shower. When she came out of the bath, Niea jumped on her, and they both fell to the bed laughing. Niea landed on top of Cal, moving her hips around on top of Cal. Cal flipped her on her back, straddling her, holding her wrist. Cal said as she held Niea down, "What are you doing, baby girl?" Niea giggled and wrapped her legs around Cal, wanting to know if this was how they did it. Cal stood up with Niea wrapped around her. Niea was pushing her hips on Cal and moaning. Cal pulled away a little, looking at Niea in wonder. Niea was turned on. This budding girl was hot. Cal asked, "What am I supposed to do with this?" Niea wanted her to teach her. Looks like this child knew exactly what to do. Niea would not let go of Cal. She seemed to be getting hotter every second, pushing her hips on Cal. Cal pulled Niea off her and stood back. She was not doing this. Niea was her baby sister. This was wrong. Grandmama would have her head. It was bad enough she was having sex with boys, but not her own sister. Niea started to cry and ran out on to the balcony. Cal wanted to just leave her there, but she couldn't. She stood at one of the sliding doors looking at her beautiful little sis. Niea was sobbing. Cal couldn't stand it. She picked Niea up and took her to her bed. She tried over and over to explain how on so many levels this was wrong.

Between sobs, Niea said quietly, "You have sex with strangers. What about love? Don't you love me? Teach me. I don't want to have sex with a stranger." She had a point, but Cal tried to explain that she was not attracted to girls that way. And that sex among family members was taboo, ignorant, and just wrong. Niea was quietly lying in her bed with her face covered. She continued to cry. Cal tried to ignore her. She couldn't. She was not having sex with her sister, and that was that. Cal sat in the chair next to the bed with her face in her hands. Niea sat up looking at Cal. "I didn't mean to upset you. I love you." Cal looked up at Niea. This broke her heart. Yes, she loved her baby sister more than anything except Grandmama. If it wasn't for Grandmama, where would she be?

This continued for quite a while. Every time Cal came home, Niea could smell it was a different boy every time. She just didn't understand why Cal had to keep doing it and doing it with different boys. She would beg Cal to just hold her. Cal would hold her, and Niea would start heating up. Cal would put her down. Niea would cry, and Cal would give in and hold Niea again. Niea couldn't help herself. She would start rolling her hips on Cal. Cal didn't understand why she couldn't just lie there.

One particular afternoon, Cal agreed to lay in bed with baby girl. Niea reached up, touching Cal's face, saying how beautiful she was. She thanked her and was so glad Niea wasn't humping her. Cal noticed Niea had her hand between her thighs. "What are you doing, baby girl?" Niea put her fingers to nose and sniffed. Cal couldn't help but think that Niea was lucky to be so hypersexual. She was a little envious. Cal was still waiting for the big thrill. She kept trying different boys to find the crescendo. It hadn't come yet.

Niea rolled on top of Cal. Her panties were off. She was turned on, sliding herself up and down on Cal's thigh. Before Cal could stop her, she screamed and was shaking all over. Cal was looking at her. "What just happened, baby girl?" Niea looked as surprised as Cal did. She jumped and ran. Cal chased her. They ended up on Cal's bed. Niea buried her face in the pillow. Cal thought she was crying or maybe laughing. Cal pulled the pillow away. Niea would cry then laugh. What a jumble of emotions she was going through. Cal wrapped her arms around Niea and blew on her neck. Niea giggled and arched her back, moaning. Then she jumped up and ran. Cal was right on her heels. She got Niea by the waist, picking her up from behind then blew on her neck. Niea was moaning and breathing heavy. She got free from Cal and ran again. Cal called out, "Where's my baby girl?" Niea giggled, and Cal caught her again. This time Niea wrapped herself around Cal. Cal nuzzled Niea's neck, and she cried out. Her legs were shaking. Cal held her this time. She had given up. Niea usually got what she wanted. Cal pulled her back so she could see her and said, "So is this what you wanted to learn?" Niea nodded. Cal looked at her sideways, "Really?"

Niea giggled. Cal knew better, "No, no, no. You just wanted to get off. You little mink." Cal pulled her close again and lightly kissed on her neck. Niea screamed in joy, arching her back. Cal kissed her neck again and again. Now Niea's leg were wrapped around Cal's waist, and she was squirming on her. Cal was astounded at how hot Niea was.

Finally, Niea was quiet and relaxed. She put her finger in her girl place and then smelled them. She offered a sniff to Cal. Cal shook her head no. Niea lay there smelling then tasting her fingers. Cal watched this in total wonder. How does one reach this garden of Eden? Whoever Niea hooked up with would be one lucky guy. Niea was hot, hot as they came.

One day Cal was lying on her back in bed, and Niea was on top of her. Her dress was over her head, and her underwear was hanging on the lamp. Cal was holding on to Niea's hips. Niea was moving her hips up and down on Cal's belly. Then Grandmama came home. She had come in on this before, but Niea was able to talk her way out of any coincidences. The genius answered the grand lady's question truthfully and vaguely at the same time.

Grandmama: What are you doing?

Niea: Practicing some movements Cal learned at school.

Grandmama: Why is your underwear off?

Niea: So I could check my pelvis placement.

Grandmama: Show me what you were doing.

Niea: We need to get it right before we show anyone.

Cal was waiting for Grandmama to see through Niea's deceit. If she did, she never let on.

Then one glorious day, Grandmama came home and Niea was deep in the middle of ecstasy on top of Cal. Grandmama was beside herself. She even cursed. That froze both her girls. She never cursed. She wanted to know if they were having sex. Cal tried to explain. Niea took over. She explained to Grandmama that she was having Cal show her the movements in the sexual act so she would know what to do when she met her husband. Grandmama just shook her head and begged her girls not to do anything that even slightly simulated the sex act. She was firm that Child Wellness would come and take both of them away. She would die without her girls.

Cal had stopped having sex after school. It was no longer interesting, exciting, or worth the time it took, and she got no reward. She actually felt better about that, and not coming home smelling of sex had its reward. Niea stop wanting Cal to play their game of "what did you do, baby girl." Then one day Niea arrived home, and Cal was sitting in a chair. She was bent over holding an ice pack to the back of her head. Niea called to her and was shocked when Cal sat up. She had been beaten up, and Niea could smell that several boys had had sex with her. She told Cal to wait here for Grandmama to take her to the infirmary and not to go to sleep. She might have a concussion. Cal nodded. Niea went to her room, got something, and left.

Niea found the area where Cal was raped. There was blood and semen there. She made sure she didn't disturb anything. One boy had dropped his student ID. Niea found him easily. She knew him and where he hung out. He was with his buddies. Niea was sure this was the rest of the rape gang. Rape gangs were given harsh punishment. The Kalifee did not tolerate such behavior. She stood there giving him that Niea stare. Finally, he said in a very sarcastic tone, "What you want, you little bitch?"

Niea spoke loud and directly to the young hoodlum, "Are you blind? I am not a bitch. Maybe if you paid attention in school, you would know that a bitch is a female dog, you idiot!"

He snarled at her, stood up, and walked toward her. "What's wrong with you? You retarded or something?" He was staring at Niea like he was going to beat her up and rape her. All she could think was, *Come on with it, moron.* This idiot doesn't know who he was messing with. He saw the stick she had in her hand. He paid it no mind. He went to grab her by her throat. Niea easily stepped aside and poked him with the stick. A volt of electricity went through his body. He hit the ground with a thud. Niea parried and got ready for the next attack. What he and his fellow rapist didn't know was they were up against one of the top-rated junior fighters in the whole school. Niea only had her magic wand, as she called it, because that would help her totally control the situation. Then he grabbed for her ankle. She stuck her wand on him and left it there. His body jerked repeatedly. His buddies were having a good time laughing at him. She released the wand and stood there waiting for another attack. She could tell by his smell that this one on the ground and shaking had done the most to Cal. She would not leave here until she got a good whiff of all these punks. Then she was going straight to the authorities. She did want to beat the living crap out of all of them. She knew all of them had been there gangraping her beautiful sister. Niea was livid. But she had her anger focus on these pathetic excuses for boys. She stood ready. The one on the ground gave an order for them to get this little bitch. One jumped out at Niea. She socked him in the nose. He was bleeding. Then she stuck her wand to his belly, and he fell back. She saw his ID and got a good sniff of him. One came from the side, and she gave him a side kick and touched him ever so lightly with the wand. Another hoodlum went for her, and she gave a round-house kick to the gut and of course a bit of the stick to make her point. Finally, they were all on the ground. Niea had all the names and smells tucked away in her perfect recall mind, and she turned to leave. But just before parting, she said, "Have a nice day, gentlemen." She headed for the Kalifee safety office.

Grandmama was horrified when she got home. Cal didn't look good. And where was Niea? Cal only knew that Niea left, saying that she would meet them at the infirmary. They both knew what their baby girl was up to. Grandmama was not worried about Niea's safety. She knew beyond a shadow of a doubt that Niea would take care of business. She just hoped she didn't kill any of them, although it wouldn't be a bad thing. Sex was a gift that was to be cherished, not a weapon to abuse and exploit the weak. Only thing that bothered Grandmama was she could lose Niea if she committed such a crime. Two officers were dispatched to the infirmary. One was a rape specialist. The boys would be picked up quickly with the information Niea given them. They offered Niea a ride. She declined. She knew she would beat them there, and she wanted to see Cal. Niea found Grandmama right away. She was glad to see her baby girl. She asked her what she had done. Niea gave her a moment-to-moment recall. Grandmama knew it was exactly how it went down. She could always count on her girls to be truthful and thorough with no drama.

One of the officers needed to talk to Niea. She was going to have to go the safety office with her Grandmama for an interview and to identify the boys. Cal would have to identify them also. Grandmama would have to wait for Cal. Cal would have to go to, but when would depend on how she feels.

Cal had a concussion and a black eye with a hairline fracture on her right orbital bone. She will need to take it easy for a few days and watch for signs and symptoms of any complications. She should be okay in a few days.

Turned out all five of them left semen in Cal. This was hard evidence, but they would need all of them to make their statement. When Cal heard what Niea did, she nearly laughed herself into a bad headache. Statement would be taken, then identification could be made. Niea said she needed to smell them to be absolutely sure. The chief officer never heard of such thing, but Niea insisted. Niea was just not the kind of person one says no to. When she went into the holding area, each suspect was asked to approach Niea. They were obviously scared of her. This amused everyone but the boys. Then Niea stepped in close to them. She said, "Hello, boys. How are you feeling? Got a bit a headache? Back hurt? Feeling a bit nervous?" She stepped away. The ringleader told them of her stick. The officer did have a hard time believing that one small girl could bring down five boys. But from the injuries they all had, it was obvious she had used some serious skills. Besides, the wand didn't leave a mark. Niea had made it that way. Niea said she didn't know what they are talking about. Niea didn't really lie; she just used different words. She called her weapon a wand. They simply used the wrong word. Cal identified them also. The nasty little ringleader made a vulgar jester at Cal, and Niea put him on the ground. The officer was glad she did that. They couldn't. They were restricted by convention.

Later that same day, Niea made a pact to Cal that baby girl would stay in the past and that Niea would have nothing to do with any man until she met her true love. She said it in her matter-of-fact way, but Cal knew she meant it.

When Cal finished her story, Jamal was smiling. "You ladies are amazing. I am so sorry that happened to you, my love." Cal lay next to Jamal, rubbing his six-pack abdomen. He was looking at her and said, "You know what you are going to do to him, right?" He was ready to love his woman again. She rolled over on top of him and slid herself down to his large penis, kissing it all over. Soon she sucked it into her mouth. She knew Jamal never knew how she got all that in her mouth and down her throat, but he loved it. The few women that had tried to do this to him couldn't get all of him in the mouth, much down their throat. But Cal was a different story. She had him all the way down her throat and looked to be in ecstasy. It felt like she was using her throat to stimulate him. Jamal watched her every move. She kept her eyes close most of the time but did look up at him every now and again. The way he looked at her made her heart sing. He stopped her before he let go. He wanted to please his woman again. He knew she liked to lie on her stomach and for him to go in her slow from the rear then get her up on her knees and wrap his huge hands around her hips. This made Cal go wild.

Grandmama had been keeping tabs on Theodosia. She was sure she was selling information to this Leit character. She wasn't sure what information she was selling. So, she went through the library use catalogue. Some of the information had to be confidential, and that registry was encrypted. It would take some time to decipher. There had to be a faster way. She needed to be stopped before some real damage was done. And there was the question of who was helping her on the inside. Grandmama knew Theodosia was not sharp enough to know about how to use to an encrypted system. Grandmama was not sleeping many a night going through all the logs. She also wanted to talk to Malik again. She had a proposition for him if he wanted it. He was still at Central. Grandmama got a message to him. He reported to her quarters as requested. He thought he might be able to do what she asked; besides she offered him a nice bit of coin, and he certainly needed it. His men, the ones left, were still camped behind the hostel. Malik had been selling some of the goods they had made like belts, vest, pants, shields, and knives. He even participated in fighting for coin and had done quite well for himself. But it would be nice to take home a good bounty. The Gogatt did not come through on their payment.

Later that night, Miguel and Niea were lying in bed. Miguel asked how she was feeling. At first she said fine, but that was not the truth. She was not okay. She was disturbed about several things and didn't really want to talk about them. Miguel insisted. She was a bit embarrassed about Cal and her performance of baby girl. She was sure Miguel felt some kind of way about the way Niea got so hot so easily. No, just the opposite. He told her that was one of the hottest things he had ever seen. He reminded her of how she felt about his sexual escapades with all the queens he had been with. Besides baby girl took the both of them to new sexual heights. He had always wondered how a virgin had been so sexually aware and free. Baby girl explained a lot. If any queen could do that, she could become quite wealthy. The rest of it wasn't going to come out as easy. Miguel could see Niea was having a real hard time knowing how to start. Then she wrapped her arms around him, and he held her. She loved being held. Although she felt a little better, this was going to be a hard one. Niea slept for a few hours then woke in a jolt. Miguel was not here. Was he afraid? Why wasn't he here? Had she attacked him, even murdered him? Was he lying somewhere injured or even dead? She ran outside, calling for him. Where was her husband? She sat down hard on the floor and started to weep. It didn't feel like he was dead.

She finally cried herself to sleep. She woke in the morning to find it had all been a dream/nightmare. Miguel was asleep on the floor.

For several months, Niea continued to be a danger to her team, her friends, and her husband. The attacks came more often. Then one night, she injured Cal, Miguel, and herself. An emergency transport was called for, and all three were taken away to Central. Niea was locked up in the psych unit once she was stabilized medically. She had cut herself in several places. Cal and Miguel had head injuries along with several deep cuts. Miguel had a subdural hematoma. They had to drill into his skull to release the pressure. The report was that Miguel was not doing as well as they needed. Cal had a mild concussion. A urine specimen confirmed she was pregnant. She was elated. She was released in a few hours to Grandmama's. She messaged Jamal. He would be on the next liner to Central. They were both so excited.

Niea remained very sick and dangerous for some time. Cal and Jamal decided to stay at Central for a few days They decided to go get some of their things and Jay and return to Central. Jay was happy to be having a sibling. Miguel was still unconscious. Zek and Margo stayed at the hostel. They had a few guests and kept the place up and running. Tulie didn't want to be an assassin anymore. She wanted to help people. She went to Central to be trained as a tech to work in the infirmary. Keddie had always wanted to be a soldier. He went to Central and joined up. Boot camp would start in a few days. The team was moving on.

Grandmama came by every day to see Niea and Miguel. Neither of them was well enough to have a proper visit. Grandmama just had to see them. Niea had been put on some strong psych drugs and was out of it most of the time. She looked like she was in a stupor all the time. But at least she was calm and not trying to hurt anyone or herself. Miguel had not come out of coma since Niea hit him in the head with a cooking iron. She asked to see him every once and a while.

Cal's pregnancy was coming along nicely. With each passing day, she, Jamal, and Jay were getting more and more excited. They were living with Grandmama, and she was loving it. But they wanted their own place. Cal still had lots of coin from her fighting. So, house shopping they went. They wanted a place with three bedrooms and two baths, a master bedroom, a room for Jay, and a nursey.

Grandmama had put a sniffer into the archive so she would be alerted if anyone tried to use her passage into the system. She was sure Theodosia was the culprit. She place several firewalls around classified information. She had devised a trap for Theodosia. And strangely enough Theodosia had been quiet for some time now.

Miguel woke up one day. At first he didn't remember anything, but with a bit of time he did. Only thing he remembered about Niea were the attacks, and he would not see her. Of course, this broke her heart, but what was she to do? She was pretty numb most of the day. The drugs were necessary, but they took a toll on her. Finally, one day, Niea was released with a large pack of medicines. She spent a few nights with Grandmama. She stopped by Cal's new place and was so pleased to see how beautifully she had decorated her home. Cal was due any day now. She wanted Niea to stay for the birth. So, she did. Cal had an eleven-pound baby boy. He was brown and beautiful. Niea got to hold her nephew. She fell in love. Cal and Niea picked out the name Aaden. It means fiery or little fire. Jamal thought that was a fine name. She stayed a few days with Cal doting on this beautiful child. Then she decided to return to the hostel. She had been happy there, and memories were all she had of Miguel. She tried one more time to see him. He was doing much better and would be released soon. He still didn't want to see Niea.

When Niea arrived at the hostel, she was greeted by Zek and Margo. They were glad to see her. But Niea was not the ball of energy she had always been. They both hated to see her this way. Margo told her of the plans they have to open a women's center that would have many features, from job training, classes in all the arts, and child daycare for working women. Niea thought that was a fine idea. They had made some coin from the guests they had cared for at the hostel and their pension from the Kalifee. They were close to their goal. Niea said she could help them, but they wanted to do it on their own. They asked Niea to join them. She thanked them graciously, but she wished to remain here.

The days passed in solitude. Although she missed her crew, the quiet and calm were just what she needed. She had her dog. There were a few guests every now and then, but for the most part, she was alone with her four-legged friend. At first the silence bothered her, but as time went on, she grew to like it. She spoke to Grandmama and Cal daily over the video chat. Aaden was growing, and he was going to be a big man. Well, his parent were not small people. Cal wanted to get pregnant again. But the doctor told her she needed to wait and give her body a rest. Cal and Jamal took precautions, but the lovemaking would continue. Cal knew she would never grow tired of sex with her exquisite man. As soon as Aaden was old enough, she would go to work training recruits. She did miss fighting, but it could wait.

One day a posted script came addressed from Central. It was from Miguel. He wanted a divorce or an annulment. Niea almost collapsed. Of course, he would want to be free of her. She had injured him inside and out. But why wouldn't he at least talk to her? She videoed Grandmama and told her the news. Niea was so sad, but she was holding her own. Grandmama asked if she should talk to Miguel. "No need" was all Niea could say. He had made up his mind. She asked Grandmama if she had seen him. She had not lately. He would every now and then come by and cook for her. Niea never responded to Miguel's post. She just couldn't. There would never be anyone else for her.

The hostel needed repairs. She really did have enough coin to do all the things that needed to be done. Miguel had kept this place going with things he had found in dumps, abandoned houses, and along the roadside. So Niea started visiting dumps and salvage yards to rummage around for parts. Eventually she got very good at finding what she needed and at fixing things. She did enjoy it. More and more guests started to come. Since the Gogatt had just plain ghosted, more and more people were traveling. This was a beautiful place. Niea had made some really nice improvements.

The medications she had to buy were very expensive. She simply could not afford them. She had already gone through her much of pension paying for them. She researched herbal medicine for psych problems and found what she needed. Then she bought some seed or plants and started a garden of Saint-John's-wort, chamomile, blessed thistle, and kava. Once the plants were ready to crop, she started weaning herself off the medications slowly. She monitored herself for symptoms and did have a few bad nights as she replaced the psych meds and slowly introduced one herbal medication at a time. Then one day she felt she had reached her goal and was satisfied at the results.

One day a video message came from Miguel. He wanted to know if she got his post. She assured him she did. Why hadn't she responded? She informed him she wasn't going to and that he could do what he wanted. He had a girlfriend now, and she wanted to get married. "So? Marry her," Niea said. She wasn't going to say anything to anyone. His girlfriend knew he was married and insisted. Niea said nothing. Then she told Miguel not to call again and hung up.

Cal, Aaden, Jay, Jamal, and Grandmama came to visit Niea's new and improved hostel. They were all impressed. Grandmama was concerned about Niea taking herself off her meds. Niea reassured her that she was doing better than ever and Grandmama could see it. This made her very happy. Then she asked about her love life. Niea laughed hard. No, she was celibate and was enjoying it. Grandmama started talking about Miguel, and Niea stopped her. That chapter of her life was closed. She didn't need to hear anything about him. This made Grandmama sad. She would love to see them get back together. She did ask Niea why she didn't want to talk about him. She told Grandmama that Miguel had a girlfriend that he wanted to get married. Grandmama guessed that him not talking to her for such a long period of time gave her the distance she needed to move on.

Miguel sat alone in the dark in his girlfriend's apartment. His contract was done with the defense ministry. He had developed a lot of ready-to-eat food for the troops. He also had trained many on all his techniques of cooking. He and his girlfriend were not doing so well. She wanted to make love with the light on, but Miguel couldn't perform that way. She looked a bit like Niea, and with the lights off or very dim he could perform very well. He did have Niea on his mind more than he could admit to himself. He had not realized it until one night in the pitch dark he yelled out her name. This infuriated the girlfriend. She wanted to throw him out. But she let him stay. He wasn't a bad fellow. She realized that without sex, there wasn't much else between them as far as she was concerned. She knew he felt the same way. She had been so enthralled with their lovemaking. She thought it was love. But as the days went by, the relationship fell apart like a house of cards. One card falling each day until she was sure he had to go. She would have to work. Miguel had supported her for all this time, and she wanted no more coin from him. She would go back to the brothel. At least there she could get paid to pretend that it was love. She couldn't do that with Miguel anymore. Miguel wasn't sure where to go. No, he was not going to his mother's. She didn't even come to his wedding. He was sure she didn't want to see him anyway. He stopped by Grandmama's to prepare supper. He had done this more often as of late. She was glad to see him but knew something was wrong. He filled her in on breaking up with his girlfriend. He wasn't sure what to do or where to go. She told him he could stay here. He thanked her so much, but he wanted to leave town. She told him how good the hostel was looking and all the work Niea had done. Niea might need some help. A successful guest house would need a good cook. She also told him there were many things he could do here at Central. He really wanted to leave town. He had plenty of coin and didn't need to work right away. He made a wonderful dinner for her. They sat and ate in quiet. Grandmama knew he wanted to see Niea. She asked if he wanted to give her a call. He shrugged his shoulders. Grandmama stood up and went to her laptop. She got Niea on the screen right away. They chatted for some time. Then Grandmama said that she had someone that wished to talk to her.

When Niea first saw Miguel, she was stunned. They were pleasant to each other. Niea told him about all the appointments she had coming into the hostel. She also was looking for a name for the place. Then he asked her if she needed any help. Yes, she did. She asked when he could be here. He said in a few days. He gave the screen back to Grandmama. They chatted for a while. She thanked Niea for giving him the job.

Grandmama looked at Miguel. He knew that look. He knew he had to at least try to get his wife back. He felt so empty without her. Miguel went shopping in the morning. He wanted to pick up some herbs, spices, and a few cooking utensils. He saw a beautiful long peach silk dress in the window of a ladies clothing store. He just had to buy it for Niea. With his old girlfriend, he would have to let her pick it out. But with Niea, he could pick out the perfect gift.

Miguel arrived at the hostel the next day. He was excited to see Niea. She was heading out the door when he got there. She was going to look at a horse just south of Gaba. He could come along if he wanted. She told him to take any room, but come the weekend, they would be full. He was hoping he would be in the bed with Niea by then.

Theodosia had cloistered herself away. She thought that she might have been doing too much with the archives. She also thought her plan might need tweaking. She had lost some support with many of the right faction. So now she would wait. She knew she needed the Gogatt to come out of hiding to help cause a distraction of chaos, destruction, and death so she could get back to her so-called work.

Niea found the horse she wanted. They also had a carriage for the horse to pull. This animal was large and black, and Niea fell in love with him. He was eight years old, the woman said, and was gentle as a kitten. She asked if she could get on him. He had pulled many a wagon or carriage, but no one had ever ridden him. Niea didn't hesitate. She went right to him. Then she kissed him on his nose and pointed to a wagon that she could get up on to mount this magnificent animal. He complied, and she straddled him no problem and took off without a saddle or bridle. The woman looked worried, but Miguel knew of Niea's special connection with animals. He leaned back on the wagon and watched the show. She looked good on that glorious huge beast. She wanted him. But she would have to barrow a trailer from someone to transport him. Miguel asked about the carriage. It was more coin than Niea had. Miguel offered to buy the carriage. She was thrilled. She could drive him home. Miguel wanted to ride with her, but someone had to drive the ground car home. She decided to name him Epona, which was the Celtic protector of horses and the goddess of fertility. There was a really beautiful lake not too far from here. It was a longer way back, but they could have a picnic. Niea pointed out they had no provisions. Miguel smiled at her and pulled out a bag he had. He had brought wine, cheese, fruit, and bread. He never seemed to forget to feed people. Niea loved that about him.

They sat under a tree with their picnic while the horse grazed. Niea had remove the bit and the carriage so he could picnic too. She kept a close eye on him. He wasn't tied. As they sat and ate, Niea asked if Miguel had seen Aaden. "Aaden who?" he asked.

"Jamal and Cal's boy," she replied.

No, he hadn't. He wanted to apologize for being so busy. But really there was no excuse. He had not wanted to see them. It would have just hurt too much.

In the morning Tulie called asking if Niea needed any help. She did. Tulie asked if she could return to the hostel and do just that. She had grown tired of management at the infirmary. They seemed more interested in meetings, politics, and chain of command. Tulie loved taking care of folks, but she had a belly full of the ill-focused ideations of management. Besides she loved working with the elderly, and they never let her go to the geriatric unit. She said she would be there in a couple of days. She had somethings she had to do first.

It was just past noon when Tulie arrived. Niea was overjoyed to see her. They hugged for the longest. She was surprised to see Miguel but glad he was here. He was such good help. Niea showed her the rooms. Tulie wanted to sleep in the bunk room. She might have to move when the guests started arriving. Niea realized that she needed an employee quarters and mentioned it to Miguel. Once he got the turkey in the smoker and the kitchen readied for the upcoming festivities, he would start on it. There was a fairly large building at the edge of the property that should do just fine. Miguel would work on getting it ready. Niea would have to decorate it. Give it the woman's touch. His decoration had been bare essentials only.

Tulie helped Miguel in the kitchen. Niea was riding her horse. She had a small pasture for him. She had planted some grass earlier that spring. He had a small shelter and access to running water. But now he needed a friend. That would come later. The coin was coming.

After all the guests had left and the place was cleaned up, Niea went to sit in the swing by the lake. Miguel asked if he could join her. She patted the seat next to her. Miguel wanted to kiss her so bad. She could see it in his face. She said, "I would like to wait if you don't mind." He nodded. She was right. Although he was married to her, he had just gotten out of a relationship. He hadn't seen her in over a year. He didn't want to bring any of those issues with him, so the passing of time would help leave all that behind. He and his ex had argued a lot. Well, she yelled at him, and he just took it. The day he would get to kiss Niea would be wonderous. He said he had a gift for her. She wanted to see it. He led her into her room where he had hung it up. She was thrilled. She had to try it on now. She pushed him out of the room and closed the door. When she was ready, she opened the door. He was standing right there. She looked so beautiful. She spun around. He was so glad he had pleased her. She kissed him on the cheek. Just for a moment or two he held her close to him. He breathed in her smell. It gave him great comfort.

Niea called Cal. Cal had rigged up a laptop so they could see each other. Aaden was growing, and Cal was in mama heaven. Cal was telling Niea she wanted to get pregnant again, but the doctor wanted her to wait. The birth was not easy for Cal. She had narrow hips. She did push her boy out, but it was hard. And it took a long time. Niea wanted to get pregnant too. Cal asked about Miguel. Niea told Cal he was here at the hostel. How did that happen? He asked for a job. Cal said, "He could help you get pregnant." Niea changed the subject and asked about Jamal. He was still working with the city planners. They were making Central bigger, more underground. So when the Gogatt came back, it would be more safe for the Kalifee people. Niea wanted to know when they could all come down. Cal said she and the boys could leave tomorrow. She would have to talk to Jamal first. She was holding her year-old son. He looked like a brown version of Cal. Cal said he acted like her too. Niea loved his bushy head of hair. It was sandy brown with blond streaks and very wavy. Niea asked for Jay. He stepped in front of the screen. He had grown a foot at least and filled out. What was

Cal feeding him? He was glad to see Niea. She told him about her big black horse. Now he had to come down to visit. He asked if he could ride. Niea said yes. She didn't have a saddle or a bridle for him, but they could hook him to the carriage that Miguel bought. Cal said, "He's trying really hard, isn't he?" Niea wanted to wait, and she might not hook up with him again. After all, she did like being celibate.

Tulie, Miguel, and Niea had been very busy for the last few weeks, and it was time for a break. Miguel was finishing up the new quarters that they would be living in. Niea was amazed he had finished it so soon. It really looked good. They sat down at the picnic table with a bottle of Miguel's finest. Even Niea had a glass. They toasted their success and relaxed. Tulie finished her wine and excused herself. She was tired, but she was happy about the way things were going. Miguel was sitting next to Niea. Suddenly she looked at him. She was mad at herself for not noticing sooner. He was depressed, sad. She could feel it. This had been going on for a long time, and she just didn't notice. She said to him in a pensive tone, "You're hurting!" He nodded. He really didn't want to talk about it. Niea insisted, "How are we going to get through this if we don't talk about it."

Miguel looked her with his golden-brown watery eyes. Niea felt his pain. It was awful. He knew she was right. He said, "You know I will never leave your side again. Wherever you go I will be right there. I don't care if we ever get into our marital bed again. I can't leave you ever again. It really hurts me that I quit talking to you. I must have been out of my head. I had no idea what I was doing with another woman. It was terrible. I would have to keep the lights off or low just to make love to her. She would get mad about everything. I wasn't allowed to cook in the apartment. She didn't like the smell.

She didn't like my hair long, so I cut it." Niea had wondered about Miguel's thick black mane of hair.

"She didn't love me and couldn't admit it. I never told her I love her because I didn't. She would get livid. Especially when I would say I couldn't love her because she didn't love me. I know I sacrificed a lot of myself so I wouldn't be alone. And you're right, I need to work through all that. I am sorry I'm so down, a real sad sack. I just feel I royally screwed things up. After I got out of the hospital, I only seem to remember the attacks and was afraid to see you. I thought it would happen again. She consoled me, and it felt okay at first. Then I got us an apartment, and things went sideways from there on out. She didn't want to work. She just wanted to shop, be pampered, and eat out. So, I paid for everything. She wanted coin when I got ready to leave. I would not give her anymore. She went haywire, throwing things, breaking furniture, smashing dishes, and more. I left with my few clothes and some of my cookware. I went straight to Grandmama's. Can you imagine? I am married to her granddaughter, and I went to her place after leaving another woman. I didn't give it another thought. I knew she would help me. She wasn't even mad at me." Miguel turned toward Niea and said, "Can I touch you? Hold your hand?" As she reached out, he took her hand and kissed it like he always did. Any contact with her just made him feel better.

Niea knew beyond a shadow of a doubt that she wanted to be in bed with her husband, but she was so afraid it might trigger her. She told Miguel of her fears. He understood. He would take that chance. They sat for what felt like forever to Miguel. He would not hurry her. Her fears were a grave possibility. He kept his eyes on her as he kissed her hand and held it to his cheek. It had been more than a year since she had a flashback. But this could be a real trigger. Was she willing to live with what could happen? She finally said, "You still won't kiss me first. Just like the first time we met. I had to make the first move." He smiled ever so tenderly. Then she straight up shocked him. She pulled up her dress. It was the one he had bought a few weeks ago. She took his hand and placed it between her legs. She was so wet. He put his fingers ever so gently on her vulva, caressing it. She got wetter. Then he held his fingers to his nose and took in the delicious smell of Niea. Then she took his fingers and placed them on her lips and in her mouth. She gently licked and sucked them. They both were breathing heavily. He dropped down on his knees, putting his head between her thighs, slowly nibbling on her labia. Finally, he stood up, picked her up, and took her to the new quarters. He had a new bed there. She was surprised. She didn't know he had done all this. There were wildflowers in several vases around the room. The candlelight was so magnificent as it flickered about the walls and ceiling. He had pictures of the crew and of their wedding on the dresser. The sheets on the bed were a pale peach. He knew this was her favorite color. Miguel was a hopeful romantic. He had hoped this was where they would end up. He laid her down on their new bed, and she opened up her legs. He put both hands on either of her warm wet entrance. He slowly began to massage her. Then he put his tongue on her and rolled her around in his mouth. She was moaning and crying out. When her body relaxed, he lowered himself into her, stroking her ever so easily. Niea went wild. She rolled him over and sat up with him in her and rocked him, changing rhythm. He never took his eyes off her. He was home.

In the morning, Cal and her boys were at the front door. Tulie answered. She gave out a shrill noise of delight. Jamal picked her up and hugged her. He gave her to Cal. Cal kissed her over and over on her cheeks. She hugged Jay. He was now taller than her and was starting to look like a man, not a scrawny little boy. Aaden was just the cutest thing she had ever seen. Cal handed him to Tulie. She wanted to know where Niea and Miguel were. Tulie told them of the quarters out back. Cal took off. Tulie was enthralled with this beautiful boy and he with her. In the back of Cal's mind, she was concerned that something might have had happened. She slipped into the room and found Niea and Miguel asleep wrapped around each other. She propped herself in the doorway. This was what she wanted to see. She stood there for a long time taking in this picture. She was smiling from ear to ear. This was a long time coming. Then she got into bed ever so quietly and snuggled up behind Niea. She whispered "baby girl" in her ear. Niea moaned, stretched, and rolled over. She still hadn't opened her eyes. She kissed Cal on the lips. Cal said, "Oh! Baby!"

Niea yelled, "Cal!" Then she gave Cal a big wet kiss. They both laughed. Miguel sat up and looked at both of them. He looked at peace. Cal knew he was. Cal said, "Hey, brother-in-law. I see things are right where they need to be!" All Miguel could do was smile. He got out of bed. He was not dressed. Cal couldn't help but check him out. She said, "I see why Niea's so happy this morning." He had a morning hard-on.

Niea said, "Put something on, Miguel! You're going to get big sis all excited."

Cal was still looking Miguel up and down. "You know, my man is a bit bigger than you, Miguel! But you are a good-looking man, even your ball sack is beautiful, dude."

No one could bother him today. He had what he had asked the Spirit for on all those lonely nights dreaming of Niea. He just stood there and glared at Cal with a sexy look on his face. Niea stood up. She was nude also. She picked up Miguel's loin cloth and threw it at him. He dodged the cloth. He was grinning from ear to ear. He looked down at his penis and shook it from side to side. He looked directly at Cal and grinned holding out hands in a gesture of come get it girl! Then he shook it back and forth again. This was enough. Niea got up and pushed him into the bathroom and threw his loincloth in behind him. Niea pulled on her dress, took Cal by the hand, and headed for the main building. She wanted to see all of them and hold her nephew.

Niea took the young lad from Tulie and whirled him around. He laughed. Niea held her nephew and kissed him as much as he would let her. He was a solid child. He was going to be tall. Didn't know if he would be thick like Jamal or long and lean like Cal. She couldn't wait. She wanted to see him every day. At lunch, they all sat down together to eat as they had always done here at the hostel. Jamal said the blessing, thanking the Great Spirit for the bounty, the beauty, the love, and their growing family. As they were eating and catching up on all that had happened, Niea asked if they would want to come here to live. Cal loved her house, but this felt more like home. Jamal was still under contract to Central, but that would be ending soon. Cal was his home. Cal had been homeschooling Jay, which she found to be easy. The lad took so much initiative in reading, looking up information, and asking a thousand questions. He did have some children he played with at Central. He was a very social child that also played very well all by himself. He wanted to move into the country. He would get to roam again, and he loved the horse. Maybe he could have one of his own. Even Aaden seemed happier here. Why not? Jamal had another week off. He and Miguel could work on a place for them to stay just on the other side of the lake. Miguel had already cleared a nice-sized plot that would do just fine. It was settled—they were returning home.

Late one evening, they were all at the picnic table enjoying supper together when a woman appeared at one of the side gates. Miguel went to see who she was and what she wanted. He was shocked. It was his old girlfriend Eda. She was upset. He had seen her in this state many times. Miguel asked, "What's wrong now, Eda?"

She looked at him with that face. Miguel knew to just keep quiet and take it. "May I sit down?"

Miguel led her to where everyone was. He looked at Niea and gave a slight shrug of his shoulders. He introduced her, not mentioning who she was to him. Niea guessed but asked how they knew each other. She said that Miguel and she had lived together about a year. Miguel said, "What is it you want?" She wanted to speak to him in private. He told her that this was his family, and they all knew everything about each other, so she might as well speak right here.

First she wanted some water. Niea got it for her. She drank the whole glass, gathered her thoughts, and said, "I'm pregnant." They all kept quiet, looking at Miguel.

Miguel sat down beside her and asked how far along she was and who was the father. She said she was about three moons along and either he was the father or one other fellow. She had started seeing him when things started falling apart between them. She had told him, but he wanted nothing to do with her anymore, and he certainly didn't want a baby. She had joined a Kalifee traveling brothel. They were in Gabba for a week or so, depending on the revenue they got from the place. It was the only work she had ever known. Miguel asked her what she wanted to do. She said she couldn't have an abortion. She would have to give it up for adoption. She wanted to know if Miguel wanted the baby. Miguel looked at Niea. She sat down on the other side of Eda, took her hand, and told her that they wanted the baby. Miguel looked at her sideways. What if it was not his? Niea said, looking directly at Miguel, "I don't care whose baby it is. We want it." Miguel had a questionable look on his face. He would take the child if it was his, but another man's baby from a woman he cared nothing for? He wasn't sure about this at all. But Niea wanted it, so be it. Cal gave one of her oops faces and came in closer. Niea had some questions and ideas. She introduced everyone and then took Eda inside. She didn't want Cal making clown faces, trying to make her laugh.

Niea said as she stood up, "Let's go inside where it is cooler." Once inside, Niea offered her a seat and more water. She sat and drank another full glass. Niea cut right to the chase. "So, how do you want to do this?" Eda said that the travelers would let her stay with them as long as she needed. They had a well-trained medic with them at all times. Niea suggested she could come here and have the baby, that Cal, her sister, and Tulie were excellent medics. Eda thought that would be hard. Surely, neither Niea nor Miguel wanted to see her every day. Besides she was making good coin and needed to continue to make coin especially for the baby. There were clients that will pay very well to lay with a pregnant woman.

Eda couldn't believe how kind and incredible Miguel's wife was. No wonder he loves her so. She had not hesitated one second in wanting this child. Eda could tell she was a woman of heart. Eda told Niea she wanted her to have this child and would do anything Niea wanted her to do. They came to an agreement that Eda would stay close. Either with the brothel, here at the hostel, or somewhere close. It would be her choice. She would give birth here at the hostel and could stay as long as she wanted. Eda said she would pay. No need, Niea assured, they all had their own coin and were making more every day. But Eda was insistent. She would pay child support until the baby was old enough to find its own way. If nothing else, the coin could be saved and given to the child on its eighteenth birthday or whenever they wanted. Niea thought that was a very good idea.

The days passed, the new house went up, Jamal finished his contract, and they moved to the hostel. Niea couldn't find a name she liked for the place. She had been through so many. Nothing seemed right so far. Eda was spending more time at the hostel. She was as big as a house. Jay was riding Epona with a soft strap around his beautiful neck. He was totally in love with this horse. Epona loved him too.

One morning, Eda's water broke. Only Miguel and Tulie were at the hostel. They both knew what to do. He had been preparing healthy drinks of roots, vegetables, and fruit for her. He also made butter to help with the stretching skin of her abdomen. Tulie had made her a long pillow to help her get comfortable on the bed and rest. She was so glad she had come here. These people were taking real good care of her and her unborn child. Her labor lasted six hours. Cal had returned without her boys. She was feeling a bit ill. Miguel had some of his juice made with beets, apples, peppermint, and ginger. It helped a lot. She was able to assist with the birthing of their latest member of the family. When he came, they all cheered. Eda was able to breastfeed without problems. Cal was looking at Miguel. He knew what she was thinking. The baby was brown like him with jet-black hair, and he had Miguel's good looks. It was his child. Once the infant finished breastfeeding, Miguel took him and rocked him to sleep. He needed a name. Tulie suggested Elijah. Miguel wanted to know what it means. Tulie told him that it meant he belonged to the Great Spirit. Miguel liked it a lot, but Niea would have last say. "That's right," Tulie told Miguel. "She is the mama that will love and care for him all his days." Miguel was holding his son, and tears of joy ran down his cheeks. He never knew love like this—the love for a child.

When Niea, Jamal, and Jay returned to the hostel, Tulie came out and told them that their latest member had arrived. They were all excited. Tulie gave the hush sign. The baby boy was asleep. They entered the sitting room. Miguel was holding his son. Niea came in close for a peek. She looked at the baby and then at Miguel. She said, "This is our son. He is as beautiful as you. How's Eda?" Miguel and Tulie filled her in on the birth. Eda was resting well. He had come a bit early but was doing well. Miguel put the boy in the crib he had made. He covered him up, kissed him on his forehead, and returned to Niea. He told her Tulie's suggestion for a name, and she liked it. Jamal said it meant one who belonged to the Great Spirit. Niea was so excited. She slept in the room with Elijah. She waited on Eda hand and foot.

It had been two moons since Elijah was born, and he was growing. Eda was thinking it was time for her to go. There was a brothel a few towns from here. Miguel offered to take her. Miguel, with Jamal's help, had rigged up a small freezing unit. They had been saving breast milk that Elijah had not consumed on a daily basis. It could stay frozen for six months. He could be on baby food then. Of course, Miguel had read up on making baby food and was well up to the task.

When Eda was packed and ready to do. Miguel put her belongings in the ground car and waited for her to say her goodbyes. She held on to Niea for a long time, telling her she was the best person she had ever known. When she could, she would be back to see their boy. Niea reminded her that he was all their boy. She got into the car and waved bye to everyone. She had had an incredible experience here.

When they arrived, the brothel was setting up for a show that evening. Miguel helped her with her bags and walked her to the entrance. She said she could get it from here. She thanked Miguel again for all he had done. Then she told him to take care of Niea and that if she ever got sick again, he won't abandon her. She then said how sorry she was for being such a self-absorbed bitch. If she had known how important cooking was to him, she wouldn't have made him take her out to eat all the time. "You never told me how you were feeling."

Miguel said that he was a hard person to know, very withdrawn. Niea was probably the only person who could feel what was going on with him and could help him. Even Grandmama had known he belonged with her. "Grandmama? The leader of the Kalifee?" Eda was dumbfounded. He told her about how Niea and he had gotten married and all that Grandmama had done for him. She looked at him. "You know who else needs Niea?" He shook his head. He didn't know where she was going with this. She looked him straight in the eyes and said,

"The Kalifee people need her." She kissed him on his cheek, turned, and walked away.

On the drive home, Miguel kept thinking about what Eda had said. She was right. Niea was definitely what they all needed. But would she ever accept the role? He really did not know. But for now, he was excited to get home and see his beautiful son.

Cal was feeling sick again. This time it was a bit more intense. It had started the day Elijah was born. She was having very irregular periods with little blood flow. She thought she might go to the infirmary at Central. Niea wanted to look her over so, she had Cal lay down. She and Tulie did a full head-to-toe exam. Tulie got urine and blood samples then tested them. She showed the results to Niea. Niea turned to Cal and said, "Sister girl, you're going to live and live large." She stood there just looking at Cal. Cal was getting nervous. Then with a huge smile, she said, "You're pregnant." Cal screamed in delight. She wanted to know how far along. Niea said, "From all the information I can gather, about two moons." The excitement reverberated throughout the hostel. Jamal was beside himself. This was what he and Cal wanted, a big family.

Niea had moved Elijah into their quarters. The smaller room was perfect for him. Once Elijah was sleeping, Niea took a shower and put on the dress Miguel had bought her. It was almost seethrough, and he loved looking at her in it. It clung to every curve moving over her like stars moving in the sky. He had lit some candles and put her favorite jasmine oil in the burner. She was delighted when she entered the room. He couldn't take his eyes off her. The last time she wore the dress was the first time he had made love to her in over a year. She lay on her stomach, pulling her dress just above her buttock. She push her buttocks up leaving her face on the pillow. She arched her back, putting her hand down between her legs. Niea always started lovemaking in a different way every time. He dropped his loin cloth, stepped in behind her, and gently put his hand on her. She was wet. Then he slowly pressed his penis against her. She could feel him rubbing up and down on her without entering her. This drove her wild. He slowly turned her on her back. She stretched one leg up, revealing her warm inviting road to nirvana. She was very flexible. She was rolling her hips, looking at him with so much desire. He rubbed the shaft of his penis all over her groin area. She had to taste it. She sat up, snuggling his penis into her face. She licked it, then rubbed it all over her face, especially her lips. She wanted to taste and smell all of it. She lay down, and he went into her very slowly. This drove her wild. He kissed her sweet neck, and he held still while Niea brought her legs closer together. She moved around so she could feel every nuance of him. He was so excited. He whispered to her, "I can't hold back anymore." Whenever he was with any other woman, he could hold off. Not now. Not with his exquisite lover, his wife.

Niea whispered to him, "Me too." They both held on to each as the whirlwind of love and sex took them over. Miguel stayed in her. They continued to hold on to each other. Miguel rolled her on to her side, and they intertwined their legs and fell asleep. They both woke and started the dance of love again. This time Miguel was able to wait longer. He sat his beauty up and rocked her ever so slowly on him. He took one of her breasts in his hand and rolled the nipple around between his fingers. Niea was calling out. Then she remember the baby and muffled her groans of pleasure in his neck. He made sure she reached her pleasure several times before he let go in her. They both tumbled over into the bed and fell asleep.

Eda told anyone at the brothel who wanted to listen about her incredible experience she had with the people at the hostel. She spoke highly of Niea, the granddaughter of the Califia. She felt so good about where her son was. The Spirit had smiled on her and her baby. She was glad she got to apologize to Miguel. She was awful to him. He was a warm, gentle soul who deserved a woman like Niea. Eda had learned a lot from Miguel and had started using the techniques she had learned from him. It had started coming back to her once she let go of her anger and her angst. Apologizing was definitely good medicine. Within a few moons, she was declared an exalted queen. She now could choose to perform or not. She could also choose whom she had relations with.

The price was high, and she would send a healthy amount of coin to Niea every moon. Niea saved every bit of it for Elijah.

A message came in from Central. A small village just south of Central had been attacked. There were no fatalities. All of their provisions were taken or burned. This was a change. Not at all like the Gogatt. No one was raped either.

A recorded video message had come in from Grandmama. She was worried that the Gogatt were coming their way. Central had gone underground. The communication system was not quite finished. They were working on it. So, they should not be alarmed if they can't message them from down under. That was the end of the message. Niea turned and saw they were all here looking at her. Cal was holding Elijah. She was starting to show. This pregnancy was turning out to be very different from the first. Cal just knew this was a girl. She wanted to name her Shona. She wanted to know if Jamal like it. He did. He thought it was the name of a flower.

Grandmama had gone back to her quarters. She needed to check the archives. She could live a year or so on the provisions she had stored there. Her laptop was working just fine. She went to work. There was a knock at her door. It was Zane, one of the techs.

She had known him a long time. He was concerned, looking to make sure Grandmama was okay. He informed her that most of the people were underground. She invited him in and offered him something to eat and drink. He admitted he was hungry, but he didn't want to take any of her supplies. She let him know that she had more than enough, and by the way, wasn't he one of her grandchildren just like all the Kalifee people? He ate and drank some wine. She asked him if he could help her. Of course, he would certainly try. He saw some pictures laying on a table. He asked if he could see them. She nodded with an enormous smile. She was so proud of her growing family. He was particularly taken with Cal and Jamal's boy, Aaden. He said, "My word, he looks like Cal, except for his caramel silky-looking skin. Aaden's eyes were a deep blue like Cal's, and what a head of hair— sandy brown with streaks of blond. He asked about Jay. Grandmama told him how he had found Cal and more than likely saved her life.

They talked for some time. He had had two daughter. Fighters in the Kalifee. They both had been killed by the Gogatt. They were fine women, and he missed them terribly. Grandmama wanted to know their names. The oldest was Kendra and Malia the younger. He had Malia's son, Mac. He was growing into a fine young man. Kendra had a girlfriend. They had adopted a girl named Tyra. Both of them lived with him. They were underground with all the other children. Zane asked if he could look at her system in a different way, especially the encrypted areas. Of course, he could. Grandmama needed help. He worked all day except to take a lunch break and call his grandkids. He found some very interesting stuff. Someone was removing information on anything from projectile weapons to mitochondria DNA, which was passed only through the female. Projectiles were highly forbidden. Why there were plans still in the system was twisted to him. Theodosia had something to do with that also. Whoever they were had been using Grandmama's pass codes. But the footprint was all wrong. With a closer look, it was traced to an account set up by Theodosia. There was the connection Grandmama was looking for. But Grandmama wanted more evidence. If she could catch that traitor in the act, it would be the end of her betrayal, and hallelujah! The Kalifees don't tolerated traitors.

They sat going through all that Theodosia had accessed. It was getting late. Zane called his children. They were sleeping now, so he could stay the night if she didn't mind. No, she didn't mind. She asked him to please stay. They sat for a while talking about their children and grandchildren. She offered him some more wine. He shook his head no. He was not much of a drinker. He reached over her and poured her another glass. He placed the bottle back to where it was. Now he was very close to her. He looked her in the eyes and said, "You know, I am extremely attracted to you." Grandmama was thrown. She did not see that coming. He can be hard to read, she told herself. She had not been with a man in many years. He saw she was nervous. He apologized and said maybe he needed to go. She looked at him with a curious smile.

Then she pulled the clip out of her hair and shook out her hair. She had long straight black hair. It was beautiful like Niea's. He loved it. She did want him to stay. But he was certainly too young for her. He didn't think so. He was sixty, and he was sure she was really close to the same age. Turned out she was a year younger than him. He asked her what her given name was. Grandmama blushed. He smiled. He was sure no one had seen this side of her in some time.

She looked at him with a wryly whimsical smile and said, "Ladia."

He knew many meanings for her beautiful name. But the one that stood out was queen. And she was certainly a queen in so many ways. She had been an exalted queen and still was but in not practice. But most importantly she was the queen of the Kalifee, the Califia, beloved by all. She laughed. Everyone but Theodosia. He asked if he could help her with taking down this awful woman. She gave a hardy nod. She stood up and dropped her kimono. She always wore one as an outer garment. She had on a single suit. Her figure was not that of an older woman. Her curves mesmerized him. She always had on a kimono. She stretched her back and then sat back down close to him. Then she said, "I would love to do this, but maybe you have a wife somewhere."

He took her hand and kissed it. "She died years ago, and there has been no one that interests me but you."

Ladia tilted her head and said, "I am not interested in a onenight stand. Maybe this is a bit forward, but I am only interested in love."

He stood up and held his hand out for her. She took it and stood up and stepped dangerously close to him. His breath quickened, and he put both arms around her. He pulled a small controller out of his pocket and pressed a button, and a song came on. It was an old tune that Ladia loved—"Sugar Man." He said, "Will you dance with me?" She started to rock slowly in his arms. He kissed her neck slowly, going to where her single suit was zipped. She reached up and very slowly pulled the zipper down a little. He looked down at her breasts, then he put his hand on the curve of her back. She took that hand and moved down onto her buttock. She guided him to explore her well-formed derriere and squeeze it. He did just that, and Ladia moaned. It was one of her favorite things for a well-chosen man to do to her. She swayed on his body, and he squeezed both buttocks. She started to moan and shake ever so lightly. He thought, *Oh my god. She is getting off.* This drove him wild. She was so responsive. His wife was never like this. Then he kissed her so passionately that she swooned and fell back on the couch. He stood there watching her put her arms over her head and open her legs. He kneeled down in front of her rubbing/massaging her body over her single suit. He looked at her beautiful pale-blue eyes. They enthralled him. This was happening. He had dreamed of this moment for years. He had wanted her for such a long time. No, Ladia had never thought of him in this way. Truth be known, she had not had sex with any man since her husband was killed. She had not even considered having a sexual partner. She had put all her energy, sexual too, into her work and her girls. But now she was ready for love, and so was he. He had no other since his wife died. She had not been that sexual, but he did love her in a way.

Ladia stood up and said, "Are you going to help me out of this suit?" He stood up, took the zipper in his mouth, and ever so slowly put it down just above her groin, never taking his eyes off her. He was on his knees again. He could live the rest of his life right here with his face buried in her mound of Venus. He blew his hot breath into her groin area. She almost squealed. She freed her shoulders and arms from the suit. Her breasts were small but beautifully shaped, and now they had been revealed. He was sitting back on his heels watching her. She wiggled out of her suit, rolling her body in a rhythmic way to the music he had put on. This song was "Talk it Over in Bed." She looked down at him and lifted her eyebrows and looked toward her bedroom. He stood up and picked her up. He was a strong older man, rugged-looking, and that excited Ladia. He was all man, and he was certainly strong enough to be her man. He sat her slowly onto the bed and stood there looking down at her. He was in love. This expression was not lost on her. She stared back at him. She felt it too.

He stepped back and started to undress. Removing his clothing in a purposeful, subtle ways that surprised her. There was so much more to this man than she ever saw. Surely he had kept this well tucked away. Ladia would have surely seen it otherwise. She was smiling from ear to ear as he moved up on her. He wanted to feel her body pressed against him. He pulled her to her feet and pulled her up on him. He was rock-hard. Ladia had to touch it, kiss it, suckle it, lick it, but first she rubbed her body all over it. He picked her up and lay her down on the bed. He kneed before her and put his mouth on her wetness. She was arching her back and moaning. He put his tongue all the way in her. He had a very long thick tongue. She had never felt something like that before. She came all over his tongue. He just couldn't help but keep comparing this to the subaverage sex he was used to having occasionally. Once again he thought about his wife never letting him go down on her. He was so turned on, and they hadn't even gotten started good. If Ladia would have him, he was hers forever.

He just had to say something to her. "Ladia, if I die tomorrow, I will be complete, satisfied, and grateful."

She pulled him up on her with her legs wide open. He was enjoying the taste of her so much. She wanted him inside of her. She love the depth he had gone in her with his tongue. She just had to see what he could do with his beautifully large hard cock. This man had talent. She wanted all of it. He could see the burn in her. He entered slowly, moving in so he could feel all of her. Oh god, she was incredible. He had dreamed of this so often, but he had no idea it would be anything like this. He had been a starving man and never knew it. He came so hard he passed out. Lidia was worried. He was only out for a few moments. When he came to, he grabbed her and rolled around in bed with her laughing and crying at the same time. They enjoyed two more times and fell asleep wrapped around each other.

In the a.m., he kissed her neck. He knew this would wake her up. She rolled over and said, "I thought I was dreaming all this."

He smiled. "I've been dreaming about this for years, but my dreams were nothing like last night." He rolled over, pulled her on top of him, and squeezed her buttocks. She got very wet straddling him. He sat up putting both hands on her beautifully foamed buttock, entering her slowly. She opened her legs very wide. He pushed himself up against the headboard holding on to her buttocks, keeping his cock deep in her. She screamed. With her legs that wide open, he could move her girl parts in many ways. She held very still while he did this. She whispered to him, "Do you mind me being still?"

He looked down at her warm, wet self, taking all of him deep into her, and said, "There is nothing still about you." He began massaging the sides of her, rolling her warm wet flesh all over his cock. She was going insane. Somehow he stood up, keeping himself deep within her. She wrapped her legs around his waist and started rolling her hips and her wet self on his strong hard abdomen. He squeezed her buttocks firmly, which made her gasp in delight. Then he sat her on the high dresser and made even more passionate love to her than he had done last night. Ladia couldn't believe this. Never had she known sex like this, and she had known some incredible lovers. Yes, she would keep him if he would have her.

They got some breakfast. He was going to have to work down under today. He would check on the children and then get to work. She said she had to be down under later in the afternoon. He had a small place down there; it was a modest accommodation. Would she have supper with him? She could meet his grandchildren. They could all eat together. It made her a bit nervous, but she wanted to know everything about him.

Ladia had some ideas she wanted to run by Zane. She wanted to bug Theodosia. She would have to come out of hiding, of course. When she told him about it, he liked the idea. They would have to be clever where they placed them. The range could be a bit troublesome, but he thought he had an idea for a booster.

There were people all around working, scurrying about down under. Everyone spoke to the grand lady. After they discussed her ideas, he took her by the arm and walked with her to his place. He had a meal prepared for them. His kids wanted to go with the other children to a picnic. He and Ladia could join them later. He escorted her to his place down under. He had another place near hers. She never knew until now that he had always made sure he was close to her. She never questioned that he was the main tech that always came to her place to assist her. She got where she would ask for him because he was so good at his job and with the wonderful company.

They ate. It was good. He had some wine for her. He also had some vaping THC, if she wanted it. She did love its effect and asked if they could try that later. He looked at her with longing and disbelief. He wanted to touch her, but they both knew if they started touching, nothing else would happen except hot, romantic love. Yesterday he had made up his mind to stay with her that night. When she pulled that comb out of her hair, he knew it was on. That was such a sexy move. He was grateful. They finished up their food. He had to run. He grabbed her and kissed her. "My place or yours?" Hers. He would need to stay up top for a while. So, move in. If they don't get any work done, she said she would take saltpeter.

The Gogatt had hit Gabba hard. Zek and Margo showed up at the hostel with some of the women from the center. They hoped that would be okay. There were several women, children, and men taken. They weren't killing or raping as far as the ladies could tell. They were taking supplies and slaves. There was a good possibility they were coming here. Niea messaged Grandmama and waited. She knew the system was being worked on.

Grandmama saw the message from Niea, but she couldn't reply. Zane should be here soon. Hopefully he would get it to work. He was a marvel with electronics, computers, and now her heart. She was glad she had him to think about. It kept her from worrying about Niea and her team so much. Niea didn't need to go into battle anymore. She had become fragile as far as Grandmama was concerned.

Zane worked until late. When he knocked on Ladia's door, she was sleeping on the couch. He apologized deeply. Ladia was just glad to see him. He got her communicator to work. The video portion would have to wait. She and Niea got several messages back and forth. Most of Central was down under. That was where Niea and her crew were at the hostel. Gabba had been hit hard, and there were already some refugees here. They had plenty of supplies and water. Jamal had even made a place for Epona. She couldn't find her dog. But she knew he knew what to do. All they could do now was wait. Zane said he needed a shower. Ladia had a hot tub. They could both get in. He was already hard. He was still whirling from yesterday and this a.m. He had the love of his life, and he would love her until the day he left this world. He had brought the vaping THC. Ladia loved it. He enjoyed watching her get high. Hell, he enjoyed watching her sleep, walk, talk—you name it.

They lay in her bed. She told him that this was his bed too. There had been no one else in this bed but her until yesterday. He was lying at her feet. He rolled her onto her belly and started with her toes, sucking, licking them. He worked his way up her leg and down the other. Then he finally landed on the wet cave of heaven. He turned her over, and slowly he slipped his generous long thick tongue up in her. She must have climaxed on him two maybe three times. She was screaming. He had never heard a woman go into that much ecstasy. She went limp. He crawled up to her lips and brushed his lips slowly on hers. He guided her onto him. She mounted him, looking down at him in wonder. He was pure magic. He reached around to her buttocks. He knew how sensitive she was there. He squeezed and pulled her buttock. He was stretching her in ways she never knew. Then he would thrust into her just the way she like it. How does he know to do all these things? Once again she went into hyperdrive. She called out his name. That was a first for him. He never knew he could do all this especially for a woman of her experience. It seemed like he was the exalted queen. This was what love had done for him. In the morning he informed her he was going to have to stay down under for a few days. He wanted her to come with him. She really needed to get to work. She had started a dossier on Theodosia. As soon as she could be located, Ladia wanted several bugs to be planted. He got down on his knees and begged her to come down under with him. She tried to get him to stand up. He wouldn't. Then he said, "Marry me, Ladia. Oh, beautiful queen." She said yes, but they would wait until Central was back to regular function. She wanted a big wedding. He did also. He reached into his pocket and pulled out a rose-gold ring. It was simple and very beautiful. She couldn't believe it.

Ladia wrapped her hands around his face and said, "How long have you had this ring?"

He seemed embarrassed. He mumbled, "Years." Then he added, "I will miss you so bad if you aren't with me especially at night." She was still dumbfounded. This man had been in love with her for years, and he was right down the hall.

She got him to stand up and asked, "what took you so long?"

He didn't think she liked him that way. But he asked her to let him stay, and she said he could. So, he went for it. Then she let down her hair. He knew beyond a shadow of a doubt it was on.

Ladia didn't see Zane for days. It made both of them lonely. He spent his off time with his grandkids, and Ladia focused on the dossier and her plans for the traitor. The communication system was down completely. Central was locked down. They had to be sure it was an internal problem and not a Gogatt attack. Ladia couldn't talk to anyone, to Niea, or Zane. She focused on her work. She hadn't changed her sheets. She love to smell them with all their smells on them, especially Zane. He was so masculine and helpful. She did spend time running over in her mind all their interactions. She doesn't usually miss much. Especially something as strong as what Zane was feeling. She didn't understand. She knew nothing of what he was feeling until he told her that he was attracted to her. She also kept running their lovemaking over in her mind. She couldn't wait to see him again. She wanted to know more about this love he had cared for her all these years.

The Gogatt had disappeared with women, children, men, and supplies. There were very few bodies, and they had about ten captives as far as anyone could tell. They had taken grain, sugar, and yeast. It looked like they were going to cook some liquor? Who knew what these monsters were up to. They definitely had some strong outside influences. These actions were so unlike them. They usually plunder, burn, destroy, and rape.

It was late one night, almost early in the morning, when Ladia heard a knock at her door. Usually she wouldn't open it that time of the night, but she had forgotten to give Zane a pass card. She opened the door with a beautiful kimono on with nothing else under it. She saw Theodosia and Vahar. She tried to shut the door, then a dart hit her neck and she was drugged, conscious but paralyzed. That was how Theodosia wanted her. She wanted her to hear everything she had to say. First they ransacked her apartment. Luckily Ladia never left anything out of place. She and her girls were meticulous, especially with their work. Ladia had locked all her papers away. She always did. They did not find her lock box. They found her ring that Zane gave her and threw it in the garbage. They teased her terribly about being nude under her kimono. She must be waiting for a man. It was just too bad about Gabba. Theodosia said that the Gogatt were furious about the manufacturing area being blown by Niea. They will finish that little bitch off soon. That was their next stop. Theodosia was going to kill her and make it look like suicide. Theodosia wanted to drag it out. But Vahar wanted her to just get it done so they could be on their way. First Theodosia would torture Grandmama, as she liked to be called. She took out a very sharp knife and ran it down Ladia's abdomen, making a long bloody cut. Vahar said to at least tie her up. But that wouldn't look like suicide. What was she doing? Vahar got nervous. Theodosia told her to just go. She cut Ladia across the chest this time. Vahar was panicking. "What the ef are you doing?" Vahar said. "I'm leaving." She went to the door. It wouldn't open. Theodosia got up and pulled out her master door card, but it didn't work either. Vahar yelled, "What have you done to the system? You fool!"

Theodosia turned to Ladia. "Open this door and I won't stab you through the heart." Ladia couldn't move or talk.

Vahar yelled, "You drugged her, and she can't talk. Are you really that stupid?"

Theodosia turned to Vahar. "Don't tell me a damn thing, you fat-ass whore. I'll kill you too." She turned and walked slowly toward Vahar. She looked mad. Why had she agreed to this? She wanted Niea, not the

Califia. Vahar deflected the old woman, went to the balcony, opened the sliding door, and yelled. Theodosia hit her from behind with the handle of the knife she had. Vahar hit the floor with a thud. She was out cold.

Theodosia tried a device she had that could read and unlock codes. It did not work. Someone must be blocking the signal. There had to be another way out. She went to the service door. It would not open either. She was trapped. She put the knife in Vahar's hand and waited by the door.

Zane flung the door open and ran to Ladia. She was alive. Oh god, he could breathe again. Then Theodosia hit him in the back of the head, and he was out. She ran. He had signaled the safety office when he found the tampering going on at Ladia's place. Soon two officers arrived. They found Vahar with a head wound. Zane was coming to. He would not leave her. He was worried about Ladia. One of them was a medic. He wanted to check Zane first, but Zane got up and took his love to her bed. He pointed to Vahar as he picked up his woman. So they started an assessment on her. He cleaned Ladia up and put ointment on her cuts. Thank the Spirit she was not injured bad. She was starting to come out of it. She saw his concerned face and started to cry. He held her face and kissed away her tears. The medic came into the room. He wished to transport Grandmama and the other woman who was unconscious to the infirmary. Zane agreed then put her kimono on and carried her to the bus. He rode holding her and did not leave her side. That was it; he was never going to bed without her again. She would have an armed guard at all times, especially when he could not be with her. He was not going to lose the only woman that he truly loved.

The problem with the communication system was Theodosia. If Zane had not put that sniffer on Grandmama's quarters, she would be dead. Some people at Central were still wondering why Theodosia would do such a thing. The queen Vahar had very little to say. This was now her second offense. She had not actually killed anyone, but two attempts and she got life. It would be a very short trial. The reason she got out before was Theodosia had a lot of influence, and she had fixed the record so Vahar was let off easy. Now that Theodosia had tried to kill the Califia, she would be considered armed and dangerous. She was now public enemy number one. How Theodosia was able to tamper with the computer system was a mystery that Zane was going to unravel.

The infirmary kept Grandmama for five days. Her blood had to be clear of the substance before discharge. Zane was there every minute they didn't have him working. He would sit and do anything she wanted. He couldn't wait to be in bed with her again. They played cards, watched videos, and talked about their children. His dead daughter Kendra's girlfriend Bet had come in with battle wounds. She was ordered to stay at Central. She didn't see her wounds as that bad. She knew Zane had his hands full. So she was now staying in the down under with the children. Her wounds were not so bad that she couldn't take care of her daughter and her nephew. She loved Zane. He was just the best to all of them. He had always treated her like a daughter. He wanted to adopt her. That sounded funny to Bet. Now he was freed up a lot. He told her of his involvement with the Califia. She was impressed. What a high-status woman he had. She could tell he was so in love with her. This made her very happy. She could help Zane out and be with the kids. Not a bad outcome at this turn.

The day came for him to take Ladia home. They were so excited. He had moved some of his personal things into her apartment. He had the whole place rigged for her safety. He carried her in and put her on the couch. He handed her a controller that would be tuned on to her voice. It controlled everything here. She had a direct line to the safety office and many more features he would show her later. Right now, he would fix her supper. She was hungry. He wanted to feed her. She assured him she could pick up her own spoon and eat. They would play a food sex game later. She still felt a bit off. He didn't mean it like that. She knew. He sat next to her on the couch, and they watched an old movie he found.

Ladia almost forgot; she needed to talk with Niea. She was still out of sorts. The medic said the head fogginess could take a few weeks to wear off. Zane sat down next to her with the controller and showed her how to activate her direct line to the hostel. She was thrilled. She got Miguel on the line, and then he showed her how to switch to video. Miguel saw Zane first and said, "What a big man you are, Grandmama." Zane laughed and introduced himself as Ladia's special friend. She chided him. Didn't he ask her to marry him? He felt foolish. He didn't know how much she wanted to tell her family. "They are family. You tell them everything. They are going to know it anyway." They all had a good laugh.

The away team had been in their down under for a week. Nothing had happened yet. There had been no reports from any of the scouts of the area. Miguel thought maybe he and Jamal should take a trip to the hole that they blew. He still had the map of the caves in that area. Grandmama thought that was a good idea. Grandmama started to cough. Zane called her name, asking if she needed some water. Miguel had never heard her name called. He loved that name. It was as beautiful as she was. Miguel could see she had some excellent company. Zane truly loved her. Miguel couldn't help but smile. He thought about their family. Only Tulie and Keddie didn't have anyone. There was Zek and Margo, Cal and Jamal, he and Niea, and Ladia and Zane. He had an idea. He was going to see Keddie as soon as he could. Finally, Niea came in holding their son. He was growing, and he looked like Miguel. The bone structure of his face was a bit different, but that was his boy. Ladia was so happy to see him, and she couldn't wait to hold him. Cal stepped in front of the monitor and showed off her baby bump. She knew it was a girl. She told Grandmama she wanted another as soon as she was told it was safe. Aaden came running in with Jay and Jamal right behind them followed by Margo and Zek. They all waved a warm hello. He was loving these introduction to his fiancée's family. He already felt like he was a part of this growing conglomerate. He only hoped they all could stay alive. He missed his two daughters so bad. At least he had Bet and his two grands. He thanked the Great Spirit for all three of them and his bride-to-be.

Once the call had ended, Ladia did what she always did—cried. Now there would be someone who witnessed this. She always tried to keep any sadness away from her girls, their family, and her people. Zane held her for a long time until she sat up and wiped off the wetness from her face. He looked at her. He even loved her more. He didn't think that was possible. She had a beautiful tender heart and the emotional strength of a fighting lion. What a woman, and she was his. He started to cry. She looked at him. He assured her it was tears of joy.

Then when she could completely compose herself, she turned and looked at him. It was time to ask those questions she had. He got nervous. What was she thinking? He kept trying to stare at the monitor, but she was looking at him so intently. He turned the video off. He turned around to face her and said, "What is it, my love?"

Then she remember her ring. He had found it and figured out what happened. He had her ring. He would put it on her finger the day they were married. She was relieved. But she still wanted to ask him about how long he had been pining for her. He had been smitten with her for over seven years. When he left the infantry due to injury, he was home every night. His late wife liked it better when he was away most of the time. She could handle sex once and a while, but she did not want to have it anywhere near the level that he desired it. They slept in separate bedrooms. Once the girls were grown, she asked him to move out. She only needed him to help raise them. He was a much better parent than she was. So he moved to Central. They had a real nice tech job for him there. That was when he saw her. She was in an apartment just down the hall from him. He became her main tech. His boss liked that. He knew she would be safe if Zane was around. He was famous for his fighting skills. He fell for her really quick, and he knew there was no need to look for another. One day one of his daughters called. His estranged wife had committed suicide—overdose. That had been five years ago. Then both of the daughters were killed within six moons of each other. That sounded so sad to her. It made her cry all over again.

Zane was upset that he had made her cry. He apologized over and over again. Once she could talk, she stopped him. Crying was how she got the sadness out of her. He had noticed that about her. She was a very positive person, always encouraging people. She took his hand, kissed the palm, and laid his hand over her heart, holding it there until she was finished. Then she looked him in the eyes and said, "Life is the lesson. The earth is the schoolhouse. Everything that happens is a lesson. What we need in life shows up when we take our power. Just like you did when you asked to stay over and were real direct in the next sentence when you told me how you were feeling. Emotional honesty is what my Niea is having trouble with." She now knew why she had not been able to read him. He had hidden his feelings so he would not lose her. He also had lived with a woman that demanded emotional distance. No, this was not cash-register honesty. It was being honest with yourself about one's emotions. Owning up to feeling vulnerable and weak. The ego rides high, doing too much for others to avoid the self and how the self feels. She was going to have to pen Niea down one day on the feelings she has tucked away inside her. But for now, she had a long way to go. She would encourage Niea not to fight anymore until she had faced herself. She was so glad she had that baby. Sweet little Elijah would keep her home. It was so interesting Cal had faced her darkness and had truly learned that her strength came from the inside, not a bottle. Niea was still wrapped up in being a strong leader, not admitting to the weakness within, and helping others will help her feel strong and not face her internal turmoil. It would just go away if she never was weak. What is denied within the human spirit will come to be the master.

Ladia had fallen asleep in Zane's arms. She was still worn out from her ordeal. He kissed her forehead and told her he was putting her to bed. She moaned softly as he carried her. Her moans were so intoxicating to him. He got hard hearing her. He laid her down, went and did his evening hygiene, and returned. She had removed her gown and was fast asleep in the nude. He realized that he had been with her only a few nights in bed, and of course she slept in the nude. He looked down at her. Everything about her was so sexy. He had instinctually known they had the same appetite for sex and so many other things.

Niea called Grandmama in the am. Zane answered. She was taking a long hot bath. Niea had met Zane before, and she understood that Grandmama was alive because of him. He had put sniffers on her system that had worked so well. She thanked him profusely. He smiled his warm broad smile saying that she was the love of his life. It was so odd to hear about her Grandmama with a man. She knew she was an exalted queen, but she had never seen her with a sexual partner. It was good though. Niea could feel his sincerity and knew he was an authentic person. His only agenda was he loved her with all he had. They talked about her new son. He couldn't wait to see him. He was excited for Cal too. He said that babies are good luck. She liked that. She was a real good mama. He could tell. Niea knew she had a good teacher in Cal. She knew how to talk to children, be their parent, and be their friend. That was tricky. Niea paid attention. Ladia came out in one of her kimonos, listening and watching all that they had to say. When he saw her, he said good night to Niea and her crew. Then he gave the screen to Ladia and they chatted for a while. Then Niea need to go feed her boy. She threw Grandmama a kiss and told her she loved her. She also said that Grandmama had found herself one hell of a man. Grandmama said she loved them all and to please call first thing in the a.m.

No Gogatt had been seen.

Ladia went into the bedroom. Zane was showering. She lay down in bed and waited for him. When he came into the bedroom, she was asleep. He tiptoed to the bed and lay down quietly. He turned away from her so she could sleep. Then she scared him. In a husky voice, she said, "You're going to leave me like this?" He jumped, turning around, and saw her in a provocative pose.

He said, "I thought you were asleep." She motioned for him to come to her. He was already hard. He moved in close, and she took one of his hands and placed it on her breasts. Then she raised up for him to suckle her. He gave generously to every part of her breasts then he moved down to the delight of her wet self. It felt like he had not had her in weeks. He placed his tongue lightly on her gently, fondling that lovely tiny G-spot with the tip of his tongue. She was amazed. She had wanted that glorious tongue deep in her, but this was making her tingle all over. When he had her on the verge of orgasm, he pushed his tongue deep into her, and she went wild. He held his tongue deep in her, and she came again. He wanted to be in her so bad, but he was going to take his time. He knew his woman had a passion for love that rivaled his. She opened her legs wide for him. He propped up her hips with a pillow and began to massage the side of her, not touching the wet place driving her wild with passion and desire. He was able to rub her vulva with just the end of his penis. He was driving her crazy and making her so hot. Then just when she felt she couldn't take the tease anymore, he plunged deep into her, and she screamed with all she had. He leaned in and kissed her with that fabulous tongue of his. She sucked on it as he stroke her into orgasm, and he shared that moment with her. His body went limp on top of her. She held on to his buttocks and whispered, "Stay in me." For some reason, he was still hard. Maybe because he had not been with his woman in so long. People like the two of them could have sex every day, several times a day. Why couldn't he just stay in her, and in a few they could have some more of their wild love again. He held on to her and rolled the two of them on their sides, and he stayed in her. He loved this. He stayed in her, and maybe they had a nap. He didn't know. He was so swept up in passion and love with this woman. A length of time went by, and she rolled on over on top of him and began to slowly ride him sitting straight up. She rocked evenly like the ocean on a gentle night. She continued to ride even and slow until he went wild. He pushed himself deep in her, putting his hand where he could feel all her parts. Then he sat up holding onto her. He got to the end of the bed and stood up. He sat her on the same dresser and began to move side to side. He wanted to feel all of her. He reached farther around her backside until he was slightly stretching her girl place with his fingers. She had arched her back so he could reach her better. That did it; they clung to each other. The powerful force of both of them coming at the same time was almost too much. He held on to her as she did to him, and it was explosive magic. They both were out of breath. He could no longer stay in her, but he picked her up and turned toward their bed, almost falling into it. They both were asleep within a few minutes. It was some deep, wonderful sleep.

Miguel discussed with Niea about going back to the hole they had blown. She tightened. Then she said it was a good idea and she would go with him. He was thinking Jamal would go with him. She sat there saying nothing. She said in low tone, "You don't want me to go." He decided to be honest with her. Yes, he thought it would trigger her. She knew he was right. She remained silent and left the room. He didn't follow. She hated feeling like this. She was going. She called Grandmama and told her that she was going with them.

Grandmama was clearly upset with her. "This is a bad idea. That baby boy needs you."

That slowed her roll. This confused, even angered, Niea. She stayed quiet for the rest of the day. Miguel and Grandmama spoke. She wanted to know if Niea was within earshot. Miguel assured her she was not. She encouraged him to just leave her alone, and he did. They discussed her emotional state and agreed Niea had some inside work to do.

It had been a few weeks now, and there was no sign of the Gogatt. They had straight up ghosted. Central had sent relief forces to Gabba. Things were getting back to normal. Miguel and Jamal had built down under areas under both their dwellings. They worked on tunnels to connect them both. Zek and Margo went back to their center. It was now for anyone left homeless, grieving a loved one, or any issue that could arise. They had several Kali workers there helping with the relief, distribution of food, clean water, and clothing. Central had thought of everything.

Jamal and Miguel headed out in the a.m. They would not enter the cave. It was still considered dangerous, poisonous. It was just after daybreak when they reached the high ridge. Miguel pulled out a spyglass. There was some movement down there, but it turned out to be wild pigs. They decided to split up and meet at the designated area. Miguel would take the low area and Jamal would remain on the high ground. They would use birdcalls that had been assigned a certain meaning. A couple of hours had gone by and nothing. Miguel didn't want to give up yet. Jamal wanted to go back. Miguel would spend the night and continue to scout out the area. He wanted to go in that cave so bad.

Central had come out from the down under. Things were getting back to normal. Zane had been working most of the day. Ladia had been meeting with the relief program manager, funds appropriation committee, and so on. It had been a very busy day. When she got home, Zane had drawn her a bath and made her favorite cocktail. She sat in the tub and chilled. They had supper and were now sitting on the couch making out. He loved to just kiss her and touch her all over. A video message came in. It was Niea. She was beside herself. Miguel was missing. Ladia sat and waited for her to settle down and give her all the details. Yes, she knew Miguel went to hole east of the hostel. Yes, they had talked about it. Niea said, "Why did you tell him to go there?" Ladia assured her it was his idea. Niea was furious. "Why didn't you stop him?" This went on for a few more moments.

Ladia had had enough. "Will you calm yourself?" This made Niea feel worse. Niea started pacing. She was in a whirlwind of emotions. She wanted to blame Grandmama. She wanted to blame someone, Jamal, anyone. She was losing it and losing it fast. She had caught the attention of Cal and the rest of the crew. She was yelling and stomping about. The baby was crying. Aaden started crying. Jay was standing there staring at her. He was thinking she was gonna get sick again. Ladia barked out a command, "Stand down, Commander. Now!" Niea stopped in front of the screen. She was breathing heavily. Her pupils looked black. Her eyes were red from crying. She was triggered and close to the edge. Ladia used her command voice again. "You are out of control. If you can't get control of yourself, I will have a liner there in no time to pick you up, and you'll go directly to the infirmary. You understand?" Niea dropped her head and put her hand over her face. Ladia continued in that tone, "You understand, soldier?" Niea still didn't answer. Ladia barked again, "You understand?" Finally, Niea answered her with a nod. But she wasn't under control. She was a mess. Ladia's voice returned to being Grandmama. "You need to come here before something happens. You understand?" Niea was contrite. She had way too many ifs in her head.

Niea dropped her arms to her side, stood up straight, and said, "Yes, Califia."

Ladia said, "I am sending scouts there now, and I am putting out feelers everywhere. Now, are you leaving the baby with the crew or bringing him with you? He needs you. He needs his mother."

Niea said, "I am bringing him with me."

Niea was picked up within the hour. Cal had gotten little Elijah to settle down. Niea felt awful. She was losing control. Her emotion were ruling her, and she knew it. This made her dangerous to everyone.

When she arrived, it was way dark, and she was starting to see things. One of the medics was holding the beautiful baby boy so Niea could see him. She was taken straight to the infirmary. Ladia and Zane met her there. She had little to say to anyone. Ladia knew she was reeling inside, and she was maintaining fairly well at this moment. Zane took the baby to their apartment. Cal had packed his bag, and he had everything he needed. Ladia stayed at the infirmary until Niea was sedated and put to bed. The restraints were just outside her door. These people were very acquainted with her.

When Ladia arrived home, she was greeted by a beautiful picture. Zane was holding the baby, softly singing to him. He looked up at her and asked about Niea. She was sedated and hopefully would sleep through the night. Zane had made Elijah a place to sleep with a baby monitor he had rigged up. He love babies, children, and Ladia. He was still having a hard time believing where he was. Had he died and gone to heaven? Here he was holding this sweet innocent baby that was now his great grandchild, and soon he would be married to the Califia of the Kalifee. He would stay home and care for Elijah. That would delight him. He could do a lot of his work from here. Yes, this was his home, being with Ladia.

A week had gone by. Niea was not progressing. She had become very quiet, sullen, and continued to refuse any medication. She had not let anyone know she was hallucinating. She had not been violent. Actually, the opposite was true. She had been cooperative with whatever was asked of her.

Scouts were sent out to the area that had been destroyed by Niea and her team. They found tracks into one of the caves, a few clicks south of the huge hole. There was evidence of a scuffle and someone being dragged away. A lot of blood was found and tested. The DNA was not something they had on file. Miguel's blood was found in small traces. There was a good chance he was alive. He had put up one hell of a fight. The leader of the scout team messaged Central for permission to enter the caves. They would have to wait for special equipment. It would arrive in the a.m. They decided to go to the hostel for the night. Commander Keddie led the way. Not only had he learned to fight, his style was very effective. He also was a very good leader. He had learned a lot from Commander Niea. He wanted to see Tulie. He had received a message that she wanted to see him. The message had actually come from Miguel. Keddie had been with quite a few women, but none of them compared to Tulie.

When the scout team arrived, Tulie, Jay, and Aaden were out back playing with the dog and dancing to Rage. The dog finally got a proper name, Shags. He had not been fixed and was running after any bitch that was in heat. So, the name was directly related to his looks and his activity.

Keddie called out, but no one answered. The team waited for Keddie to find the proprietor of this beautiful place. He went around back and saw Tulie with Aaden and Jay playing and dancing with Shags. He stood there smiling from ear to ear. Aaden saw him first and ran to him. Aaden loved anyone in Kali war garb. He picked the boy and knew right away he was Cal's and Jamal's son. Jay threw him a high five. Shags remembered Keddie and was jumping around him. Keddie kneeled down to pet this wiry dog and put Aaden down. The boys chased after the dog. Tulie turned around and froze. It was Keddie. He was filled out and not a bad-looking man. Tulie was staring at him. He was a fully realized Kali solder. Keddie stood up and saw Tulie. He walked slowly toward his love, excited and scared. What if she didn't want anything to do with him? They hadn't parted on bad terms. They had just drifted away from trying to have a relationship. She looked up to find where Aaden and Jay had run off to. They were still dancing and chasing Shags. Finally, Tulie broke into a huge smile. She was so happy to see him. He was tall, lean, and she was so attracted to him. When he left for boot camp, he was still a scrawny boy. She looked him up and down, grinning. He walked up close to her, picked her up, and kissed her. She wrapped her legs and arms around him and received her delicious gift of love. She leaned back and laughed. Her Keddie was home. He put her down slowly, sliding her down his abdomen, and she felt his other soldier standing at attention. With that, she knew he had really missed her. They sat down at the picnic table, and he filled her in on what his scout team had found and that they needed a place to sleep for the night. She was so excited. She took his hand, and they walked around to where his team was. She was introduced to all of them as his once-a-upona-time girlfriend. They both showed the team where they could sleep and get cleaned up. As they began to settle in, Tulie went to check on Aaden and Jay. They were out back still dancing and playing with the dog. Aaden was definitely his mother's child. Jay had even picked some moves from Ma-Cal. Keddie followed her, asking where she slept. She showed him her little cabin that Jamal and Miguel had built. He stood in the door of her bedroom, looking at her. She nodded, and he put his gear in her room. He wanted to bathe. She showed him the bathroom. He asked her to join him. She said she would join him later. She was going to get supper ready for all of them. He said he would help her as soon as he got cleaned up. Miguel had plenty of leftovers that would impress the team. Once they had bathed, ate, and had as much wine as their leader would allow, the team fell out. They were tried. But Keddie was energized and wanted to lay down with Tulie. He was beside himself with excitement, and there was a dose of fear. He knew Tulie was a virgin, and he was a large man. He would not want to hurt her. Once Aaden and Jay were asleep, she joined him on her patio. She had a bottle of wine and two glasses. He liked the way things were going, but first he wanted to talk to her about what he was feeling and his concerns. He knew she really wasn't comfortable talking about her feelings, but it had to happen. He would not get into her bed until they have a good chat. They sat and watched the moon come up. It was full.

Keddie leaned forward and poured himself some more wine. He looked over at Tulie, then he patted the seat next to him. She sat down, and he put his arm around her. Tulie could hardly believe how muscular he had gotten. Keddie was a strapping man. She snuggled up to him and laid her head on his chest. She wanted him but had no idea how to get started. He read her very well. She was looking at him with so much desire. He smiled and was glad he had on some loose shorts. He was so hard it hurt. He had dreamed of this day for way too long. He started going directly to it: "I love you Tulie, you know that. I want to make love to you."

He looked at her, waiting for a response. He could tell she was enjoying his excitement. She sat up, turned toward him, and kissed him so passionately he forgot what he was going to say. He picked her up and carried her to her bedroom, kissing her the whole way. He couldn't believe it. She always kissed him with her mouth closed. And now she was sucking on his tongue. She loved the way he kissed.

They made out for a time. Tulie got up and went to the patio and got the wine and glasses. She had removed the top of her dress before she came into the bedroom. Keddie had never seen her breasts. In that moment, he realized she had kept them well hidden in a sports bra. They were beautiful, perfectly round, and fit her small frame to a tee. She saw him looking at them. She dropped her dress to the floor, and for the first time, he saw her perfect little body she had kept under wraps. Her waist was tiny, her hips perfectly round, voluptuous. She was so well proportioned. He was staring, stunned. She stood there and did some girl poses for him. Then she jumped in the bed and stood over him. He was still in a state of shock, staring up at her. She pulled the string on his shorts and pulled them off him.

Tulie was looking at his generous cock and said, "You never told me you were so healthy." Keddie was still staring at her. Words were gone for him. She sat down lightly on his cock. It was lying on his abdomen. She rubbed herself on him until she got very wet. She stood up and said something that he still didn't believe she had said, "You are going to use all of it." It wasn't a question. She didn't act like a virgin.

She acted like a queen. He couldn't wait to taste and feel this perfect-shaped little woman. She straddled him, saying, "I will get us started. I will go slow. I have never had a penis in me." What had she had in her was all he could think. But as she lowered herself onto him, he could tell that her hymen was intact. He wanted to dive into her. He didn't have to. Once Tulie got the head of his wonderful man self in her, she was right where she wanted to be. She was shifting back and forth, rolling her hips around, enjoying the descent onto his glorious cock. He could tell by her face she was in full pleasure mode. Keddie didn't move. He had never witnessed anything like this. She rolled her hips until he was all the way in her. Then she came, screaming, panting, looking at Keddie with total desire. He rolled her over, holding himself over her. He loved her until they were both spent. He lay on his side and pulled her up close and said, "God knows I love you." She cuddled herself into the crook of his well-formed arm, looked up, and whisper words of love to her man. They slept well.

Before Keddie and his team had arrived in the area, Cal had gone into labor. Tulie had checked her; she was almost fully dilated. Her baby girl was coming. But the baby was breeched. Days before, she and Tulie had tried everything they could think of to turn the child. Cal had even stood on her head many times. She and Tulie had tried to manually shift the unborn infant. But now it was time. Jamal and Cal packed up the ground car and headed out to Central.

Before dawn, Keddie, Tulie, and the team were all geared up and ready to go. Tulie served protein wraps and tea with a mild stimulant. Soon the liner would be in a field a couple of clicks from the hostel. Commander Keddie sent two soldiers to pick up their needed gear. Margo and Zek had come to pick up Aaden and Jay. They were going to the center. There were lots of other kids there, and they loved to go play. Zek and Margo were happy to see Keddie. Both of them were amazed at the man he had become. Zek asked if they needed any help. Keddie had his team, and he had Tulie. They should be okay. Zek and Margo told him to message them if they did and off they went.

Cal and Jamal arrived at the infirmary in record time. Cal's water had broken. Her contraction were every three minutes. Her baby girl was coming. Cal was handling the pain like a champ. They took her straight to labor and delivery. Jamal wanted to go with her, but they asked him to wait. He remembered no one had called Grandmama. He decided to go to her apartment. When he arrived, Zane opened the door and invited him in. Zane called out to Ladia. She entered the room with just a kimono on. Jamal couldn't help but stare. Her body was beautiful. She apologized and wrapped her kimono up around her. Zane didn't blame Jamal for looking. She was something to see. Ladia got so excited when she heard Cal was having her baby. She told Jamal that a scout team might have located Miguel. Then he asked for Niea. She wasn't doing well. This made him so sad. He asked about Elijah. Zane said his daughter had him. Jamal and Ladia headed to the hospital. Zane was sure no one would try to hurt his woman with Jamal there. He was a very intimidating man, not unlike himself. He had some work to do, and then he would go see his new great-grand baby.

When they arrived at the infirmary, Cal was in a room hooked to a monitor and a drip of Pitocin—a very old drug but effective. It was going very slow. Cal knew the positions she needed to be in to help the baby turn. A tech had put a chair reversed so that Cal could sit on the bed and use the back of the chair to lean forward. When she was tired of that position, the tech would come in help her lay on her side, placing pillows to her back. Cal was lying on her side palpating her abdomen. She could feel the baby's whole body. She could also feel her daughter hiccupping through her belly button. She called for the tech. She was sure the baby had turned. The tech checked her. She was fully dilated, and yes, the baby had turned. The head would be fully engaged soon. Cal was so excited. The tech had never seen a woman this elated to have her baby.

Jamal knocked on her door. Cal looked up and grinned from ear to ear. She looked down at her belly, rubbing it ever so gently, and whispered, "Da is here, Shona!" Jamal leaned down and kissed her lightly on the lips. He put his hand on Cal's very large baby bump, then he kissed it. Cal was having another contraction. She leaned forward, holding on to Jamal. She said in a painful whisper, "Shona is coming!" Jamal got into bed behind Cal. She lay back on him in between his powerful legs, just as she had done when Aaden was born. She crooked her arms around his capable legs and called the tech. He wrapped his large dark arms around her upper abdomen ever so gently. She turned her head so she could see her magnificent man and said, "I love you, Jamal." He always had known Cal was a phenomenal woman. But she had shown herself to be so much more. She was the best mother he had ever seen.

Grandmama knocked at the door. She had a beautiful bouquet—pink baby's breath. She looked at Jamal and Cal, and her heart felt like it would burst. Her eyes watered up. She was so glad she was here. Her third great-grand would be entering the earth in minutes. She hoped Zane would be here in time to welcome their great-grandchild.

The tech entered the room. She checked Cal once more and said, "Let's have this baby." Ladia started to cry, which made Cal cry. Jamal held on; he didn't want to cry, but he couldn't help himself.

All his dreams and prayers had been answered. He had the woman of his dreams, two sons, and very soon he would meet his daughter. The tears rolled down his cheeks. His beautiful smile lit up the room.

Ladia said between sniffles, "Aren't we all a watery mess."

Tulie, Keddie, and the team geared up and headed to the caves. If today was a good day, they would find Miguel alive. They walked quickly and quietly. Tulie had to walk in front of Keddie. His walk was mesmerizing her. He had more swag than Cal. His body was lean, muscular, and so masculine.

Soon they were at the cave where it was believed Miguel had been dragged into. Tulie told Keddie in Kalifee battle language she would go in first. Keddie's number one was perturbed. Who was in charge? The commander or this little woman? Keddie started to dress him down, but Tulie stopped him. She had this. They were in the shadows to conceal the team from any onlookers. Tulie disappeared from right in front of them. In the next instant, she was standing in front of the naysayer with her needle long blade drawn at his groin. He gasped and jumped back. Tulie said, "If you have any problem with me, you need to address me directly. You understand?" He nodded. He had heard stories about her being a shadow warrior. He didn't believe them until now. Keddie laughed quietly to himself. Don't mess with Tulie.

Tulie shadowed her way into the cave. She found him in a jail cell. It was locked. She looked in. and there was Miguel. He was dazed, drugged. He was lying on his stomach and had on no pants, just a shirt. Tulie was worried he had been raped, possibly more than once. She shadowed her way through the entire cave. It had three separate rooms. She counted a handful of Gogatt that could be taken down no problem. Then she saw that man Leit. He was angry. He was cursing at these men. Had they raped Miguel? She remained still, listening intently. He was angry at them, telling them that Miguel was his and they had better leave him alone. The men were angry with Miguel. He had out fought them, killing several before they knocked him unconscious. She decided to report back to the team.

Tulie told them everything she had seen. The lock on Miguel's cell was an old key lock. Keddie was sure he could open it. He had on his shadow suit. He gave orders for them to wait a few beats then follow him and Tulie into the cave. Tulie would lead the way. Once they hit the cave, she and Keddie disappeared. She tapped out on Keddie's leg where the cell was. She headed to the room where she heard Leit. She would start her dispatching of this filth. Keddie was having a bit of trouble with the lock. Miguel was coming out of the stupor. He looked at Keddie as if he was dreaming. He couldn't really believe it. But help was here, and he was going home. He started to cry. Leit had raped him. He had ordered his men to leave Miguel alone, and they disobeyed. Only one had actually penetrated him. His backside was sore but intact. He knew the Gogatt were famous for destroying a man through his rectum.

Tulie killed five of them without a hitch. She couldn't find Leit. She rejoined Keddie. He was still working on the lock. Tulie asked him to step aside. She took her short needle blade and opened the door. Miguel was in pain but happy to see her and Keddie. Keddie picked him up. Miguel was grinning at Keddie. He couldn't believe how big and strong Keddie was. He passed out again.

The team was going through the entirety of the cave. They found the dead Gogatt. They knew Tulie had killed them all due to the where she had stuck her blade. If there had been any doubts left about little Tulie, they were gone now. She was a master assassin hands down. One of them found where Leit had gotten out. Too bad; they would have loved to drag his nasty self to Central.

Cal was holding her baby to her breast and feeding her. She had strawberry-red wavy hair and green eyes, and she was darker than Aaden. She looked more like Jamal. Jamal was sitting next to the bed, smiling so hard his face hurt. He loved his boys, but a girl was this daddy's heart and soul, just like her mama. Baby girl Shona had finished nursing and was fast asleep in her ma's arms. The tech came in with some nutrition for Cal. She took the baby and placed her in her crib.

Ladia went upstairs to visit Niea. She wanted her to come downstairs with her to meet her niece. Niea just shook her head no. She continued to be depressed with little to say to anyone. She had little energy and didn't sleep well. She looked haggard and old. Ladia was so worried about her girl. She had been like this for way too long. Zane came into the room and found Jamal, Cal, and Shona sleeping. Jamal woke the minute Zane stepped into the room. Zane apologized. No need—Jamal was hungry and asked Zane if he would like to get something to eat. Zane called up the psych unit and spoke with Ladia. She said that there was no need to visit Niea. She has gone to her room wanting to be alone. She asked that he and Jamal go ahead. She would meet them there. It was one of her favorite places. She wanted to look in the gift shop for a present for baby Shona. Zane sent a guard up to be with Ladia. She thought she would be all right, but he reminder her Theodosia was on the loose and very dangerous.

Ladia went back to see Cal and Shona. They were both sleeping. She sat on a chair and fell asleep herself. It had been a long day. Her heart had two conflicting songs—one was buoyant and full of joy, the other was a dirge.

Jamal and Zane arrived at the tavern in a very gregarious mood. Jamal was passing out cigars to all the men and was giving really nice chocolates to the ladies, unless they wanted the cigar. They ordered a drink each, swapped war stories, and talked about their families. Zane complimented him on his beautiful daughter and his hair. Jamal had braided it up in alternating patterns. Zane had long hair and wondered if Jamal could twist his up sometime like that. Jamal said he would be honored. They both had a pint of ale. Zane liked this ale better than any alcohol he had ever drunk. They both ordered another one. Zane had never had more than one drink. At the end of that drink, he was feeling tipsy. People were congratulating them both. Men were shaking hands. Women were giving them kisses on the cheek. One female came up to Zane and introduced herself. She complimented him on his new great-grand. She didn't believe he was old enough to have a grand, much less a great-grand. He actually blushed a little. Alcohol had taken some of his cool exterior away, and he put his arm around her. She stepped up close to him and kissed him. He kissed her back, and she grabbed his ass. Ladia was standing at the end of the bar. She watched the whole scene. The kissing and the ass grabbing lasted just way too long. She walked up on them, and he caught her out of the corner of her eye. He took his arm from around this woman and stepped back. The woman asked if he would like to have a go at it. Ladia said, "Yes, Zane would you like have a tumble with this beautiful lady." He shook his head, keeping his eyes on her. Ladia was so composed. It would be hard for anyone to see the wound that scene had put in her heart. She excused herself. She was tired and was going home to sleep. Zane excused himself and followed her. Jamal's expression was almost comical. His eyebrows were up, and his eye were rolling about. He wouldn't want to be Zane, especially in that moment.

Jamal decided to stay and eat. He hadn't eaten all day. The young woman tried to make a move on him. He was not ugly to the lady, if that what one would call such a forward woman. He said she needed to find someone else. His wife had just had a baby, and he had no need for company. She moved on down the bar.

Zane kept calling after Ladia. She walked with her guard and ignored him. She had not looked at him or spoken to him all the way home. He followed her home, walking into the living space behind her. She turned around and said, "Will you go and get me some silver tequila?" He did and returned fast. She poured herself some and offered him a glass. He had more alcohol than he obviously needed. She sat and drank. He kept trying to apologize. She just cried. She did let him hold her, but she said nothing to him. Eventually she was drunk, and he was very tired. He carried her to bed, took off her dress, covered her up, and kissed her on the forehead.

Morning came. Ladia was hung over. Zane got her some strong tea and a piece of dry toast, just like she asked. She ate and drank in silence. If she looked at him, she would cry. It was that silent, still cry that came from a broken heart. This was killing Zane. You know men; they want to fix the woman. But there was no fixing this. Only time would tell if she could get over it. He had to go to work. She still said nothing to him. She had a faraway look in her eyes, like a piece of her soul had just gotten up and left her. Finally, he excused himself. He checked with the guard to stay with her no matter what. The guard said, "Of course, Captain." He went to the gym and beat up a punching bag. He was so angry with himself. Why in hell had he done that? He felt so stupid. If he lost Ladia, he had no idea what he would do.

The team took off running. Keddie was carrying Miguel. They found a good hiding place. Tulie did a full assessment of Miguel. He needed to go to the infirmary. His rectum was pretty torn up, and God knows what they gave him. Keddie sent a message to Central. Tulie was debating whether to go with them or stay at the hostel. Keddie asked her to come with them; she could return to the hostel tomorrow. They waited at the edge of the field designated as the pickup area. Tulie messaged Zek and Margo. They would check on the horse, the dog, and the place this evening. The boys could stay with them.

When the team arrived at Central, Zane was there to meet them. Ladia had asked him to do this. He went to the infirmary with Miguel. Keddie recognized the captain and was glad to see him. Zane had an impeccable reputation. Once he got Miguel settled, he went to see Cal. She looked like the happiest person in the world. She apologized for not recognizing him on the video call. She was so excited about her baby bump. Not a problem. She could tell that something was really bothering him. She would not let up until she got it out of him. He told her what had happened. Cal said she, of all people, knew where alcohol can take a person. He knew of Cal's drunken escapades. They were legends. He talked at length about how upset Ladia was and how withdrawn she was. He was worried he couldn't fix this. Cal said she would talk with her. He thanked her. Jamal had gone down to see his friend Miguel. Everyone was so happy he was alive. Zane went to see Bet and his grands. He decided to stay with them a few days. He left a message for Ladia that he was with Bet and the grands and did not know when he would be back. He asked Bet if she would like to move into his apartment. He might be living there after all. He told her what happened. She just shook head. She knew he was in pain.

Miguel wanted to see Niea, but she wouldn't. Ladia told him how sick she was. The depression really had a hold on her. As soon as he could get up and move around, he was going to see his beautiful bride. He was going to see her if it was the last thing he would ever do. Ladia would like to bring Cal and Shona up to see him. This made Miguel feel better. He wasn't allowed out of bed until he had healed enough. Leit had not torn his rectum up like the Gogatt did. Ladia was curious that Miguel didn't seem emotionally traumatized by what they did to him. He knew it had nothing to do with who he was. Ladia thought to herself if only Niea could do that.

Ladia was good when she was around her people, but alone she was a mess. She hadn't seen or talked to Zane in days. Zane would talk with her guard but avoided seeing her. He decided he would rather her break it off with him in person, so he continued to avoid her.

One evening she sent a message to him. She wanted to see him. He showed at to her apartment. He had made up his mind he wasn't going to stay, and he wasn't going to apologize anymore. He felt that this was the end. He had become attached to her blended family. He would not cut any of them out of his life. They were all fine people. He especially loved the grands and wanted to watch them grow up. Jamal and Cal's kids were so exotic, and Elijah was just plain beautiful. He did not use his pass card. He knocked. She opened the door. A guard was standing at the door with her. He stood just inside the door and waited as a good soldier did. She invited him to sit. His military formality was disconcerting to her. He walked into the sitting area but remained standing. The guard went into the hall and shut the door. She motioned for him to please sit. He finally did, but he sat on the edge of the seat. She started talking around the subject, which perturbed him. He finally had enough and said, "Please, Ladia, say what you want to say."

She thought for a few moments and said, "I don't mean to make you mad." He looked away and blew out a long breath. Then he looked at her with a hard look. She knew he had looked at many a soldier this way. His face said get to it. Ladia smiled as best as she could and said, "I love you. You are the only man I have ever really loved. I have never had sex like the way we make love. I miss you." He sat there with his back straight and his hands clasped. He was thinking what he should say to this woman. He said nothing. She stood up and walked over to him. She wanted to kiss him but saw no way in. She touched the side of his face. She couldn't read him at all. She went to the table and sat down. She said, "If only you hadn't made out with that woman, and you did it in front of family! Do you have any idea how bad that hurt?"

He didn't move. "Well, it seems to me that you made some real bad choices. Life is full of trials and choices." She continued chatting away about life and choices, his choices. Suddenly he stood up and turned toward her. He was staring at her. God, she couldn't read him. Then she said, "If you want this thing to be over, so be it." With that, he turned over the table she was sitting behind. He grabbed her by the shoulders and stood her up. She truly didn't know if he was going to hit her or what. He could see the fear in her face. He kissed her so passionately. She had to admit to herself all this was turning her on. She loved Zane taking charge with his masculine self. At that moment, the guard heard the commotion and came into the apartment. Ladia looked over her shoulder and said that everything was okay. He left shutting the door behind him. Zane sat Ladia on the counter pulling off her kimono. Now she was nude. He dropped down on one knee and buried his face in that warm, delicious place between her legs. God, he had missed her. He slowly licked her until she was very wet. Then he did what he knew she loved. He buried his tongue into her, and once again she came. Then he picked her up and took her into the bedroom, kissing her the whole way. He laid her on the bed and removed his clothes quickly. He lay on his back and motioned for her to mount him. She did, then he scooted to the edge of the bed, dropping his legs to the floor. He pulled her down onto him, stretching her until she screamed so loud the guard knocked on the door. Zane barked out an order for him to stand down. He stretched her over and over, rocking his legs and hips. Ladia screamed again and again. Then it was Zane's turn. He kissed her with his tongue deep in her mouth. He came and went limp. She lay on him for a long time. He held her so tenderly, humming a tune he knew she loved.

After a time, she sat up and asked him to forgive her. No, he was the one that needed forgiveness. She said, "I can't live without you." He felt the same way. They made a pact that if there was ever a problem they didn't know how to handle, they would consult their family first. Then she wanted to know how he always knew what to do for her. It was always so perfect.

He sat up looking at her very intently, then he said, "This will sound crazy, but I have known you for a long time. I don't mean just the past few years. I have known you for eons. I have loved you for eons. I know every centimeter of you, physically, emotionally, mentally, and spiritually. I don't have any idea how I know this, but I do. I knew this the first time I saw you. I'm a left-brain person—weapons, computers, military strategies, thing like that. I am not the esoteric type. But this will never happen again between you and I." He kissed her again. He dismissed the guard. He went back to his woman, and they went to sleep curled up on each other.

Niea continued to be withdrawn and somber. She missed Elijah. She tried not to think of Miguel, but a tech told her that he was in the medical unit. No, she did not want to see anyone, and she wished Grandmama would stop coming by to see her. Serge knocked on her door. She was genuinely glad to see him. He wanted her to come with him. She finally said yes. But first, Serge insisted she must get cleaned up. She had let her personal hygiene go for far too long. He assisted her especially with her hair. There were many tangles, and he worked them all out. Then he braided her hair. He found her a dress that would do. She did feel and look better. He was going to take her to Miguel. He didn't tell her where they were going. When they arrived at the medical unit, Grandmama was there with Elijah. She was waiting for Niea. Serge had called her saying he would get Niea out of that room. Grandmama was elated to see her baby girl. Niea started crying. Ladia handed the baby to her. He had grown and was almost ready to start walking. She kissed and kissed her baby boy. Niea and Grandmama went in to see Miguel. Ladia went in and kissed the beat-up-looking Miguel. She handed him his son. He was so happy. While he was in that cave, he thought he would never see his son and wife again. Then he asked for Niea. She was hanging back afraid. Then she stepped into the room and ran to Miguel. She begged and begged him to forgive her. Ladia took the baby from Miguel and slipped quietly out the door. Niea walked sheepishly up to Miguel. She sat down on the side of the bed. He pulled her ever so gently so she would lay down with him. He held her for a long time. She could tell he was in pain and tried to get up. He held on tightly to his Niea. Now he was all right.

Later that same day, the therapist came in to see Niea. Maybe today she would start talking. Niea knew she had to open up about all the crap inside her. She talked about Elijah, Grandmama, Cal, and her new baby. She just wouldn't or couldn't talk about herself. She had avoided herself for so long it was difficult to know where to start. She talk about the rape briefly. She said she didn't remember much, but that wasn't true. She didn't want to tell the therapist about the hallucinations. But she admitted she was seeing things that she knew weren't real. The therapist complimented her. If she could tell the difference between reality and a hallucination, she was well on her way to unraveling some of her issues. This made Niea relax a little, and she started talking more freely. She hated the part of herself that pulled away from the ones she loved. She just didn't understand how she could be so fragile. When she was a girl, she was fearless, fierce. There was nothing she couldn't tackle head-on. It really bothered her she was afraid of the dark now. She talked about refusing medication and the herbal combination she had come up with. It worked so well. The therapist said she would speak with the psychiatrist. Niea liked that. She asked the therapist if she could see Miguel in the morning. The therapist said he could come to one of their sessions. Niea did not like that, but she agreed.

A tech brought Miguel in a wheelchair, who was sitting on a doughnut pillow. He was still quite beat up, and his rectum was very sore. He had been through a hell that would rival what Niea had been through; his had lasted for weeks. She knew none of what had happened to him. The therapist was well aware of Miguel's ordeal. They sat and chatted for a while, then the therapist asked Miguel if he could recount what had happened. He spoke clearly with an even tone. He left nothing out. Niea sat with her mouth open in shock. When he had finished, the therapist asked about what had happened to Niea. She dropped her head and breathed in deeply. Her mind went to the cave where she had fought and killed so many of those monsters, but when it came to the rape, she froze. Miguel took her hand and held it to his heart. She cried for some time. Then she looked at Miguel. In between sobs, she said, "How do you do it? How?"

Miguel didn't know how to answer her. Then he said, "You do what you have to do to stay alive."

That was not exactly what she meant. She thought for a bit then said, "You seem like you're over it. How do you do that?" She was staring at her incredible husband. He had suffered so much more than she could even imagine.

Miguel took her other hand and held them tenderly, saying, "What happened to me had nothing to do with me. It was their crime, not mine. I refuse to let that evil live in me. It belongs to them. I left it there. It's not mine."

The therapist thanked Miguel and turned to Niea. Again, the therapist asked her to tell them what happened. She stood up and started to pace. The therapist asked her to sit. She continued to pace. She went back and forth for a few. Niea did sit down, putting her face in her hands. Miguel put his hand on her back and rubbed lightly. She took a deep breath and cried. She was so tired of crying, tired of being so sick. Then she said, "I failed. I was a virgin when Miguel and I got together. I am ruined now. Those horrible men raped me. I failed my team. I became weak, dangerous and…" She trailed off. "I am worthless. I failed my team. I failed my husband. My beautiful man suffered more than I ever did, and now I am the one that is all screwed up."

The therapist said, "What else, Niea?"

This infuriated her. She had told them all, hadn't she? Why was this woman pushing her? She went to the wall and started punching it. She wanted to hurt something and hurt it bad. Her knuckles started bleeding. Miguel got up slowly. He was very sore, but he wanted so badly to take her pain. He motioned for the therapist to hold off for a bit. He wrapped his arms around her and held on tight. She relaxed a bit. He guided her back to the chair. He sat her down and kissed her ever so lightly on the lips. They waited. Finally, Niea said, "No, I haven't told it all. I don't know how."

The therapist said, "Are you ready to tell us the rest?" The therapist had suspected all along that Niea was holding back, not wanting to admit something even to herself. They waited. Niea sat with her eyes closed, tears streaming down her face.

Then she screamed it out, "I had an orgasm!"

The therapist said, "Tell us about it."

Here was the big secret she had held on to for far too long. Niea said, "There were three different men that raped me. The last one started choking me. I wasn't showing any fear. He didn't like that. He started choking me. Then it happened. That was when my team intervened. Miguel kicked that piece of garbage off me. I thought they had witnessed it. But none of them said anything about it. I guess I buried it deep inside me. I was so ashamed. I felt like a piece of worthless nothing. Then I started reliving it. Over and over again and again. The hallucinations were so real. That's when I injured my husband several times. I almost killed him. Then when he went MIA, I lost it. I recessed deep within myself."

The therapist told Niea she was very proud of her. That was not an easy thing to do. The therapist said, "Have you heard of erotic asphyxiation?" Niea nodded. "I understand how upsetting something like the horror that happened to you would trigger you. How are you feeling?" Niea just shook her head no. She felt horrible, embarrassed. She felt like she had let everyone down. She sobbed for long time. Then she got angry. Miguel went over to her and held her. He whispered in her ear that nothing could ever change the way he felt about her. He also told her that she wasn't ruined. She was his beautiful baby girl. This made her smile, remembering the game that she and her sister had played.

Miguel was getting very tried, so a tech came and wheeled him back to his room. Cal, baby Shona, Jamal, Ladia, and Zane were there. The tech helped him into bed. He held his niece. He couldn't get over how beautiful she was. He teased Jamal about having a beautiful woman. That was the only way his big ugly self could produce such incredible children. Jamal laughed and said, "I sprinkle a little black magic and Cal, she brings the rainbow." They all laughed. Miguel did need to rest. So they all said their goodbyes and went to see Niea.

Niea was better. But she was still having bouts of depression. She still felt like a failure, like she had let everyone down. She just couldn't let go of that feeling. The staff agreed she would need some kind of medication. Niea and the psychiatrist agreed on an herbal formula. He would have enough made up for her to go home with. She and Miguel could make more with the herbs they would grow at there. She was excited and afraid.

Zane had moved all his things into Ladia's place. She had lots of room. She would have Miguel, Niea, and Elijah stay here until they were ready to go home. Cal wanted to get back to the hostel and see her boys. She knew Tulie was doing a fine job with them. They loved that little woman. They were in awe of her shadow abilities. Bet and the grands had moved into his old place. They would throw a party when all of them were here.

Niea's depression got worse. She would stay in her room much of the time. Miguel would come to see her, but she had little to say to anyone. Miguel was discharged from the infirmary. He and Elijah moved in with Ladia and Zane. Bet was sad to see the beautiful boy leave. He would be right down the hall, and she could babysit anytime they wanted.

One night at dinner Ladia's communicator went off. It was disturbing news. Niea had made a serious attempt on her life. If Serge had not come by to see her, she would be dead. Ladia was beside herself. Ladia, Zane, and Miguel took off to the hospital. They left Elijah with Bet. When they got to the infirmary, Niea was in surgery. She was going to need blood. She had lost a lot. They would have to do it in a direct transfusion. Zane was a match and he did not hesitate a second.

Once everything settled down, Ladia went to find out just what happened. Zane went with her. Miguel sat and waited to see his wife. Ladia interrogated everyone, anyone that was even slightly involved in Niea's care. First she talked with Serge. She was eternally grateful to him. He had come by to visit Niea. When she would not come to the door or at least talk to him, he entered the room and found her bleeding out on the floor. He found the scalpel she had used. He had not disturbed the scene. Ladia had a safety team come and gather all the evidence. They would thoroughly analyze everything they found. As it turned out, no one could tell the Califia how Niea got the scalpel. She was angry, but she held it. She called to the surgical unit. Miguel told her that Niea was out of surgery, but she was heavily sedated. Ladia, Zane, and Miguel sat in silence. No one knew what to say. The sadness prevailed throughout the unit. They waited.

Niea had a one-one tech assigned to her care. Ladia was glad to see it was Serge. She probably would be out until morning. Ladia knew she couldn't sleep. She wanted to stay. Miguel said he would stay. That way Zane and Ladia could go home and get some rest. Ladia knew she had better contact Cal. Cal would be so upset if she wasn't told right away. The best way to contact Cal was on the laptop she had at home. She and Zane left. When Ladia told Cal what had happened, she wanted to leave for Central right away. Ladia encouraged her to wait a few days. Cal agreed. When she told Jamal what Niea had tried, he was shocked. He and Cal would have never guessed she could do such a thing. Cal knew her sister was really sick.

Miguel was there when Niea woke up. He smiled so warmly at her that it made her cry. She had bandages on both arms. It had taken the surgeon quite some time to repair her veins, ligaments, and tendons. Yes, she had made several serious cuts up both arms. Thank the Spirit she had not cut an artery. Miguel kissed away her tears. He asked Serge if they could give her something. He was sure they could bring her an antidepressant. Miguel would not leave her side. Inside he was horrified, but all anyone could read on him was the love he had for his beautiful baby girl.

Niea stayed on the surgical unit until her wounds had healed. She still didn't want medication. Serge convinced her that she should. She had to get better; there were so many people pulling for her. He just had a way with her. He had shared his struggles with depression and suicidal ideation with her. His story had warmed her heart. She trusted him. He knew what it was like to have your brain turn on you.

Niea would be on the psych unit for some time. Suicide wasn't a crime, but it was not taken lightly by the Kalifee people. She still was having suicidal ideations. She shared them with Serge. With Miguel she was more reserved in talking about her psych issues. She thought it might upset him, but he never showed it. He was here for her no matter what. She tried to convince him to go get some rest. Sleeping in a chair was not good. Besides he had on the same clothes for days. No, he didn't smell. Miguel would never let himself get that way.

Miguel gave in and went to Zane and Ladia's. Besides he wanted to spend some time with his son. Ladia and Zane were glad to see him. He looked exhausted. He played with his son for a bit. Then he had a bath and went to bed. He slept. He was mentally and emotionally exhausted. Bet was more than happy to keep the boy. When Miguel woke, it was too late to go see Niea. He asked Ladia if he could cook. Of course, Ladia agreed. Cooking helped him keep his mind busy. He made them a late delicious supper. He called the unit. Serge was not there. Niea was sleeping. Serge would be back in the a.m. Miguel would be there then.

Miguel arrived with a present. It was a dress. He loved buying anything for her. She was awake and in a fairly good mood. She kissed her husband ever so sweetly. It made Miguel think of them in bed, but he knew it was out of the question. But one day he would hold his beguiling bride and love her. Serge was there, and they both helped her get dressed. There was some damage to the ligaments and tendons in her arms. Getting her hands to move correctly was difficult at times.

Ladia was going through everything she could think of that might locate where and how Niea had gotten hold of a scalpel. Zane was going through the patient log, and he found something. A prisoner had been admitted to the unit, a female. When Ladia saw the name, it made her blood run cold. Vahar!

Vahar was brought to an interrogation room. Zane and Ladia were waiting for her. Her wrists were chained to her waist. The guard brought her in and pointed for her to sit down. Ladia had the guard remove the wrist restraints. The guard looked to Zane. He nodded.

He was here. No one was going to do anything to Ladia, not with him around.

Vahar sat down rubbing her wrists. She looked around the room, not knowing what to say. What do these people want? Ladia sat at the table looking hard at Vahar. No, Vahar didn't recognize her. She thought she knew the older man. He was so sexy. Vahar had a hard time keeping her eyes off him. The way he looked at her was so tantalizing. He was mesmerizing to her. She would have a hard time manipulating him. All she wanted to do was lie down with him. She knew beyond a shadow of a doubt he would be spectacular in bed. Vahar was hardly ever attracted to any man. But this man was something special.

Ladia said, "How are you, Vahar?"

Vahar said, "I don't think I know you, do I?" She kept looking at Zane. Ladia couldn't detect if he was doing anything. When Vahar would look at him, he would just look at her. Vahar felt herself getting excited. He was a specimen of a man, and it was so distracting. She turned toward him and said, "Do I know you?" Zane shook his head slowly and smiled. Vahar said, "Are you sure?"

Zane said, "I remember you from a very long time ago."

Vahar said, "A brothel somewhere?" He nodded. She continued to look him up and down. "You were a performer?" He nodded again and gave that crooked smile that drove her wild. All she could think was she wanted to be alone with this man.

Ladia slammed her hand down on the table. "I need your attention, Vahar!"

Vahar snapped her head around and looked at Ladia, annoyed. Ladia said, "I can see you are interested in this man. Yes, he is a specimen. But I need for you to pay close attention. My daughter had an incident, and I believe you had something to do with it."

Vahar looked at this elegant woman, and she knew. "Sorry, Califia, but I have no idea what you are talking about."

Ladia stared at Vahar, biting her lip ever so slowly. She was angry. She said, "It has come to my attention you were a patient at the infirmary." Vahar wanted to look at the man. He was so sexy. Maybe he could stay with her tonight. Again, Ladia slammed her hand down on the table. Vahar jumped, and her chair went straight back. She hit the floor hard. Zane went to her and picked up the chair with her in it. Her head was bleeding in the optic area. He pulled a handkerchief out of his back pocket and held it to her head. She held on to his hand that was supporting her neck. She looked at him, and he knew. He could have her anytime, anyplace. He got the bleeding to stop and left the room for some ice.

Ladia wanted answers, and she wanted them now. Her beautiful baby girl had tried to kill herself. Ladia's heart was torn into pieces. Zane returned with a bag of ice with a small towel and held it to the back of Vahar's head. Now she was looking at the Califia. She swore she was not there when Niea had her incident. Zane handed Ladia the patient roster from that day. There was Vahar's name. Ladia leaned forward and shoved the roster into Vahar's face. She was going to have to dance faster if she was going to skirt this one. She knew she could. Maybe if she told the Califia the truth, the man could stay with her tonight. She had not had a man in a long time. She would get a prize she never dreamed she could have. She found him more desirable than Miguel.

Ladia interrogated her for hours and got nothing. Vahar had mastered not only manipulation but also lying. Finally, exhausted and ready for sleep, she stood and motioned for Zane to join her outside. He opened the door for Ladia and turned, giving Vahar a wink. She sat up and pushed her breasts out slightly and smiled at him.

Ladia asked, "What do you think?" Zane and she agreed. She was lying and definitely hiding something. They rode home in silence. Ladia turned to Zane, saying, "You think she will talk to you?" He thought maybe if they were alone. Ladia said they should at least give it a try.

Ladia entered their apartment and just fell onto the bed. She sat up slowly as Zane helped her out of her single suit. He never understood—a woman of such wealth and status would have more clothes and jewelry. Not her. Over the years she had given away a fortune to anyone in need. She was very good at reading people and knew whom to give what to. She had seven single suits, ten or more kimonos, and wore only a ring that was her great-grandmother's. She wore her hair up with a single large comb. She looked years younger than her actual age. He marveled at such a woman.

In the morning, Ladia went to see Niea. She seemed in a much better place than she had been in a while. Ladia wanted to ask her why, but she thought better of it. Ladia hired Serge to stay with Niea. He would do twelve to fourteen hours at a time. He even told the Califia he could just stay with her all the time. Ladia thanked him graciously, but that would not be necessary. The staff here could fill those spots just fine.

Zane had been out for a run when Ladia came home. She asked if he had talked to Vahar. No, he hadn't. He had just gotten out of the shower. He walked over to Ladia drying his long thick salt-and-pepper hair. Usually Ladia would braid it back in a Kalifee warrior style, flat to the head, for fighting. But today she was in her single-mindedness mood. Zane knew she would not or could not focus on anything else. So he twisted up his hair as best as he could. She wanted him to go now. He thought maybe they could have some lunch together somewhere nice. No, she had things she had to get done, and there were a couple of meetings she had to get to. The guard would go with her today. Zane finished dressing. She told him he looked nice, but sexy might be better. Sexy? What in hell's name was she thinking? He said nothing. As she was leaving, she said, "Do what you have to do to get her to talk." Zane knew she didn't mean torture. He felt a little tortured right now.

Zane walked slowly to Vahar's containment cell. The guard let him in. He had a bag with him; the guard didn't search it. He was very much aware of Captain Zane's reputation. Vahar was genuinely glad to see him. He had on his game face. He asked if she had eaten. She wasn't tolerating the food here very well. She had lost weight. Zane told her that she had not lost any of her luscious ass. She laughed. She hadn't done that in a while. She started rolling her hips. She was, after all, a prized belly dancer. The one thing the Kalifee people liked the most was live shows and talent. Zane was smiling so big. He started shadowing her moves. She was delighted. He didn't miss a beat. Vahar started a shimmy. He followed that movement but not as well as Vahar. But he was amazing to watch. He was this strong sexy man, and he could dance. Vahar asked if he could sing. He nodded. She wanted him to sing his favorite song, and he did. When he was finished, she had tears rolling slowly down her cheeks. He looked at her and said, "I didn't mean to make you cry."

Vahar said, wiping the tears away, "No, it isn't that. I just haven't had a friend in a long time." Zane walked over to her. She was leaning forward. He put his hand on her back and gently rubbed. She continued to cry. He sat down by her and put his arm around her. She laid her head on his shoulder. She asked, "Why are you being so nice to me?"

Zane move away a bit so he could look at her and said, "You are a spectacular woman. To tell the truth, I was ordered to see if you would tell me more about Niea and that day at the infirmary."

Vahar sat up and looked him in the eyes. "So, I am an assignment." She stood up, walked over to the table, and sat. She hung her head and cried hard. This was breaking Zane's heart. He didn't want to hurt her. Yes, she had done things to get herself locked up. Maybe he could help her out. He had an idea.

Zane held out his hand and said, "Want to go for a walk?" She looked up at him and smiled through tears and nodded. She would love to get out of this cell. They did allow them to walk in the fenced-in yard but never outside. She was still sniffling. He handed her a handkerchief. She dried her eyes and went to wash her face. She had one jumpsuit she was issued. She had lost all her clothes, jewelry, and coins. She felt she just couldn't go out wearing a prison outfit.

Zane took her hand, guiding her to stand, then twirled her around. Then he said, "I will get you something that should do." She was taken back. She started crying even more. He said, "I will be back in no time." He kissed her lightly on the cheek and left.

Vahar lay down on the bed and cried even more. She wished she hadn't been so stupid trying to hurt the Califia's granddaughter and then going into the Califia's home with that awful woman Theodosia. She could blame it on the drugs, but Vahar knew no one made her take any of those drugs. No one made her do to Miguel what she did. He was the only man she had ever loved. She had really messed up her life. She had run one of the more successful brothels.

But it wasn't family friendly with the drugs, and crossover sexual practices were not appropriate for young Kalifee people. She would never go back to that life. She would rather be killed than work as a queen again. Although Vahar was an incredible lover, she didn't want to ever service another man or woman.

It wasn't long before Zane returned. He handed Vahar the bag and asked her to try it on. He still had the bag of scones and some fresh juice. He didn't tell her who had made it. He wasn't ready to reveal just how close he was to the Califia. She said that she would like to eat something first. Then she would look at what he had brought her. She loved the scones and fresh juice. It was a welcome change from prison food. She finished up doing her hygiene. He handed her the bag. She looked inside and pulled out a spectacular ice-blue tight-fitting dress. She stood there with her mouth open. She couldn't believe it. She stepped behind a half wall to change. Zane couldn't help himself. He had to peek. Her body was something to behold. She was exotic, and her skin was a beautiful honey brown. When Zane had first met her, he thought she had tanned her skin. As the light hit her in a different direction, her skin shimmered. She saw him trying not to look. She thought he was such a gentleman and a man. She stepped out, and he was mesmerized. She said, "This is perfect!" He smiled, never taking his eyes off her.

They had a wonderful walk. Zane brought some picnic supplies, and they ate in the park. He had a bottle of wine, but drinking in public was not allowed. They both ate, talked, and had a fabulous time. As they were walking back to the prison, she held his hand tightly. When they arrived at her cell, she asked him to stay a while. It would be wrong not to drink the wine he bought. He agreed.

Zane was nursing his glass of wine. Vahar said to drink up. It was a great topper to a wonderful day. Her radiant smile couldn't be resisted. He finished his glass and held it out for her to pour him some more. They talked and shared Kali show stories. They were both performers.

Zane helped Vahar into bed. She hadn't drunk in a long time and was tipsy. Zane was a bit high himself. He decided to walk home. When he arrived, Ladia was at her laptop working on something. She spoke to him without looking up. He said he was going to bed. She said she would be in soon. When he woke in the morning, she was gone. There was a note for him to keep up the good work and she would be late tonight.

Zane arrived at Vahar's cell midmorning. She had on the lightblue dress he had given her. She looked incredible. She looked happy to see him, unlike Ladia, who hadn't even looked at him. He loved Ladia, but she had not been with him as of late, especially since Niea had tried to kill herself. He had breakfast and a flyer. They ate and drank some wonderful tea he had made. Then he showed her the flyer. It was a Kali show, one of the biggest and best. It would open tomorrow night. He asked her if she would like to go. Yes, she wanted to go. Would that be allowed? Of course, he would be her escort. She said that she could wear the beautiful dress he had bought. No, they were going shopping. She jumped up and down, clapping her hands. He tried to not watch her breasts, but he couldn't help himself.

Zane and Vahar went shopping. He enjoyed watching her try on different dresses. He would love to be doing this with Ladia, but she just wasn't into this. While she was in the dressing room, he went through the racks of ladies' dresses. She came out not really happy with anything the store clerk had brought her. There he was holding a beautiful long orange-red satin dress with a slit up both legs in the front. The bodice covered her ample breasts with a plunging neckline. The waist area was cut out in a form-fitting V. Wow. How did he pick out this dress this fast? He just knew what would look really good on her.

They had a wonderful time at the show. Zane introduced her to the promoter during the halftime. He asked if she was going to enter the amateur contest. She said she would if the captain danced with her. She turned those large brown eyes on him, and he said yes. They danced several different styles. But when Vahar started her belly dance moves, Zane stepped back. The crowd went wild. Zane was beaming with pride. The promoter offered Vahar a job as a dancer. He was sure she would be headlining in no time. She said she couldn't. She was in custody. Zane said something could be arranged if the promoter was still interested. Yes, he was. Besides Vahar kept very good company. The promoter winked at Zane. Vahar was elated.

As they were leaving, a man recognized Vahar and approached her. "Excuse me, I don't mean to bother you, but aren't you Vahar?" She turned. Oh my god. It was a man that had saved her so many years ago.

She hugged him with so much gratitude. Zane thought maybe he had been one of her regulars. He then recognized Zane. "Captain, so good to see you."

Zane loved seeing any of his men from his team. "My man, so good to see you. How do you know our lovely Vahar?"

He said, "I was on safety patrol in her neighborhood for years. I'm surprised to see her." Then he turned to Vahar. "You are one of the strongest people I have ever known." Then he hugged her again, and he shook Zane's hand. "Have a wonderful evening. You both deserve it." Then he was gone.

Zane stopped and looked at Vahar. "Just how do you know him?"

Vahar sat down on one of the park's many benches. They were all alone now. She didn't know how to start. Zane would be the perfect person to tell it all to, but how does one begin?

Zane sat down beside her and asked, "What is it?"

She looked at him. Tiny tears were streaming down her face. She took a deep breath and said, "My childhood story is a sick one, if you want to hear it. You are the one person I would tell it all to." He put his arm around her and nodded. "I grew up with a mother and an uncle. He was cruel. He beat and raped my mother whenever he wasn't passed out from drinking. Then one day, when I was seven, he turned his perversion on me. At first it was him feeling on me. If I tried to stop him, he would beat my mother. So, I would hold real still, and he did what he wanted. The rape started about a year later. I always held still so he wouldn't beat my mother. Then he grew tired of my stillness. He started beating me if I didn't act like I was into it. He was the reason I started keeping my head shaved. He always would catch me by my hair."

Zane thought she was the only woman he knew that was beautiful with her hair shaved close to her head.

She continued, "It was one way of getting away from him. He loved to drag me around by my hair. I would hide outside waiting for him to pass out many nights. That was where I met Officers Marcus. He saw the bruises all over me. He did all he could do for me. I begged him not to contact the authorities. My uncle would beat both of us, even kill us. He became a quiet benefactor for me and my ma. He tried to come by every day. He would leave food and coin for us. He would make sure there had been no new beatings. He even threated the uncle to the point that he left both of us alone for a long time. Then my ma got very ill and became bedridden. I think her spirit was broken. One night, the uncle got very drunk. He was into drugs too. He started in on me first. My ma was yelling. He yelled for her to shut up, and she wouldn't. He started choking her. He was killing her. I got a butcher knife and yelled his name. He turned and came for me, and I stabbed him. My ma sounded like she couldn't breathe, so I dropped the knife and ran to her. I propped her up, and she began to breathe better. I felt him behind me. He had the knife. He lunged at me, and I jumped out of the way. He stabbed my ma instead. He and I fought and fought. There was a loud knock at the door. It was Officer Marcus. I yelled, and he broke down the door. He got a hold on my uncle, who by the way was my father. He got him by the throat and killed him. He cleaned up the scene according to protocol and reported a murder-suicide. He took me with him. He had said there was no need getting me involved in this mess. Then he got me a room where I could clean up. He brought me food, some clothing, and gave me some coin. After that, he took me to a brothel where they hired me as a dancer. Here is where it gets better, until I started using and selling sexual-stimulating drugs, along with other mind-and mood-alerting substances. Then I saw Miguel at one of my shows. He always thought I was from the breeding program. Truth be told, I am from an incestual, abusive, twisted home trash from the wrong side of town." Zane held her for the longest time.

Vahar and Zane walked back to her cell arm in arm slowly. They both wanted this evening to last. The water in the many lakes at Central were glimmering with the soft light. They walked in the glow of the evening and all that had been revealed. Zane wished Ladia would take the time to go with him. But in this moment, he was so glad to share with someone who loved the same things he did. This woman deserved some good moments in life. After a long time, Vahar asked, "How I'm to be in a cell and travel with this wonderful Kalifee show?"

Zane smiled, saying, "I want you to come with me tomorrow to the wellness center." Vahar was apprehensive. "I want you to tell your story. I will be there the whole time." She looked scared. He nodded and wrapped himself around her, and she kissed him lightly on the lips.

Zane showed up at Vahar's cell early in the morning. She was concerned she didn't have the proper clothing to go. Zane was way ahead of her. He had the cutest yellow sundress that covered her beautiful bosom. It was knee-length. He also brought some wedge heels that went perfectly with her dress. She smiled so big. This man knew her so well. She couldn't help herself; she kissed him with passion he hadn't felt in way too long. All Zane could think was he wanted to lie with her. But he kept resisting. How much longer he couldn't say.

While Vahar was having a bit of breakfast, which he also had brought her, he went to use his communicator. First he spoke to Miguel and asked if he was still coming to the wellness center. He was. Then he asked to speak to Ladia. She was in a hurry. She was late. No, she would not be able to make it. Zane had gone past the point of being disappointed with her. It had become the norm for her not to be available to be with him. So he turned his attention to Vahar. Every day he had grown closer to her.

When they arrived at the wellness center, Vahar didn't think she could go through with it. Zane pulled her aside and said, "If we make out, will that give you courage?" She smiled so big then planted one on him that took his breath away. They both turned and entered the building. The signs were clear. The rape survivor group would be in the second hall. Vahar was nervous. She couldn't do any of this without Zane Kedif. She loved his whole name. They sat down in the back. He held her hand. He knew she was scared. She had only told her story for the first time yesterday.

A statuesque, poised woman entered the room. She introduced herself as Schade, a healer. One of the patrons asked her what kind of healer she was. She was a spiritual healer, but the mind and body are one. She explained that dis-ease in the spirit becomes disease in the body. She also explained how the body gives signals. That is what pain is, a signal for attention to the spirit. Schade was a mesmerizing, confident, and in the center of her power. Niea was sitting out of sight. She really liked this woman. She listened intently to everything she said. Then Schade called on Niea. Niea shook her head. Schade stood there looking at Niea, holding both hands out to her. Niea couldn't resist her. She walked to the front of the room. Schade motioned for her to sit in a lone seat in the middle of the group. Niea told her story. Schade walked up to her and hugged her for a long time. Then she thanked her and gestured for her to sit with the others. She did. Then Schade looked at Miguel and motioned for him to take a seat in front of the room. He didn't hesitate. He sat and told his story of repeated rape by Leit and a Gogatt man. Then he saw Vahar and Zane. Vahar smiled at him. She seemed different to him. He was intrigued. Once he was done, Schade thanked him. He sat down by Niea and took her hand. He kissed it ever so tenderly. Schade spoke of the difference of holding on and letting the eagles fly. She asked if anyone could see that difference in these stories. Yes, they could. Niea could see it but didn't have any idea how to really let go. Maybe she just didn't understand what to let go of.

After several stories, Schade called on Vahar. She stood up slowly and walked to the chair in the middle of the room. Niea watched her closely. She could see that something was very different about this woman. Niea's empathic ways were on high alert. Vahar was becoming whole. Her true nature was that of a loving person. Niea smiled so warmly at Vahar. Vahar stopped and looked at Niea. She moved her lips slowly in a whisper, "I am so sorry." Niea could feel the sincerity in her and was blown away. Vahar turned her chair so she could see Zane. He nodded to her. She told it all. Then she hung her head. Schade walked over to her, put her hand gently under her chin, and raised it. Looking deep into Vahar's eyes, she saw an incredibly strong woman with bounds of love to share with anyone.

Schade said, "Hold your head high. You have endured horrors that the rest of us couldn't even imagine. You are here today not only for yourself but as a monument. Not just to survive but to live life, to thrive. It is never what happens to us. It is what we do with it. I see in you the past of a very dark road you chose. You have walked forward into the darkness and now into the light. A person cannot know the light until they have walked in darkness. The dark defines the light. I congratulate you."

Vahar raised her hand ever so slightly. Schade nodded. "I have hurt too many good people for any congratulations. I would like to make amends. A lifetime might not be enough time to make anything up to any of them. Two of them are here today." The room went silent. Zane was so proud of her. She had stepped out and claimed her crap.

Schade looked around the room. She could tell it was Miguel and Niea. She asked everyone here, "Does anyone here object to those two coming up here with Vahar?" No one objected. Schade was looking directly at Niea and Miguel. She pulled out two more chairs and gestured for both of them to have a seat. When everyone was settled, Schade said, "Vahar, you want to start?" Schade stepped back.

Vahar turned toward both of them. Then she moved her chair in front of them. She took Niea's and Miguel's hand. "Whatever I could do, I would. The two of you are meant for each other. I allowed the green monster called jealously to rule me, and I made one of the worst mistakes of my life. If you never forgive me, that would be fitting. I don't deserve anything from you but to be forgotten like an old worn-out shoe with no mate. Niea, you helped Miguel become the person he was meant to be. I just took advantage of him. He would have died if he had stayed with me. Thank the powers that be that you, Niea, came along. He has flourished with your love. Now you need to let him help you. I think that is very difficult for you. He has the capacity to do just that. Let him. Miguel, you were the tenderest, dearest person I had ever met, and I used you so sorely. I never stopped to see who you really were. Thank the Spirit Niea did." She kissed both of them on the cheek then looked at Schade. She nodded slowly. Then Vahar returned to her seat next to Zane.

He was grinning from ear to ear. This had turned out better than he had ever imagined.

Several more survivors shared. But no one was as moved as they were by Vahar's. It was just her horrific childhood or her heartfelt apology but the deep sincerity that she projected. It touched everyone. Once all was done. Niea wanted to talk to Vahar. She wanted to know how Miguel could help her. Schade asked if she could join them. Vahar looked at Niea. She nodded yes. They all sat off to the side. Niea grabbed Vahar's hand with huge tears watering in her eyes. Schade encouraged Niea to say what she had to say. Niea said, "I never knew." Vahar thought to herself that no one would have ever known if it wasn't for Zane. Then Niea said, "How did you live through years of such horrors? How do you let go of those horrors?" Vahar looked to Schade for answers. All she knew was to keep going.

Zane asked Miguel if he needed a ride back to Central. He said no, he was going to stay with Niea as long as they would let him. Vahar and Zane drove back, both in high spirits. He came into her cell for a few. He was working on something but would be back within the turn of the clock. He had an apartment for Vahar to stay in until she left with the Kali show. He made sure all was ready for her, and he stopped by Ladia's place. She was actually there. He knocked on the door. She let him in and wondered where his key card was. He handed it to her. She was confused. He said, "I have decided to leave Central for good. I will be moving to the hostel within one moon time. If by any chance you want to see me, you can visit on the weekends." She said she had too much to do, blah, blah, blah. Zane laughed. He reminded her she had an entire staff that was totally capable of handling anything she needed done. She got quiet. He knew it was going to be hard for her. He reminded her that she needed to come and see her family every once in a while. She froze. She realized she had been there only once. She felt ashamed. Couldn't he just wait for her to get a few things done, and they could go together? He told her that she would never leave here unless someone made her.

Ladia changed the subject. She was not comfortable being put on the spot for her shortcomings. "So did you find out that Vahar gave Niea the scalpel?" No, Vahar didn't. Ladia started to protest. He directed her toward Niea. She needed to talk to Niea. She had stolen the scalpel days before Vahar was admitted to the unit. In fact, Vahar tried to talk her out of it. Ladia was still indignant. Of course, Vahar got the scalpel and gave it to Niea. Then she told her to kill herself. Zane had had enough. He said for her to talk to Niea. He kissed her on the cheek and left. She sat there stunned. Deep down inside herself, she knew she had driven him away. But why? Why had she treated him like any other soldier that took orders from the high command? She had to admit she made him take time with Vahar.

Zane hadn't told Vahar about the apartment. He blindfolded her and led her to the door. He pulled off the blindfold. She knew right away this was where she would be staying until she left. Also, all the things he had bought her were here with a few more new things hung up around the room. She looked at him longingly, but he had given her more than she had ever imagined. He had helped her free her soul. She kissed him on the cheek and said good night.

Zane and Vahar spent the rest of the month doing all the things they loved. Vahar would be in rehearsal for six hours in the morning. The rest of the day was theirs. In the evening, they would eat and work on Vahar's costumes. She had never seen a heterosexual male that loved to style, tailor, design, and create women's clothing or costumes, and he was good at it. She had been making her costumes for years. They both were having fun. She asked him if he would come with her. He explained he had to be with his grands. His daughterin-law and his two grands had moved to Gabba. Bet was now working with Zek and Margo at their woman's center. She was worried she would never see him again. He assured her he would have to see her again. Then Vahar asked, "What about your woman, the Califia?" Zane asked how she knew. She informed him she was not dumb. He laughed so hard he almost choked. He told Vahar that he was leaving for the hostel in one moon. He would not be coming back to Central anytime soon. The Califia could come there if she wished to see him. Vahar asked if she could come see him. He said he would find her.

The day came that Varah and Zane had to say goodbye to each other. Even Zane cried. They kissed a tender kiss. Vahar boarded the bus with the other performers, never taking her eyes of Zane. He was real close to being over Ladia. He would send her a note or a message every now and then. She would answer, but she was still not really available to have a real relationship. He required time with his lover, and she just couldn't give that to him.

Everyone at the hostel was excited for Zane to come live with them. Miguel was still at Central, and Niea was at the wellness center. Her progress was slow. Schade had taken over her therapy sessions. Schade used ancient methods of spiritual healing, teaching Niea the difference between the body mind and the mind. The body mind communicates with pictures and visions. Niea was a very cerebral person. But sitting and talking about her problems was not working so well. She knew that. Schade had something different to bring to the table.

Zane settled in at the hostel. The kids fell in love with this grandda. They called him Papa Zane. He was in heaven. He helped Cal with their homeschooling. He also kept up with their physical training as well as the adults and the folks at the woman's center in Gabba. Everyone needed to be ready to fight. He kept busy. Ladia never came. She would say she was coming, but somehow she never showed. He knew she wouldn't.

Zane would contact Vahar through messaging. The show was coming to Northdale. Zane was so excited. He was going. He was there for the first show. She saw him and smiled so big. She put on the best show of her life. He met her backstage and asked if she was hungry. He had brought her some scones and juice. Just like she liked. They walked through the town. It was a real charming place. He had a room at a lovely bed-and-breakfast. He was unsure if he should ask her up. She smiled at him and said, "You are scared to have sex with me." He was. She was thirty years younger than him. He had had daughters around her age. She knew that was part of it, but what was the rest, her history? She knew he was a man of character. She was not good enough for a man like Zane.

Zane looked at her and said, "You don't know what you have done."

She said, "I know exactly what I have done, and it's not what one would call good."

He took her by the shoulders, looked at her in the eyes, and said, "You have done what I have never seen many people ever do. Ladia can't do what you have done. You, my beautiful Vahar, you have stood up in front of God and the Kali people and admitted what you have done wrong. You have owned all that crap. You walked through the fire and came out on the other side. Poor Niea can't do it at all. Ladia is too busy to say to anyone what she has done wrong."

She smile. "I could do that because of you, Zane Kedif. Your strength and caring gave me what I needed. If you don't want to have sex with me, so be it, but please say you will always be my friend." He stood staring into her beautiful face, then he kissed her.

Zane said, "Will you please come to my room? I want you to be my lady. I am very proud of you."

The show was in town for four days. They spent every moment together. Vahar had never experienced love or sex like that in her life. She was still amazed at everything that happened.

Niea had been progressing under the tutelage of the healer Schade. She knew Niea still had a long way to go. She asked Miguel if he minded leaving for a while. He didn't want to leave his Niea. But maybe he did need to go back to the hostel. After all, it was his home. He asked if he could spend the night with her. Schade had no problem with that. There were some cabins just behind the center they could use. Niea was so emotional at times that Schade thought they should stay close, especially with their history. She didn't want any repeats of violence. Niea had not had an incident in quite some time.

Miguel and Niea went to the cabin that was the nearest to the center, just in case. They lay together for some time. Miguel didn't want to hurry his beautiful fragile woman. He would be so happy when they could go home for good. He would wait forever for Niea. She was the only woman he had ever loved.

In the middle of the night, she woke in a cold sweat. A recurring nightmare was haunting her. Miguel got her a cool rag to wipe her face. He kissed her on the forehead. Her mood changed. She looked at him kind of sheepishly and a bit naughty. She lay back on the bed stroking her long black hair, posing for her excited husband. Then she pulled him on top of her. He had not been with his lady in a long time. She was wet and ready for her lover. Miguel went slowly and tenderly. They made slow, gentle love. In the morning, Miguel kissed his Niea goodbye and left. He was hopeful that one day soon he would come and take her with him. But for now, he would keep praying for that day.

Miguel was glad to see the hostel. He noticed there was another structure being put up. He stood for some time just looking at the place. It was beautiful here. He was looking all around, remembering so many things that had happened here—mostly it was full of Niea. He was determined not to be down. His son needed him. He certainly didn't need to be moping around making everyone miserable. Cal saw him and came running. She was followed by Jay and Aaden, and Shona was papoose to Cal's back. He was elated to see her and her growing pride. She had really come a long way. She was a fabulous mother and a good friend. She hugged Miguel and kissed his cheek. She told him that Elijah was at the hostel with Jamal. They were all glad to see Miguel. He and his cooking had been missed terribly. When he saw Jamal, they hugged for the longest. They had been friends for such a long time. He asked for Zane. Zane was in Northdale. He should be back soon.

Zane wanted to take all the kids to see Vahar dance. He hoped Cal wouldn't mind. Cal was still not keen on Vahar. So Zane spoke with her. She said out of respect for the captain she would be civil with her. He gave Cal a big hug. Cal thought to herself that he's got it bad. She regretted Grandmama had never come to see Zane here. Cal knew how Grandmama was. She would never change. She worked all the time when they were growing up. Cal had raised Niea pretty much, kept their home clean, washed the clothes, cooked the food, and did the shopping for the most part. She trained Niea to do chores every day along with her.

They all went to the Kali show in Gabba. It had been sometime since one had come to town. They even had Elijah. He was walking now and into everything. Shona was close behind. Cal was so grateful for Zane. He really helped out with the kids. He was just as good as Cal at kid wrangling. It really does take a tribe to raise a child.

They all loved the show. There would be an adult show later that evening. Everyone went back to the hostel but Zane. He waited like a backstage Jonnie for Vahar. She saw him standing there with a bunch of beautiful flowers arranged just right. She knew he had gone out, picked them, and arranged them. She stood there looking at him waiting for her. He hadn't seen her yet. He looked like he was going on his first date.

She walked up slowly and kissed him on the cheek. He turned toward her and handed her the flowers, then bowed his head. She pulled his bowed head into her bosom and whispered, "I love you." He had water in his eyes. He said it was allergies. He wrapped his arms around her and held her for the longest. Zane stepped back and looked her up and down. Vahar looked at him and sighed. She said, "Yes, I have gained weight." He said it looked good on her. She asked him if he would mind if she gained more weight. He told her of course not. She was glad. She looked him in the eyes and said, "I have some news. You may or may not like it." Oh my god, what could it be? Was she breaking it off with him? She took him by the hand and led him to a sitting area. They took a seat next to each other. First she kissed him so intently it scared him. She said, "I don't know how to say this. I'm pregnant." His jaw almost hit the floor. Of course, it was his.

Zane had a thousand questions. "How far along are you? I just assumed you were on birth control."

Vahar couldn't tell if he was happy about her news. She said, "I have never taken birth control. I was told I had to much scarring from the forced rape done by my uncle. I had no idea I could get pregnant. If you want me to have an abortion, I can't do that. I will raise him on my own, but I would rather have you with me." How did she know it was a boy? Vahar told Zane she just knew. She always wanted children. She had told Miguel she didn't want kids. She didn't think she could be a good mother with her background anyway. She believed she was just too messed up inside to ever carry a child to term.

All of a sudden, Zane broke down and started sobbing. He held on to Vahar like a frightened child. She didn't know what was really going on with him. Was he happy, sad, or just losing it? After what seemed like an eternity, he wiped his face and nose with his handkerchief. He apologized for being so emotional. It was just that he was so happy. He kissed her over and over. Then he asked all kinds of questions. When was she going to come be with him? How far along was she? Had she been taking care of herself? Was she eating right? Did dancing hurt? Vahar started to laugh. He looked at her with red swollen eyes, not knowing what she found funny. She informed him with correctly ordered answers: today, two months, yes, yes, no. She said, "Any more questions, my love?"

He started to laugh and cry at the same time. There were a thousands more questions, but they could wait. Tonight, they would stay in Gabba. Bet wanted them to stay at the center, but she knew of a cozy bed-and-breakfast at the edge of town. She knew they would love it. So Vahar gathered a few things, and they headed out to be alone. She wanted to be with him and all his talents.

Ladia called the hostel. She asked for Zane. Tulie explained that he was in Gaba at the bed-and-breakfast. Ladia wanted to know more, but Tulie thought it best not to talk about what Zane was doing there. She changed the subject. When was the Califia coming to the hostel? As always Ladia made excuses. She was just too busy.

Miguel prepared a wonderful meal for them all. They all wanted to wait for Zane, but no one did. As they were finishing up supper, Zane came to the door. He was glowing. Everyone was looking at him. Then he went back outside and led Vahar into the hostel. No one said anything. Vahar just stood there. She wanted to apologize to them but stood frozen. She whispered to Zane that maybe she should leave. Zane shook his head no. Cal had a predator's stare locked on Vahar. This was not lost on Zane. He stepped in front of Vahar. "I have something to tell all of you. First, let me say if you need Vahar to leave, I will have to leave with her. She's two months pregnant with my son. She says it's a boy. I don't care if the baby is a boy or girl. It's mine, and I will be there to help raise my child. Now I am hoping she can come to term here. If she does anything questionable, I will deal with her behavior." He looked around the room at each and every one of them. No one said anything at first. Then Cal stood up, giving Vahar a bit of the stink eye. Then she turned to Zane and shrugged her shoulders.

Cal said, "I would never turn away a child or mother in need. But she had better be on her best behavior, and I will be watching." Baby Shona started to cry, and Cal excused herself.

Jamal gestured for Zane and Vahar to sit. Miguel served them a plate each. Jamal poured Zane a glass of wine, and Miguel gave Vahar a glass of juice. Vahar was amazed at the food. She looked at Miguel in wonder. It was just so good. She ate it all. Jamal wanted to show Zane what he had done on the cabin they had been working on. They headed out back chatting about what had been done and what they needed to finish the place up. The kids had all gone to bed. Miguel went to kiss his son good night. He returned and found Vahar softly crying. He had never seen her cry. He wasn't sure what to say. Then he asked why she was sad. She said it was hormones. But that wasn't the total truth. She was scared. Then she looked him in the eyes and said, "I am so sorry about the way I treated you. You deserve so much better." He handed her a napkin to wipe her tears away. This made her cry more. She asked him not to be nice to the likes of her.

Miguel took her hand and said, "I'm glad you are here. I can't wait to meet your baby." He might just have the best heart out of anyone she had been acquainted with. Zane came into the room and saw Miguel holding her hand. He sat down beside Vahar saying that she had friends here. These were some fine people, and they would help her see to her every need. He wrapped his arm around her and held her until she could compose herself. Then he asked her to come and see their place. He got her bags, and they headed to the cabin where they would be living for at least a few more moons. But he knew they would be here much longer. He also knew when Cal saw that baby, she would be in love. Cal might be tough, but inside she had a big heart and was a lover of all children.

Back at the wellness center, Schade and Niea were discussing the possibility of some different ways to deal with Niea's fractured spirit. Schade was sure this could be the healing Niea needed. It was a bit unconventional but very effective. She would prepare Niea for soul retrieval. She was sure together they could put Niea's shattered spirit back together again. It wasn't going to be easy, but it would well worth it in the end. First Schade would have to introduce Niea to some meditation and ceremonies to wake up and call in the spirits of place. Then Niea would need to do some centering meditations and exercises. Although Niea had suggested others meditate, she never did. Niea had never done anything like this before. But she was open and ready to be whole.

Several moon turns came and went. Vahar gained much of her weight right in the abdomen. Zane and she spent every moment together. She had never been this happy. Even Cal had lightened up on her. When Cal couldn't find her toddling Shona, she knew she was with Vahar. The little redhead loved Vahar. Aaden and Jay had taken to her also. They would bring her presents of flowers, bird feathers, pretty rocks, turtle shells, and anything from nature. She would make things out of their gifts. It was strange that the children taught them more than the adults taught them. Vahar wondered at what age they closed their hearts to unconditional love.

Schade had built a meditation lodge. It was in a very old teepee. Ancient. Today she had Niea sitting in it with white sage burning in an abalone shell. Niea had on a long blue dress. The color would help her remain calm. All she had to do was focus on it. Schade taught her proper deep breathing. Niea had been breathing shallow and high in the chest for some time now. She sat looking at the purple geode Schade had placed in the middle of the teepee. Suddenly the flap opened up, and just for a second or two Niea saw a black wolf and a large spotted cat. Then the image disappeared, and there stood Schade. Niea kept her eyes on her. Was she hallucinating? Should she tell Schade what she had seen? Why wouldn't she? She did. Schade sat down across from her looking all around Niea. Then she said, "What you saw were my guides, spirit guides. So, you are a seer. But this is not for me to define. I think you are ready for your first journey." Niea thought they were going somewhere. Yes, they were, but not in the physical. They would have one foot in the physical and one in the spiritual. Niea had asked if she would see anything. Hopefully she would meet her guides. And there was the cave of the unknown self—the shattered self in Niea's case. She asked if Schade would see the same things. Schade said no, but she would see the energy, and she would hold power for Niea to assure her a safe journey. Niea closed her eyes, breathing deeply then relaxing. She felt good, and she felt strong. She hadn't felt that way in a long time. Niea continued to breathe deeply and fell into a trance. It happened fast. Suddenly she was in the cave where the Gogatt had raped her. She was alone. Then a whitish shadow figure came out of the darkness and lay down beside her. It appeared to be a wolf, a white wolf. It felt vaguely familiar, a source of great comfort. It was female. The energy whirled. There she and her wolf companion stood in front of several Gogatt. She recognized the one who had raped her last—the one that had choked her. He stood with his sword drawn and grinning an evil grin. At first Niea couldn't remember any of her training. She could feel the wounds on her lower arms. She froze. She heard Schade's voice reminding her that she could change the dream/nightmare at any time. Niea had learned how to be awake in her own dreams, the master of her dreams. Yes, find your hands. She raised her hands and looked at her palms. Then she imagined a weapon in her hand. She felt the wolf stand up and take an offensive pose. They both stared at the man with a slow predatory gaze. Niea gave a Kalifee warrior yell. The she wolf howled. Slowly they inched up on this evil man, never taking the eyes of the prey. She and her companion struck at the same time. The Gogatt was gone, but there stood several more. Niea felt overwhelmed. The wolf nudged her forward like any good pack animal would do for a pack member that had frozen up. She stepped out and through the Gogatt. They all disappeared. Then she saw an image of Miguel. He was being raped repeatedly by Leit. She felt the anger bubbling up inside her. The wolf bumped her again. This brought her back to being focused on the task. The image of Miguel being raped disappeared. Now she stood in front of Cal. Cal was passed out drunk. A shadow went across her. It looked like a bird, like a large raven. Niea heard Schade whisper, "The keeper of secrets and war." In that moment, Cal moaned and sat up in a drunken haze.

She couldn't fight. She looked at Niea, and in that moment, Niea knew she had kept too many secrets and almost helped ruined one of the Kalifee's finest, her sister and her number one. Keeping other's secrets can be deadly in so many ways. The raven landed on Cal and started picking at her. She couldn't shoo the bird away. Niea tried, but the bird turned a golden yellow eye on her. Then Gogatts showed up, and Niea went into fighting mode without hesitation. She fought with full force. Cal stood up and turned, looking at Niea. This was Cal's battle, and she would fight it. Niea stood back. Cal disappeared. In that moment, the cave and all the images faded, and Niea found herself sitting in the teepee again staring at Schade.

Schade spoke in a low soothing voice, "The images you saw are the things you need to let fly, like the eagles."

Vahar was around eight and a half months pregnant now. She needed to have this baby soon. The pressure was taxing, to say the least. The menfolk and kids had gone to Gabba to hopefully buy what they needed for the finishing touches on Vahar and Zane's new cabin. They dropped the kids off at the women's center. Cal and Tulie decide to go east and look around the caves, more curiosity than anything. Varah wanted to get out, so she tagged along. They took the other ground car as far as they could. Cal and Tulie got out and started having a look around. Vahar waddled off to find anything she could make into something. Cal's boys had gotten her into this. It wasn't long before Vahar heard a blue jay's cry. She knew its meaning. One of them was in trouble. She made her way toward the sound. There was a ravine, and Vahar could see Cal at the bottom. It wasn't real deep, but it was going to be difficult for Vahar to maneuver. She whistled back she was coming. When Vahar reached Cal, she could see a thin sharp wire wrapped around her leg. It had cut her pretty deep, and every time she moved, it would cut deeper. Vahar pulled out the blade she had strapped to her thigh and cut the wire. When she got it out from around Cal's leg, the bleeding started. Vahar quickly cut off a big enough part of her dress to help stop the bleeding. She had Cal hold pressure while she cut off another piece to hold the dressing in place. Cal couldn't walk alone. Vahar had to hold on to her, and they made their way up the ravine, getting thorns and scratches as they went. When they reached the top, they both heard a blue jay whistle. Oh god, Tulie. Vahar hid Cal in some thicket and went to see about Tulie. She also was caught in a wire and couldn't move. Vahar got her loose, cut some more of her dress, dressed the wound, and carried Tulie to where Cal lay hidden. She turned, and there was a single Gogatt. She had never seen one of them. She had heard of the smell, and it wasn't an exaggeration. She would like to have thrown up her breakfast. His weapon was sheathed, and she was not going to try to outdraw him or fight him. So, she did the one thing she knew how to do best. She turned it up. She slowly took in a long even breath. Yes, he watched her bosom go up. He looked down at her dress, which was cut all up. Then he asked, "What the hell are you doing out here? Especially as knocked up as you are."

Vahar smiled and bent over just a little and feigned rubbing a sore ankle. He had his eyes all over her. She turned ever slightly and slowly pulled out her blade. He was just so busy looking at such a woman. He was trying to decide to rape and kill her here or—

Her blade went deep into his chest, piercing his heart. He hit the ground with a thud.

Vahar was making her way back toward Tulie and Cal when two more Gogatt stopped her. This time she acted like she didn't see them and bent over, showing her deep cleavage. She stood up with her blade concealed in her hand. With the other hand, she had picked up a rock. The big one stepped up to her. She looked up and smiled so pleasantly at him that it threw him off. He had never seen a woman like Vahar, much less such a warm, inviting smile. He was thinking he would rape her here and then cut out her baby. At that moment, her blade went deep into his groin. Then she smashed the rock against the other one's head. She kicked both of them hard to make sure they were good and dead. She made her way back to the ladies. She carried Tulie to the car and returned to get Cal. Oh god, there was another one. This one was ready to rape and kill her now. She turned and said, "Hi, you looking for some company?" He was thrown by her open friendliness. He had his eyes planted on her chest. He was going to have some fun raping her and cutting off those tits. Vahar stepped up to him. He didn't look past her breasts and figure either. She had her blade in her hand and rammed it into his gut, disemboweling him. He fell back, bleeding out from the gut. Vahar gave him one more hard stab. Seeing him suffer was not her way. She finally got Cal into the car, and they took off.

Vahar got both of them into the hostel. She was working on Cal's leg, and Cal was tending to Tulie's leg. Once they were stitched up, Vahar got up to get them both some sulfa and valerian root for infection and pain. Suddenly her water broke. She sat down and leaned forward. The pain was worse than she could have imagined. She made her way to the bunk room and lay down. Cal had found her a stick and made her way to Vahar. She asked if she could check her. She was almost fully dilated. Her baby was coming. Cal had her lay on her left side and take deep breaths. Tulie had made her way to the communicator and sent a signal to the guys: "Come home now." Zane, Jamal, and Miguel took off. They had found what they wanted and would pick it up tomorrow. Zane said the kids can stay with the ladies at the center tonight.

When they got to the hostel, they found all three ladies lying in bunks. Vahar's labor had progressed. Her contractions were coming very close to each other. Cal and Tulie were sound asleep. They were tired from their ordeal, and the valerian root had taken full effect. Zane picked up Vahar and took her to a main bedroom. He had her lie on her back and propped her up with pillows. Jamal got some towels to clean up with and a blanket to wrap the baby in. Miguel looked at Zane. He was unsure if he should even be here. Zane wanted him to run the show. In all his experience, he had never even witnessed a birth. Miguel nodded, understanding, and went to the kitchen. Jamal had put on some hot water for sterilization. Miguel cleaned himself up and got a scalp, some stitching needles, and deer sinew. All the stitch kits he had made were gone. He returned. Jamal had Zane sit behind Vahar and hold her like he held Cal during the birth of their babies. He showed Zane how to support her while she used her abdominal muscles to push their son out. Zane looked worried. Jamal assured him he would coach him through the whole process. The baby was big. Miguel preformed an episiotomy, and the baby came on out with one last push by Vahar. She had to hold off holding or nursing her baby until Miguel could stitch her up. He had put lidocaine on the area and numbed it up. Vahar only felt the tug of the sinew as he stitched. Zane had been holding the baby in wonderment. It hit him for the first time. When their baby boy was Vahar's age, he would be ninety years old.

Niea was feeling stronger and wanted to know when she could go home. Schade said there was still work to do. Today Niea would have a peek at her shadow self, her dark side. To say it simply, the personality's dark side. Often referred to as our more basic animal instincts—our shadow self. It is the cave of the hidden self. It is our greed, lust, fear, envy, ego, hate, rage, shame, jealousy, judgment, deceit, and more, pretty much any perceived negativity, unacceptable behaviors, sinful, or evil characteristic we want to hide from others as well as from ourselves. But the shadow self isn't all bad.

Carl Jung said, "The shadow is ninety percent pure gold." He believed the golden shadow is where our hidden or submerged creative potential resides. It is the crack in the shaman's jewel where our enlightenment lies not in its perfection. Just as we disown our negative shadow traits, so, can we disown our greatness. It is true that in shunning our light, our potential is equally as dark as whatever is being held prisoner in our shadow self.

Niea had never liked showing weakness. She believed it would make her crumble. It was her fear of being weak that was actually holding her back. Somewhere deep inside she knew it was. There was more to it. Niea had hidden other parts of herself.

Schade said, "Today, you begin to meet all of you." She explained that the concept could be confusing. Many ask how hiding our light is equal to ignoring our darkness. Because light can only be hidden when trapped in total darkness. But now Niea had met two of her animal spirit guides. They will help her look into the mirror of the unmet self and make some hard truths easier to discover, acknowledge, and accept.

Schade spent most of the afternoon and half of the night trying to guide Niea to seeing her total self. It was so hard for her to see she had done so much covering up for Cal just to feed her fragile ego. And that much of her concern for others was her way of avoiding herself. Her fighting was her way of dealing with unresolved anger. Schade had wondered way this hadn't crumbled in on her until now. Niea was a strong woman. But sometimes you have to surrender to win. That said, if you wish to be healthy, whole, and happy, discovering and dancing with your demons is an imperative part of your spiritual journey.

Niea knew Schade was right on the money. But admitting all this to herself made her head throb. She just wanted to run and never stop. Ego and pride were not something she thought was her problem, but it was. She had been avoiding all of this since she was a young girl. For one thing, she had never really failed at anything. In fact, she was one of the best students and fighters that the Kalifee had. Schade said, "No one learns from the things they do right. That's a pat on the back, and here you go. We learn from what we do wrong. And again, what one must remember that this Mother Earth of ours is a schoolhouse. We are not punished by the Great Spirit. Every mistake is a chance to go deeper into knowing who we are. We actually call in our lessons with our actions and deeds. The who is not what we do, like a job. It is a lifetime of providing mirrors for each other. We are the one thing we cannot see." She told Niea that she had a great tribe to provide her with all the mirrors she would ever need. And to never forget we make our own reality. Niea soaked all this in. She didn't want to be lost for the rest of her life. This course of action would lead her back to where she was. Learning to meditate would help her stay in touch with her center. They had many journeys together. Her soul was being retrieved.

Finally, the day came when Niea knew she was ready. She would be leaving early in the morning, and she was packed and ready to go. Keddie had been reassigned to the hostel. He was there to pick her up. No one knew they were coming. Grandmama was there to say goodbye. No, she couldn't come along. She had too much to do. Niea was beginning to think she was afraid to leave Central. Niea said goodbye to the staff. She told Schade she had an open invitation to come to the hostel anytime. Niea knew she would see this gifted healer again. She hoped soon.

Keddie and Niea arrived at the hostel just after breakfast. Niea stood outside and look around the place. It looked so good. The crew had done a marvelous job with all the improvements. Then she saw Miguel and started running. He picked her up and whirled her around. His beautiful baby girl was home. Keddie carried Niea's and his bags. He wanted to see and hold Tulie. She came limping up. She told what had happened and how Vahar had worked those Gogatts. No one had ever seen a scene like that. Both couples kissed for a long time, then Tulie offered them some breakfast. Niea wanted to see her son. Miguel said all the kids were at the center in Gabba except Vahar, Kedif, and Shona. Miguel said they could go to Gabba after they eat. Niea grinned at him. Maybe they could be alone for a while. Keddie and Tulie agreed to that.

They ate, and Miguel just sat there staring at Niea with the sweetest look on his face. Vahar came through the door holding Kedif and Shona's hand. She hugged Niea for a long time. Cal, Zane, and Jamal had gone hunting. Tonight, they would party.

Miguel, Tulie, and Niea prepared a feast fit for a queen. Cal, Jamal, and Zane returned with the biggest deer anyone had ever seen. Everyone was there. They even had Ladia on video chat. Wine and juice were served to the appropriate persons. Zane raised his glass to give a toast. "I hold this glass up to the finest Kalifeeians I have ever known. We are family, blended with the colors of the rainbow, a tribe with strength, love, and a bright future. I thank you all for staying alive. We have all fought to live another day. We train, we live, and we love. With the undying help of the Great Spirit, we will live to fight another day."

ABOUT THE AUTHOR

I am a sixty-nine-year-old white female from South Georgia, who worked as a nurse (RN) for almost thirty years. I always wanted to write fiction stories! When I became unemployable (bad case of burn out, I do believe), I began to see my situation as some kind of sign. Now is not going to wait. So, I purposefully called in the energies I needed to write my first story. Four months later, I had written this. I have learned that a person choses their own reality. So, that is what I did. I remove words like try and want. I will do this, and I will have that. My prayer is to never forget the consciousness; they deepen the lessons of the journey.